W9-BEB-098

Books by
Virginia Swift

BYE, BYE, LOVE
BAD COMPANY
BROWN-EYED GIRL

Forthcoming in hardcover

HELLO, STRANGER

VIRGINIA SWIFT

BYE, BYE, LOVE

A MUSTANG SALLY MYSTERY

AVON BOOKS
An Imprint of HarperCollins*Publishers*

This is a work of fiction. Names, characters, places, and incidents are products of the author's imagination or are used fictitiously and are not to be construed as real. Any resemblance to actual events, locales, organizations, or persons, living or dead, is entirely coincidental.

AVON BOOKS
An Imprint of HarperCollins*Publishers*
10 East 53rd Street
New York, New York 10022-5299

Copyright © 2005 by Virginia Scharff
Excerpt from *Hello, Stranger* copyright © 2006 by Virginia Scharff
ISBN-13: 978-0-06-054332-7
ISBN-10: 0-06-054332-9
www.avonmystery.com

First Avon Books paperback printing: December 2005
First HarperCollins hardcover printing: November 2004

Avon Trademark Reg. U.S. Pat. Off. and in Other Countries, Marca Registrada, Hecho en U.S.A.
HarperCollins® is a registered trademark of HarperCollins Publishers Inc.

Printed in the U.S.A.

10 9 8 7 6 5 4 3 2 1

*To Bob and Martha, Sam, Patty and Steve,
Liz and Mike, and Dick*

Acknowledgments

Once again, during the time I've been working on this book, I've been the recipient of more love and friendship and support than I deserve. I'm grateful to the friends who've kept me sane despite my own best efforts: Karen Anderson, Mim Aretsky, Beth Bailey, Audie Blevins, Melissa Bokovoy, Hal Corbett, Katie Curtiss, Paul Hutton, Nancy Jackson, Katherine Jensen, Catherine Kleiner, Monica McCormick, Les McFadden, Maria Montóya, Judy Morley, Jessica Moseley, Harriet Moss, Greg Nottage, Craig Pinto, Richard Sanchez, Ernesto Sanchez, Wendy Schmidt, John Schmidt, Bev Seckinger, Jane Slaughter, and Laura Timothy. A special word of thanks to Chris Wilson, whose generosity, eye for beauty, and love of life are an inspiration.

Writers owe a lot to the people who make books possible. Thanks to Kay Marcotte, Lindsay at Bookworks, Bonnie and Joe at Black Orchid, and the incomparable Barbara Peters at Poisoned Pen for encouragement and great events. To my splendid agent, Elaine Koster, and wonderful editor, Carolyn Marino, thanks for your continuing faith in me. To Tara McDonald, Jon George, Yolanda Martinez, Helen Ferguson, Dana Ellison, Barbara Wafer, Cindy Tyson, and Scott Meredith, thanks for smoothing out the kinks and keeping me on the forward path, in just about every way.

Thanks to the Scharff, Levkoff, Swift, Bort, and Broh families, especially Cheryl Swift, scientist, environmentalist, feminist, and sister. To Peter, Sam, and Annie, I am endlessly grateful to you for keeping the ship afloat in stormy seas. To my brothers and sisters, who've put up with me longer than anybody else: I love you very much.

BYE, BYE, LOVE

1

Darlin' Tommy J

The first time she'd heard his voice, sweet and clear, coming through the wire on this new thing called FM, Sally Alder had been totally, utterly gone. Gone, gone, gone, from the moment she'd stood in the record store, looking for the album with the hit song, "Last Night," and found herself staring open-mouthed at the photograph of Stone Jackson on the front. His penetrating, wounded blue eyes conjured a fantasy of passion and intelligence, a vision ignited again and again as she wore out the vinyl, reveling in his songs of warm whimsy and earthy blues, invitation and anguish, loss, love.

Like there'd been this instant connection between them. Fate. Destiny. Please. His debut album had gone platinum. American females by the millions had paid their—what? $3.50?—had mooned over that album cover, had fantasized the moment when they'd give him the comfort he so clearly needed. And by the millions, the women of America had managed to grow up and get over it.

Not Sally.

Truly it *was* embarrassing to admit it, but through albums, tapes, CDs, and live concerts, she'd followed the heady highs and desperate downs of his story. She'd dreamed, vividly, of hearing him say the words:

"I need you to help me, Sally."

The precise words Thomas "Stone" Jackson was saying this very minute, sitting in her cluttered office at the top of Hoyt Hall, at the University of Wyoming, in the glory of the last fine day of September. The voice was the same: gentle, mellow, pure, hinting at irony. The long, graceful, string-bean body was just as she'd admired so many times on stage, slung with a guitar, swaying with soul, bopping with the beat, rocking out.

The face, however, had a whole lot more miles on it than the one on that long-ago album cover. It was as if every sign of innocence had been burned away, leaving sharp bones, arched brows, wry mouth. Crow's-feet winged at the corners of those ever-remarkable eyes. His forehead was deeply etched, and there was a whole lot more of it.

Which mattered to her not a whit. She, too, was on the dark side of forty. Guys who managed to keep up appearances in the middle of the long strange trip suited her just fine.

Still, experience had taught her to be wary of appealing men. Here came Jackson, saying he needed her help. Over the years, she'd extended aid and comfort to enough guys to remember to check her wallet.

"Why me?" she asked Thomas Jackson, keeping her voice low, trying to sound neither eager nor suspicious. "Where'd you get my name?"

"Our mutual friend, Pete," Jackson explained, naming an old boyfriend of Sally's who'd had his own ups and downs, but was currently riding high in the upper echelons of a southern California multimedia empire. "I've just bought a little place outside Cody," Jackson continued. "When Pete found out I planned to spend time in Wyoming, he suggested that I look you up."

A little place! Everyone in the state had heard about Thomas Jackson's purchase of a prime property he called the Busted Heart Ranch. The brand? What else? Two offset halves of a heart. Next to Harrison Ford, Thomas Jackson was pretty much the biggest Hollywood rancher in Wyoming. "Oh yeah?" she said. "That was nice of Pete. We keep in touch, from time to time."

Thomas Jackson grinned faintly. "Pete says you're a nag and a bit of a diva, but that you're brilliant, sexy, and can sing some. And that he's had reason, in tight situations, to find you trustworthy."

"Pete's definition of trustworthy isn't most people's," she replied, trying to ignore the fact that Jackson had blithely announced that he'd casually discussed her sexuality with one of her old lovers. What was that, some kind of blasé Hollywood move? She went for Wyoming blasé. "So what's the problem?"

Jackson leaned back in the dilapidated easy chair usually occupied by students whining for grade changes. "You know Nina Cruz, of course."

Of course. Angelina Cruz, known as Nina: his ex-wife, folk singer icon. Nina had retired from the fast lane in L.A. to seek peace of mind in a gracious, but relatively modest, log house on eighty pretty acres west of Laramie, a spread she called Shady Grove, near the town of Albany, Wyoming. Nina was an ardent wilderness lover, animal-rights activist, and feminist. She drove a Range Rover with bumper stickers that said, MY OTHER CAR IS A BROOM and FRIENDS DON'T LET FRIENDS WEAR FUR. She had once told Sally she believed that, at the deepest level, plutonium, the endangerment of species, and professional football all came from the root toxin of patriarchy.

Who in hell would leave *la vida buena* in southern California for *la vida blizzard* in southern Wyoming? Nina for one, evidently; Sally for another. Sally had left UCLA to direct the Dunwoodie Center for Women's History at the University of Wyoming. She and Nina had feminism in common, though Nina was the type of feminist who believed that all women were extensions of the earth goddess, and Sally was more inclined to the view that women and men were all too human, equally capable of Nobel Prizes and bonehead moves on a planet ruled less by goddesses than by chance and choice.

But Nina was also the kind of feminist who wrote big

checks. Sally was the kind who cashed them. When Nina's first substantial donation to the Dunwoodie Center had arrived, Sally had called Nina to say thanks and invite her to dinner at the Yippie I O Café, the only place in Laramie one dared take a vegetarian to dine. They'd since had several cordial dinners together, and, happily, more checks had followed. "Nina has been a very generous contributor to the Dunwoodie Center," Sally said carefully.

"Nina's big on her causes," said Stone. "So am I, come to that." He grinned. Serious wattage. Sally tried to remain calm. Failed.

Stone continued. "Anyway, you probably know that right now, she's putting a lot of time and money into her latest project, the Wild West Foundation."

Sally nodded, though she wasn't quite sure what Wild West was all about. Some kind of wilderness and wildlife protection thing, it could involve anything from holding tofu potlucks, to saving prairie dog villages from bulldozers, to crusading against grazing on the public domain. So far, Nina hadn't pissed off the people who thought Wyoming was spelled "B-E-E-F," but the time might come.

"I haven't talked with Nina about Wild West. We've had some nice evenings, done a little business, but that's about it. I'm sure you'd know a lot more about it than I would," Sally told him, trying to tell him nothing.

"A little more, maybe," Jackson said, scooting the broken-down easy chair forward, leaning over, resting his elbows on the edge of Sally's messy desk. "I had lunch with her today, out at her place. She wanted to introduce me to some of the Dub-Dub staff."

"Dub-Dub?" Sally inquired.

"Short for WW, shorter for Wild West. My invention. The long version makes me think too much of Buffalo Bill."

"How does Nina like the short one?" Sally said.

"She laughed. But then, she's humoring me. She wants me to headline a benefit concert in Laramie."

Stone Jackson, playing in Laramie! It would embarrass both of them if Sally got down on her knees and told God she was sorry she had ever flirted with agnosticism. She'd have to contain herself. "That'd be great," Sally managed. "What's the venue?"

"Nina wants to raise real money, so she's thinking a big place. The university's basketball stadium was mentioned."

Stone Jackson at the Dome on the Range! Sweet Jesus in a wind tunnel. Basketball stadiums tended to be echoey and loud as hell, and the Dome was no exception. But then, if Thomas Jackson had been playing at the Laramie municipal landfill, Sally Alder would have stood in line for hours to get standing room in the ooze. "I'd buy a ticket."

"Nina was hoping you'd do more than that. She said maybe your band could open the gig, kind of a showcase for the hometown before the national acts come on."

No. This was way past too much. Sally's band, the Millionaires, was easily good enough for an average Saturday night in Laramie. Sally herself had once had a minor hit on the country-rock scene with "The Goin' Home Alone Again Waltz." But were they ready for this?

And then there was the fact that this was a benefit put on by tree huggers and sprout heads. At least three members of her current band were even now probably oiling and sighting high-powered rifles in preparation for the opening of deer season on the morrow. Those guys might have some reservations about donating their talents to the kind of outfit that referred to eating eggs as "ovacide."

But she wouldn't worry about that now. "When, exactly, is this event?" she asked.

"Thanksgiving weekend," said Jackson. "Eight weeks from now."

Don't panic, Sal. In less than eight weeks, Sherman had marched through Georgia. In eight weeks, Helen Keller had probably read all of Shakespeare in Braille. Certainly the Millionaires could work up a respectable dozen songs, if they weren't too busy terminating Wyoming ruminants. "I'll have to talk to the guys about it," she said.

Stone smiled. "Yeah. See what they think. I, myself, don't know quite how I feel about this gig."

Sally bristled. "I'm sure this must seem pretty small time to you."

Jackson tilted his head, looking compassionate, but just insulted enough to make her feel ashamed. "Eventually," he said, "we're all small time."

It wasn't for nothing that the man had spent the better part of two decades in recovery. "I'm sorry," said Sally. "You're making me incredibly nervous."

He laid his hand on hers. "Don't be."

Oh yeah. Stone Jackson, touching her very own hand, was sure to calm her down. As her blood pressure approximated that of an astronaut adrift in deep space ("Open the door, Hal"), she struggled to remember what they were talking about. "You said you're uncertain about doing the show?"

He squeezed her hand, nodded, and then let go. "And it isn't the town or the venue. It's the cause." He swallowed. "Don't get me wrong. I'd do anything for Nina. The woman saved my life."

The end of their storybook romance had made good tragic copy in *Rolling Stone*. Thomas Jackson had been off on a two-week bender in Hawaii with some of his drug buddies, leaving Nina Cruz back in Topanga Canyon. He'd promised her he was trying to stay clean, but there were more than enough obliging folks in the islands who could help a man get royally fucked up if he had half an urge. Old Stone Jackson had urge to spare.

He'd come home a junkie once again, to find that Nina had emptied her drawers and packed up all her books and instruments, and left a copy of *The Twelve Steps* on the dining room table. Along with a note that just said, "Get a grip, Tommy."

The life he'd gotten was about the worst he could have chosen, spinning lower and lower, more and more out of control. And then, finally, painfully, he'd taken her advice. For years and years now, according to *Rolling Stone*, he'd lived day by day. In time, Thomas and Nina had divorced, headed in different directions. Then, music and the depth of what had once bound them brought them back together. Sally had seen them, featured in a *People* magazine spread titled "Friendly Exes." There had been a picture of them, laughing with Bonnie Raitt at a "no nukes" benefit concert where they'd all performed.

Even in a black-and-white photo in a weekly magazine, Sally had (as usual) seen more than laughter in his eyes. It was said that Thomas Jackson had dragged himself out of hell by living on the hope that he could make it up to Nina Cruz, and she would come back to him. He'd never stopped hoping, the Hollywood gossips said, but she'd never come back.

Ever.

Talk about your busted hearts. Sally's own quest for a second chance with a first love had come out better, so far. But she remained cautious. "Nina," Sally said, "is a remarkable woman. So, what's wrong with her cause?"

Jackson sat back, put his elbows on the chair arms, massaged the hard contour of his jaw with the long fingers of his left hand, then rubbed the calloused tips of his fingers together. "I can't say if I'm being fair, but I just have this feeling that there's something really off about those Dub-Dub people. Did you have some friends, back in the day, who took one too many acid trips, or whatever, and just never came back down? People who seemed to have tuned in to a different frequency, and never gotten back on the main channel? Mostly, they were harmless—hell, some of them probably had visions of computers and ended up ruling the world. But these guys. I don't know," he said, massaging his forehead.

"Old hippies?" Sally asked. "People who seem like they fell into an iceberg in 1974 and are just being thawed out?"

"Oh yeah. As far as I could tell, there are more than a dozen of them out there; who knows how many more we expected. They've even got an old school bus parked out by her barn, probably half of them crashing in it. Lots and lots of dope smoking going on. While I was there, Nina happened to mention to several of them that she'd posted 'no hunting' signs along her fences, but that hadn't kept hunters out during antelope season. By the time I left, they were firing up fatties and debating further measures, everything from stringing fluorescent flagging along all the fences to painting every tree trunk on the place DayGlo orange."

"I can't imagine Nina'd let them get away with that kind of idiocy," Sally said.

"She wasn't listening to them. She was too busy introducing me to her foundation director, a guy named Randy Whitebird." Stone shook his head. "I've never been able to figure why she hangs around with guys like that. African beads on a leather thong around his neck, Birkenstocks with socks, calls everybody 'man,' hugs you when he doesn't even know you."

Sally laughed.

"Yeah, it makes you laugh," said Jackson, "until he gets wound up and starts using phrases like 'the carnivore holocaust.'"

"In Wyoming?" Sally asked. "Is he suicidal?"

"I don't rightly know what he is. Probably just off the plane from the People's Republic of Santa Monica," Jackson said.

"Aren't you?" Sally asked.

His eyes gleamed. "Yep. But at least I grew up in a real place."

If you could call growing up in Lexington, Virginia, as a great-great-great-grandson of the second-most-famous Confederate general "real." Jackson's nickname didn't derive solely from his storied susceptibility to addictive substances. His people were southerners, and not all of them had been Reconstructed. Living down the mother of all Lost Causes had put some of the shadows in Stone's depthless blue eyes.

"This Whitebird," Sally continued. "Is he Native American?"

"I suspect," Jackson said, "that he gave himself the name."

"Probably on a vision quest. I hate that," said Sally.

Once again, Jackson made her feel like a shallow bigot. "I try to cut people a lot of slack when it comes to their spiritual stuff. But as I was explaining, something about this guy isn't quite right. Then there was the foundation administrator, Kali."

"Kali? Hindu goddess of death, sex, and apocalypse? You're kidding," said Sally.

Jackson shook his head, letting a little amusement show. "Nope. Little bit of a thing, spent most of the lunch answering her cell phone and whispering into it. According to Nina, this Kali's got a Ph.D. in molecular biology. Evidently, she's spent years in the biotech industry, even after she started working in environmental politics."

"Did Kali talk about the carnivore holocaust?" Sally asked.

"Not to me. Didn't say a word to me, come to think of it. There were half-a-dozen other people kind of hanging around, and when she wasn't on the phone, Kali was working up things for them to do. Nina's still running the operation out of her home office, but they're looking for space in town. When they find a place, Kali and her crew are supposed to move into Laramie, but for now, they're camped out all over Nina's place."

"Oh wow," said Sally.

"Mmm-hmm," said Jackson. "Woodstock in Wyoming."

"Well, the good news is that there's a big snowstorm forecast for tomorrow. That might inspire them to find some real shelter someplace, hopefully not in her house. I'm kind of surprised," Sally mused. "I've had the impression that Nina treasures her privacy. Why else would she have bought that place and moved out here permanently? Why would she want to go and collect a gang of wackos who, if I know my hippies, may or may not ever get around to moving out?"

Trouble in the blue eyes. "Beats me. And that's the worst part. Nina isn't acting like herself. I've known the woman twenty-five years. She's always had a regrettable tendency to collect hustlers and strays, but she's sharp. She notices everything. She's liable to let one thing or another slide by, but she always has her reasons. And when she's inclined, she'll tell you exactly what she thinks, and if you don't like it, tough."

Jackson pondered a moment. "She called me a month ago to talk about the benefit, and we've had several conversations since. She's seemed distracted, like she's having trouble concentrating. She complains that she's tired a lot, and I've never known anybody with that much energy. I'm worried that there's something wrong with her, and the Dub-Dubs are taking advantage of the situation."

Sally wanted to help. Not just because she had this life-long thing about Thomas Jackson being the man of her dreams, but also because it did sound as if Nina might have a problem. But really, she and Nina Cruz were only acquaintances. "Shouldn't you be talking with her close friends about this?"

His mouth quirked, softly. "Half of Nina's good friends wouldn't speak to me if they were in a burning building and I was the guy with the fire hose. The other half, well, let's just say I don't regard them as likely possibilities. But her sister Caterina is solid gold. Unfortunately, Cat's in Brazil on some kind of UN goodwill ambassador gig, and the only way to get in touch with her is satellite phone.

"Look, I have the impression that Nina hasn't met all that many people in town, but she speaks highly of you. And of course, our friend Pete does, too."

Sally looked at the ceiling. She could only imagine what kind of recommendation had come from the latter source.

"I'm not sure what you're asking me to do," she said.

"Take the gig," he replied. "And if you've got the time, see what you can find out about this Dub-Dub thing. I'll be back and forth from Cody, but hang out with me while I'm in town, and keep in touch when I can't be here. Share your impressions."

Now that would be a hardship, wouldn't it? Sally thought.

Might be, come to think of it, if Hawk Green, the love of Sally's life, took a dislike to the idea.

He might have done so back when they were in their tempestuous twenties, when Sally had been a wild girl flirting with danger, and Hawk had been a rambling guy with a tendency to get mad and move on. But happily for Sally, Hawk Green was the kind of man who gave aging a good name. He was still as lanky and broad-shouldered as he'd been at twenty-one. He still wore jeans and boots or sneakers, T-shirts or flannel shirts, and kept his mass of straight black hair, now shot with silver, tied carelessly in a ponytail at the back of his neck.

He'd mellowed some over the years, in Sally's opinion, just exactly enough. But Hawk was anything but laid back. His immense, deep-set brown eyes radiated intelligence and curiosity. He woke fast every morning, springing out of bed with a list of the day's obligations already fixed in his head. Daunting, to say the least. Good thing he could sometimes be very happily convinced to return to the horizontal.

He might not be as easy to convince about the wisdom of her spending any quantity of time with the idol of her youth.

"In case you're interested, Margaret Dunwoodie is one of my favorite poets," Jackson told her. "In fact, I'd like to talk with you about making a contribution to your Dunwoodie Center. I read that biography of her that you wrote. Thought it was great." He paused. "Word has it that particular research project nearly did you in."

Thomas Jackson had read one of her books? "Glad you liked it," Sally said, blushing.

Thomas Jackson's eyes glowed. "I really, really liked it," he said.

2

Blood on the Tracks

"I don't like it," said Hawk Green, pouring coffee, looking out the kitchen window at fat snowflakes drifting groundward. "They're predicting at least six inches of snow by tonight and more to come. Your car handles like shit on snow without snow tires." He removed his round wire-rimmed glasses and polished them on the tail of his flannel shirt. Narrowed his eyes and frowned downward.

"I don't even have snow tires," said Sally. "Remember? You looked at them when I took them off last May and hauled them out to the dump." Tires meant a lot to Hawk. When he'd given her a set of Michelins for the Mustang for her birthday last year, she'd taken it as a sign of deep commitment. "The snow isn't even sticking," she told him, playing Wyoming's favorite wintertime role: amateur meteorologist. "It'll take a couple of hours for the ground to cool off enough for it to start piling up. Nina's expecting me. If I leave in the next half hour, I can get out there, talk to her about the benefit, and be back in time for lunch."

The temperature had dropped forty degrees overnight, blasting everybody's zinnias and marigolds and zucchini and tomato plants to shriveled black tangleweed. Yesterday, Sally had gone to work in a short denim skirt and a black cotton T-shirt. Today, she'd gotten up and put on jeans, a long-sleeved turtleneck, a fleece vest, and wool socks. For the ride out to Albany, she'd add a fleece jacket and lightweight hiking shoes, and throw a pair of sweatpants, an extra pair of socks, some heavier boots, a down jacket, a wool hat, cashmere-lined leather gloves, and a fleece scarf in the backseat. Her cell phone was fully charged, her gas tank full, her windshield washer tanks and antifreeze topped up. She'd made herself a small thermos of coffee and even laid in a supply of chemical heat packets, the kind hunters used to warm their hands and feet. She didn't want to fret Hawk, but on the other hand, she'd lived in Wyoming long enough to think ahead. She'd already put her foul-weather emergency kit in the trunk. Flashlight, granola bars, box of matches, blanket, plastic jug of water, jumper cables, tire chains, signal flares. She thought there might even be a few rock-hard Slim Jims left over from the previous year, so she wouldn't starve even if she was stuck in a ditch for a week. She'd toss in her sleeping bag. Hawk wasn't wrong to worry. In Wyoming, you couldn't actually be overprepared for a sudden onslaught of winter.

She had to get out there and see for herself what was going on before she pitched the idea of doing the Wild West benefit to the Millionaires. But there might be a slight problem with Jimbo Perrine, the Millionaires' ursine bass player, who proudly described himself as a born-and-bred Wyoming redneck. He worked a day job as a foreman at the cement plant, but during hunting season he moonlighted as a taxidermist. Jimbo handed around a business card that said, MOUNTS BY PERRINE. YOU SNUFF 'EM, WE STUFF 'EM.

Jimbo said he'd always wanted to take a trip to New Mexico just to shoot spotted owls. He referred to the Sierra Club as "the sequoia-fuckers."

It might not be so easy to talk Sam and Dwayne into it either. Sam Branch and Dwayne Langham, the Millionaires' lead guitarist and musical polymath, respectively, were also, respectively, the town's leading developer and banker. Sam's earlier thriving sales career in high-grade weed and snortable powder was one of those subjects his heavy-hitting Republican friends (some of whom were, of course, former customers) never saw fit to mention. As for Dwayne, who scoured eBay every day on the chance that a Grateful Dead bootleg he didn't own might be up for bid, his famously hyper-cautious loan policy at the Centennial Bank made even his most fascist colleagues smile faintly at his tendency to sport ties with dancing bears, or lightning-bolt skulls and roses, on the occasional casual Friday.

During the Vietnam War, Nina Cruz had been photographed in Hanoi, kissing a little guy in black pajamas. That didn't exactly bowl them over at the Rotary lunches. But maybe by the weekend, when Sally would see them, Sam and Dwayne would be in a good mood. A little bit of snow and they'd likely get their deer right off the bat. Hunters loved a nice light snow for the animals to walk through, not deep enough to create problems, but perfect for revealing tracks. With that kind of trail, even the most inept heavily armed bozo could fancy himself a heap-big frontier scout.

Some guys treated hunting as a social event. Sam Branch, for example, made a point of getting out the first day of deer season, and passing some hours at other times of the year getting wet and cold in duck blinds, chiefly to drink whiskey from a flask, tell off-color stories, and rack up karma points with the good ol' boys. But lots of Wyoming men, and a few women Sally knew, were skillful and serious hunters. Hawk, for instance, enjoyed bird hunting, and had bagged a nice goose for their last Christmas dinner. Dwayne Langham and his brother Dickie, the county sheriff, had pretty much been hunting from the time they could toddle, and they'd shot everything from rabbits and pheasants to elk and moose. Hunting was a big Langham family tradition, although Dickie allowed that since he'd gone into law enforcement, he'd lost some of his enthusiasm for putting holes in things that bled.

She hoped they'd be as jazzed about opening for Jackson as she was, but then again, if they decided they couldn't

stomach his lefty politics, she could have a tough time changing their minds. Back in 1980, after all, Sam had handed out
Reagan campaign buttons with every gram of coke.

But then who was she to take the high moral ground?
She'd spent her share of time with Sam during the Reagan
years, playing in the band and otherwise. Indeed, she'd done
five or six things she regretted right into the next millen-
nium, one or two of them with Sam Branch.

Fortunately, Hawk had developed the capacity for for-
giveness, given a decade or two.

She sighed. With Sam's ambitions and Dwayne's congen-
ital unwillingness to do anything that might be perceived as
controversial, she was going to have a tough time selling
them on the Wild West benefit. And that was before she even
got to Jimbo Perrine.

Her Michelins swished on the wet pavement as she drove
over the railroad bridge and into West Laramie. Ordinarily
she'd be blasting a CD by now, Beatles or Stones, reggae or
Haggard, whatever. But right now, she kept the music quiet.
Jonatha Brook offered up a Paul Simon tune at low volume.
Sally needed to be able to listen to the sound of her car
wheels on the road.

There were a few scattered cars and pickups in the parking lot at Foster's Country Corner Truck Stop. Almost no big
rigs. It occurred to Sally that any trucker pushing east on
I-80 was likely trying to keep ahead of the storm, while the
ones heading west would probably keep driving until it got
too bad to go on. The pavement was darkly wet but clear,
and you could still see lots of space between flakes. The
heavy heart of the front must be well to the west. Nina
Cruz's Shady Grove was forty minutes' drive from Laramie
in good weather. She'd have hours before getting back might
be a problem, Sally devoutly hoped.

If Foster's wasn't doing much business, the West Laramie
Fly Store was making up the difference. The Fly Store was a
local institution, the last stop at the edge of town for guns,
ammunition, camo gear, Vienna sausages, burned coffee in
plastic foam cups, and Goody's Headache Powder. King-
cab, step-side pickups, oversize SUVs, battered Jeeps, and

ancient Land Cruisers thronged the parking lot, abandoned at haphazard angles, as if the drivers had been too preoccupied with getting into the Fly Store for last-minute supplies to think about the fact that they were parked blocking three other vehicles.

But then, Sally reflected, it was after eight in the morning. Anybody presently buying bullets or preserved meat was already late. Conscientious sportsmen, looking to get a jump on the storm and the season, had doubtless risen in the dark, their gear packed, the Mr. Coffee programmed to drip a pot of Folgers right about the time their pajama pants hit the floor and they pulled on long johns. Here in southeastern Wyoming on the first bloody day of the season, antlered deer were already confronting mortality.

Sally drove on, deciding to pass up the turn-off for route 130 to Centennial, and continue along 230, southwest instead of straight due west. She could have gone through either Centennial, on the north, or Wood's Landing, from the south, to get to Nina's place southeast of Albany. Going down from Centennial would mean more paved road and less dirt, but would also require climbing up over a pass, where the snow would be heavier, the road, likely, worse. So Wood's Landing it was.

Twenty minutes later, her tires made a quieter sound as the road cooled and began to speckle white and frosty in spots. On a sunny day, she'd be driving close to seventy by now (and looking out for cops, since the speed limit was fifty-five). But it wasn't sunny. She was still fairly relaxed, but obeying the law, listening to the *ssshh* of her windshield wipers and taking note of the feel of her tires on the pavement. They gripped solid enough that she didn't even think about turning around, even though she had three miles of dirt road ahead, on the way to Nina's. Worse, on the way back.

Just before Wood's Landing, Sally turned north to wind her way uphill on a good enough gravel road in the summer, but a potential problem today. The creek paralleled, and then flowed under the road and right through Nina Cruz's land. That could make for a muddy, even flooded road. Happily for Sally, Nina's driveway was on this side of the creek. Still, the road could easily wash out if the culvert backed up. For now, the dirt was packing down slightly under the dusting of wet snow, not yet turning to slick and viscous gumbo.

She promised herself she'd have just a quick chat with Nina, and hope to lay eyes on a few of the Wild West crew. She was making this possibly unwise trip as much to reassure herself that taking the gig was the right thing to do as to accommodate Mr. Stone Jackson. Just because the guy was her Idol of All Time didn't mean she had to do everything he asked, now, did it?

Nina's driveway was on the left, and, as Sally took the turn, she was delighted to feel and hear gravel crunching beneath her wheels. One of the benefits of being a Hollywood homesteader, Sally reflected, was that you could afford to have somebody deliver a truckload of rock for your ranch road whenever you liked. Another benefit was that you could write a check, and some incredibly beautiful piece of Rocky Mountain paradise could be yours. The Shady Grove that had inspired the name of Nina's spread was an aspen forest. Here, more than eight thousand feet above sea level, it must have frosted a week ago. Slender silvery trunks spired up into the golden and leafy canopy, shivering in rhythm with the snowflakes that fell out of steely skies. The timbers of the log house, studio, and barn Nina had built had weathered gray in only two years. Nina had cleared as few trees as possible, and the buildings seemed to nestle into the landscape in almost organic harmony, counterpointed in bright, assertive notes by the tilting blue photovoltaic panels on the roof, the slender silver spire of the three-bladed wind turbine in the clearing.

Rhythm, harmony, counterpoint. Shady Grove made Sally imagine countryside in musical terms. Nina would like that. The house she'd built was a rambling musician's retreat, complete with three bedrooms and three baths, a vaulting central space combining kitchen, dining room, and enormous living room, full of light from windows and skylights. A short walk through the aspens, down a flagstone path, led to a smaller building, a studio housing recording equipment and instruments, a large office space, a futon bed, and another full bath. More room than a solitary occupant would need, but plenty of space for the occasional houseguest or three. Not enough for an occupying army of Californians, but sufficient for friends to drop in.

The ordinary Wyoming homesteader would have found Nina's place palatial. The average visitor from Malibu or Marin would see it as minimal, remote, rustic. Nina had told Sally that her agent, a lifelong Angeleno whose idea of roughing it was to sit in the second row at a Lakers' game, referred to Nina's Wyoming abode as "Dogpatch."

For the first time, Sally had some sympathy with the agent. The dirt-and-gravel turnaround between the house and the barn, big enough to accommodate a dozen vehicles without crowding, was packed. The school bus Stone Jackson had mentioned stood adjacent to the barn. It was painted lime green, its windows festooned with tie-dyed curtains. Any Wyomingite would instantly notice three things about the other cars, vans, and SUVs filling up the area. First, they all had out-of-state plates, mostly from California, but Oregon, Washington, and Colorado were also represented. Second, with the exception of the Ford F-250 Nina had bought for hauling, there were no pickup trucks. Third, nearly every vehicle was a foreign model, with the emphasis on European manufacturers. Northern Europe was heavily overrepresented, with Volkswagen vans and bugs, Mercedes sedans and sports cars, Volvos and Saabs. A couple of BMW SUVs represented the "roughing it" crowd. The sole Japanese vehicle she saw was a curiosity—a forest-green Toyota Prius, a hybrid gas-electric jellybean of a car favored, Sally knew, by science nerds who wanted to drive green and stay ahead of the technological curve.

Sally managed to slip the Mustang in between a yellow VW bug and a silver Mercedes Sport, opening her car door carefully so that she wouldn't leave a Mustang-red ding on the Mercedes. She had no sooner squeezed herself to a standing position than a shot rang out, then two more. She ducked, then felt incredibly stupid for doing so. By the time you heard a shot, after all, it was too late to do anything about it. Some hunter was a damn sight closer to the house than any hunter ought to be.

The front door slammed open, and Nina Cruz rushed out onto the porch and down the steps. "Damn damn damn!" she yelled. "I've posted so many signs on my fences, the place looks like Hollywood Boulevard. What part of NO HUNTING are these assholes not getting?"

Nina was wearing faded purple sweatpants, cut off above the knee, a long-sleeved gray sweatshirt with UNIVERSIDAD DE NUEVO MEXICO printed on the front, and fuzzy pink bedroom slippers. Her spiky-cut hair, once blue-black but now bright white, stood up in clumps around her head. The bones of her face, always prominent, now threatened to knife right through taut olive skin. Her immense black eyes were frantic.

At that, she was by no means the strangest sight to greet Sally's eyes. As Nina stood glancing wildly around the yard, the pink tufts of her slippers collecting fast-falling snow, two long-haired young people, a boy and a girl, ran out of the aspen grove, trailing long bright orange and hot pink streamers of plastic surveyors' flagging, giggling and stark-raving naked. Nina stared in horror at the streamers stretched tight, as the young people skirted the edge of the clearing, sprinting from one aspen to another, wrapping circles around the trees. "This oughta show those murderers a thing or two!" hollered the boy as he and the girl separated and ran in opposite directions around a final tree, colliding, pulling each other upright, and tying off their streamers in a bow. They embraced, laughing, and dragged each other off to the school bus, folded open the accordion door, and disappeared inside.

"Wh-what in the h-hell is going on out here?" Nina exclaimed. Her teeth had begun to chatter in the cold, and her bare legs were stippled with goose bumps. She turned and hollered toward the still-open front door of the house, "Wh-whose idea was it to t-turn my woods into s-some kind of D-DayGlo cuckooland? This m-mess comes down right n-now!"

Dashing to the first tree, Nina ripped the flagging off, and then ran off into the aspens, leaving a trail of large, flat, fuzzy-edged slipper prints in the deepening snow. The storm was getting going in earnest now. Nina disappeared surprisingly quickly, darting between the silver tree trunks, into the dancing swirl of snowflakes and shimmering golden heart-shaped leaves. Even her tracks filled fast with snow, vanishing before Sally's eyes.

Now a bearded, bare-chested man ran out onto the front porch, a pair of Gore-Tex boots in one hand. "Nina!" he yelled, sitting down on the porch swing and pulling on the boots before he caught sight of Sally. "Where'd she go, man?" he asked Sally.

Sally pointed into the aspen grove. "I think Nina's taking down the flagging," she told him. "She didn't seem too pleased."

The man looked up from lacing his boots, a puzzled expression on his face. "But she told us she needed to do something more to discourage the hunters," he said. "We talked about it, and came to a consensus that the best thing to do would be something colorful and nonconfrontational, sort of a conceptual art piece." He shook his head. "Oh well, I'd better go after her. She's hardly dressed for the snow."

Sally looked at his chest. "And you are?" she asked.

"Oh. Oh wow, man, you're right. It's cold out here," he said, standing up, running a hand through his mane of graying brown hair, looking down and apparently noticing for the first time that he wasn't wearing a shirt. He fondled the African beads hanging on a leather thong around his neck. Mr. Randy Whitebird, if Sally didn't miss her guess. "Guess I'd better get something on," he said.

As Whitebird was turning to go back inside, Sally heard another shot. The snow muffled the noise some, but still it seemed to have come from even closer to the house than the first three.

And then a scream.

All at once, the clearing was full of people, streaming out of the house and the school bus, coming out of the woods. A few dressed for the weather, others were in various stages of stunning unpreparedness. A more than middle-aged man, in jeans and a heavy fisherman's sweater, stumbled out of the aspens. His hair was in two long braids, red threaded liberally with gray. His hands were covered with blood, and the tracks he made in the snow were stained pink and spotted with dark red. "Oh God, oh God," he said over and over.

"What's wrong? Nels, what's happened?" shouted the shirtless man, running out into the snow and taking the bloody man by the shoulders.

"Deer. Oh man, Randy, I found a deer. Oh God, one of those bastards got one."

"Was that you screaming, Nels? Are you all right?" asked the formerly naked girl, now wearing jeans and a down parka with, Sally suspected, nothing underneath.

"No. No, I couldn't make a sound. Oh my God . . ."

The scream came again, trailing off into a moan.

Whitebird left the girl in the parka to deal with the man with the braids, and ran off into the woods, toward the place they'd last glimpsed Nina. Sally, instincts too alert, dreading against dread, ran after him. Her light hiking shoes made soft crunching noises in snow that was packing down and piling up. The snow was falling now thick and fast enough that she might lose her way within a few dozen yards of the house. Whoever had screamed was now moving into full-bore hysterics.

And no wonder. There in the midst of her own Shady Grove, Nina Cruz was sprawled on the white ground, her arms and legs at wrong angles. She was twitching very slightly. Blood gushed from a ragged hole that seemed at once too small and too large, neatly drilled through the DE between UNIVERSIDAD and NUEVO MEXICO on the front of her sweatshirt. Bubbles of bloody saliva were gathering at the corners of her mouth. A thin blonde woman in an anorak parka and jeans stood a yard from the fallen Nina, keening and sobbing.

Nina's mouth was moving. She was clearly in very grave shape, and she knew it. She was trying to say something. Sally and Whitebird bent down to try to hear over the blonde's wails.

"K-k-k," Nina said. "M-m-m-m."

Sally took Nina's hand. Her pulse was thready. "Don't try to talk, honey," she said. "We'll get help. You just hang in there."

Whitebird, shivering as snow caught in the thatch of graying hair on his chest, was leaning in to pick Nina up. "Don't!" Sally yelled. "Don't touch her. Is anybody here a doctor?"

Randy Whitebird stared at Sally for a second. "Yes," he said finally, kneeling down to take Nina's hand. "Nels Willen used to be a surgeon, before his epiphany."

The man who couldn't stand the sight of a shot deer had been a surgeon? Before his what? Half-a-dozen people had followed Whitebird and Sally to the spot where Nina Cruz lay. "Go to the house," she said far more calmly than she felt, "and call nine-one-one. Tell the dispatcher to get the ambulance out here right now."

"But it's snowing," said a woman in rainbow balloon pants and a black leather jacket.

Sally glanced down at Nina. Her skin had turned ashen, and the hand clasped in Sally's had ceased to clasp back. Life was leaking out of Nina Cruz far faster than an ambulance could drive or fly.

It didn't matter. Sally turned to the rainbow/leather woman. "Strange as this may sound," she said in a flat voice, "it snows in Wyoming. It's the busiest time of the year for the emergency folks." Sally was still holding on, but Nina had slipped off to another place. Sally's voice felt like it was coming from another person. "Just call fucking nine-one-one. And the sheriff. Tell them there's been a fatal shooting at Shady Grove."

3

The Corpse Magnet

It shouldn't have surprised Sally that several of the twenty people who were at Shady Grove at the moment when Nina Cruz was shot made an attempt to leave the scene the minute the word spread about the shooting. Sally was still crouching over Nina's body, gulping air as if it were cold water, when she heard the sound of the first car engine starting up. She was dimly aware of ex-doctor Nels Willen kneeling next to her in the snow, feeling for a pulse in Nina's neck, rising, shaking his head.

Sally battled sick dizziness. She climbed shakily to her feet, feeling, as the snow accumulated in her hair and the creases of her jacket, that touch of arthritis in the left knee, and stumbled toward the turnaround by the house.

Half-a-dozen Eurocar drivers were trying to elbow one another aside in the dash to be first out the driveway, spinning their tires, spitting enough gravel to crack the windshield of every vehicle in the lot, getting thoroughly in one another's way. Sally began to run, shouting at them to park and stay put until the police came. But Willen was way ahead of her. Having determined that there was nothing he could do for poor Nina, he'd quickly moved on to deal with what came next.

Sally had no idea what kind of epiphany Dr. Nels Willen had undergone, or why, or when. But right this minute, grizzled, gaunt, and gentle-faced, he'd clearly shaken off the shock of finding the dead deer. Long experience of coping with life-and-death situations in an operating room must have kicked in. Willen now stood smack in the middle of the driveway, scrubbing the last smears of deer blood off his hands with wet snow, speaking to the fleeing coastal motorists (five California plates, one Oregon) in the soothing drawl of somewhere in the Southland.

"Easy, easy all, y'all," Willen said. "Everybody just find a nice place to park, and we'll all go on up to the house and set tight. I reckon when the cops arrive, they'll want statements from each and every one of us." He looked around with calm eyes. "Anybody else hurt?"

No one was, at least no one in the clearing. Sally had no idea what other people might be on the property. Including, of course, whoever had fired the shots.

"I need to call my therapist!" whimpered the skinny blonde woman who'd found Nina. "My cell phone's got a dead battery, and Randy's on the phone at the house. I can't deal with the trauma!"

Sally took a millisecond to admire the way Nels said nothing and looked sympathetic, even as Sally herself was getting ready to tell the woman what she could do with her trauma. Nels's moment of patience broke the panic. The formerly naked girl walked up to the blonde's car, holding a cell phone. "You can use my phone, Lark," she said kindly. "The reception out here sucks, but if you stand right in the middle of the turnaround, you can at least get a connection."

"Thanks, Pammie," said Willen. "You just help Lark get through to her therapist, and everybody else can call their therapists if they want, too. I bet there are as many cell phones to go around as there are therapists."

Sally suppressed a snort, reminding herself that this wasn't even remotely a humorous situation. And then she realized she was trembling.

She bit down on her bottom lip and tried hard to will away the picture of Nina dying. God, she'd never ever seen anybody die before. So she kept biting that lip until she tasted blood. Let tears fall fast and hard as they would, as she fought to control the swirling faintness that threatened to take her away.

The faintness won. She raced for the base of the nearest aspen tree and gave up her morning latte. Horribly, that seemed to help. She scooped up a handful of snow, rinsed her mouth. Repeated the process twice, and then worked a minute more on getting first, her balance, and second, a grip. Falling to pieces made her part of the problem, not part of the solution.

Sally scoured her face with snow one more time, and suddenly she felt the cold. Then she walked back to where Willen confronted the crowd. "We should leave the house line free, in case the sheriff or the emergency med techs need to get through," he told the stunned group. "Who has cell phones anybody can use?"

People began pulling cell phones out of nowhere. Half of the group weren't any more dressed than Randy Whitebird had been. Pammie had gotten some clothes on, but there were several people in shorts, a couple of bare-breasted women as well as men, one guy in a saffron-dyed loincloth. Collectively, they offered a display of piercings and tattoos that would not have been visible among most Wyomingites most times of the year.

Not much in the way of handbags, backpacks, or pouches. Not many pockets even. It'd be a miracle if nobody succumbed to hypothermia. Still, half-naked and everything, they had their phones on their persons. Really coastal.

Nels looked Sally up and down. "You stay here and keep an eye on these folks while I go up to the house and get Whitebird off the phone," he said softly. "Give me a couple minutes to clean up and see how things are, and then we'd better get everybody up to the house before they all freeze to death. Let's gather everybody in the living room and make some tea and wait for the cops. Do you have any idea which direction those shots came from?"

"I'm not entirely sure, but it sounded to me like they came from down closer to the main road," Sally said. "Off in the woods somewhere. I wish I could be more specific."

"I do, too. I had the same impression, for what it's worth." He smiled sadly and introduced himself. Sally returned the favor. Then Dr. Nels Willen strode off toward the house, red-gray braids flying behind him.

They ended up having to move some of the Californians' cars anyway. The snow was falling thick and fast, but in spite of the worsening visibility and road conditions, the sheriff and the Albany County EMTs arrived within the hour, lights flashing, a red-shirted state game warden hard on their heels. The law added another six vehicles to the already crowded lot, one of those an ambulance big and heavy enough to churn up swerving ruts in a driveway rapidly denuding of gravel and slipping into muddiness. Sally stood on the front porch of Nina Cruz's house and watched them roll in. Four deputies leapt out of the first two county Blazers, the game warden right behind them, toting short-barreled shotguns and rifles, zipping up fleece-collared jackets, the deputies fanning out in all directions, the game warden shouting that he needed somebody to show him where the deer had gone down.

They all had their work to do. Someone, after all, had fired the shots that had killed Nina Cruz and a hapless deer. That person or persons were still at large. Sally walked down the stairs, out into the rising storm, passing another deputy running up the steps of the house. She headed straight for her old friend Dickie Langham, now sheriff of Albany County, standing in the falling snow, calmly telling everyone what to do.

"You know," Dickie Langham said to Sally as they stood amid the careful choreography of cars and trucks, the headlight beams gone murky in the whirling whiteness, "if I'd known how much of law enforcement was going to be directing traffic and moving motor vehicles, I'd have given more thought to staying in crime."

"Not true," said Sally, who had after all known Dickie back in his criminal years, when he'd been Laramie's most popular dope-dealing bartender. She knew how often the line between ragged and right, for him, had been precisely a matter of directing traffic—of another kind. She had little idea where he'd been or what he'd done during the eleven years he'd gone missing, but the fact that he'd returned clean, sober, and ready to go to cop school suggested that he'd learned something about avoiding fatal collisions. "You were born to be a good guy. That's why you're here with the badge."

She looked up at him. Dickie Langham was a big, tall, pear-shaped man in a fleece-lined khaki jacket with an AL-BANY COUNTY SHERIFF patch over the chest, and a dove-colored felt cowboy hat quickly filling at the brim with an accumulation of lacy wet snow. A man who'd befriended her when they'd both been young and frigging crazy. He had stuck by her even at her most erratic and self-indulgent. She'd stood fast for him, even when he'd grown spacy and paranoid by turns, blowing off his friends as well as suppliers, customers, and the leg breakers who came more and more often to collect debts.

They had lost contact for sixteen years, reuniting only a couple of years ago. But joyously. Dickie Langham and Sally Alder were beloved friends, now and forever.

Dickie peered back intently from under his hat, trying to gauge her state of mind. "I suppose you're just out here paying a casual social call on a lady friend in the middle of a blizzard."

"No, you don't. I'll level with you. I'm here because Nina's ex asked me to come out and check on her."

"Her ex? Stone Jackson? Some old Hollywood flame you've forgotten to mention to your hayseed Wyoming pals?" Dickie asked.

"No. Don't mock me," she said. "It's kind of a complicated story. But to make it short, he's a friend of a friend, and he knew I knew Nina, so he came to my office yesterday and asked me to come see if she was okay. He was worried about her."

Dickie nodded slowly. "Why?" he asked, his voice very soft.

"He thought she was acting weird. And he didn't like the company she was keeping," Sally explained.

Dickie thought that one over. "I begin to think you ought to wear a big sign that says 'Here comes trouble.'"

Sally inspected the toe of her shoe, digging into the snow. He was right. She had become something of a corpse magnet in the past couple of years.

"Aw Jesus, Mustang, I'm sorry. But how the hell does this keep happening?" he asked. "Never mind. We'll go over all that stuff. I just hate the idea that we keep meeting over dead bodies."

Sally shook herself, took a couple of hard breaths, and began to explain. "Nina wasn't dead when I got here. She was pissed off. Hunters were trespassing on her land, killing animals. The groovy earth people she'd invited in were treating her aspens as if they were stage props in some historic reenactment of a sixties happening or something. She came running outside in her fuzzy pink slippers, looking like somebody in the middle of being driven crazy. I can definitely understand why, and as soon as you meet these people, you will, too.

"I'd already heard a couple of shots," Sally continued.

"How many?" Dickie asked.

She thought a minute. "Three. I was just getting out of my car. I ducked when I heard them."

Dickie kept listening.

"Nina ran off into the trees. Then I heard another shot. I think they came from down by the road, out in the woods. I couldn't swear to it, but that's what I think. If it helps any."

Dickie's cell phone rang. "Langham," he answered. Sally could feel herself slipping into impossible despair. She fought that slick downhill slide in the only way she knew. She had to find a way to be of use.

That had to explain why she was listening hard to Dickie's voice, speaking a little too loudly into the cell phone.

Some would say she was eavesdropping. Others might call her fatally nosy. Fuck 'em. She preferred to think of herself as possessing a lively curiosity and using her powers for good, even as her nose felt as if it might fall off and her feet were turning into lumps of ice.

"Yeah. Yeah. Three-point-four miles up the Fox Creek Road from Wood's Landing," Dickie said, giving the location of the turnoff for Shady Grove. "The parking area at the ranch is pretty jammed right now, but by the time the DCI guys get here with the lab, we'll have finished interviewing at least some of the witnesses. Course, by then the weather may be too bad to send these folks to town. They aren't from around here. I kind of doubt they know much about driving in snow."

So the sheriff had called in the Wyoming Department of Criminal Investigations, and was expecting the arrival of the big RV that housed the state DCI's Mobile Crime Lab. Sally wondered whether that was the usual procedure in what anyone would assume was a tragic firearms accident on the first day of hunting season.

"What?" Dickie was saying now. "They're where? How long? Okay, okay. Tell 'em we want 'em out here as soon as possible, whenever that is. Okay. All right. Call me when you hear."

He hung up.

Sally looked at him expectantly. "The crime lab?" she said.

Dickie looked grim. "Backed up to hell and gone. A pissed-off trucker shot at somebody who'd aced him out at a pump at Little America and nearly blew the whole goddamn place to Nebraska. And they just found three kids, a mom, and a dad on a ranch outside Torrington, every one of them shot through the head. Model family, the neighbors are saying. My guess is that Dad had a very, very bad day. We're third in line for DCI's loving attentions."

"But they'll be here, right? Even if something else happens," Sally said.

Dickie began to walk toward the aspens. "This is a high-profile shooting. If we don't put half the state's annual crime-fighting budget into the investigation, next thing we know they'll be skinning us alive on *Entertainment Tonight*: 'Did a yahoo Wyoming hunter mistake an international celebrity for a mule deer? Or was this one more violent interlude in the great American culture wars between California and New York, and everybody else?'"

"And which do you think it was?" Sally asked, blinking her eyes against the snowfall as she padded along next to him, into the trees.

He stopped walking and turned to her. Dickie Langham was a placid man, but she was pushing too hard. "My dear darlin' Mustang Sally Alder," he said. "The Albany County Sheriff's Department is currently in the process of securing the scene of a fatal shooting. The Wyoming Game and Fish Department is in pursuit of whoever trespassed onto private land prominently posted as off-limits to hunting, took a deer, and, in an apparent act of wanton waste, left the carcass to rot. Odds are this was a horrible hunting accident. We are just barely commencing to collect evidence and interview witnesses. And right now, we've gotta deal with the damn parking problem and slog around in the woods, hoping to find some tracks that aren't already buried in snow. I've been banging the DCI to get the crime lab in here, but by the time they get around to it, if indeed they can actually manage to get here in this weather, most of our evidence will be snowed over or frozen up or melted down or washed away or otherwise fucked. Why in holy hell would you think I had any idea what happened here?"

Sally held her hands up. "Okay, okay, sorry. Just trying to help."

"Right. Thanks," he said. " I know you're upset. I think you should just go on inside and wait with the others. Get warm. Have a cup of tea. Let us do our job."

She knew what that meant. The county medical examiner, working on the body, taking a million pictures and five million notes. Deputies trying to comb the site without destroying evidence, in the middle of the rising blizzard. These guys earned their keep.

And she should get out of the way. She probably should just go inside. Sally became aware, for the first time, that the snow had cascaded up over the tops of her boots, seeping in, soaking her socks. No wonder her feet were freezing.

Dickie Langham walked off into the woods. Sally turned to head into the house. Then she stopped, listened, and turned back toward the driveway.

Another vehicle appeared. A battered Toyota 4Runner, with new County 5 plates.

Detective Scotty Atkins, chief investigator for the Albany County Sheriff's Department, in his private ride. Off-duty that day, Sally deduced, but they must have called Atkins in on the emergency. He'd finally taken the Casper plates off his truck. Sally found herself wondering if that meant anything in terms of Scotty getting over his divorce from the ex who still lived up in Natrona County.

He wore flannel-lined khakis, Redwing boots, and a corduroy- collared barn jacket. Short, slightly wavy hair; no hat. Scotty Atkins was a long, lean, cold-eyed Wyoming cop who dressed like a preppie and moved like a cat. He liked his rock music dark and moody. Sally wasn't sure what else he liked. She kind of thought he liked her, but she was trying not to think about that.

Scotty played basketball with Hawk three mornings a week, and sometimes at noon. The two seemed to enjoy and respect each other. But those games occasionally got physical. Both men were taciturn and restrained. On the surface. She knew quite a bit about what Hawk was like under the surface. She had her suspicions about Scotty. She did not like to think about anybody getting a hard elbow in the mouth in a tussle for control of the ball.

"Professor Alder," said Atkins, towering over her, his pale green eyes searching hers quickly, then flicking down to her waterlogged boots. "Don't you have enough sense to get in out of the snow?"

Sally was just composing her answer to this egregious opening insult when the game warden emerged from the trees, carrying something weighty in a plastic garbage bag. He headed to his truck and gently tossed the bag into the truck bed. Then he pulled out a cell phone and punched in a number. He spoke briefly into it, finished the call, and walked over to where they were standing.

"Detective Atkins," said the warden, introducing himself. "We were at the law enforcement academy in Douglas together."

"Been a while," said Atkins, nodding a greeting. "You find the shooter?"

"Unfortunately, no," said the warden. "There are two sets of boot prints leading off toward the road, and some tire treads that look like they came from a pickup or a big SUV, over some other treads. All of it already pretty snowed over. Those guys are long gone. There might be prints in the mud under the snow, but we won't know until it melts, and by that time they probably won't be worth much." The game warden reached inside his jacket, pulled out a soggy pack of cigarettes and a lighter, and spent a few moments lighting a limp Vantage.

"So what's in the garbage bag?" Atkins asked.

The game warden shut an eye against the smoke piling up under his cowboy hat, assessing the mess of vehicles in the turnaround. "The head. The sheriff asked me to leave the rest of the carcass."

"The head was separated from the body?" Sally said, wondering what the hell kind of gun you would use to blow a head clean off a large mammal.

"Nope," said the warden. Sally had the impression that the man might be deciding that she was an amazing idiot. "I cut the head off."

"Cut it off?" she echoed, maybe confirming his impression.

"Have to get the brain to the state vet lab in Laramie. Standard procedure when we find an animal with spongiform encephalopathy."

Scotty closed his eyes.

"What do you mean?" Sally asked.

"Chronic wasting disease. It's been in the deer and elk herds around here for eight, maybe ten years, but it's really taken off in the last year or two. Nobody knows why. These days, the vets are spending a lot of time looking at brain tissue."

"So where was the deer shot?" Scotty asked.

The man sucked smoke, exhaled, jerked his head toward the aspens. "Out there in the woods," he said.

Cop hilarity.

"Where on its body?" Scotty tried again.

"Right through the heart. Looks like the slug's buried good in the chest cavity."

"The deer's brain is your problem," Atkins said, as a deputy arrived to take him to the place in the grove where Nina Cruz's body lay. "Make sure we get ballistics on the slug."

4

Professional Law Enforcement Officers

She stood in the parking area a moment more, snow falling around her. Sally pulled her cell phone out of an inside pocket in her jacket and called Hawk's office. He'd be in class right now, but she could leave a message on his voicemail. The message she left was this: "Hi, honey. Some stuff has happened out here at Shady Grove that I'd rather not discuss in an answering machine message. I'm fine, but I'll be later than I thought getting back. You can try calling me on my cell, but the reception out here isn't that great. I'll try you again later. Seriously, I'm fine, so don't worry. I love you, Jody," she finished, calling him by the nickname she usually reserved for intimate situations. As she hung up, she realized that her use of her secret name for him was certain to alarm him. She hoped to hell he wouldn't decide to leap into his pickup and snowplow his way out to Albany. So she called again, got his machine again, and said, "I mean it, Hawk. Don't worry. Don't come out here. There's no place for you to park your truck. Dickie's here, so if the weather and the roads are too bad for me to drive the Mustang home, I can hitch a ride with him."

Oh yeah. Telling Hawk that Sheriff Dickie Langham was on the scene was dead certain to reassure him.

Then she made a call to another cell phone. Stone Jackson answered on the third ring. She'd found him, he said, at the McDonald's in Riverton, where snowblindness had forced him off the road on his way to the Busted Heart. "Lovely weather you have around here. My favorite colors. White on white," he said, clearly getting ready to launch into an extended discussion of the storm. Jackson might be from Lexington, Virginia, and Santa Monica, California, but he'd developed the Wyomingite's habit of assuming that everyone else was, or ought to be, fascinated by shitty weather. This kind of talk would go on throughout the state for nine months or so, until summer came.

"Thomas," said Sally, "there's been a terrible accident." She told him what had happened.

"I'm coming down there," he said, talking over the din of a fast-food place capitalizing on the vulnerability of motorists to the inevitable fact of winter. He sounded wired, the way people who have just taken an unendurable blow will sometimes sound, inappropriately chipper. "I'll just get a cup of scalding hot coffee, and I'll be on my way."

"Stone," said Sally, "most of the roads between where you are and where I'm standing are closed. If they aren't, they should be. If I were you, I'd go on down to the best motel in Riverton and let them know you're a famous guy who needs a room even if they have to kick out some family with six kids and a hundred-year-old grandma."

"Sally," he said, "you've just told me that Nina's dead. Somebody shot her to death, and the cops don't know who it was. If I have to stay in some motel in Riverton, I'll go fucking crazy. I need to be there."

Of course he did. If Hawk had been hurt, let alone killed, she'd be fighting her way through snow wallows and roadblocks until she got to him. Through alkali wastes, boulder fields, muddy morasses of slickrock gumbo, even hails of flaming arrows. Thomas Jackson had first come to see Sally because he was worried about Nina, and now here she was calling him to say that his worst nightmare had come true. She could barely begin to imagine his state of mind.

"Look, I can't fathom how you feel, but I understand why you need to be here," she told Jackson. "It's just that right now, there's no way in hell you could get here. Come tomorrow. They'll have opened some roads—maybe they'll even have plowed a couple. All you'll miss is the interrogation."

"Interrogation?" he asked. "Did they catch the hunter?"

"No. They're still looking, but the police are going to question everybody here. About twenty all told, presumably the staff and wannabe staff of the foundation. Most seem wacky and mildly incompetent—I can see why you call 'em Dub-Dubs. But there's one guy, this ex-surgeon, who's got something on the ball. He was the one who found the dead deer, and it really freaked him out. Still, the minute he found out Nina'd been shot, he snapped back into emergency mode."

"Nels Willen's there?" said Stone.

"Yeah, that's his name. Do you know him?" Sally asked.

"Only forever," said Jackson. "He's a good ol' Texas boy. We used to go skiing at Aspen. He was the top orthopedic surgeon in town. Half the people I know had their knees scoped by him, and Nina and I got to be friends with him when we had a place out there. Twenty years ago, she ripped up her left ACL skiing in the backcountry at Zermatt, and Nels flew all the way to Switzerland to staple her back together. I'm glad to hear he made it up there."

"Wasn't he here when you came out to visit yesterday?" Sally inquired.

"No. Actually, I called him and asked him to come up, and he said he'd get right on the road. Must have arrived last night. He was always an environmentalist, but lately he's gotten real passionate on the subject of animal rights. Nina told me a couple of weeks ago that she'd recruited him to help with the fund-raising for Wild West, so I knew they were in touch.

"When I saw how weird she was acting, I wanted somebody with medical expertise to take a look at her and see if I was just overreacting, or if there might really be something wrong with her. Nels hasn't practiced medicine in five years or so, but he's a smart guy, and I trust him. When I told him how sketchy she's been, how she was losing weight and throwing tantrums, he sounded really worried. I didn't find that too reassuring."

"What part do you think worried him the most?" said Sally.

"All of it. He'd seen her in August and noticed some of the same stuff, but not to this degree." Jackson slurped something. Must have gotten that cup of Mickey D's litigation coffee.

"So Willen would have been bothered enough by what you said that he'd have managed to get himself here by last night?" Sally said.

"He's got a spread up in North Park, Colorado, now, outside the town of Rand. He could have been at Shady Grove by dinnertime yesterday, no problem. He's lived up in the high Rockies for a long time, so the likelihood of a little snowstorm today wouldn't scare him. For Nina, he'd get there as quick as possible, no questions asked."

"Why?" Against the cold and the horror, Sally could feel a puzzle beginning to buzz in her brain.

Jackson sighed into his cell phone, while somebody in the background took somebody else's order for a Quarter Pounder meal, supersized. "He loves her. Half the men who ever met Nina Cruz have fallen in wicked love with her. Hell, half the women, too. But Nels has a little more at stake than your average Nina-phile. When she left me all those years ago, she went straight to Aspen. Lived with him for two years."

"They were lovers?" Sally couldn't believe she was having this conversation in the middle of a crime scene in the middle of a blizzard.

"Everyone assumed so. I couldn't say for sure. Those were the years I spent a lot of time with swarms of imaginary bats flying around my head. I've chosen to believe that Nels was a kind of father figure to her, taking her in to help her heal from all the damage I'd done. Made it easier for me to revive a friendship with him when I got my shit together.

Anyhow, I'm glad he's there. Tell him to stick around until I get there tomorrow."

Sally had the feeling that pretty much all of the Dub-Dubs might be sticking around, given the investigation, the weather, and the likelihood that by the time they were able to get out, every motel in Laramie would be overflowing.

"Meantime," said Jackson, "I'd better put in a call to Cat. She's gonna have to come back from Brazil. Nina's parents are dead, so Cat's her next of kin." His voice broke on the word *kin*.

"I'm really sorry, Thomas," said Sally, wishing, in vain, for adequate words.

"Yeah," he said, breathing through tears. "Yeah. Okay. I'll be there tomorrow. Think I will try to get that motel room. Meantime, call me with whatever you know, and tell Nels to do the same."

"Sure. Of course. What else can I do for you?" Sally asked him.

"Remind me that it'd be a real stupid thing for me to pick up a bottle of Chivas on the way to the motel."

"You don't need reminding," Sally ventured.

"The hell I don't. But I won't. Keep in touch." He hung up.

The scene inside Nina's house was moving out of chaos and into a surreal order. As Sally entered, everyone seemed to be talking or whimpering or sobbing. Then Dickie Langham, standing in the center of the great room like a human tent pole, cut through the cacophony. "I need quiet, *right now*," he hollered.

He got it.

"Could somebody turn a few lights on in here?" Dickie asked.

Come to think of it, the house did seem dim. A couple of people walked around plugging in lamps and turning them on. Sally had to hand it to Nina Cruz. Not many people worried about phantom load, the quantity of electricity consumed by appliances that were plugged in but turned off. Nina walked the walk.

"Allow me to introduce myself to all of you," Dickie told the group. "I am Sheriff Langham of Albany County,

Wyoming, and this here sympathetic soul is Detective Scott Atkins." Dickie waved an arm at Scotty. Scotty surveyed the room without blinking.

"As you all know," Dickie continued, "one Nina Cruz, owner of this property, was shot and killed not five hundred yards from this house, earlier this morning. At this moment, we are investigating her death as a hunting accident. This is not a homicide investigation, although that could change. We've secured the scene of the shooting, and Albany County deputies are currently collecting evidence. We're awaiting the arrival of the state's Mobile Crime Lab, but that may be some time from now."

A young man with blond dreadlocks spoke up. "Are we in danger here?"

"Any time a person is shot, it should be considered a dangerous situation," Dickie said. "But we've searched the property and the vicinity, as has the state game warden. We've secured the area. We haven't found anybody out there runnin' around with a rifle, if that's what you're worried about. At least not on this property. But I wouldn't vouch for the rest of the county. It is hunting season, after all."

Sally noticed that Dickie said nothing about the boot prints and tire tracks in the snow that the game warden had mentioned to Scotty.

A woman spoke up, indignant. "You can't imagine that anybody here would shoot a deer, let alone a person! We're all here because we believe in the sacredness of wilderness and the sanctity of life. I doubt there's anybody here who even knows how to fire a gun!"

Dickie regarded the woman with bland amusement. "We're not making any assumptions about anything, ma'am. That's not our job. We will be asking you all a whole bunch of questions, and we're gonna need the cooperation of every person here. You people may think we're a bunch of dumb cowpokes, but I assure you that we are professional law enforcement officers."

Several of the Dub-Dubs sniggered.

Dickie looked from one side of the room to the other, and then said, "I can understand your skepticism. You probably think we're no more competent than, say, the Los Angeles Police Department. But I promise you that the Albany County Sheriff's Department will hold to a higher standard than our less meticulous, more sophisticated, better-lookin' big-city brethren. This is a high-profile case. The good news is that this is Wyoming. Maybe a dozen people will be dealing with the actual, physical evidence between now and the time the case comes to trial. Think about it, folks. Could we possibly fuck up as bad as the idiots who let O.J. walk?"

The Dub-Dubs regarded him in shock.

"Now we'll get on with our business," Dickie said, having made his point. "We surely do appreciate your help."

Sally had to suppress a guffaw.

"I'm sure all these folks will be glad to do everything they can for you, Sheriff," interjected Nels Willen, looking meaningfully around the room. Heads nodded, but Sally could see expressions on the faces that ranged from eager to perplexed to potentially resistant. Randy Whitebird didn't even nod. Just sat on Nina's couch, fingered his beads, inspected Dickie and Scotty with narrowed eyes.

"What would you like us to do?" Willen asked Dickie.

Dickie looked Willen up and down, regarded the motley crowd, and smiled a little, sympathy in his eyes. "For starters," he said, "I'd suggest that everybody put on a shirt and pants, and somebody build a fire in the woodstove. That fire in the fireplace looks cozy, but you all need to concentrate on keeping warm. I assume you've all got sleeping bags or whatever around, and you'd best gather 'em up and bring 'em in here. This storm's gonna get heavier before it lets up."

Sally raised her hand. "I'll get on the fire."

Dickie nodded. "You might also think about organizing a detail to get something together to feed people. We're liable to be here awhile."

Trust Dickie to get somebody on the food. Sally had seen him power down not one but *two* Quarter Pounders, supersized, on an average lunch day. At Shady Grove they probably ran more to buckwheat groats and steamed cabbage than buckets of french fries, but if that was all they had, Dickie Langham would certainly find a way to fill the void.

Pammie spoke up instantly. "I'm on it," she said, touching a couple of people on the shoulder and beckoning them toward the kitchen. Sally was happy to see that Pammie was actually wearing a shirt, and intrigued to note that it was a Wyoming Cowboys football jersey.

"Third," said Dickie, "you folks have to promise me that you won't talk amongst yourselves about what happened here this morning. Anybody here might have seen or heard something that can help us figure out what happened. But if you start comparing stories, pretty soon you won't know what the hell—excuse me—what in the world you really did see. So do Detective Atkins and me a favor, and find some other way to entertain yourselves while we conduct our interviews. We'll be using Ms. Cruz's studio out back, talking with you one at a time. Meanwhile, my deputies over there"—he gestured at two poker-faced guys in khaki, one young, one middle-aged, both looking as if they'd sell their children for a cigarette just now—"will keep you company."

The Dub-Dubs examined the deputies. The deputies glared back impassively. Quite a house party was shaping up, Sally thought.

"Is there any chance," Atkins asked Pammie, "that it'd be possible to get a pot of coffee?"

Several Dub-Dubs gasped. Randy Whitebird, dressed now in Dockers, a long-sleeved T-shirt with a Greenpeace logo, and his trademark Birkenstocks with socks, stepped forward to take Scotty on. "Do you have any idea what coffee plantations have done to the rain forest?" he asked, his voice quivering with outrage. "Not to mention what they do to the indigenous people and the workers!"

Atkins sighed.

"I think," Willen interjected, "that I might be able to scare up some coffee for you, Detective. I brought some of the stuff I mail order from an organic farming cooperative in Costa Rica."

"Don't worry about saving our souls," said Dickie. "Gotta figure the acre of rain forest in my cup is already plowed under anyhow."

Sally took her stand. "Guess I'll have some, too. It's as good a thing to go to hell for as any."

Willen grinned at her. "And we've got some calming chamomile tea for those of you who aren't going to hell. Meanwhile, let's see if we can't find a productive way to pass our time while the investigation goes on. Lark, how 'bout you lead a yoga class while we wait?"

And now Sally saw that what she'd taken for chaos was really a kind of social functioning she'd forgotten in the years since she'd been a grad student at Berzerkly. Skinny Lark, her trauma and her therapist evidently pacified, swung right into action. Within ten minutes, virtually everyone in the room (coffee drinkers and the cooking crew excepted), had gone off to find sleeping bags and yoga mats, had changed into loose pants and T-shirts, and had lined up ready to be put through their asanas.

For people who doubtless prided themselves on their technicolor nonconformity, the Dub-Dubs turned out to be remarkably tractable. All of them except Randy Whitebird. While the yoga practitioners put their hands palm to palm and got their breathing under control, Scotty Atkins asked Willen who might be considered in charge of things at Shady Grove, with Nina gone. Before Willen could answer, Whitebird stepped off his mat, stalked over to the detective, and stood an inch or two closer to Atkins than Americans generally found comfortable. He introduced himself, told Atkins that as the Wild West Foundation director, he felt it was his responsibility to facilitate all interactions between his people and local law enforcement.

"Are these your people?" Scotty asked Whitebird, raising his eyebrows. "Gosh, and I'd thought feudalism was, like, totally over in California."

"What Detective Atkins is meaning to say, Mr. Whitebird," Dickie said, smoothly inserting his oversize self into the somewhat too-narrow space between them, "is that we'll be needing to speak individually with everyone here, but we're grateful for whatever you can do to help us with the investigation." He smiled warmly into Whitebird's eyes, and even patted him on the arm. Sally suppressed an urge to laugh or maybe puke again. "Now if you'd be so kind, we'd like it if you'd just step out back to Ms. Cruz's studio with us, so we can get started."

Sally followed them out, leaving the door ajar so she wouldn't have to drop an armload of wood to open it back up, slogging through the snow toward the woodpile, next to the path between the house and the studio. She brushed snow off the pile and started digging down, looking for dry logs, when she noticed that one end of the pile was covered with a snow-laden tarp. There'd be dry stuff under it, she knew. Careful to keep snow from cascading onto the pile, she pulled the tarp off. And underneath, sitting on top of the pile, was what Sally believed to be the kind of rifle you'd use to kill a deer.

Her heart seemed to stop, then kick hard.

She ran toward the studio and managed to catch Scotty by the arm before they'd shut the door. "You need to come see what I just found out on the woodpile."

"May I ask what you're doing rooting through the wood-pile?"

Sally gritted her teeth. "I'm building a fire in the wood-stove. It would be useful to have wood."

Scotty looked down at her hand, gripping his arm, and she let go, then led the way to where she'd found the rifle.

Scotty picked up the gun and drew the bolt back. A spent shell popped out of the chamber. Sally smelled burnt gun-powder. "Thank you for bringing this to my attention. Now, if you please, get your wood, go back inside, and make that fire."

By this time Dickie and Whitebird had joined them. And several of the people inside stood at the back door, looking out.

"Huh," Dickie said. "Winchester .270. Deal with the weapon," he told Scotty. "There are evidence bags in the stu-dio. I'd better go talk to the folks."

Back inside, they were met with puzzled looks, apprehen-sive expressions, and horror all around. Or mostly around.

"I understand you folks just got a look at a rifle Professor Alder found. Anybody know anything about it?" Dickie asked.

"Yeah," said Nels Willen. "I do. I was planning to tell you about that. That there's my rifle. I used to be quite a hunter in my time. Nowadays, of course, I have a problem with it."

"Nels!" exclaimed Whitebird. "How could you bring a gun up here?"

"When I called Nina yesterday to say I was coming up, she asked me if I had a gun I could bring. She knew I used to collect guns. I sold 'em all off, except that one I kept. Shot my last deer with it," Willen said.

"But why?" Whitebird said. "Why would she want you to bring it? Nina, of all people!"

Willen pressed his lips together. "She said with all the shooting that had gone on around her place this fall, she felt like she had to have some way to defend herself. I thought it sounded crazy. That she'd gone into some kind of paranoid state. That was one reason I came. She scared me with that kind of talk. I didn't want to bring the gun. But she told me she had to have it. She said she was sure somebody was trying to kill her."

5

The Soul Mates

Nels Willen disappeared out the back door with Dickie, leaving shocked silence, then muddled murmuring in his wake.

Suddenly there was a shrill whistle, and Sally looked around to see Pammie, of all people, with her little fingers stuck in either side of her mouth. "Listen up, people!" Pammie said loudly, commanding attention. "I'm sure Nels hasn't done anything wrong, and the police will be getting to the bottom of this. Meanwhile, why don't we just do what we were doing anyhow? I'm gonna get dinner together. Why don't you all go ahead with the yoga class? I think we should focus on the healthiest, most healing things we can think of, while we wait to talk to the sheriff."

Well, hell, why not? What else could they do? Given that other muttered suggestions had included everyone heading out to get stuck somewhere on the road to Laramie, or banding together and storming Nina's studio to liberate Nels Willen from the clutches of the fascist Albany County pigs, Pammie's notion seemed an eminently sensible plan. Sally assessed her choices. The yoga class actually looked pretty good, but yoga pants weren't included in the survival gear

Sally had stuffed in the Mustang. She elected to help Pammie's crew with dinner.

Which turned out to be something of a revelation. Start with the food. Sally wasn't one of those people who believed that vegetarian meals basically boiled down to negative eating, to making do with what you didn't want, because what you wanted, you couldn't have. She was, after all, a former hippie, a longtime Californian, and a woman of the world. She'd relished porcini-and-morel-mushroom risotto at a trendy hot spot in Santa Monica, crunched savory *masala dosas* in Delhi, feasted at Berkeley vegetarian potlucks thrown by and for organic epicures. She had put in her time as a passionate gardener, shoveling compost and picking snails off lettuce leaves, and she possessed some succulent recipes for tomatoes and, yes, even eggplant.

But she'd also had maybe hundreds of meals consisting of greasy stir-fried cabbage and limp broccoli and brown rice that had been pressure-cooked to a fault, all soaked in a tamari sauce that had probably spent its youth as motor oil. In short, her expectations regarding cuisine at Shady Grove were modest at best.

She hadn't reckoned on the chef. Sally's impression of Pammie was that she was well intentioned but seriously scrambled. After all, this was a person she'd first encountered naked in the snow. Sally figured that the preparation of dinner would entail a fair bit of joint smoking, giggling, and haphazard assembling of meatless messes.

What a shock to discover that a person named Pammie was a born-and-ruthless kitchen general. She quickly assigned her three assistants their particular tasks (chopping vegetables for soup and salad, mixing bread dough, working up a couple of apple pies), as Pammie herself located ingredients, set up work stations for each assistant, and took upon herself the tasks of creating the soup, kneading and tending the dough, and finishing the salad.

Sally volunteered to chop. She nearly severed a hand discovering that somebody (doubtless at Pammie's direction) kept Nina Cruz's knives sharp enough to gut a rhinoceros. As Sally took three deep breaths and resumed chopping at a more deliberate pace, she looked around and noticed that Nina's kitchen was elaborately stocked and brilliantly organized. Open shelves held spices and cans and boxes, big glass jars filled with grains, pastas and beans, oils, vinegars, dried fruits and vegetables, aromatic herbs. There was a Sub-Zero refrigerator, a stand-up freezer, and a commercial range, all done in stainless steel. Sally would have loved to check out the freezer, to see what kinds of vegetarian culinary essentials lay within (vats of brown stock made from potatoes and leeks and carrots? Bags of flash-frozen berries? Gallons of golden curries?), but she'd have had to shove Pammie out of the way to take a peek.

Before long, the house filled with the splendid aroma produced by somebody who knew what she was doing, sautéing down the layers of a proper base for a perfect *minestrone à la Milanese*.

The formerly naked boy, clad now in jeans and a Phish T-shirt, stood at Sally's shoulder, meticulously slicing apples into a hand-thrown ceramic bowl decorated with petroglyph symbols. He glanced at Pammie stirring the contents of her stockpot, turned back to Sally, and said, "Give it five minutes, and then check out what you're smelling." He grinned goofily and sighed.

Obviously he was in love.

His name, he said, was Quartz. Sally assumed the worst (self-selection of an unfortunate nature name under the influence of shallow knowledge and hallucinogenics) but then felt ashamed of herself when she learned that "Quartz" was a contraction of his actual name: Quentin Schwartz. He'd grown up in Portland, in a devoutly Unitarian family (if that wasn't an oxymoron), had converted to environmentalism at the age of twelve. He'd been volunteering in the office of Deep Nature, an Oregon group dedicated to returning the state to the way it had been in 1800. He'd met Randy Whitebird and Kali, the director and administrator of Wild West, at a conference in Eugene. They'd convinced him that Wyoming was a whole lot more like it had been in 1800 than Oregon was, due to the fact that hardly anybody lived in

Wyoming, or ever had. It seemed pressing, said Quartz, to make sure that hardly anybody ever would.

Sally was pretty sure overpopulation would never be a problem in a state where the fainthearted would flee winter by February, the stouter of mien might last through April, and those still desperate or crazy enough to be around by Memorial Day would still be waiting for spring. Not to say that there weren't plenty of ways Wyoming could permanently wreck itself (or already had; the state, after all, had a long and abusive love affair with mining and drilling, fertilizers and pesticides). If Quartz wanted to imagine that he was single-handedly keeping the population down, he'd at least have reason to feel successful.

He said that Randy and Kali even offered to pay him, whereas he'd been working at Deep Nature for the Experience. So he'd put a new clutch in his parents' aging school bus and headed east to the Rockies.

"It must have been my karma," said Quartz. How long since Sally'd heard somebody say *that*? "I mean, I guess I was meant to come here. If I hadn't, I'd never have met my soul mate," Quartz avowed.

"Soul mate," she said, logging one more expression that hadn't often fallen on her ears since the fall of Saigon. "Pammie?" Sally inquired, watching the soul mate in question pull a small jar labeled FLEUR DE SEL off a shelf, extract a large pinch between two fingers and a thumb, and swirl an artful sprinkle onto her aromatics.

"Yeah," breathed Quartz, adding cinnamon, nutmeg, allspice, and brown sugar to his sliced apples. "There's no chance our paths would have crossed if I hadn't come here. She grew up in Laramie and she still goes to the university. The farthest she's been from her hometown is Denver."

Sally watched as Pammie critically examined the potatoes she was adding to her pot. "I wouldn't have thought growing up in Laramie would turn somebody into a future four-star chef."

"It's her calling," said Quartz. "I saw that the first time I laid eyes on her. I mean, I'm into food and everything, but Pammie connects with what we eat on a higher plane."

Much as Sally hated to admit it, she had a notion of what he was talking about. Lots of people cooked. Only a few treated making dinner as if it were making love. To somebody you really cared about.

"Pammie's training now, but she's hoping to open her own place in a couple of years," Quartz explained.

Training. Okay. Now Sally knew where she'd seen Pammie before. In the past few months, the dinner salads at the Yippie I O Café had gone from being nicely prepared and presented to being works of epicurean art. If you took away the long blonde ponytail and plunked on a calico chef's hat, you'd have chef John-Boy Walton's salad girl, an employee he bragged about and exploited with equal enthusiasm.

"So, did you two soul mates meet at the Yippie I O?" Sally asked.

He sighed sweetly. "Yeah. I'd gone to town with Nina and Kali to get groceries, and they decided to stop off for lunch. Nina ordered the black bean soup, but Kali wouldn't touch it because it was cooked."

Sally blinked and shook her head. "I thought the whole point of going to a restaurant is that you get to eat food somebody else cooked."

"Not if you're Kali," said Quartz, sprinkling fresh lemon zest into his bowl and gently turning the mixture with his hands. "She only eats raw foods—fruits and vegetables, nuts and seeds. She mixes in a little soy here and there, but it's a pretty narrow diet, and she's totally adamant about it, even though she's too shy to actually confront a waiter or anybody."

"So let me guess," Sally said, filching a perfectly seasoned apple slice. "They sent you to talk to the cooks."

Quartz was grinning in earnest. "Yeah. Lucky, lucky me. Pam was whirling around at this long open counter, pulling stuff out of undercounter fridges, chopping and assembling and arranging. She piled up this and that, and the next thing I knew, Kali was digging into some concoction of enoki mushrooms and arugula and raspberries and blueberries that looked like the garden at the Tuileries."

Sally stifled a laugh. Those Unitarian boys had almost all

been sent overseas by their parents to learn about other cultures. Some went to Ghana or Guyana. Others, like Quartz, opted for the chance to get to Paris on somebody else's money. "So who got to play Marie Antoinette?"

Quartz walked to the refrigerator, pulled out a wax-paper-wrapped parcel of pie dough, and began rolling out his crust. "Well, Nina was our queen, of course. But Kali is kind of like one of those ladies-in-waiting. You know, with the heart-shaped patch in the corner of her mouth and big schemes for the empire."

"Nice feel for the ancien régime, Quartz." How could such a person have only a short while earlier been running naked through a Wyoming blizzard?

"I was a history major at Reed. Really dug the French Revolution."

That explained a lot. But there was something serious at work under Quartz's metaphor. This Kali was assuredly an important presence in the Wild West Foundation. "So where is Madame du Barry today?"

"She left for Salt Lake City yesterday," Pammie called from across the kitchen. She had her back to them, stood maybe eight feet away, was in the middle of explaining to her other assistant, the boy with the blond dreads, how to use a potato peeler to shave Parmesan cheese. Pammie possessed the master chef's uncanny and uncontested talent for knowing what everybody in the kitchen was saying, who they were saying it about, and why, and then joining in the conversation as if she had every right to be included. "Kali goes to Utah every couple of weeks to check in with her biotech firm. Wild West doesn't pay a lot, as I'm sure you can imagine, so most of us do some moonlighting. She's pretty much kept her day job."

"I thought you were working at the Yippie I O," Sally said as she ferried a cutting board full of chopped zucchini and tomatoes across to Pammie. "Doesn't that keep you pretty busy?"

Pammie shot Sally a sidelong glance as she laid out a bouquet of parsley on a board, anchored the tip of her big triangle-bladed knife, and hefted the handle to begin chopping. "I've been working out here on a day-to-day basis ever since Quartz showed up." She had the grace to smile at her, er, soul mate. "A couple of weeks ago, Nina asked me to be her personal chef."

"I'm surprised," said Sally. "That seems pretty Hollywood for Nina. From our conversations, I'd had the impression she wasn't too concerned about food. She told me once that one of the best meals she ever had was a bowl of Raisin Bran, eaten standing over the sink, watching the sun set over the hills."

"Just because you don't mind a view doesn't mean that you don't care about *food*," said Pammie, sniffing haughtily. "Nina cared. She liked lovely, healthy food. But with the exception of coming in to make a smoothie every morning, she had absolutely no idea what people did in a kitchen."

"She was really particular about that smoothie," Quartz said.

"Yeah," Pammie agreed. "I kept telling her I could easily blitz one up if she'd just tell me her secret recipe, but she always made it herself."

"Not that the recipe was really a secret," said Quartz, pinching the top crust of his apple pie to the bottom, fluting the edges, slashing leaf patterns in the dough for vents. "A couple handfuls of fresh or frozen fruit, couple big spoonfuls of soy yogurt, a drizzle of honey, a big splash of soy milk, and a huge heaping spoon of protein powder. What's not to love?"

Pammie continued pulverizing her parsley, but she couldn't resist a comment. "Soy yogurt, soy milk, even soy protein powder—yick. Why not just add a little chalk dust? All the over-forty chicks think if they eat soy shit, they won't need the face-lift they've been putting off for like ten years. As if they don't all look like they tried to swallow a bag of marbles that only got down as far as their necks. Pathetic."

"That's a little harsh, sweetheart," said Quartz. "That protein supplement's supposed to help arthritis. Nina had a lot of pain."

Sally sympathized. Her own knee creaked like a horror-movie coffin lid. And, of course, she herself was trying to eat more soy, though that generally meant eating a bowl of hot-and-sour soup every time she went to California, and otherwise snacking on edamame laced with enough salt to cure an Iowa hog. Nina had had beautiful skin, taut and remarkably unlined. Maybe there was something to the soy miracle diet. "Do you know what kind of supplement she used?"

"Sure," said Quartz, reaching down into a cupboard and taking a large can off a shelf holding maybe a dozen such cans. "But I don't think you can get it in a store. She had some health food outfit blend it up specially for her."

Pammie looked over. "Go ahead and take a can if you want, Sally," she said. "Take the whole case. Otherwise, I expect it'll just get thrown away."

Why not? If she couldn't bring herself to relish soy yogurt or tofu surprise, maybe soy powder could smooth out a wrinkle or two. It might be worth a try. "Thanks," she said, taking the can, walking to her shoulder bag, and putting it in. "If I suddenly start looking twenty years younger, maybe I can come back and get the rest."

"You don't need to look twenty minutes younger," said Quartz, instantly winning Sally's heart for all time. "There's nothing that says a woman can't be beautiful lots of ways over a long life."

"Right," said Pammie. "At least that's what Kali kept telling Nina all the time."

"So they were close, Kali and Nina?" Sally asked.

"Oh yeah," said Quartz. "They were like sisters."

Pammie looked over her shoulder, still chopping, and smiled sweetly at Quartz. "Uh-huh. You should see my sister and me, honey. Last time I saw her she borrowed fifty bucks from me so she could get her books for school, she said. Two days later, I found out she'd never even registered for school, had spent the whole wad on crystal meth for her and her disgusting boyfriend, and had ended up running our mom's car into the back wall of the Torch Tavern after she'd been in there trying to score more."

Quartz sighed. "I'm a sentimentalist."

"Me, too," said Pammie. "About you. But not about Nina and Kali. They were always real sweet to each other, but I got the impression that Nina felt like Kali was crowding her. Sometimes it seemed like Nina couldn't go two steps without her little shadow tagging along."

"And what about Whitebird?" Sally asked.

Pammie stirred the parsley into her soup, frowning. "Kali's main competition," she said at last.

"For Nina?" Sally said.

But she never got her answer. The yoga class broke up, and people began to move around, making noise, streaming into the kitchen. Dickie Langham and Nels Willen came in the back door, both tight-lipped, followed by Scotty Atkins, unreadable as usual.

"I'll keep it brief," Dickie announced. "For any of you who've been entertaining ideas about getting out of here and going to town tonight, forget about it. We've got lots more questions to ask, for one thing. For another, the highway patrol has closed the road to Laramie. In other words, we're all snowed in together. So it's a good thing that something smells good in here. It's gonna be a long night."

6

Hellfire or Whiskey

Under the best of circumstances, Sally Alder was a lousy
sleeper. Circumstances being what they were that night in
Shady Grove, her chances of a peaceful rest were exactly
zero. Not long after dinner, Randy Whitebird had retired to
Nina's bedroom as if it were his right. Nels Willen said
nothing, watched Whitebird go, and then allowed as how if
nobody minded, he'd take the other bedroom. After directing the cleanup and talking to the police, Pammie and
Quartz went out to the bus. By and by, all of the Dub-Dubs
had been questioned. A couple decided they'd try sleeping
in their cars, despite the cold, but most opted to bed down in
the living room, clustering together, Sally supposed, out of
California herd instinct (she'd noted the same behavior in
L.A. freeway drivers) and fear of guns, stormy weather, and
wild Wyomingites. Dickie's two deputies stayed with them.
There was some grumbling about "fucking pig surveillance."

She wandered out to the studio, where Dickie Langham
and Scotty Atkins were finishing up their notes on the interviews. Nina wouldn't have been happy. There were dirty

bowls and coffee cups scattered around, the place reeked of cigarette smoke, and a hand-thrown ceramic plate overflowed with butts. Scotty, in the throes of an investigation, wouldn't have noticed if a garbage truck had dropped its load in the middle of the room. Dickie was a considerate guy, but housekeeping wasn't his strong point, and when it came to his filthy nicotine habit, he was a Wyoming libertarian through and through.

Then it occurred to her that quite apart from addiction, Dickie would have used smoking as a tactic in his interviews with the sprout eaters, a form of chemical warfare. He might look like a big galoot, but he knew how to play for advantage. She walked in and left the door open, hoping to clear the air a bit.

"How'd it go?" she asked.

Scotty was writing something down on a yellow pad, and didn't bother to look up. Dickie said, "We can't decide between Cabo San Lucas and Acapulco. Scotty likes Cabo because he says the beaches are better, but I kind of dig Acapulco because there's more to do. Then again, maybe we should just do the patriotic thing and see America first. I hear there're great Internet deals on Kauai."

She stared at him. "Very nice. What did you find out from these bozos?"

Scotty did look up now. His eyes looked exhausted. "I believe we've already conducted an interview with you, Professor Alder. What could possibly delude you into imagining we're interested in divulging the particulars of a police investigation to a civilian, no matter how meddlesome?"

She was just as tired, edgy, and hostile as he was, but having seen it all in him before, she wasn't deterred. "Look, I was here. Maybe if you tell me what you can, it'll jog something loose I haven't thought of. Was she murdered? With Willen's gun? Did he do it?"

Scotty shook his head, jotted down one more thing, and then got up and went into the studio bathroom.

She turned to Dickie. "Come on. I'm every frigging bit as beat as you are, and I want to know what's going on."

"We're not holding out on you, Mustang," said Dickie. "Although we surely would if we had something. We're still putting the picture together. We've got a lot of work to do, and like you said, it's been a long damn day. Right now, all I want is to curl up on that couch over there and get a few hours of sleep. You should do the same."

"The whole house is full of freaks. I'm not real thrilled about the prospect of going back in there."

"Then crash out here," Dickie said. "You can put a sleeping bag over there on the carpet, between the desk and the filing cabinet. Scotty can bed down over here on the floor. I don't snore much. Do you?"

Mary Langham often said her husband snored like a steam shovel, and Sally was ambivalent about the prospect of learning Scotty Atkins's sleeping habits. But the odds were that there'd be more noise among fifteen sleeping people than three. "I'll get my bedding," she said.

When she returned with bag and blanket, she found them glaring at each other. "Scotty has questioned my judgment in offering you the hospitality of our little bungalow here," Dickie explained.

"I'll go in the house," Sally said instantly, turning to go.

"No," Scotty said. "Don't bother. There's room enough for three out here. Forget I said anything. Seriously," he said, clearly his version of an apology.

And Sally realized, all at once, that she was too beat to go one step farther. The air in the studio had cleared some, but she didn't even care about the smoke. Without a word, she walked over to the desk and spread out her bed on the floor next to it. With her last ounce of energy, she pulled toothbrush and toothpaste out of her shoulder bag and went into the bathroom to brush her teeth. She barely registered coming out and crawling into her sleeping bag.

Sometime in the night, Dickie's snoring woke her. She opened her eyes. The sky had cleared. Moonlight reflected off the snow, bathing the room in silver ghost light. Scotty Atkins sat in an overstuffed chair by the window, staring out. She didn't think she'd moved, but in the stillness, she must have made some small sound. Otherwise, why would his head turn and his eyes gaze into hers for a too-long moment?

He looked back out the window. She shut her eyes again, turned over, and lay with her back to him, her mind jumbling all she'd been through, until at last sleep found her again.

As dawn broke, she woke for good, stiff from the night on the floor and royally pissed off at everyone and everything, but especially (and to be fair, unaccountably) at Scotty Atkins. Why was she so angry? He hadn't done anything more than be a little ruder than he needed to be. In her experience, Scotty never settled for merely average rudeness while doing his job. And he *was* doing his job. Just because she was feeling raw and needy, it certainly wasn't up to Detective Atkins to comfort her. Dickie Langham, she knew, would have done so if she'd acted as if she wanted it. He was the King of Hugs, even if he was a sheriff. But she hadn't exactly been Ms. Warmth either.

She was alone in the studio. Dickie and Scotty were already up and gone.

Sally got up, folded the blanket, got back down on her knees and began rolling up the sleeping bag. But as she was cinching a cord around the bedroll, she knocked over her shoulder bag and sent a lipstick tumbling under Nina's desk. She lay on the floor, stuck a hand between a wastebasket and the desk, and felt around under it in search of the lipstick. Her hand closed over a wadded-up piece of paper.

Sally sat up, leaned back on folded legs, and smoothed out the paper. It was a letter, typed, undated.

> *Dearest to My Heart,*
>
> *I know you didn't mean to hurt me when you said good-bye this morning. I shouldn't have been so angry. I need to remember all the ways we've cared for each other, not the hard words. You know me. I dwell too often in the dark.*
>
> *But trust me, love. I'm not one of your enemies. Turn to me. I know I can keep you safe and make you happy, no matter what kinds of things we said today.*

The letter wasn't signed.

What the hell was this about?

Whatever it was, the cops ought to have it. But first, Sally thought, she'd make a quick copy. She pulled out her Day-Minder, opened at the back page, and hastily scribbled down the words.

Just as she finished, the studio door opened. Lark, the blonde who'd taught the yoga class, entered. "The detective sent me to get you," she said. "They want everybody in the living room."

"Sure. I'll be right there," Sally said. The woman looked at her, registering the crumpled paper in her hand. As nonchalantly as she could, Sally folded the letter and stuck it inside the cover of her appointment calendar, then put both in her shoulder bag. Saying nothing, Lark turned and left. Sally picked up her bedding and her bag and followed.

Sally walked out to the parking area, wading through knee-deep snow, to put her things in the Mustang. By the time she got to the house, the nearly two dozen people had assembled, filling the room to bursting. They crowded the couches, sat three to a chair, sprawled on rugs and sleeping bags. Randy Whitebird sat on the coffee table, one leg tucked up with his arms around the calf, spine softly curved. Nels Willen leaned a shoulder against the wall, arms folded, legs crossed at the ankle, face unreadable. If nothing else, these guys knew how to play it casual.

Sheriff Dickie Langham glanced around, beaming a friendly smile. He looked entirely too perky after the long night, and Sally realized that he was holding a large mug of what must be Nels Willen's politically correct coffee. She edged toward the kitchen, hoping for a transfusion.

"Good morning, everyone," said Dickie, taking a big swig from the mug, and smiling again. "I want to personally thank you all for your cooperation last night, and in the weeks to come. I'm sure you understand that we'll be keeping in contact with you, in case we need a little more help. We would prefer that you stay in the area, but we understand that most of you don't live here. Given what's happened, those of you who've been contemplating a move to Laramie may be reconsidering your plans. Several of you have already told me that you intend to leave the state as soon as weather permits, and go back to California, or Oregon, or wherever."

Boy howdy, Sally thought. Most of them would have been gone like a cool breeze yesterday, before the police ever arrived, had it not been for the combination of Nels Willen and Wyoming weather.

"We'd like it if you'd stick around, but we can't force you to remain in Albany County. So we have to make reasonable accommodations. When we talked with you yesterday," Dickie continued, "we got home addresses for all of you, or at least post office boxes and e-mail addresses and cellular telephone numbers. If you expect to change any of that information, or to stay with friends, or to take a trip to Jamaica or whatever, we ask that you get in touch with us at the Albany County Sheriff's office, and give us new information. Most likely we won't ever need to contact you again, but you never know."

The Dub-Dubs groaned as one. Sally figured most of them had never been involved in a shooting before. Unhappily for her, she had. Dickie was being unusually lenient. He actually might have been able to force them to stay in the county, or at least to fake them into thinking he had the power to do so. But since he hadn't been born in a barn, thought Sally, he must have decided that the negative press he'd get from detaining peace-loving coastals in gun-toting Wyoming wasn't worth the trouble.

"Be sure to take one of those cards my deputy is handing around," he said. "And yes, in case you're wondering, some of those cards actually are refrigerator magnets. We had them made up two years ago as a fund-raiser. Consider them our gift to you, in gratitude for helping us figure out what happened to Ms. Cruz."

Pammie stuck her Albany County Sheriff's Department magnet on the refrigerator in the kitchen and requested another for the Yippie I O Café.

The boy with the blond dreads raised his hand. "I'm, like,

not sure where I'm going to be in the next few months. There's a Rainbow Family gathering, and a Wood Nymph convocation, and I might check out a couple Phil Lesh shows. I don't have a phone or e-mail or any of that other bourgeois crap."

"Luckily, in your case," said Scotty, not managing to suppress a sneer, "we have your parents' names, addresses, and contacts. They'll at least know which *gathering* they're sending the checks to."

Dickie took a less sarcastic, but more disconcerting line. "We understand that this will be complicated for some of you. But in addition to needing your help with our work, we're concerned about your safety."

"You don't think whoever shot Nina is after any of the rest of us?" a girl spoke up, her voice rising to a squeak on "us." "I thought this was a hunting accident."

Of course it was. But Sally thought about Willen's gun; it had clearly been fired recently. And she thought about the letter in her bag. Whoever had written it had mentioned "enemies." She'd be jumping to conclusions to assume that Nina had been the recipient, but she had, after all, found it under Nina's desk. The fact that it had been wadded up and tossed in the direction of the wastebasket suggested to Sally that Nina hadn't welcomed the offer of help. But who had written it? Who were the enemies? What did they intend?

And what kind of good-bye had been exchanged between the writer, who "dwelled too often in the dark," and the reader, Dearest to—somebody's—Heart?

Was the note from somebody who lived at Shady Grove? As both a historian and a former hippie, Sally knew a little something about the dynamics of communal households. When people who lived together started communicating in writing, instead of talking face-to-face, it was definitely bad news for the future of the group. To say nothing of the relationship between writer and intended reader. She recalled once leaving a note for a particularly odious housemate in a fast-deteriorating collective pad, telling him to get food and kitty litter for his badly neglected cat, or else she'd take Little Whiskers to the animal shelter. The guy had written back to say that kitty litter was a housewife's affectation, and if Sally did anything to his cat, she'd better watch her back. Not exactly Woodstock Nation.

But this wasn't the moment to lose herself in reflection on old rages or, for that matter, speculation on the sociology of communes. Dickie was explaining to the group that he'd called the county to get them all plowed out, so they would soon be able to leave and head to Laramie, if not to other destinations. It might take a couple more days before all the roads were open again. While they waited for the plow, he was also happy to report that they'd located a snowblower in the barn, and he asked for a volunteer to clear the parking area. "You don't want the plow doing that little job," he said. "Or at least not if you don't want your cars buried."

Your average Wyoming snowplow driver would enjoy nothing more than avalanching a bunch of Volvos with out-of-state plates.

Within the hour, the plow came and set them free. To Sally's surprise, Dickie asked if he could ride back to town with her. "No point waiting for the DCI Mobile Crime Lab," he said. "They've got messes to clean up all over the state. Seems that sometime between the mishap at Little America and the family tragedy at Torrington, a meth lab blew up in Thermopolis. The soonest those guys could get here would be tonight, more likely tomorrow, celebrity or no celebrity." He inspected the blazing blue sky. "By then, the snow will have melted and frozen and melted and the weather will have screwed whatever forensics weren't wrecked by the storm in the first place. Atkins is as good a crime scene guy as any cop in the state. We'll just have to manage on our own for the moment. The coroner will take the body, and Scotty'll go over this place with an electron microscope."

"I hope I didn't screw up any fingerprints on that gun," Sally said in a very small voice.

Dickie just rolled his eyes.

"Oh, by the way," Sally added, "I found something out in Nina's office."

She reached in her shoulder bag, pulled out the crumpled piece of paper, and handed it to Dickie.

He pulled the note flat with his fingertips, spread it out, and read it without comment.

"That was on the floor under her desk," said Sally, trying to gauge his reaction.

"Thanks," he said, reaching down into his briefcase, extracting a medium-size plastic bag, putting the note inside, and zipping the bag shut. He put the bag in his briefcase and went on with the conversation they'd been having before she told him about the note as if nothing had happened.

Then he asked one of his deputies to drive his Blazer back, helped Sally chain up the Mustang, and now sat in the passenger seat, as he said, just to keep her company. Their breath froze into little streaming clouds in the cold car. Her tire chains cut into the plow-packed snow. She turned on the heater and prepared to be cold for the next ten minutes while the Mustang heater labored toward warmth.

"I fucking hate dead bodies," he said at last. "I hate violence. I don't even much like it when Mary and I have a fight. A lot of cops are like that. That's why cops are so weird."

"So how do you deal with it?" Sally asked.

Dickie reached inside his jacket, took out his pack of Marlboros, and looked at her. She decided that it would be churlish to tell him he couldn't smoke in her car. She made a face, but nodded.

He cracked open his window, lit up, inhaled, blew smoke toward the crack. "You don't deal. Sometimes the mind is merciful. The worst stuff you see doesn't register immediately. Your brain turns off long enough to secure the scene, get the investigation started, calm down the bystanders, and, God help us, call the relatives. You just keep doing your job.

"You think you're all right for a couple of days. Then you start forgetting stuff, like where you were going when you got in the car, or how to stop at a red light. You get the shakes for no reason. You feel like shit a lot of mornings. Not that it's news to you, Mustang, but lots of cops drink." When she shot him a questioning glance, he added, "I been down that road, as you know. So far, I'm still headed in the other direction." He took another drag. "Good thing we catch the bad guys now and then."

Sally took a deep breath, nearly choked on secondhand smoke, cracked her own window. "So, what do you think about this one? Did some reckless trespassing hunter get his deer, then leave it, then accidentally shoot Nina?"

"More likely, some nearsighted hunter mistook her for a deer."

"I'd buy that if there were two hunters. One who shot the first deer, and then the second who shot her. There were two sets of tracks, right?"

"How'd you know that?" Dickie asked her.

"I heard the game warden tell Scotty," she said.

Dickie shook his head. "Well, at least I'm not the only leak in this police operation. Keep this shit to yourself, Mustang."

She nodded.

"There's another obvious possibility. Ms. Cruz went out into the woods, saw the deer, and confronted the shooter, who panicked and shot her," Dickie said.

Sally thought a minute. "That makes sense," she said. "Except that I didn't see the deer anywhere near Nina's body."

Dickie closed one eye, squinted at the glowing coal of his cigarette. "When you put it that way, it sounds pretty unlikely."

"I'd say so. Especially when you've got this deer rifle of Dr. Willen's that ended up in her woodpile, recently fired, sometime in the middle of a morning when there were—what was it, eighteen people?—milling around her place."

"Nineteen, counting you," Dickie said.

"I wasn't milling when those shots were fired," said Sally. "I was ducking."

"You still count. As a witness, if nothing else," Dickie said.

"So you don't consider me a suspect?" Sally asked.

"Theoretically, I suppose, you are, but since you were seen out in the parking area by more than one person at the moment that Nina Cruz was shot, I consider you an unlikely possibility."

The car skidded a bit on an icy patch, but Sally steered into it, and the chained tires found purchase. "Watch the road," said Dickie, "but keep talking."

Sally thought about what she'd seen and heard over the course of the day and night. "I can't say anything about hunters lurking in the woods, but as far as I can tell, there were three people who couldn't have shot Nina. Pammie and Quartz came running out of the woods right after the shots, and they didn't have a stitch of a place to hide a hunting rifle. Then they went into the bus to get some clothes on. Randy Whitebird was on the porch, putting on his shoes."

"Interesting that so many of those people were going around at least half naked, blizzard or no blizzard. You think that goes on a lot out there?" Dickie asked.

"Nina never struck me as the get-naked-with-everybody type. But then, I didn't know her very well. Of course, up until yesterday the weather was still really nice, but for all I know, being naked in the snow is the latest health craze in California. I've been gone a couple of years," Sally said.

"Nels Willen wasn't naked," Dickie observed. "The man was dressed for the cold, and shortly after the shootings, he came out of the woods covered with blood. Judging by the holes—sorry Mustang—judging by the wounds in Ms. Cruz and the deer, it appears that a gun a whole lot like the one Willen brought onto the Cruz property was used in the shooting."

"So despite Willen's supposed hatred of bloodshed, you assume he was the one who shot both the deer and Nina Cruz. I don't know why he would have, but then, it's up to you guys to figure that out, isn't it? I mean, I wouldn't want to presume to interfere in police business—"

"Of course not, although that would be a first," said Dickie, lighting another Marlboro off the butt of the first, and flicking the butt out the window. "Look, Sally," he said, turning her way, "I am very much inclined to believe we've got a hunting accident on our hands. But we're covering the bases. Every fucking sensationalist reporter in the country will be hollering murder by tomorrow morning. And what if it is murder? Just in case you're interested, we police officers believe that when we have a weapon, the individual who brought it onto the scene is generally the person who intended to use it."

"There is one small problem with that finding," Sally said. "Willen came out of the woods right after the shots were fired. The next thing he did was to go back up to where Nina was, and then he was down in the driveway, talking to people. He wasn't out of my sight until he went in the house, so if he fired the shots, he'd have had to have ditched the gun, gone back for it, and then put it in the woodpile. That would have taken some pretty careful planning in what seemed to me like a frigging free-for-all situation. And he looked completely flipped out, except when he was dealing with people even more freaked than he was."

Sally felt the trembling building in her chest. She could see why Dickie considered this moment a good one for chain-smoking. She listened to the clicking of tire chains on snowy pavement, looking for some way to focus her mind, and at last she had a couple of coherent thoughts. "Okay, Dick. What about Lark, the woman who found the body? She was dressed for the weather. Admittedly, she seemed as distraught as Nels Willen, but she was the first one on the scene, and she might have had a little time to hide the gun in all the chaos afterward."

"We're checking her out," said Dickie, declining to elaborate.

Sally could see she wouldn't get anywhere on that tack. "Okay. Another question: Who else, if anybody, knew that Nels Willen had brought a rifle with him to Shady Grove?"

"Good question," said Dickie. "So far, nobody admits to having known. But we've got some hunches we're looking into."

She could just imagine. Scotty Atkins, looking into a

hunch, would be Wyoming's version of the Spanish Inquisition. "Guess you also have to find out whether Willen's gun fired the shots that killed the deer and Nina. Do you know whether it was fired more than once?"

Dickie declined to answer.

"And then, there's the matter of whether the same gun killed both," Sally continued, hoping to get him talking again.

"That's the thing about doing an investigation. You're liable to find out all kinds of things you didn't know before," said Dickie evasively.

"Like the fact that out of all the people who were there, there was at least one who should have been and wasn't," Sally said.

"You're referring to the foundation administrator, a woman known as 'Kali,' " Dickie said.

"Nothing surprises you," said Sally.

"Not much," Dickie answered. "I'm not even surprised at all the stupid hippie names these Wild West people are still using. Lark. Quartz. Whitebird. Kali."

"Quartz is short for—"

"I know," said Dickie. "Quentin Schwartz, Oregon greenie boy. Getting it on with little Pammie Montgomery."

"You know Pammie?" Sally asked.

"Sure. She and my girls went to Laramie High together. Everyone's expecting her to open a restaurant and put the Yippie I O out of business," he said, proving once more that Laramie was the kind of town where everyone knew everyone, sooner or later.

"Quartz says Pammie's his soul mate," Sally noted.

"Which proves Quartz is a schlocky name," said Dickie.

"What do you know from schlocky?" Sally protested. "Or from Schwartzes?"

"Enough to know that he's an airhead like the rest of 'em. At least in his case we've got a real name. The ones with just one nature-type name, or an alias like Whitebird, will be a whole lot harder to trace and keep track of, unless they have police records and got in trouble using the same name."

"Or friends who know their other names," Sally said. "Pammie told me that Kali had gone away for the weekend, back to Utah where she used to live."

"Did she say why?" Dickie asked.

"No. But I bet Whitebird knows. He's the foundation director; she works for him. According to Pammie, they weren't exactly tight. More like rivals than boss and employee, or fellow activists, or whatever. Pammie said Kali was Nina's shadow, and Whitebird evidently didn't dig it."

"From what I heard, he wasn't the only one who didn't exactly cotton to this Kali woman. We heard of at least one other person who didn't like the way she'd appointed herself as Nina Cruz's gatekeeper."

Sally thought about what she knew. "I'm guessing you're talking about Stone Jackson," she said. "No need to worry about him. When I got him on his cell phone, he was stuck in Riverton, at a McDonald's, on his way to the Busted Heart Ranch." She thought a moment. "Then again, since it was a cell phone, he could have been anywhere. But I know it was a McDonald's. I distinctly heard somebody order a Quarter Pounder."

"Just like I do, three days a week, right back home in Laramie. You're really something, you know, Sal? A full-grown kick-ass feminist like you getting all googly over some geek with a guitar." Dickie cocked his head and gave her a narrow-eyed glance, then tossed his spent butt out the window, but not before using it to light yet another Marlboro.

"You know what happened to the Marlboro Man," Sally nagged.

"Yeah," said Dickie. "He got to go on *Sixty Minutes*."

They rode on without speaking for a while. At last Sally said, "I've never seen anybody die before."

"It's a big drag, isn't it?" Dickie said, patting her right hand as she gripped the wheel.

She expelled a no-longer-frosty breath. "Worse for the victim," she answered.

"Far as I can tell," said Dickie. "But then again, for all I know, Angelina Cruz could be up in the great blue beyond,

floating on a cloud and singing beautiful harmonies on radical labor ballads with the Weavers and Woody Guthrie and
Joe Hill. It's worth at least imagining the possibility," he
added. "Beats hellfire or whiskey."

7

If You Don't Do It, Somebody Else Will

There was smoke coming out of the chimney when she pulled up in front of the little house on Eighth Street. That could be a sign of welcome, or might be an ominous reflection of Hawk's state of mind.

Hawk, after all, would be justified in being in an I-told-you-so mood. He hadn't wanted her to go to Shady Grove, and last night, when she'd finally gotten the chance to call and tell him a little of what had happened, he'd said only that it sounded horrible, that he was sorry she was stuck, that he'd see her in the morning. He hated the phone anyway, but he sure hadn't prolonged the conversation.

He'd built a cheery blaze in the living room fireplace, but Hawk was sitting at the kitchen table, reading the *Laramie Daily Boomerang* when she came in. He looked up from the newspaper. "How are you?" he asked.

"I've been better," she answered. "I need to add a foam pad to my emergency kit. The floor of Nina's studio was carpeted, at least, but there was a concrete slab underneath."

"Flat," he said. "No rocks or sticks or prickly things."

"It was fine," she said, "considering. I'm not whining."

Sorrow and concern showed in his eyes. "I made coffee. Have some."

The glass Melitta pot was on the stove. She lit the burner under it to warm the coffee. It occurred to her that after what she'd been through, coffee might not be the answer. Her shoulder bag sat on the kitchen table, the bulky can of protein powder poking out the top. Maybe what she needed was a bracing health drink instead of a caffeine fix.

Of course. She told herself that if she'd had what she needed for Nina's blended panacea, she'd have whipped one up on the spot. But she knew what was in the fridge, and it didn't include the yogurt, or the lovely fresh fruit. There was probably a bear-shaped squirt bottle of honey in the cupboard, a sticky, crystallized archaeological artifact purchased with the idea that they might entertain mellow tea-drinking friends. But she couldn't swear to it. In fact, about all she had in the way of ingredients for the Nina smoothie was a little bit of 1 percent milk and a big jar of soy powder. So she'd have to settle for coffee. Oh well.

With the best of intentions, she put the can of protein supplement on the shelf where they kept the dry ingredients they used all the time. And the next time she went to the grocery store, she vowed, she'd not only get the necessaries for the smoothie, but toss in some broccoli, brown rice, and buckwheat noodles.

But for now, she poured a cup of Hawk's fine, strong brew. She added milk and then turned to him and said, "I would like to be held now."

He unfolded his legs, got up slowly, walked to her and obliged.

At length, he said, "The paper gave the story its usual balanced coverage."

"Oh yeah?" she said. "I can hardly wait to see."

"Go ahead and drink your coffee and check it out. It probably won't make you feel any better, but it'll remind you how things are from the Wyoming perspective. I'll make you some breakfast."

"Thanks." She wasn't hungry, but she'd eat if he was cooking. It wasn't about food.

Presently, Hawk set a plate of eggs and hash browns in front of Sally, along with a bottle of Tabasco sauce.

"Poor Nina. They made her look like a Commie," Sally said, dosing her breakfast with Tabasco.

"I thought she was a Commie," Hawk said.

"Well, yeah, back in the day. Before Tom Hayden ever dreamed about being a state legislator. Before Eldridge Cleaver got into fashion design and the Republican Party. Back when they were still sending César Chávez to jail instead of talking about giving him a national holiday. It's worth remembering that all through the sixties and seventies, the FBI was opening Nina's mail, and following her around, and hassling her friends and relations." Sally dug into her breakfast, then continued. "They audited her tax returns for like ten years running, tried to plant cocaine in her suitcase when she was coming back from Europe, and forged her signature on letters to her record company, her agent, and her concert promoters, saying she was retiring from the music business so she could devote her life to making bombs with the Weathermen."

"Your point being," Hawk said, sitting down with his own breakfast, "that paranoids have enemies, too?"

Sally forked up crispy potato and runny egg yolk. "My point is that the fucking *Boomerang* reporter, and thus his readers, haven't got a ghost of a clue who Nina Cruz was, or what she went through, or what she meant, or how amazingly great she was. Hell, most of them probably never heard her voice, even on a record. They wouldn't know that when she sang, you'd hear what angels sounded like. And she was so smart, and so brave, and just so goddamn *big*. Her life could read like the story of America in the late twentieth century. She deserves a hell of a lot more than this stupid shit." Sally threw the paper on the table, contemptuous.

"Then give her more," said Hawk.

"What? Like send a check to that woo-woo foundation of hers, so that Randy Whitebird can go around claiming that he's channeling her deepest desires? Not hardly." Sally snorted.

"That's not what I meant," Hawk said, putting his hand on

Sally's. "It just occurred to me that you ought to think about writing her biography."

Sally just stared at him.

"Why not?" he asked. "You've been fishing around for a new big project. You proved with the Dunwoodie book that you could write biography. You're a women's historian, and Nina Cruz was a pretty historic woman by any measure."

Sally extracted her hand from his, rubbed a knuckle over her lips. "It's a cool idea, actually. But wouldn't I look like a disgusting opportunist? I hate people who make a career out of gravy-training dead heroes."

Hawk took her hand again and smiled a little. "Look at it this way, Sal. It's obvious you don't believe she was shot accidentally by some nearsighted yahoo. I know you. You've probably already been driving Dickie and Scotty Atkins nuts. Nobody can stop you from butting in when you're like this."

"I might already have butted in," she said.

"How so?" Hawk asked.

She got up and extracted her DayMinder from her bag. "When I was rolling up my sleeping bag this morning, I found a note crumpled up under Nina's desk, next to the wastebasket. I made a copy."

Hawk read. "Wow," was all he said.

"Yeah," said Sally. "It's downright intriguing, don't you think?"

"Did you give the original to Dickie?" His eyes were grave.

"Of course!" she said, trying to work up a little indignation, without much effect. "But as you can see, I made the copy first."

Hawk shook his head. "You are a real piece of work, Sally. Obviously you understand how much trouble you could get in for tampering with evidence in what might well be a murder case?"

Boy howdy. "Hey, I gave it to him, didn't I?"

Hawk sighed.

Sally changed the subject. "I really do like this book idea."

"And you've already decided to start mucking around in this business. There's probably not a damn thing I can do to stop you, so I guess at least if you're writing a book, you'd have good reason to go around asking a bunch of questions. Some might say you're making a target of yourself. On the other hand, it would put you in enough of a public spotlight that it might be easier to keep an eye on you."

"Not to mention that I'd have plenty of excuses to hang around Stone Jackson," Sally said.

Hawk's smile returned. "I'm not worried about Jackson. He's not your type."

"He's not?" she said.

"No. He's too talented, too introspective, and too rich," Hawk explained.

"You forgot too tall," Sally said.

"Exactly so," Hawk agreed.

She thought about it. She couldn't imagine that they'd go ahead with the benefit concert, under the circumstances. That would eliminate her only reason for contact with Jackson, or, for that matter, for staying on top of the investigation into Nina's death. She really did need a new project, and Hawk was right. Nina deserved her historical due.

"Call your publisher," said Hawk. "If you don't, somebody else will. And there's no guaranteeing that whoever else writes about Nina will give her the treatment you think she ought to get."

"And what about you?" Sally said.

"What do you mean?" Hawk asked.

"You're being awfully nice, even though you warned me not to go to Shady Grove, and I ended up getting stuck out there, and it's kind of likely that my getting involved with this thing could cause a problem or two. I've had a rough night, and I imagine you did, too."

"Yeah? So? So I'm glad you're back, and you're okay, and I'm really sorry for what you've been through. I wish to Christ that Nina Cruz was still alive," said Hawk.

Sally was wired and tired, but this man of hers had a way of holding the demons at bay, at least temporarily. She leaned over and put her hand on his thigh, under the table.

His worn jeans were soft to the touch. The muscles of his leg weren't. She licked her lips and met his eyes. "What kind of treatment do you think you ought to get?"

Hawk moved her hand slightly up and to the right. "I think I ought to get very attentive, very thorough sexual stimulation, involving both tactile and visual techniques and maybe some naughty language."

"I think," said Sally, making slow circles with the palm of one hand, unzipping her fleece vest with the other, and beginning to untuck her shirt, "that is exactly the treatment you deserve."

"If you don't do it, somebody else will," he said. "Ouch! Gently there, darling."

8

Rumor Mills with Hot Pans and Sharp Knives

"The show must go on," declared Thomas Jackson, when he called from Santa Fe ten days later.

"No way," Sally said.

"Yes ma'am," Stone replied. "Nina's sister Cat is back in the States, and says that's what she wants. I had a long talk with Cat after the memorial service in Santa Fe."

"Memorial?" Sally asked. She wondered if the police had released Nina's body. She assumed that given the suspicious circumstances of Nina's death, there would have to be an autopsy, though she'd heard nothing.

Stone answered her question, somewhat euphemistically. "There'll be a more formal funeral when the medical examiner, um, finishes his work. Meanwhile, Cat's planning to fly to Denver, rent a car, and drive up to Laramie to meet with Whitebird and Kali. As far as she's concerned, doing the show and getting Wild West off to a big start was Nina's last wish, and Cat's going to see it through as a tribute to her sister, and then think about what to do with the proceeds and the foundation. She asked me to take charge of the benefit arrangements, so I'll be at the meeting, on my way back to the Busted Heart."

"Makes sense," said Sally. "You've done a million of these things."

"Yeah," said Stone. "They always call me. Don't matter if the cause is HIV education, oil spills, or women's shelters, I'm on the mailing list. Back when Nina and I were together, we did a lot of gigs to get people out of jail. Turned out half of them belonged there. I'm a little pickier these days.

"But I got the scene wired. By now, all I have to do is make a couple of phone calls. Nina'd already lined up the promoter, so it's just a matter of getting my publicity people to give it an extra thump and getting the talent together. Thought I'd see if maybe Bonnie and Emmylou and them are interested."

Stone Jackson in Laramie was miracle enough. But Bonnie and Emmylou and them? Sally would really have to reconsider religion. "Sounds like you won't be needing the Millionaires," she said, relieved.

"Sure we will," Stone said. "I always like to promote the local talent."

"Thomas, I haven't talked to the boys in the band. I'm not sure they'd want to do the gig. There are a couple of them who aren't big fans of tree huggers or Californians." She'd almost said, "whose idea of a good time is shooting tree huggers," but had managed to stop herself in time.

"Or Chicanas?" he asked, his voice acquiring an edge.

"You're a Wyomingite now. Draw your own conclusions," Sally said, giving him edge for edge.

"Then that makes it even more important that you all play. Show everybody that Laramie folks aren't a bunch of pencil-neck dickheads," he said.

"I'll see what I can do," Sally answered. Several members of the Millionaires might actually be pencil-neck dickheads, at least when it came to what humans had the right to do with and to animals. But she'd raise the subject tonight, when the band had their weekly practice.

"I hope you're free for a lunch meeting next week, at the Wild West headquarters," Jackson continued. "They've rented some space in Laramie, on Second Street. They're just getting set up, but it seems like that would be most convenient for everybody."

"So are all those Dub-Dubs still crashing out at Shady Grove?" Sally asked.

"Nope. Most of them lit out for the coast after the roads opened up. Right now, Wild West has just a skeleton staff—Whitebird and Kali, and two assistants who seem to be sleeping in the office. Oh, and Nels Willen's around, too. He's helping out with the fund-raising side. I'm hoping he starts with himself. Got more money than God."

"Willen's involved?" Sally couldn't hide her amazement.

"Listen, Sally. I know he brought that rifle out there that day."

"How?" Sally asked.

"He called me up and told me so. But at this point, the police haven't announced anything about a murder weapon, and even if it turned out that somebody . . . well, even if that gun was used, I know in the heart of my heart it wasn't Nels pullin' the trigger. If anybody could begin to understand how he felt about Nina, it's me. He wouldn't have done it any more than I would."

"Maybe it was an accident," Sally offered lamely.

"Yeah. Maybe. Do a lot of people get shot randomly during deer season in Wyoming?"

Sally admitted that they didn't.

"And does it occur to you that deciding you want to look into her life puts you a little too close to her death, in the event that there was somebody who deliberately went about killing her?" he asked.

She hadn't thought about that, and decided not to. "I think you're just trying to scare me off."

Jackson took a breath. "No. I'm not. I want to know what happened, Sally Alder. So does Cat. That's one big reason we want you around. You can help us find out."

"You really ought to let the police do their work, Stone. You haven't met the sheriff," said Sally.

"I'm about to," said Stone. "He called. I'll be going to see him first thing when I get to Laramie."

"He's a good guy, a really smart guy. A lot of people make the mistake of thinking that because Dickie Langham's big and sweet, he's kind of slow. But I've known him most of my adult life. More often than not he's two steps ahead of everybody else. And he's got good people. His detective is the kind of pit bull you want on your side. You can trust these guys," Sally finished.

"I'm sure we can," Jackson agreed smoothly, "but Cat and I need somebody who can help us communicate with them, too. We need a friend," he said.

"He wants me to be his friend," Sally told her friend Delice Langham, two days later as they sat down at a table at the Wrangler Bar and Grill. Sally knew the Wrangler's menu a little too well to make lunching there a habit, but she had ordered a side salad with Italian dressing and an order of onion rings. A Wrangler version of a vegetarian lunch, if you didn't count lard. The wind had picked up over the course of the morning and was pounding away at the front window of the Grill, whistling through the shingles on the roof. The temperature had dropped, too, and Sally might have regretted deciding to walk downtown rather than drive, but she figured the fat content of the rings would keep her warm on the walk home.

"His friend? Uh-huh," said Delice, silver bracelets jangling as she set down her coffee cup and began to sort through the day's mail. "Stone Jackson probably doesn't have any friends. Having lived all over the world, and made every woman in America fall in love with him, and having more money than Jimmy Buffett, I bet he's just lonesome as hell. What was it he said in that song of his, 'Lost Boy'? 'Out here in the cold, one more lost soul . . .'"

"That'll do, Delice," Sally interrupted. "You've got a thing for lost souls yourself. Who named her kid after Jerry Jeff Walker?"

"Who named her dog after George Jones?" Delice shot back.

It was a draw. They were a couple of suckers for feckless losers. More than twenty years ago, Delice had hired Sally for her first Wyoming gig, playing happy hours at the Wrangler. Delice looked pretty much the same as she had then. Her black hair (mighty black indeed) fell halfway down her back, her jeans were still tight and trim, and she still sported half her weight in silver jewelry. Her cowboy boots were custom-made now, and the black leather vest and black silk shirt she was wearing probably cost as much as her car had back then. They'd both come up in the world, but they still knew how to ride each other hard, and come out grinning.

Sally's salad and onion rings arrived. She dipped a hot ring in ketchup and bit in. "Would it make you feel better if you thought I was getting involved with Stone Jackson out of self-interest?" Sally asked.

Delice looked up from a credit card offer she was tossing in a pile with all the other credit card offers, and eyed Sally narrowly. "Depends what you mean. You don't still have that picture of Darlin' Tommy J on the sun visor of your car, do you?"

Sally glared and took a bite of middle-age iceberg lettuce and bottled dressing.

"Okay," said Delice, taking a sip of the Wrangler's translucent coffee and managing not to grimace. "What's your angle?"

"I think I want to do a biography of Nina Cruz," Sally said.

"Oh that," said Delice. "Everybody knows about that."

"What?" said Sally. "How the hell could you know? I've only told . . ."

"I heard it from Dwayne," said Delice.

"Dwayne?" Sally sputtered, setting down the next rapidly cooling onion ring. "Your brother's heard—"

"Of course. He said Nattie thinks that's why you're going to try to talk the Millionaires into doing the benefit with Stone Jackson. Nattie figures you've already got some kind of six-figure deal with a New York publishing house, and you're just using the band for your own selfish purposes."

"Nattie's talking about *my* selfish purposes?" Sally said, incredulous. Nattie Langham, Dwayne's wife and sister-in-law to Delice and Sheriff Dickie, was a realtor who'd virtually invented selfish purposes.

Delice drank another swig of coffee and reached for one of Sally's rings. "Eat up, Sal. You don't want to let these get cold. Five more minutes and you could use them to do a valve job on your Mustang."

The onion rings had already reached a state that made them all but indigestible.

"As for the gig," said Delice, "recall that Pammie Montgomery works at the Yippie I O, and she's not a moron. She's seen and heard all kinds of things out there in Albany, and restaurant kitchens are nothing more than rumor mills with hot pans and sharp knives. Nina Cruz was the biggest thing to hit Laramie since the railroad came through, and now add Stone Jackson to the mix and it's pretty juicy stuff. Did he really come to see you in your office?"

"I'm a shitty best friend," said Sally. "I should have called and told you as soon as he left."

"I may never forgive you. So does he want the Millionaires for the benefit?"

"Yeah. It's freaking unbelievable. He told me this morning he was going to ask 'Bonnie and Emmylou and them' if they'd be willing to help out."

Delice fell back against her chair and put her hand on her heart. "Oh my God. Do you think Emmylou'd autograph my copy of 'Pieces of the Sky'? I swear, I could die happy."

Sally pushed the unfinished plate of room-temperature rings aside. "I ought to mention this to Dwayne and Sam. I know they were never big fans of Nina's, and I'm sure they wouldn't want anything to do with this Wild West outfit, but Bonnie and Emmylou might make them a little more willing to put principle aside and do the gig."

Delice chuckled. "Fortunately, Sam Branch wouldn't know a principle if it was hanging between his legs. And as for my brother, I believe he'd stand naked in the snow and sing all seventy-seven verses of 'El Paso' if it meant he'd get within a hundred yards of Bonnie. They'll piss and moan, but in the end they'll give in and act like you owe them big-time."

"That's what I figured. The problem," Sally said, trying to decide whether to give the salad another shot, "will be Jimbo. The only celebrity he gives a damn about is Charlton Heston."

"This time of year," Delice said, "the only thing Jimbo Perrine cares about is bagging his limit. Or maybe more than his limit. He was in here yesterday morning, pounding down the Ranchman's Big Breakfast."

"Jesus. How often does he do that?" asked Sally. She'd seen the menu. The Ranchman's Big Breakfast was equivalent to ingesting a pig and a cow, with a side of poultry protein and extra animal fat.

"Nobody ever died from eating a good breakfast," Delice insisted, a Wyoming meat patriot to the end. "But this is what I'm trying to tell you. Jimbo was working on one of his pals to give him his deer tag. Admitted he'd already bagged three, but his point was that time was a-wastin', and his pal wasn't going to use his tag, so it shouldn't go to waste."

"You'd think he'd be more discreet about poaching," Sally said, disgusted.

"He was being discreet," Delice replied. "I just happened to accidentally overhear the conversation."

Sally got a mental image of Delice "overhearing" that looked a lot like the 1974 *Newsweek* photograph of Nixon's secretary, Rosemary Woods, spread-eagled across the entire Oval Office reception area, "accidentally" erasing the eighteen minutes of White House tape.

"Isn't Jimbo worried about the game warden?" Sally asked.

"Jimbo's been hunting around here his whole life, and the Game and Fish are pretty busy these days," said Delice. "This whole chronic wasting epidemic thing is really scary. It's all over the elk and deer herds in southern Wyoming and northern Colorado, and it's basically the same thing as mad cow disease. The Game and Fish guys don't like to talk about it, but the vets at the Ag station are doing a whole lot of research to try to determine whether it could jump species and infect the cattle herds."

Mad cow disease in Wyoming? The state that had far more Herefords than humans? Bad enough that the elk and deer were infected. A bovine epidemic would be nothing short of catastrophic. "And what do they think?" Sally asked.

"From what I hear, there's no evidence that it could jump to cows. But they haven't got it near figured out yet. It's fucking scary. If it gets out of hand, a whole lot of people around here will be in deep shit."

No kidding. Everybody from ranchers to bankers who made loans to ranchers to businesspeople like Delice Langham, who staked the better part of her monthly profit on Americans' insatiable hunger for animal protein. "So are you doing anything about it?" Sally asked.

"Doing anything? Like what, start firing up tofu stir-fries and alfalfa-sprout souffles?" Delice scoffed. "I'll let the geniuses at the Yippie I O deal with that stuff. As far as the Wrangler is concerned, I've decided not to worry about it until Jimbo Perrine and my brothers stop ordering the Double Roundup Burger at lunch."

9

The Taxidermist

"You're shitting me," said Jimbo Perrine, chewing the second gigantic bite of a Quarter Pounder with Cheese, mouth slightly open, crumbs of burger dropping unheeded into the great tangle of his wild brown beard.

"No. Amazing, isn't it?" replied Sally, choosing to miss his drift. "I mean, we're barely competent to play the Laramie Elks' Steak Fry. Can you believe we're actually being asked to open for Stone Jackson, and maybe even" she drew it out—"Bonnie and Emmylou?"

The Millionaires had gathered for practice in the usual place, Dwayne Langham's airplane hangar of a living room, in Dwayne and Nattie's outsize house on the east edge of town. No snow was expected, but the forecasters had rightly surmised that the weather would turn much colder and brutally windy. Not the still, bone-deep below-zero cold of midwinter, but the kind of blowing cold that made meteorologists think about measuring wind chill.

Jimbo finished his burger in three humongous bites, reached into the cardboard container, and crammed a handful of fries into his gaping mouth. Once more, he chewed, and once more spoke before swallowing. "Fuck Stone Jackson," he said, masticating french fries to saliva-softened paste. "Fuck Bonnie and Emmylou. For all I fuckin' care, they could have the fuckin' Queen of England."

He took a swig from a can of Keystone. Sally took a sip of Robert Mondavi Fumé Blanc. "The queen," she said, "never sang with Gram Parsons. Come on, Jimbo."

Much to her surprise, Dwayne chimed in. "I don't have any of the queen's CDs," he said, "but I have all of Bonnie's."

"I have 'Bohemian Rhapsody,'" observed the drummer, toking up in the corner.

Sally, Dwayne, and Sam guffawed. Jimbo was unamused. He shot a hostile glance at Sally's wineglass. "Gimme a break, Alder. These Left Coast faggots are exactly the kind of outside agitators who're gonna wreck Wyoming. That Nina Cruz comes in here and buys up a prime piece of deer and elk habitat, and then closes it off to locals whose great-granddaddies were hunting that aspen grove when her people were still swimmin' the fuckin' Rio Grande. The way some people around here think, the bitch got what she deserved."

Jimbo looked around for support, but he'd gone too far. Dwayne stared down at his pedal steel. The drummer sat motionless at his traps. Sam turned toward the wall, making a big deal of tuning his low E.

She slammed down the rage, but pedant that she was, she at least had to correct Jimbo's history. "Nina Cruz's family was settled in New Mexico a hundred years before George Washington crossed the Delaware," she said quietly, trying to keep the fury out of her voice.

"Wetback's a wetback," replied Jimbo, draining his Keystone and reaching for another. "We oughta just put up electric fence all along the border, and fry every fuckin' greaseball who tries to sneak in and steal our jobs and our property."

"Don't be confused, Sally. He means the Colorado border," Sam observed.

"All the borders," Jimbo asserted, crumpling the empty fast-food cartons, shoving them in the paper bag, and hauling himself to his feet. "I gotta take a whiz."

The thing was, Jimbo was a mighty tight bass player. He'd gigged with different Laramie bands for years, but joined the Millionaires six months before, when Jimbo's predecessor had moved to Denver. Sally had played music with enough disgusting but gifted people to understand that artistic talent and excellence of character were not necessarily connected. Or as Sam Branch, no Boy Scout himself, had once said after a particularly hot set, "That Jimbo plays real good. Too bad he's a total asshole."

Well, Sally reminded herself, struggling to emulate Stone Jacksonesque goodwill toward humanity, everybody was at least a partial asshole. Jimbo happened to be more fully realized in that department than most people.

When Jimbo returned from the bathroom, they'd just about finished tuning up. Time to do a few songs, drink a couple more beers, get loose. Then maybe they'd warm up to the idea of doing the benefit.

But Jimbo wasn't leaving the matter alone. "Boys," he said, deliberately addressing everyone but her, "no way can we do this fuckin' gig. It ain't just that my taxidermy business would be up shit creek if the animal rights nuts have their way. You're all hunters. They'd take your guns and your God-given rights and pretty soon we'd all be chantin' the fuckin' Hare Krishna and livin' on soybean squeezin's." He turned to Sam. "Plus that Nina Cruz was some kind of commie, you know? Fuckers don't even believe in property rights."

"Commies like her do," said Sam. "You don't catch 'em inviting the homeless for a swim at their beach houses in Malibu—and those beaches are *public* property. Nina Cruz did damn near everything she could to protect her property rights out in Albany, Jimbo, including her right to post her land off-limits to hunting. That's what's got your knickers in a knot. You and your buddies have taken a lot of deer and elk out of that aspen grove over the years. It pisses you off to be told you can't do it now. Though from what I hear, having the Cruz place posted off-limits hasn't slowed you down much this season."

Jimbo feigned wide-eyed innocence. "Wouldn't want to

shoot anything out there anyhow. That herd's so full of the wasting disease, the meat wouldn't be worth a bullet."

"It'll be interesting to see what happens to her place now that she's gone," Dwayne said. "Ought to be a prime piece of property for subdivision. Wonder if her heirs want to sell."

Sally looked at Sam. If there was any rumor of a sale, he'd know about it, and probably be trying to get a piece of the action. She grinned at him. "Gosh, Sam," she said, "might be a friendly gesture on your part to do this benefit after all."

He gave her a cynical smile. "Hey, I'm all for saving Wyoming's birds and bees."

"Even if it means paying tribute to the woman who once kissed a Vietcong commando?" she asked.

"We might all have reasons to do the gig. Especially if it means shakin' hands with Emmylou," Sam said.

The drummer, happily stoned, beamed. "I'd like to shake more than that with Emmylou."

"Son, you're so ugly, the only thing you could shake is her good manners when she has to look at you," Sam observed.

And so they moved on to good-natured insult, and then into a relatively placid practice. Jimbo had a few more Keystones and moved from glowering into laying down his usual reliable chops. At the end of two hours, they'd done a reasonable evening's work, leaving them all feeling pretty good. "I've got to go to a meeting with the Wild West people day after tomorrow, to talk about the benefit. You guys are in, right?" Sally asked, as they packed up their instruments.

They all nodded, except Jimbo. He looked at the floor and made harrumphing sounds.

"We can do it without you, bro'," Sam said. "Dwayne can play bass. But it would be a hell of a lot better to have you along. You could even wear your MOUNTS BY PERRINE hat if it'd make you feel better."

Jimbo sulked. "I don't know," he said. "I'll give it some thought. Might be good for business."

"Slow this year?" Dwayne inquired.

Jimbo shook his shaggy head. "Worst I ever saw. Drought's cut the total population down over the past few years, and the wasting disease isn't helping. Too many sick animals, not enough trophies. Half the guys I know aren't even using their tags."

Sally had heard who might be making use of those tags, but she kept her mouth shut.

"That's incredible," Dwayne said. "Can't imagine not getting out there and trying my luck. If people don't get around to it right quick, the season will close and that'll be that."

"Yeah," Jimbo agreed. "I hate to see a good deer tag go to waste."

Those words could have been his epitaph. The next afternoon, Sally got a call from Delice. "Did you hear?" she said. "There's been an accident. Jimbo Perrine went out hunting this morning and well . . ." She swallowed. "He's been shot. Hit in the lung—guess he somehow got between a hunter and his game. They've got him down in Ivinson Memorial. Been doing surgery on him for a couple of hours, but things look terrible. They don't expect him to pull through."

"Oh my God," said Sally, thinking instantly of Nina. "How could this happen twice in two weeks?"

"It's weird. Your friend Nina Cruz was one thing—from what I heard, she wasn't wearing orange, and whoever shot her was already trespassing. But Jimbo knows what he's doing. What's even more bizarre," Delice said, "is that he was out by Albany. I know he likes to hunt out there, but I'd have thought, with all the recent stuff at Shady Grove, he'd have avoided that place like the plague."

"And last night at practice he said he wasn't interested in hunting out there. Too much wasting disease in the herd," Sally told Delice. "So who was he with?"

"That's another strange thing. He went alone. People don't generally go after deer alone. Maybe he does, though. Especially considering that he seems to be in the habit of using other people's extra tags, huh?" Delice said.

"So how did they find him?" Sally asked.

"Evidently, somebody driving by on the road happened to look into the woods and see him lying there. They called nine-one-one from a cell phone, and then stayed with Jimbo until the ambulance came. Lucky for him, the person who found him was a doctor, so the guy did what he could. That's how Jimbo made it this far."

"How'd you hear about it?" Sally asked.

"My cousin's an ER nurse at Ivinson. She was there when they brought him in," Delice said.

It occurred to Sally that the person who'd found Jimbo was as likely to have shot him as anyone. "What about the doctor guy? Did he come in, too?"

"Yeah," said Delice. "He insisted on riding in the ambulance. My cousin said he was a dead ringer for Willie Nelson."

10

Hello, Darkness

Throughout Sally's afternoon class, and on through her office-hour appointments, she debated going to the hospital. Jimbo Perrine, while hardly a close personal friend, was nonetheless a Millionaire. On the other hand, if he wasn't still in surgery, he'd be in the intensive care unit, where they only let family visit, and the waiting room tended to be overcrowded with very worried friends and kin of terribly sick people.

By five o'clock, she decided she just had to do it. She didn't know Jimbo's wife, Arvida, very well, but she knew that they had two little kids and assumed that things would be very tough if he didn't make it. Sometimes it helped just to have somebody else there, worrying. If she wasn't welcome, if she was even the least bit superfluous, she'd quietly disappear.

Outside Hoyt Hall, you'd never know there'd already been a blizzard. It was fall, to be sure, crisp and clear. Marigolds and zinnias planted in beds the shape of a U and a W were frosted to cinders, but heads of purple and green ornamental kale remained bright. The cottonwoods had turned brilliant yellow a week before, but the leaves had only just begun to fall. The wind whispered through the leafy canopy as she walked home in the twilight, picked up the Mustang, and drove to the hospital.

The ICU waiting room was packed, as she'd expected. Arvida Perrine was huddled there, sharing a "sleeping chair" (hospital oxymoron) with the two kids and her mother, a remarkable achievement given that Arvida probably tipped the scales at about 180, and Arvida's mother made Arvida look like Gwyneth Paltrow. Jimbo, they said, was still in surgery. They all looked absolutely miserable.

Sally offered to go down to the hospital cafeteria and get them some dinner. Arvida wasn't hungry, but said she was sure the kids could use something to eat. Maybe they could even go to the cafeteria with Sally. The kids shook their heads vigorously, much to Sally's relief. "They ain't real comfortable with strangers," Arvida said, "but you could get 'em a sandwich or some chicken nuggets or somethin'." Arvida admitted she'd take a cup of coffee. Arvida's mother allowed as how she could use a hot meal and a piece of pie, and she was partial to Salisbury steak.

If she'd been one of the other visitors spending long hours in the waiting room, Sally thought, she wouldn't have been too keen on the aroma of hospital cafeteria Salisbury steak just then. But she told Jimbo's mother she'd see what she could do.

The cafeteria had made an attempt at cheer that fell some ways wide of the mark. There were "country" touches— warped wicker baskets stuffed with dusty plastic flowers in unnatural shades of pink and blue, tacked to the walls; straw brooms tied with calico bows behind the cash register; some kind of strawberry potpourri that must have been an attempt to mask disinfectant, if indeed that wasn't the smell of the actual disinfectant. Sally got a tray and went through the line, choosing grilled cheese and tater tots and chocolate milk for the kids, and for Arvida's mother, a truly monochromatic boxed dinner: chicken-fried steak with white gravy, mashed potatoes, a square roll, and a matching piece of gluey coconut-cream pie. The vegetable of the day was steamed cauliflower, but on behalf of the other waiting room folks, Sally demurred.

She paid and walked out into the dining area. There, at a corner table, Scotty Atkins sat staring steely-eyed at Nels Willen. She'd have loved to accidentally overhear what they were saying, but there was no way Scotty would have permitted her within a mile of their table. Sighing, she headed back upstairs and delivered the food.

But she'd forgotten Arvida's coffee. A perfect excuse to make another pass.

She hustled back to the cafeteria, got the coffee, and nearly ran headlong into Scotty, who was on his way out.

He gave her the narrow-eyed once-over. "Visiting a sick auntie?" he asked.

"My bass player's in the ICU. I'm taking dinner to his family."

Scotty looked down at the cup of coffee Sally held in her hand. "They gonna share that?" he asked.

She blew out a breath.

Before he could say anything more, she decided to go on the offensive. She might as well. He'd be offended one way or the other. "What's Nels Willen doing here?" she asked.

"I have the impression you know the answer to that question, although I'm damned if I know how."

"I never divulge my sources," Sally said, deciding she could use the coffee herself. She took the plastic lid off the plastic foam cup, inevitably spilling a little hot coffee on her hand, took a sip, and wondered if somebody had decided to reuse grounds from an earlier pot, maybe more than once. "I understood that a doctor found Jimbo, somewhere out near Albany. Nels Willen is a doctor, or was, anyhow. And he's got business in Albany. I draw the obvious conclusion. You can try to bluff me, Scotty, but I think I can get that far on my own."

"Forget about it, Sally," said Scotty, shaking his head. "Do what you have to do for Perrine's family, if you want. But stay out, I repeat, stay out of this case. You've got your million-dollar publishing deal. Go sit in a library, or punch a keyboard, and do some research. Don't deceive yourself that you're equipped in any way to assist the police in the investigation of suspicious shootings. You can't help. You might get yourself shot in the bargain."

At least Scotty hadn't added another zero to her fictitious book contract. "So you consider this a suspicious shooting? Homicide, maybe?"

Scotty's lips thinned. "You don't give up, do you? Are you some kind of crusader, or do you just have a thing about violent death?"

The shock registered in her eyes.

"I'm sorry," he said. "That was out of line."

They stood glaring at each other, pain—and something else—silently passing from him to her and back. And as they stood there, Nels Willen got up from the table and walked over to join them.

Willen nodded. "Hello, Sally," he said.

Scotty looked from one to the other, as if he were choosing his words. "Stay close, Dr. Willen," he finally said. "We'll be in touch."

"Whatever I can do to help, Detective," Willen answered. "And if I think of anything more, I'll call right away."

Atkins pursed his lips. "Yeah. You do that." He turned pale eyes on Sally. "Better get that family a fresh cup of coffee." He walked away.

"You know the Perrines?" Nels Willen asked her.

"Jimbo's the bass player in my band. When I heard he'd been shot, I came down to see if I could do anything. So, it was you who found him," she said.

He closed his eyes, rubbed his stubbled jaw. "Yeah," he admitted.

"I better get that coffee," she said, fumbling for words.

"I'll wait for you," he said. "I want to go up and say goodbye to the family."

Hospitals, Sally thought, were places that seemed to have had the sound vacuumed out of them. As she and Willen got out of the elevator on the ICU floor, the hallway seemed audibly silent. Hello darkness, my old friend.

They rounded the corner by the nurses' station. A choking sob tore the air. Halfway down the corridor toward the waiting room, a tall, tired-looking man in green scrubs put a hand under the elbow of a crumbling Arvida Perrine. Within moments, she began to cry in earnest, and he moved to put an arm around her back, to hold her upright.

Sally looked at Willen. "I think," she said, "we ought to leave."

He nodded. "In my experience, his folks will want to be alone."

They turned, took the elevator to the main floor, and walked out into the parking lot. The night was clear, lit by a crescent moon and a million stars. Their breath came in clouds.

"So are you driving out to Shady Grove tonight?" she asked him.

"It hardly seems worth it. Think I'll get a motel room in town tonight," he said.

"Feel like talking?"

He offered a wan half-smile. "What's to talk about?"

She took a deep breath. "I don't know. If I'd found him, I'd want to talk about it to somebody besides Detective Atkins."

Willen laughed softly. "He isn't the most sympathetic listener."

Sally took a chance. "Why don't you come over to my house and have a drink and something to eat?"

Willen's face relaxed a notch. "That would be good," he said. "Where are you parked?"

She gestured at the Mustang, halfway down a row.

"I'll follow you," he said.

As she walked to her car, it occurred to Sally that Nels Willen had been early to the scene of two fatal shootings. Anyone might reasonably conclude that he'd been involved. Some people, indeed, might think it a supremely stupid thing to do, to invite a possible murderer to come on over for a beer. She needed backup.

She unlocked her car, got in, dug in her big leather shoulder bag, pulled out her cell phone, and dialed her home number. Hawk answered.

"What are you doing?" she asked.

"Sitting around naked, imagining that you're similarly attired, standing in the kitchen, whipping up a batch of hollandaise sauce. And I've got this basting brush, and you've got those very lovely—"

"Seriously," she said, "what?"

"Drinking a beer and thinking about ordering a pizza," he said. "You coming home?"

"Yeah," she said. "Order enough pizza for three, and hold the pepperoni. Get the deluxe veggie."

"How come?" he asked. "You aren't bringing a Californian home to dinner, are you?"

"Certainly not," she said. "A Coloradan. And with any luck, he's not exactly homicidal."

"I guess that's good news. Do you care to explain?" Hawk asked.

"It's a long story." She took a deep breath. "There's been another shooting death. Jimbo Perrine," she said.

"Christ." Hawk exhaled. "What happened?"

"He was out hunting."

"Another hunting accident?" Hawk asked.

"It's possible. But then there's the fact that he was found by Nels Willen."

"The doctor from Shady Grove? What the hell's going on?" Hawk said.

"I'd really like to know. That's why I asked Willen if he wanted to come over for a drink."

Pause. Then Hawk, master of understatement, said, "Are you sure that's wise?"

Sally gave it one moment's thought. Willen's Saab had pulled up behind her Mustang; he was waiting to follow her home. She could just tell him she'd changed her mind—was too tired. But, she reasoned, the poor man must be emotionally and physically exhausted. The least she could do was offer him a helping hand. "I don't think he'll shoot us tonight," she told Hawk.

"Okay," Hawk said. "In that case, there's plenty of cold beer. I'll order a couple of pizzas and put the Smith and Wesson in the silverware drawer."

"It's a comfort knowing you're always prepared," Sally said.

"I love you, honey," he answered. "Just thought you ought to know that in case he shoots you on the way home."

"You're such a sensitive guy," she said, and rang off.

An hour later, they sat in their living room, an open pizza box and a healthy array of long necks on the coffee table. Nels Willen had managed one slice of pizza and was working on his third Budweiser. He sat on the couch, hunched forward, forearms on his thighs, the beer dangling from the fingers of his right hand. They were beautiful hands, Sally noticed, strong and graceful. Musician's hands, she'd have said under other circumstances. But, of course, his were surgeon's hands.

He hadn't seemed to be inhibited by Hawk's presence. Sally had offered him a sounding board, and he was using it. But he'd yet to mention Jimbo Perrine. What he wanted to talk about was Nina.

"You have to understand about Angelina Cruz," he said, raising the bottle to his lips and taking a swig. "She was the most passionate woman—the most passionate person—I've ever known. It extended to everything. First time I met her was in Aspen, at a party a friend of mine gave. She was just learning to ski. Thomas had brought her to Colorado. He'd skied for years, and he was damn good at it, but then, that's how it is with him. Anything old Stone wants to do, comes pretty easy.

"But not for Angelina. She didn't take more than one or two lessons before she got off the bunny slope and attacked the mountain. She told me that first night that by the end of two weeks, she'd be skiing right along with Stone, and since he was pretty much sticking to the black diamond runs, I thought I'd better keep an eye on her. Lucky thing. On the third day, she racked herself up good, sprained an ankle and an elbow, and I thought she was done for the duration.

"I didn't know Angelina. Three days later, she had me taping her up tight and pushing her back out on the mountain. Skied the rest of the vacation, eating codeine at night."

"Eating codeine? That doesn't sound like Nina," Sally said.

"Maybe not the Nina of now," said Hawk, "but this was— what, back in the seventies?"

Willen nodded.

"Hell, I knew people whose idea of getting back to nature was living on fruit juice, marijuana, and enemas," Hawk observed. "Coke-snorting vegetarians and bodhisattvas facing paternity suits. I knew one guy who insisted the only way to find harmony in the desert was to survive on roasted mesquite beans and rattlesnake jerky. He got pretty skinny and dried-out before he broke down and hit the Taco Bell."

"Yeah, I guess you're right," Sally said. "There was a lot more room for creative mania in those days."

Willen drained his beer. "Angelina wasn't lacking in that department. With her, it was all or nothing. Take the time she busted up her leg in Switzerland, back in eighty-four. By the time I got there, Stone had gone off on a toot, and she'd spent four days in the care of some Teutonic quack who'd convinced her that the best way to get her body ready for surgery was a diet consisting solely of organ meats. Cows, pigs, sheep, and goats; kidneys, livers, brains, and balls. She was by God gonna stick to it, until I told her that, at the very least, she was working her arteries a hell of a lot harder than she had any business doing. Not long after that, she gave up meat entirely."

No wonder she'd gone over to soy smoothies, thought Sally. "Goat liver, really?"

Willen ignored the question. "And once she'd decided to be a vegetarian, that was it. She made up her mind about things fast. First impressions counted—if she liked you on sight, she'd stick with you long after everybody else had decided you were boring or full of shit or bad to the bone. She had an incredible capacity for love and loyalty."

"She loved you," Sally told him. She had only Stone Jackson's word on that subject, but she wanted to give Willen some comfort.

"Yeah," said Willen, and sighed. "Among others. I think she even loved you a little."

"Me?" Sally said. "She hardly knew me."

"But that was how it was with her. Snap judgments. She read your Dunwoodie book. She'd heard what you'd been through on that project. That was all she needed."

"She talked to you about me?" Sally was incredulous.

"I asked her if she'd made any friends in Laramie. She mentioned you."

Friends. Sally had considered Nina Cruz an interesting, pleasant acquaintance. A person who might someday become a real friend. But not yet. Maybe she'd been a little intimidated by Nina's celebrity. Maybe fame made Nina a lonely woman.

"Unfortunately, Angelina could be a little too quick to trust sometimes. Especially in the last couple of years, she let people take advantage of her."

"Stone Jackson said the same thing," Sally offered.

Willen put the beer on the table and leaned back on the couch, eyes closed, braids trailing down his back. "Funny thing. The way we each felt about her, you'd suppose we'd hate each other's guts. But it's never been like that with Stone and me. Maybe it was because by the time Nina came to me, he knew he had to let her go, at least a little. Maybe I wasn't jealous of him because—well, how could you be? It'd be like being jealous of John Lennon or Jesus or something. Or maybe it's that when she moved on down the road, we both just went on loving her and trying to protect her."

"From what?" Hawk asked. "She must have known there were people trying to scam her. It's not like there's any shortage of bullshit artists in L.A."

"Sure," said Willen. "Or Aspen either, for that matter. For Stone, it was dope dealers. For Nina, it was people with causes. Back in the sixties, it was radicals who needed lawyers, or somebody's foundation that was supposed to set up medical care for migrant workers. Later on, they'd come pitching women's shelters or Andean indigenous agriculture. Always sounded good, and the people were so convincing. Then she'd find out that the radical lawyers were buying condos in Maui, and the indigenous farmers she was bankrolling were growing coca."

"What would she do then?" Hawk asked.

Willen paused and took a drink. "She'd be terribly, terribly hurt," he said. "And then she'd pick up and go on, gung ho for her next crusade. She said she wasn't willing to let a few bad experiences trash her faith in the human race. She believed in progress."

That sounded like Nina. Who else would move to Wyoming with the idea that you could convince people to give up their addiction to beefsteak and the Broncos in the name of living a more enlightened life?

"So what's the deal with Wild West?" Hawk asked the question. Sally realized she had absolutely no idea what the answer might be.

"Angelina grew up in northern New Mexico," Willen replied. "Some of her cousins are still hanging on to pieces of what's left of a Spanish land grant, trying to make a living running cows and herding sheep and cutting a little timber. She did what she could to help them stay on the land, became a silent partner in their operations, sent checks for feed and seed and to pay the lawyers when the government canceled their grazing leases.

"She cared about their determination to hold on to their land. But she told me she thought they were killing the very thing they loved. Too many cows, too many sheep, too many hooves and teeth grinding and chewing that grass right down to bare dirt. Riverbeds trampled, erosion, streams drying up—you probably know what happens to a place that's been overgrazed."

"It's a vicious cycle," Hawk said. "The worse shape the pasture's in, the harder the ranchers have to struggle to pay the bills, so they run more animals. Was that why Nina didn't get a place in New Mexico?" he asked.

"She wanted to start fresh, without the family baggage. A lot of the folks were already pretty mad at her for the Vietcong stuff, and they wouldn't have felt any warmer toward her once she started telling them to get rid of their cows and let nature take its course, maybe bring a couple of wolves onto the place."

Sally could imagine the reaction. The ranchers she knew in Wyoming would have politely suggested that maybe such a person would be happier in California, living on redwood bark and roots. "What in the world made her think it would be any better here?"

Willen smiled. "The optimism of the ignorant, maybe. Or just plain longing. She fell in love with Wyoming when she came out to visit me and I took her up in the Snowies on a fishing trip. The land here's still a bargain, compared to a lot of the rest of the West. Sort of a last best place."

"That's Montana," said Sally. "A lot of people get confused."

Willen grinned weakly. "No need to be touchy. I ain't here to Coloradicate you all."

"So Wild West was her attempt to do something about rangeland in Wyoming?" Hawk asked.

"Mmm-hmm. The foundation could support a number of activities, from green range management research to sponsoring public mediation of grazing disputes. I was advising her on some possibilities. But, of course, she was also concerned about the animals themselves. It wasn't clear what direction she planned to go with that part of the agenda."

"The animal rights part?" Sally asked.

"Right. You're probably aware, there are all kinds of animal rights activists."

"Sure. Everything from Ducks Unlimited and the Humane Society to people who throw blood on fur coats and bust up labs where they experiment on animals," Hawk said.

"Well actually, most animal rights activists wouldn't put themselves in the same basket with duck hunters and people who kill cats and dogs because there are too many of them," Willen said. "Animal rights folks believe, pure and simple, that animals don't belong to humans for food, clothing, experimentation, or entertainment. We're against causing needless pain and suffering to animals." His tone was mild, but it was clear that he counted himself among the faithful.

Now she noticed his clothes: canvas boots with rubber soles, cotton denim blue jeans, and the fisherman's sweater she'd taken for a heavy wool knit on the day that Nina had died was in actuality some kind of patterned fleece. No animal products there (although, Sally reflected, to clothe Nels Willen, rubber trees had bled on plantations in the Putumayo, petroleum had been pumped and pipelined and refined halfway across the world, and scarce desert water had been lavished on behemoth cotton plantations, maybe in Egypt, or maybe in Arizona). Once again, Sally wondered about Willen's celebrated epiphany.

"Angelina believed in animal rights, and she wanted Wild West to support the cause," he said. "But, even so, there's some difference of opinion among the Wild West people on those matters. It's still being worked out," Willen said.

"What do you mean?" Sally was pressing.

"Let's just say there are various views as to whether the land or the animals are most important. It's a little complicated. I don't really have the energy to explain just now," Willen said.

"Thomas Jackson thought there was something wrong with Nina." Sally tried another tack.

Willen put his head in his hands. "He was right about that," he said. "She'd walk into a room, start a sentence, and trail off in the middle. Then she'd walk out. She'd get really angry for no reason. Memory lapses, disorientation, all the signs of what looked to me like a brain problem. I was worried about a tumor, and was going to suggest a CAT scan."

"So why in the world would you bring her a gun?" Sally asked. "I'd think that'd be the last thing you'd want to do with somebody whose mental stability you doubted." Not to mention the fact that your average animal rights supporter wouldn't want much to do with something that could blow a terminal hole in a living creature.

"Seems pretty obvious in retrospect," Willen agreed. "But she said she was scared. There were a bunch of people around her place she didn't know. She suspected somebody was out to get her. She just wanted it for protection. I should have told her to get a dog." He took a long pull on the latest beer. "I finally had to take it away from her when I saw her shoot into the woods on the morning she died."

Sally and Hawk exchanged a look. "When that morning?" Sally asked.

"Maybe half an hour before we heard those other shots," Willen said. "She was out behind the house, by the woodpile. I couldn't see who or what she was firing at. Then she just slumped over and started to shake. I grabbed the gun, stuck it under the tarp on the woodpile, then took her into the house. She couldn't speak. I took her up and put her to bed, then went out into the woods to see if she'd hit anyone or anything. The next thing we knew, there were more shots. You were there, Sally. You know what happened after that."

Willen pulled the elastic bands off the ends of his braids and began combing out his hair with his fingers. They waited. He rebraided his hair, and said at last, "Think I'd better find that motel room now. I'm so beat, I might just crash out on your couch here in about a minute."

"You're welcome to do so," said Hawk. "Maybe you shouldn't drive."

Willen left the remains of his fourth beer on the table. "Thanks, but I think I need to be by myself for a while," he said. "I'll be okay. Reckon I can find my way to the Holiday Inn. Thanks for the pizza."

They watched him walk out to his car, dejected but steady on his feet, and decided they'd let him go.

The moment he'd driven away, two things occurred to Sally. First, if Willen's prints were all over the gun he'd brought to Shady Grove, a gun that had just been fired, he'd offered a neat explanation. Second, he hadn't said one word about the recent trauma of finding poor gunshot Jimbo Perrine.

11

The Goodwill Ambassador

The morning of the meeting, Sally dressed with unaccustomed care. Not that she wasn't fussy about clothes, as Hawk had often pointed out. But then, he was one of those people who got up and put on a pair of jeans and a shirt and never gave it a second thought. If you held your hand over his eyes and asked him what he was wearing, he might have a little trouble coming up with the color of the shirt. She, on the other hand, generally had to try and reject various permutations of three or four different outfits, grimacing at herself in the mirror, twisting and turning in the effort to get a look at her backside and seeing every onion ring she'd ever consumed showing up somewhere between her shoes and her earrings.

But this particular morning presented a daunting fashion challenge. How could she avoid sending up red flags with animal rights partisans at the Wild West meeting? She could manage with jeans or cotton pants, or a skirt and any number of cotton or synthetic blouses or sweaters. The leather jacket would have to stay in the closet; ditto the wool overcoat. The nylon ski jacket was just too woodsy, the fleece still too bulky and casual, but it would have to do.

The problem was the shoes. Among the forty-odd pairs crowding the closet she shared with Hawk (another thing he liked to mention), she owned only three pairs of shoes that weren't made of leather: rubber beach flip-flops, wedgie canvas espadrilles that tied around the ankles, and a pair of red Keds she'd bought on impulse after listening to Elvis Costello sing "The Angels Wanna Wear My Red Shoes." It was too cold for the first two, and the Keds had turned out to look dorky rather than cool, even with jeans. Stone Jackson was going to be at this meeting, and she had no intention of facing him in dorky shoes.

So in the war between sensitivity and vanity, vanity won. She went for the boat-necked dark gray knit top, form-fitting with the three-quarter sleeves, and the snug ankle-length black skirt. Put together, in control, an edgy touch of sex. There wasn't much she could do about her high-heeled boots, but maybe she could tuck her feet under her chair and the skirt would cover her sins.

She did make some concessions. She'd put aside the cashmere sweater she really wanted to wear. She didn't need some righteous Dub-Dub explaining that because of her, some poor wrinkly sheep was walking around naked in Mongolia.

Which was pretty much what Randy Whitebird said to Thomas Jackson when the latter walked into the meeting with Caterina Cruz, forty minutes late, sporting what looked to be a well-loved ski sweater.

"Nina bought me this sweater almost thirty years ago in Switzerland," Stone told Whitebird. "I don't think the sheep's suffering much anymore."

Cat Cruz was shorter and less angular than Nina, and clearly more concerned with elegance. Where Nina had embraced Wyoming's easygoing attitude about dress, Cat's idea of casual made allowances neither for Rocky Mountain informality or animal lovers' sensibilities. She wore black wool pants, soft leather boots, and a cowl-necked pink angora sweater, along with an array of tasteful but noticeable gold jewelry. She could have been mistaken for a Beverly Hills socialite, heading for a little power shopping on Rodeo

Drive. But she had her sister's shiny black eyes and acute expression as she surveyed Wild West's makeshift headquarters, not much liking what she saw.

The operation looked to be running on a shoestring. They'd rented a three-room office suite, relatively spacious but bare, with fluorescent light fixtures and a restroom of its own. The furniture in the main room consisted of a sagging thrift-shop couch; a rickety coffee table, probably acquired from the same source; a banged-up gray metal desk; and a small assortment of plastic lawn chairs. They also had a fiberboard bookshelf that held files and books. In a second room, a mini-refrigerator, a microwave, an electric tea kettle, and a metal and Formica dinette set did duty as a kitchen. Through a door opening from the main room, Sally could see that the third room was empty, except for two sleeping bags laid out on inflatable camping pads, with a desk lamp between, attached to a wall outlet by a long extension cord. Two backpacks stood propped against opposite walls.

"Well, Thomas," said Caterina Cruz, raising an eyebrow and turning to Jackson, "it doesn't look like they're squandering my sister's money on fancy furnishings anyhow." Then she turned to the people who'd sat around cooling their heels, waiting for her to arrive, and said, "Sorry we're late," looking not one bit sorry, in Sally's opinion.

"We've just been visiting with your local law enforcement," Stone explained. "It took a little longer than we'd planned."

Sally could imagine. Two celebrity-size egos walk into the Albany County Courthouse, expecting to give the Deputy Dawgs maybe ten or fifteen minutes of their valuable time. Old Scotty Atkins wouldn't need more than a whiff of high-falutin' attitude to decide to back and fill and stall and stonewall until they'd gotten sick of him. For that matter, Sheriff Dickie Langham might have taken a turn at them himself, putting on the "aw shucks" and besieging them with seemingly stupid questions until everybody was ready to puke cornpone.

Not to mention that Dickie Langham's awareness of the presence of McDonald's franchises everywhere might inspire him to ask Stone Jackson some questions.

Jackson and Nina's sister did look a little weary for so early in the day, and Sally evidently wasn't the only one to notice. Nels Willen pulled himself out of one of the lawn chairs and gave Cat a big hug. "It's been a while, darlin'," he told her, "I'm so awful sorry." And then he moved to hug Stone in turn. The expressions on their faces nearly broke Sally's heart.

But they pulled themselves together, as everybody got acquainted. Sally noted that Cat seemed to have heard of Whitebird, but not met him. Whitebird was sitting next to a mild-faced man with a receding hairline and thin graying ponytail, who'd been introduced as Terry Kean, the genius behind thirty years of all-star benefit concerts. If there were whales or farmers to be saved, wolves or prisoners of conscience to be freed, Terry Kean had been there to make sure that tickets got sold, that the sound system worked, and that all the performers had their contract-specified brands of vitamins, mineral water, and massage therapists.

Far more important, the artists had learned that, more often than not, benefits lost money. Of course, lots of concerts lost money. But there were other problems. Many people in the music business regarded doing good as, at best, a clever cover for self-interest (good press) and, at worst, a waste of time better spent overtly feathering one's own nest. In L.A., they might talk about good karma, but they believed in above-average marginal returns. That was why even the most cynical respected Terry Kean. He seemed to have the knack of turning a profit, while looking noble.

Cat hugged him hard, saying, "It's been like ten years, T.K."

"Yeah," replied the man, grinning. "Back when we thought raising five mill for Amnesty International was going to liberate the world."

"Well," said Cat, "I haven't entirely given up hope. Appears you haven't either."

"Nope," said Kean. "But I'm too homely to be a goodwill ambassador for UNICEF. Glad to see they're still sending out the pretty ladies."

"Right. And if pretty ladies were all it took to defeat world hunger, we'd be doing benefits for eye jobs and liposuction," Cat replied.

Sally cracked up. If this was UNICEF, she was prepared to sign on for trick-or-treating.

Pammie Montgomery, Quartz, and Lark, the blonde who'd taught the yoga class (and walked into Nina's office that morning, just in time to see Sally sneaking the mysterious note into her DayMinder) were in the other room, setting up the lunch on the dinette table. They were called in to introduce themselves. Cat shook their hands and immediately dismissed them as bit players.

Sally, on the other hand, was treated to a dose of the Cruz charm that had attracted her to Nina, and that had evidently earned Cat her UNICEF gig. "My sister said really nice things about you and the work you're doing," Cat told her, grasping both of Sally's hands, leaning over for a Hollywood air kiss, and whispering in Sally's ear, "and she put her money where her mouth was. Let's have a drink after the meeting, okay?"

That was intriguing, to say the least. But Sally was even more interested in the way Caterina Cruz greeted the woman who'd been introduced as Kali. Sally had never seen a mongoose approach a snake, but she'd bet there was some of the same energy in the air.

"Hello, Kelly Lee," said Cat, putting a hand on the woman's arm not as a gesture of familiarity, but more as if she didn't want even the impersonal intimacy of a handshake. No eye contact, no follow-up, no "How are you?" Just nothing.

Kelly Lee? Sally thought the name might suit better than Kali, but now she had some idea where the goddess title might have come from. Stone had said that Kali was a "little bit of a thing," and he hadn't exaggerated. She couldn't have topped five feet or a hundred pounds. But Kali was a figure to be noticed, even at first glance: sharp-featured as a ferret, dressed all in white fleece down to her clogs, blonde hair cropped in the same short, spiky cut Nina had worn. In that outfit, she should have looked like a lamb. That wasn't even close. Sally tried not to stare, but suddenly, she understood why the encounter between Cat Cruz and Kali had put her in mind of the mongoose and the snake. Kali—Kelly Lee?—

wore long, dangly silver-and-onyx earrings that were, on closer inspection, lifelike renderings of writhing snakes.

"Hello, Caterina," whispered Kali, in a voice hardly louder than the sound of leaves rustling in the wind. "Our cherished sister is gone, but I swear to you that I will do everything in my power to see that her splendid vision lives on."

Our sister? Nobody had said that Kali was actually related to Nina; probably she was just doing a particularly inappropriate and insensitive rendition of the all-women-are-sisters-in-Mother-Earth thing. Sally didn't know Cat Cruz, but if her own sister had been killed, and somebody else came around claiming some kind of phony kinship, she'd have wanted to ram a fist down the somebody's throat.

"I assure you, I have every intention of honoring Nina's vision," Cat replied, staring unblinking into Kali's deep blue eyes. Then she turned her attention to the group. "I'll be going through Nina's papers out at Shady Grove this week, trying to pull together a full accounting of the foundation's finances and projects. I'll expect you to assist with any materials you've moved to this office, or anywhere else. The sooner the better, but no later than this time next week. It's going to cost money to put this benefit together, and I need to know where that money's coming from, and where Nina intended it to go. I'll need copies of all correspondence on those matters along with bank statements, investments, spread sheet summaries, and any other relevant records. Naturally, I'll want to see your salaries and job descriptions. No games here, people. As executor of my sister's will, I'll be stepping in as acting chief executive officer of Wild West. If I have to pull the plug, on the benefit or the whole operation, I will."

So much for the goodwill ambassador portion of the program.

"Absolutely, Cat," Whitebird interceded. "With everything that's happened, we haven't had the chance to catch up with all the paperwork. But just as soon as this meeting's over, we'll start putting it all together. It's a little more difficult, of course, since you've asked the staff to vacate the ranch, but we can do it."

Vacate the ranch? So she'd kicked them all out of Shady Grove? And Cat was planning to stay out there? There'd be no better opportunity to get started on the book about Nina. Sally would have to see if Cat would let her come out and take a look at the papers.

"See that you do, Mr. . . . Whitebird, is it? I loved my sister, but I'm not a sentimentalist. I've spent the better part of the last weeks meeting with lawyers, and now with cops. I still don't understand how she had some kind of freak show running at her house, and all over her woods, and somebody still managed to shoot her and disappear."

Nobody said a word.

"We don't understand it either," Whitebird finally ventured. "But as we've all heard by now, she's not the only victim this year. Sometimes even the ones carrying the guns get in the way of a bullet. It appears that hunting season in Wyoming is as dangerous to humans as it is to other animals."

Nels Willen slouched lower in the lawn chair, a picture of wretchedness.

The meeting might have broken up there and then, but Kali stepped in. "I'd suggest that everyone get some lunch, and then we can get down to the business of planning a concert that will be a fitting tribute to Nina."

Stone put his arm around Cat. "Why don't we do that?" he said. "It's been a long morning, and I'm feeling a little peckish."

Whitebird retreated. Cat conceded the moment. She and Stone led the way into the room where the buffet had been laid out on the Formica-topped table.

It was a Pammie Montgomery triumph, an abundant and appealing vegan spread. There were gorgeous grilled vegetable sandwiches on focaccia, alongside plates of more such vegetables for those who disdained risen bread, Sally assumed, on account of feeling compassion for yeast. There was a pot of a rosemary-scented white bean soup keeping warm on the hot plate, a bowl of sesame-flavored slaw salad, made with red cabbage and cucumbers, dishes of plump dried fruit and mixed nuts, a platter of chocolate-dipped strawberries. There were bottles of sparkling and still water, tea bags for herb tea.

"You," said Cat, shooting an index figure at the beaming Pammie, "are hereby appointed our official caterer. This totally rocks. I assume you do real food," she said, and then added, in response to Pammie's polite puzzlement, "not just vegan menus."

"Whatever you want," Pammie replied, handing Cat a business card that said PAMELA M. CATERING FOR ALL OCCASIONS with a phone number and e-mail address. It wouldn't be long before the Yippie I O lost a salad girl and gained a competitor. Sally wondered if a restaurant called Pamela M had a chance in a place where most people liked a steak that was pretty much indistinguishable from the plate.

"Don't forget to leave room for the strawberries," said Quartz, clapping an arm around the genius-chef-in-training. "Or eat dessert first."

They were using paper plates and cups, paper napkins and plastic flatware. Sally guessed that the caterer had decided that the inconvenience of washing dishes in the restroom sink trumped the desirability of not adding to Wyoming's solid waste problem.

Still, the buffet was clearly calculated to give the least offense possible. Pammie had even prepared special dishes to satisfy the most stringent dietary rules. Kali and Lark each received a plate heaped with beautifully colorful, carefully cut, enticingly garnished and uniformly raw fruit and vegetables. Each was handed a paper-wrapped pair of wooden chopsticks and a bottle of spring water. As everyone went back into the main room, arranging him- or herself on a chair or the couch, Kali and Lark sank into cross-legged positions on the floor, setting their plates in their laps, and went to work with the chopsticks. Quartz was last to arrive, with a heaped-up plate. Pammie remained in the kitchen room, restocking platters, checking the temperature on the soup, nibbling a chocolate strawberry with a huge grin on her face.

A catered vegan lunch, complete with custom-made raw meals. It had to be a milestone in the history of Wyoming. Sally half expected somebody to come running in with a bloody cow carcass, or, at the very least, a bag of burgers, either to save the luncheon guests from malnutrition, or to protect the state's endangered cultural identity.

This was, however, a business meeting held in the temporary offices of Wild West, and everyone seemed to be waiting for Stone Jackson, obviously the most powerful person in the room, to make his move. He made pleasant small talk, efficiently polished off his soup and sandwich, drank a cup of tea, and powered down two helpings of slaw. And then, without appearing the least bit aggressive or assertive, he assumed control and opened the meeting. "Let me begin by asking for a volunteer to take notes," he said, brandishing a yellow pad.

Quartz raised his hand, and reached down to retrieve a laptop computer sitting by his side. Good lad, Sally thought. Raised late enough in the second feminist wave not to have absorbed the notion that the secretarial grunt work belonged to women, and long enough into the information revolution to be accustomed to taking notes into a computer.

Stone nodded thanks at Quartz, and moved on. "Why don't we start by summing up what we know so far," he said. "The concert will take place on the Saturday night of Thanksgiving weekend. That gives us not quite four weeks to ramp up. Terry, ticket sales are looking good, right?"

"They've been selling like crazy, even though the talent isn't completely nailed down. We've had phone and Internet inquiries about everything from motels and restaurants to RV hookups. Looks like people will be flying and driving in from as far away as Phoenix and Seattle."

"Hope it doesn't snow," Sally couldn't help saying.

Everyone glared at her. She vowed not to open her mouth again. If they didn't want to think about the oh-so-predictable Thanksgiving blizzard, fine. Let them figure out what to do with ten thousand irate would-be concertgoers, demanding refunds because they were iced down in Colorado Springs, or freezing their asses off at Little America, or spending a night in the Denver International Airport. Or because half the talent was sitting on the runway at LAX, waiting for global warming to take effect.

"I've been working on the lineup," Stone said. "So far, it's looking pretty good. Bonnie can't make it, unfortunately—"

Uh-oh. That might dampen Dwayne's enthusiasm.

"But Emmylou's on board, and she mentioned that Linda and Dolly might want to come."

Linda and Dolly? The Millionaires would be ecstatic, especially Jimbo, who'd even made a pilgrimage to Dollywood. And then Sally recalled, with a blast of hot grief, what had befallen the bass player.

"David and Graham are in, too," Jackson added.

Sally broke her vow. "Linda and Dolly and David and Graham. Wow! It really sounds to me like you've got more than enough without my band," she said.

"Not at all," said Stone, fixing her with a let-me-handle-this look. "We support local music."

"Thomas, we've just lost our bass player, in case you hadn't heard."

"Of course. I'm sorry, I did hear," he said, looking at Nels, who closed his eyes. "Another one of these hunting accidents. Was he an old friend?"

"Well, no," said Sally. "He's only been with the band a little while, but it's horrible, nonetheless. The guy had a wife and a couple of kids, and a job at the cement plant. I'm sure they're hurting every which way."

Stone looked thoughtful. "Would you be willing to go on with somebody else sitting in?" he said. "I could get you a bass player, if it came to that. Or if you've got somebody else who could fill in, I could sit in on guitar or piano and sing some harmonies."

Stone Jackson could sit in with the Millionaires? Sally could actually be singing harmony with beloved Tommy J? "I guess we could manage. Dwayne's played bass for us a lot anyway."

Stone turned to Terry Kean. "Hey T.K., would it be possible for us to earmark some of the proceeds from the benefit for a fund for the widow and kids? A gesture of compassion to a local guy who died the same way Nina did?"

"Not a problem," said Kean. "It's up to you all."

"I think that's a great idea," Cat said. "Gun violence is a terrible problem."

"I don't believe this," Kali said, quiet but adamant. "I

can't believe you think Wild West should be subsidizing people who go out into the woods with deliberate intent to kill."

"But that's not what we'd be doing," said Whitebird, looking not at Kali but at Cat. "We'd be reaching out a helping hand to the needy family of a local victim of gun violence. It'd be excellent community relations."

Sally had pegged Whitebird as a PR type. Now, as Cat nodded in agreement, she knew he was also a pretty shrewd ass kisser.

"I think it's a decent thing to do," said Cat. "I also think it's important to make the local connection. In every project I've ever been involved with, success has depended on that link. Wild West needs to be about the West in general, and Wyoming in particular," she finished, looking around the room to see who agreed. Stone obviously did, since he'd made the suggestion in the first place. Whitebird wagged his head emphatically. Quartz smiled pleasantly; Sally wondered if he might not be just the tiniest bit high. Willen said nothing, and Kali and Lark glowered.

Sally had her doubts. "I don't know. Maybe you'd better ask Arvida Perrine, Jimbo's widow. If she's willing, I guess we could do a couple of songs in his memory." She wouldn't dwell on the irony of doing a tribute to Jimbo Perrine at what Jimbo would doubtless consider some kind of pagan treefucker festival. Maybe they could really show their respect and display some of his taxidermy while they performed.

"I don't know about the songs, but we can certainly kick in some bucks. And let me be very clear about this: We want you involved," Cat said bluntly, closing the subject. Sally still wondered why.

Kali had fallen silent, finishing her lunch. Now she set her empty plate on the coffee table with deliberation. "You've recruited some impressive performers," she told Jackson, and then looked around the room. "But who will speak for the foundation? Who should deliver the political message?"

"As director," Whitebird said quickly, "that would be my job."

"And what," Cat asked, "is the political message of Wild

West? That hasn't been clear to me, but then, I've been out of the country a lot in the past couple of years. I'd assume that we're talking about the kinds of environmental and social objectives Nina and I have believed in since we were kids, and supported with money and time since we've had enough of both to spare a little. Protection of wildlife habitat, restoration of riparian environments and grasslands, and, at the same time, sustainable, vibrant rural communities. It's a balancing act that involves paying attention to tradition and a sense of place, keeping on top of the latest scientific and humanistic research, thinking hard about growth, details, deadlines, and practicalities, and keeping ordinary people in the loop when big decisions are being made."

Nels Willen nodded vigorously.

"The UN's got projects in places like Ghana and Bangladesh," Cat added. "Working with NGOs. With everything from forest conservation programs to rural manufacturing co-ops. All about the small scale and the local. Incredibly important, totally nonglamourous work," she said.

Whitebird nodded, but his eyes were remote. The man was not listening. "Of course, of course," he said vaguely. "Although we've been thinking that in order for Wild West to get some initial attention, we should pick a cause that makes a splash. A hot-button issue."

"And that would be . . . ?" Cat asked.

Kali spoke softly, but with vehemence. "Animal abuse," she said. "I've never seen anything like what they do to animals in this place. Between the legalized murder of everything from pheasants to moose, and the death-camp cattle culture, it's intolerable."

"Death-camp cattle culture?" Cat asked.

"You know what she's talking about," Lark put in. "The castrations and the ear notching, burning hot brands seared into their hides, pens where they force-feed them drugged-up, chemical-laced corn, railroad cars to the slaughterhouses, poking them all the way with electric prods. And they have no more idea of what's happening to them than the Jews who were rounded up and—"

Jeez. Such a promiscuous mixing of cows and Jews. In Sally's informed opinion it was, to say the least, not kosher.

"That'll do, Lark," Nels Willen said softly.

Stone's response was diplomatic. "I'm sure some of you feel passionately about animals," he said. "And there's a time and a place for that message. But I'm hoping that this concert can be a way to bring people together to remember Nina, and to pledge to support a broader message of caring for the earth, for the place and the places each of us call home." He sent a warm look around the room. "We should mention some specific goals, but we don't want to push people away.

"Look: You all loved her. That makes you kin, in a way, with millions of people who had the pleasure of hearing her glorious voice, of admiring her deep commitment to what she believed, even when they didn't agree with all of it. We want to put up a big tent."

Lark sulked. Kali's face was expressionless. Whitebird played with his beads.

"We had a call yesterday morning from an Internet zillionaire in Palo Alto," said Terry Kean. "Said he went to a concert at the Cow Palace in sixty-eight where Nina sang 'I Ain't Marchin' Anymore.' He was so inspired, he decided to drop out of Stanford and do what he'd always dreamed of doing, which was to invent a language that a machine could understand. Now he runs a Fortune 500 company and owns two major sports teams and the newest hotel on the Vegas Strip, and he wants to buy a block of a hundred tickets and fly his top managers in for the show. He'd also like us to forward Wild West's prospectus and annual report to his wife, since she handles their philanthropy."

"Prospectus and annual report?" asked Whitebird.

"Or whatever you have on the projects you've done, and what you're planning. This guy could turn out to be a big benefactor."

"The prospectus won't be available for some time." Kali's voice didn't rise above whisper volume, but it carried a heavy chill. "Most of our projects are in the drawing-board stage."

"I expect you to show me the drawings," said Cat, "and we'll decide what needs to be inked in, and what gets erased. We won't have time for a prospectus, but we can at least work up a nice-looking brochure to circulate to potential donors. Who does your publications work?" she asked.

"We're, uh, still working on that," said Whitebird.

Cat narrowed her eyes, shook her head, and aimed her gaze at Terry Kean. "What," she asked, "have we already had to advance? No numbers—you and I can talk about that later. Just tell me who's already cashing foundation checks, and who's expecting a check in the mail."

Kean began to tick off items on his fingers. "The ticket-booking consortium, the stadium, the light and sound people, the trucking company, the travel agent—"

"Enough," Cat said. "I get the picture. And I assume the checks haven't bounced," she added.

Whitebird looked at Kali.

"No," she whispered, licking her lips. Sally noted that her tongue was very pink and pointed, but it wasn't forked. "The checks are quite good. The endowment has more than enough cash on hand to cover the advance expenses. I've made sure the bank account is in order."

Sally wondered if mongooses got as still as Cat Cruz, before launching into battle. "I'll look forward to seeing the checkbook and the bank statements. It'll be interesting to see how Nina planned to allocate that cash, before she was killed. I'd be surprised if there's enough to cover the losses if the benefit tanks, and I'm wondering what you all would have me do about that."

"I can write a check," Stone volunteered.

Cat put a hand on his cheek. "That's sweet of you, honey. Let me check out the books, find out what's what, and maybe line up a few other big donors. Get me your zillionaire's name, Terry," she said, "and I'll give him a call."

Quartz looked up from his keyboard and spoke for the first time. "Ms. Cruz, I know how busy Kali's been, just getting everything up and running. I'd be glad to work with you on getting the books in order. I took a couple of accounting classes."

"At Reed College?" Sally was incredulous.

"Nope. Portland State. The summer after my senior year in high school. Actually, I've been freelancing with H&R Block during tax season," he admitted.

The French Revolution, and apple pies, and laptop computers, and smoking weed, and tax returns. Those Unitarians, Sally reflected. Always hedging their bets.

12

Hollywood at the Wrangler

"That oughta do it. Everybody here knows what they have to do between now and November 24. Just be sure to keep T. K. and me in the loop on everything. We can be in touch by phone and e-mail until then," Stone finished, giving them his e-mail address, home phone, and cell phone numbers.

"Keep me posted out at Shady Grove as well," said Cat. And then, with a look at Kali and Whitebird, "I'll be in touch with requests for information I can't find out there. If there are any problems, I'd like to be able to handle them before we spend a lot more money," she finished ominously.

Cat Cruz willing and weather permitting, this was going to be one hell of a show. With Stone Jackson headlining an all-star program, and Terry Kean managing the enormous job of pulling together a major musical happening in Wyoming in the winter, you had to get excited in spite of yourself. Randy Whitebird said that the Night for Nina (as they'd decided to call the event) could be the biggest thing since Farm Aid. For Sally, that put things in perspective. Had Farm Aid actually made money? She couldn't remember what she'd heard. Willie Nelson had top billing, and everybody knew how good he was with the financial stuff.

"I can really use that drink now," Cat told Sally as they got into their coats. The skies had been calm and sunny when Sally arrived, but she'd seen clouds building up over the Snowies as she'd walked from her house to the Wild West office, bundled in her warm fleece jacket and gloves.

Sally looked at Stone, assuming he'd be coming with her and Cat. "You two go ahead," he told her. "I want to visit with the folks here a little longer, then catch a ride back over to the courthouse. Cat, I'll call you on your cell and find out where you are, and let you know if I need to be picked up."

Sally could understand Stone not wanting to hang out in a bar, but what was this about the courthouse?

"Detective Atkins," said Cat, as if the name were an answer. "He wasn't quite finished when we were. He asked Thomas to come back after the meeting."

They went down the flight of dingy stairs and out the door, into genuinely crappy weather. Big globs of icy mush plopped on their jackets and in their hair as Sally followed Cat, at a run, toward the car. Cat Cruz did rental cars Hollywood style. Sally wondered which car company doing business at Denver International rented Lexus SUVs.

"Where shall we go for a drink?" Cat asked.

"Depends what you're in the mood for. Bistro or saloon?" Sally offered.

"When I'm in the U.S., I live in the Santas—Monica and Fe," Cat explained. "My life is lousy with bistros."

"All right then. The Wrangler it is."

The Wrangler it was, complete with the aroma of stale beer, the slightly sticky plank floor, and the thin twilight illumination of a barroom on a cloud-shrouded afternoon. It wasn't Sally's favorite atmosphere, but, she had to admit, it wasn't altogether unknown. Or altogether unwelcome.

They found a table in a back corner by the pool tables, where they'd neither disturb nor be distracted by the hard-living crowd of regulars at the bar. Sally had developed a fairly firm rule against drinking hard liquor before five, and it wasn't even four. But when Cat ordered a double vodka martini, very dry, three olives, it seemed antisocial to settle for a beer. So Sally requested coffee with a shot of Jim Beam, a compromise drink. The coffee would suck, but it would be warm and caffeinated and vastly improved by the addition of whiskey. She took a sip and remembered those long-ago times, playing the summer rodeo circuit, when she'd considered this particular drink a breakfast beverage.

Cat slipped out of her coat, a perfectly tailored, glove-soft leather job the color of corn silk, and inspected the places where melting slush was leaving water spots. "This particular garment might have been an unwise choice today," she observed, draping it across the back of a chair, reaching for her drink, raising her glass in salutation. It was a squat old-fashioned glass, not a fancy-stemmed martini glass (saloon, not boutique). She took a large, grateful swallow.

"You never can tell about winter weather here," Sally said.

"It's not just the weather. I assume you understood that I was making a statement," Cat told her.

Sally drank a little more coffee, watching Cat's eyes, and nodded over the rim of her cup.

"Thomas told me that some of them were animal rights fanatics," said Cat. "The Dub-Dubs, as he's named them."

"Looks like," said Sally, wanting to coax but not divulge.

"I thought I'd let them know where I stood," Cat said, setting her glass on the table.

"I think you succeeded," Sally said.

"I'd better watch my back," said Cat. "That Lark looked like the type who might decide to come pour pig blood on me some day when I'm lunching at Chinois."

"She's a woman of firm convictions," Sally agreed.

Cat snorted. "Fuck her convictions. I've seen places where thousands of people are sick with AIDS because the men in charge, from the village chief to the president of the country, are too damned ignorant and evil to admit that the plague spreads through sex. I've seen women who know how to make the most beautiful crafts go begging in the street because they can't get a loan of thirty-five dollars to start up a little business that would make them self-sufficient for life. I've seen people bathing in and drinking out of rivers so polluted, they get sick before they get dry. I've spent the better part of the last five years in places where children have worse lives than most dogs in Wyoming, or any place else in the U.S., for that matter. Let's just say animal rights isn't a high priority with me," Cat said, draining the rest of her drink and motioning to the day bartender, who had his professional radar on. Looked like he'd been expecting a refill request from their table in fairly short order.

"And so you think . . ." Sally prompted.

"That this is abso-fucking-lutely ridiculous," Cat said, enfolding her empty glass with her hands, interlacing her ringed fingers, staring down at her stacked thumbs. "I can't believe that this is what Nina left behind."

"Wild West?" Sally asked, taking the last swig of her coffee and welcoming the arrival of another cup, glad to see that the bartender had taken the order as not simply another martini, but another round.

Cat looked up from her thumbs. "Yeah. Nina had a lot of money," she explained.

"I'm not surprised," Sally said, expecting elaboration.

"Most people would be. She played the whole 'screw capitalism, I'm an artist' thing to the hilt," Cat said.

Sally made the obvious assumption. "But while she was doing that, she had you managing her money."

"Mmm-hmm." Cat nodded. "Not that I didn't have high ideals. We used to sing protest songs together. Even did a kind of Mamas and Papas thing with Stone and my ex," she began.

"I know," Sally said. Cat's husband, one of Stone's tight drug buddies, had OD'd. *Rolling Stone* had run a really heart-wrenching story.

"I didn't much feel like singing anymore, and Nina's career was taking off. So we made a deal. We'd stay true to what we believed, and she'd keep on singing. I'd handle the financial end of things, and kind of look out for her. I'm two years older. It came naturally. Especially after our mom and dad died."

Sally wondered if there had been some tragedy that had taken both parents from the Cruz sisters. Cat understood. "No, no, nothing like that. My mom died in eighty-six from lung cancer. She was a two-packer, and it was horrible—drawn out, excruciating. My dad went in ninety-three. Heart attack on the golf course. We decided we should never smoke or learn to play golf."

Oh Cat. Oh Cruz sisters.

"It was a good partnership. It turns out I'm good at managing money, and Nina, God knows, was good at singing, and not half bad at songwriting, either. You can't imagine how much a song like 'Ruby Rose' or 'Down to Dust' makes in royalties every year," Cat said.

Sally had no idea, but it must be big money. Everyone from Lucinda Williams to Vanessa Williams had covered Nina's timeless "Ruby Rose," and the last time Sally had been in New York, much to her horror, she'd heard the Hollyridge Strings version of "Down to Dust" in the hotel elevator.

"She trusted me. Not that we didn't get into it from time to time—we're sisters, right? But Nina understood that her money made shitloads of money in my hands, and she pretty much left it to me to manage things. We did great, if I do say so myself. I ended up handling some things for other musicians, who'd come to me on her recommendation. Did pretty well for them, too.

"But in the last eighteen months, she started doing stuff without telling me."

"What kind of stuff?" Sally asked.

Cat shook her head. "Everything. This whole Wild West project, for one. Incorporating the foundation, hiring people, and who the hell knows what else. That's what I'm going to try to find out by going through her stuff, although I wouldn't be surprised if Kelly Lee and Mr. Whitebird have squirreled away some documents they'd rather I didn't see."

"Why?" Sally asked.

"Because Kelly Lee Brisbane is the most deceitful, manipulative, self-serving creep on the planet," Cat answered.

"Don't hold back, Cat," said Sally.

"I'm serious. Why the hell do you think she calls herself Kali? Talk about goddess complexes," she finished.

"How long have you known her?" asked Sally.

"Forever. Nina brought her down to Santa Fe, to a family thing, maybe fifteen years ago. They'd been friends for a couple of years by then. They met in Aspen. Nina had a way of collecting acolytes. A select few, like Nels Willen, actually became friends. Most of them worshiped her for a while and then moved on. But not Kelly Lee. She sank her hooks in and never let go."

"Did she call herself Kali back then?" Sally said.

"Nope. In those days, she even had a last name. She was just a little blonde Utah snow bunny who worked for some biotech firm in Salt Lake City and spent her big paycheck on lift tickets."

Snow bunny? An odd way to talk about a woman Stone Jackson said had a Ph.D. in biology. But Cat was on a roll. "As the years passed, she began to imitate Nina in ways that got weirder and weirder. It wasn't just the clothes and the haircuts and the politics. Her sentences, her phrasing, every opinion about everything. About eight years ago, they both got heavily into green politics, and, I guess, animal rights. That's when Kelly Lee started referring to herself as Kali."

"Were they lovers?" Sally asked.

Cat took a deep breath. "Yeah, they were. Nina believed that heterosexuality and monogamy and sexual convention of all kinds were hang-ups. She thought human desires were a whole lot more complicated and varied than our society permits, and she wasn't going to be hemmed in. As a matter of fact, I agree, and I didn't have any problem with her being bisexual. I reserve the right to decide who's a jerk and who's not. I liked a lot of Nina's women, but this girl was bad news from day one."

"Did they live together?"

"Not at first. Nina bought a condo in Sundance, and they used to get together there. Sometimes Kali would come out to California to visit. They were in and out of each other's lives. I don't know about Kali, but there were plenty of other people who were close to Nina. That is, until she found Shady Grove and moved out to Wyoming."

"And since then?"

"Who knows? Wyoming's a million miles from anywhere. I assume lots of her admirers thought she'd gone to the dark side of the moon," Cat said.

Sally laughed. "No offense taken, Cat," she said.

Cat appeared surprised that any offense might have been given, and plugged on. "Kelly Lee, of course, was from Utah, so she probably thought settling in Wyoming was just kind of like going to Oregon or something. She moved right in, as soon as she could. I was only out here once, but I paid attention to what was going on. They kept separate bedrooms, but they were definitely living together."

"From what those kids Quartz and Pammie told me," Sally said, "they were inseparable. Or at least Kali made a point of sticking close to Nina. When did Whitebird come into the picture?"

"Less than a year ago. I don't know exactly how or where or why. And it blew my mind, when Stone and I got up here last night, that Whitebird was staying in Nina's bedroom!"

"Sounds cozy," Sally said.

"Sounds like a setup for somebody getting shot," Cat replied coldly. "I know Kali was supposedly in Salt Lake when my sister was killed, but I told your Detective Atkins that if it were me, I'd be checking her story out pretty carefully. Especially since Nina got this idea about changing her will six months ago. Without consulting me, or even telling me about it! The first I knew was when she sent me a draft for my files."

"Were there a lot of changes?" Sally asked.

"Not many. It had been years since she'd made a will, and apart from not mentioning it to me, it made sense to update. She'd made a few new bequests, eliminated a few of the old causes she didn't care about anymore. The one big red flag was a huge endowment for the Wild West Foundation, which, to my knowledge, didn't even exist before that. She didn't use our lawyer to set it up. Which is why I'm going to rip her place apart, and tear every one of those fools a new asshole, until I get to the bottom of what's going on." Cat polished off her drink. "Seriously, that was the only thing that stood out. Mostly the changes weren't any big deal. There was some stuff that I didn't understand at first—like a donation to your women's history center, for example—but that was easy enough to research and figure out. I took a look at your website, then went and got your book about Meg Dunwoodie. Plus, as I said, Nina told me how much she liked you, and, of course, she was big on women's history. So I had no problem with the idea that she'd want to leave you a couple hundred thousand to do your work," Cat said, as if such figures were chump change in her world.

"Glad to hear it," said Sally. "Did you say a couple hundred thousand?"

"Yeah," Cat answered. "Two-fifty, to be exact. Our lawyer will be in touch with your lawyer."

"Right," said Sally. Two hundred fifty thousand? "Wow. I'm dumbfounded."

"Don't be. I'm sure you'll put it to good use," said Cat. "If I hadn't already had two martinis, I'd have them bring the wine list and order a bottle of champagne."

Sally thought that Cat Cruz would find the wine list at the Wrangler a big disappointment.

Cat stared down at her empty glass. "Despite what her toadies think, Nina wasn't a saint. She liked to play the martyr, and it was a pretty convincing act. But she broke more hearts than you can believe. She'd throw herself into a relationship, and then one day turn it off, and treat somebody who thought they were the love of her life like a total stranger."

"Not Stone Jackson, surely," Sally said.

Cat shook her head. "She had poor Thomas convinced that he was the root of all evil in her life for years. I think he still believes that, in some way. He's never understood that she was part of his problem. The more sanctified she acted, the worse he looked. I'd call it codependency, but that's such a hack word."

"Not if it's the one that fits," Sally said.

"I guess. I just think that what happened wasn't all his fault, or even the fault of his disease. They adored each other, and were bad for each other."

"That's not the way he tells it," said Sally.

"Oh, he's figured it out by now. A few months ago he called to let me know he'd bought a place in Wyoming. I asked him why he suddenly felt compelled to spend a big chunk of change on his own personal wind tunnel, and he laughed and said, 'You know.' And then, when Nina told me she'd asked him about him doing this benefit, I called Stone and told him I was sure he'd lost his goddamn mind, letting her jerk him around. And you know what he said? 'Look, Cat. I've given up all my other joneses. Can't you leave me just this last little addiction to pain?' "

"You really care about him," Sally observed.

"I've known him more than thirty years. He was married to my sister for eight," Cat said, fighting back tears. "He's the only reason I'd let this insane hootenanny go on. He needs to say good-bye this way."

Strong feelings. Sally made a mental note and moved on. "If you don't mind, I still don't understand why you want my band on the program. You've got world-class talent. We don't suck, but we're not in their league. And as for raising money for Jimbo Perrine's widow, you need to know that Jimbo was one loathesomely reactionary bad ol' boy. Not that Mrs. Perrine and the kids don't need the money, but they may not even want to accept it."

"Oh, I'm not worried about that," said Cat. "Not that many people turn down free money. And if she's got issues, I'm sure you can talk her out of them."

"Me?" said Sally.

"Of course. You're the obvious choice to approach her."

Sally sighed. Of course she was. "Cat, what do you really want?" she asked, wishing there was more Jim Beam than coffee in her cup.

"First, crazy as it may seem, I actually do believe in giving local folks a voice and a part. From what I've seen, it's the main thing, whether it's in Lhasa or Laramie," Cat said. "I don't know whether Wild West will survive three more days, or four more weeks, or into the cosmic future, but if it does, it'll have to have local support."

"Okay. But you could do a whole lot better getting a bunch of elementary-school kids up there singing 'We Are the World.' Why the Millionaires?"

"They're your band. I want you around and in contact with these Dub-Dub fools, because Stone Jackson and I are convinced that you can help us nail whoever murdered my sister," Cat finished fiercely.

"Easy, Cat. The police haven't called it murder—"

"But they will. You know it. Especially with this Perrine guy getting shot, and Nels happening to find him. Something really bad is going on."

"Do you think Nels is in on it?" Sally asked.

"I hope not. I've always liked him. But I don't feel as if I can trust anybody," Cat said.

"You don't even know me, and you're trusting me," Sally pointed out.

"Look, Sally. As I understand it, you've solved one or two ugly cases, at some personal risk. The sheriff is your good buddy, and it's clear that he and his guys think Thomas and I are a couple of candy-butt Californians who'd like nothing more than to turn Wyoming into one big cappuccino bar. You're part Californian yourself—you might say you're practically bicultural. Frankly, we can use that. Maybe most important, Nina had a hell of a lot of respect for you, and considered you a close friend."

"I wasn't her close friend," Sally said, a little more vehemently than she needed to. "Both Kali and Whitebird were a whole lot tighter with her than I ever was, and you hardly trust them."

"There's a big difference between parasites and friends," Cat declared. "You had no idea she was leaving your center any money. You didn't have any idea that you stood to gain from Nina's death. Both of them are named in the draft of the will she sent me, as is this foundation they're so devoted to. Maybe they'd seen the will. Maybe one or both of them decided to hurry fate along. Or maybe they know who did.

"You're good at asking questions," Cat pointed out, "and you're nosy enough to ask them. You're a historian. You have a sense of what to look for, rooting around in somebody's papers." She pulled out the carrot. "It'd help both of us if you'd come out to Shady Grove and work with me. See what you can dig up."

And now she pulled out the stick. "You, and your Dunwoodie Center, have got at least two hundred fifty thousand reasons to do what I'm asking," Cat Cruz told Sally. "Before you ever write a word of a book I might or might not end up authorizing."

"Okay, Cat. Yes, I want to write about Nina, but I don't like threats," Sally said. From what she'd seen of Cat Cruz that day, she couldn't afford to look like a patsy.

"Sorry," Cat said, putting a hand on her arm. "Really. With all the time I've spent dealing with people in the entertainment business, I sometimes catch myself falling back on playing Hollywood hard-ass. How about a deal instead of a threat?"

Sally said, "Let's hear it."

"Come out to the ranch. Look through her papers. Ask some questions around town. See what your pals Langham and Atkins are willing to share with you."

"Atkins isn't my pal," Sally said, not quite knowing the name for what he was to her.

"Probably not, though he's sexy in a hard-boiled kind of way, don't you think?"

Sally declined to offer her opinion.

"Do what you can," Cat said, "and I'll do two things. I'll promise not to challenge the part of the will that deals with the bequest to Dunwoodie. And I'll sign an agreement authorizing you as her biographer." Cat took a breath.

"If you do that," Sally said, leaning in on her elbows and looking Cat straight in the eye, "I'll expect you to stipulate that whatever I do, nothing will in any way jeopardize the bequest to the Dunwoodie, that I will have unlimited access to her papers, and that you have absolutely no authority to censor anything I write."

Cat smiled slowly. "Who's a Hollywood hard-ass now?"

13

Trigger Points

"Why is it," Sally asked Hawk, "that I get the distinct feeling that I'm being set up, but I don't know what for, or how, or when, or by whom? Oh, yeah, baby, that's it," she said as he set the tip of his index finger in the middle of her right trapezius muscle, leaned down, and applied pressure, holding the finger down ten seconds, then letting go slowly, changing the angle, and repeating the process. Sometimes he used an elbow. She lay facedown on the bed, with Hawk straddling her hips, working on his trigger-point-massage techniques. He'd decided he wanted to develop a repertoire of massage moves: Swedish, Thai, trigger, Shiatsu, deep tissue, maybe even hot stones. Sally was doing her best to encourage his efforts.

"Uh-huh," he said, trying another point and eliciting a satisfied reciprocal "unh" from her. "This could be a setup. But until you know more about what's going on, you won't be able to avoid it. You'd better talk to Dickie anyhow, and maybe Scotty, too. Breathe out," he instructed.

She tensed at the mention of Scotty Atkins, then blew out a long breath and felt the tightness go out of the muscle

Hawk was addressing. "Yeah. Dickie, anyhow. He probably already knows that there's a hell of a lot going on among the Dub-Dubs, but maybe I can fill in some detail after that meeting this afternoon."

"You can do more than that," said Hawk, working his way down the right side of her spine, heading for her hip. "You can let him know you're getting deeper and deeper, even when you're trying to hold back. I can't quite tell if it's you who manipulated the situation, or if things are kind of developing as they go along, or if you're being used. Probably all three."

She heard and felt her bones crack. Aaaah.

"Adjustments are free," he said genially. "Put it this way. It looks like you're going to be spending time with Nina's sister and her ex."

"Cat and Stone," she embroidered, unnecessarily.

"Sounds like the title of a seventies folk-rock album," Hawk observed.

Sally laughed, then grunted when he inserted his elbow in a gluteal muscle crease she hadn't previously known existed, and leaned down solid. "Agh. Man, that's great," she said. He leaned a little harder, just hard enough, and then gradually let up. He rubbed her hip with the palm of his hand, kneading away stiffness she hadn't even realized had been there.

A thought occurred to her. "Wait a minute," she said, and started to sit up.

"I'm not done," he said, pushing her back down on her stomach on the bed, and laying a calming hand on her left shoulder.

Sally sighed. "Please, by all means, continue," she said. "But let me work a little on this thought. Less than a month ago, I was sitting in my office minding my own business, when the fabled Thomas Jackson came waltzing in and gave me an ego massage the likes of which I've never experienced in my whole, fairly well-massaged life," she said.

"Fairly well massaged?" said Hawk, leaning in over her deltoid. "Shall I take that as an insult or a challenge?"

"The latter, by all means," she said, exhaling as the weight of his upper body came down on his elbow. Mmmph. "But keep listening. Since that day, two reasonably close personal acquaintances of mine have been shot. One of them I liked a lot. The other?" She paused. "Surely he had his virtues."

Sally believed wholeheartedly in the old adage about not bad-mouthing the departed. What good would it do to point out that Jimbo Perrine had been a nasty redneck son of a bitch?

"Apart from the fact that they were both shot near Albany, both during hunting season, and you knew them both, is there anything else they had in common?" Hawk asked.

"That's the obvious question, isn't it?" Sally answered.

"You'd think," said Hawk. "In fact, you'd think that coming up with the answer would go a long way toward figuring out whether the same person shot them, and, if so, who it might have been, and why."

"And, of course, that's what I do think," Sally said. "But I'm not coming up with any answers. Aside from the fact that both of them lived in Albany County, and both had pretty strong opinions about hunting and wildlife and nature in general, I can't imagine two people who had *less* in common. If you'd put them in a room together, the air would've gotten so toxic, you'd eventually have had to seal off the building.

"Meantime, there's this whole Wild West thing revving up, with the truly goofy result that there'll be a grand public event at which both Nina Cruz and Jimbo Perrine will be fondly remembered, and their memories fondly funded. What the hell do you think that's about?" she asked him.

"I have no idea. Nels dropped some hints yesterday, but he didn't give us much to go on. From what you've told me, it sounds like your Dub-Dub friends are fixing to have a big battle about the direction this outfit goes. That Kali seems to want to zero in on animal rights, which strikes me as a pretty hopeless strategy in this state. She seems like an extremely strange character in any case. Cat Cruz, on the other hand, is a world-renowned humanitarian who apparently has a much broader, more sensible agenda. Or at least the stuff she tells you makes her sound like I'd agree with her. As for Randy

Whitebird, despite Stone Jackson telling you that the man uses expressions like 'the carnivore holocaust,' he's acting like the kind of opportunist who knows how to latch onto money and power. The rest of them don't really matter, do they?"

"No, they don't," Sally agreed, "except insofar as I can get them to tell me stuff I want to know. With one exception. What about Nels Willen?" Sally asked.

"What about him? He's a puzzle, huh?" Hawk said.

"Oh yeah," said Sally. The main thing she knew about Nels Willen was that he had managed to beat back panic and rise to the occasion on the morning Nina Cruz was shot. Apart from that, he seemed like a smart, nice, interesting man. Sally had known any number of beguiling men who had handled one or more crises pretty well. In her life experience, the perils of mistaking such good behavior for trustworthiness had become painfully clear, soon enough, sometimes even before the tequila wore off. "I like Willen," she said.

Hawk didn't see fit to mention her track record, but he found a way to tactfully bring up the necessity for independent verification of good behavior. "Willen's been involved with environmental organizations besides this one. I can call one or two people in the Wilderness Society, the Trust for Public Land, the Conservancy. Find out what they know about him. You want me to make some inquiries?" he volunteered.

Sally flinched. "Yeah, you do that," she said, as he resumed his ministrations. "Maybe the fact that you're checking up on him will get around, and you, too, can get yourself shot."

"More likely you can," Hawk retorted, digging in perhaps a little extra hard with that elbow.

"Ouch!"

"Sorry. I forgot what I was doing. Temporarily distracted by the thought of bullet holes in you. I'm sure you understand," he said.

She surely did. "Apology's all mine," she acknowledged. "Clearly, I'm opening myself up to stuff again, this time. And as always," she said, stretching a hand back toward his leg, "I'm so glad you've got my back, no pun intended. But you know how I am, Hawk. Until I figure out if anybody's setting me up, and if so, who it is, and if they are, what that has to do with Nina Cruz's death and maybe Jimbo's as well, I'm not about to leave this alone."

Hawk rubbed her left hip, signaling the end of the massage. As a final flourish, he swept his palms slowly and heavily up her spine, from the sacrum to the nape of her neck, and then leaned down to kiss the valley between her shoulder blades. "I'm not about to leave you alone," he whispered.

"Good," she said, smiling into the pillow. "So just think with me one minute more. I'm trying to get a clear picture of the people I'm dealing with, starting with the ones who got shot. What's your take?"

Hawk's voice, soft, warm, came from half an inch from the top of her spine, sometimes closer. "Nina was a diva and a lover and a martyr, and from what you tell me, a whole lot of other things. She planned to drop a bunch of money on a foundation that is either a thoughtful, flexible land trust and wildlife protection organization, or some kind of wacko animal rights fanatic society, depending on who you're listening to. Jimbo Perrine was a decent bass player, but a reactionary bastard, about as unlovable as they come, and just about all he left behind was a wife and two kids."

"And a grieving mother," said Sally.

Hawk kissed the back of her neck, very softly.

Sally shivered and went on. "And now I'm suddenly on the job, at the urging of a couple of big-time Hollywood types, trying to figure out why these people died, what's going on with the foundation and its assorted hangers-on, and what the Albany County Sheriff's Department is doing about all this. Not to mention keeping the Millionaires in line, and dealing with Jimbo's widow. And just for fun, diving into writing Nina's life story, and taking in a substantial bequest to the Dunwoodie Center from the very same Nina Cruz."

Sally spoke into the pillow. "I think I ought to tell them I'm too busy. Got classes to teach and the entire history of women to account for." After a great massage, she always contemplated the thought that she worked too hard, and needed to reduce the stress in her life.

"Right. That's what I think you should do," said Hawk. "Tell them you're too busy with your day job to do this benefit and have to sing with Stone Jackson. While you're at it, let them know that a serious women's historian like you has better things to do than writing a potentially best-selling biography of some second-rate folksinger. And that, by the way, you don't want a quarter of a million dollars for your center." And then he pinched her ass.

"Hey!" she said, slapping his hand. "Watch yourself, buddy!" Another sigh. "Why does this feel way too good to be true, and at the same time so awful I can hardly believe it?"

"Because it's both," he answered. "But you're ignoring some obvious things. Nina told Jackson and Cat that you were her good friend. And you're not just some small-town college professor, Mustang. I mean, you *are* that, of course, but not every college professor reveals international conspiracies, tracks down killers, finds treasure, unveils the lives of mysterious poets—"

"Okay, okay. You're talking about that *People* magazine story," she said, twisting her body and pushing up on one elbow to look at him. "That was totally embarrassing."

Hawk rolled off her and onto his side, facing her. "No, I'm not talking about that story. I'm talking about the fact that while you're wondering why famous people are bothering with you, you've forgotten that you're a little bit famous yourself. Everybody around here ignores that fact as much as they can, and most of the time it doesn't make a damn bit of difference. The snow will still snow, there'll still be whiskey to drink, you'll still have to deal with brain-dead students, grade papers, and digest the food at the Wrangler.

"But in this case, Stone Jackson and Cat Cruz have sought you out because you've somehow gotten yourself in the middle of murder, solved the crimes, and written some damned good biography while you were at it. They really do have reason to think you can help them figure out what Nina was up to, and what might have inspired somebody to decide to kill her. If you want to believe they're using you, fine. But if they are, it might be because they think you'd be, well, useful."

Sally lay still a minute, trying out the idea. "When you put it that way," she said, "it throws a different light on things. So maybe instead of being suspicious, I actually ought to try to help out."

"As you wish," said Hawk. "I'm just a humble masseur."

Sally laughed.

Hawk leaned down and put his face close to hers. "All I ask is that you keep the police—and me—informed about what you're doing and where you're doing it, while you're doing good deeds." Kissed her again, a little less softly.

"Naturally," said Sally. "I always tell my masseur everything." But then she got serious again. "Seems to me that when people get killed, it's usually because the killer decides that the victim either has the potential to do harm, or has already done so. I can imagine any number of reasons why somebody like Jimbo Perrine might get himself into a place where somebody else thinks he did them wrong— even leaving aside the possibility that some careless hunter really did shoot him by accident."

"Having shot my fair share of state-regulated game animals," Hawk said, "I'm dubious. Most hunters are careful to a fault. According to the *Boomerang*, Jimbo was wearing a DayGlo orange vest and an orange stocking cap. It'd be damn hard to mistake him for a deer. I'm sorry, but I can't buy that one as an accident."

She sat up, cross-legged, leaned an elbow on her knee and put her chin on her fist. "But what about Nina? Nels Willen says she was shooting at somebody on the morning of the day she was killed. He could be lying, but then there's that letter I found, the fact that at least half the people involved with Wild West have apparently been Nina's lovers at some time. Plus there's the fact that Nina had a whole lot of money, which she was giving away at a nice clip. So it's not far-fetched to assume that one or more of those once-and-future lovers had been sufficiently hurt by Nina Cruz, and/or had enough to gain from her death, to maybe do something about it."

Hawk reached out and put a hand on the inside of her thigh. "You know what I love?" he said, stroking. "I love when you get so wrapped up in speculating that you forget you're naked."

Sally looked down, a puzzled expression on her face. Looked up, eyes wide. "Naked?" she said.

Hawk grinned. "Naked," he said, and moved closer.

The telephone rang.

"Fuck," said Hawk.

Sally answered. "Hello? Oh, hi, Delice," she said.

"Delice," said Hawk. "Fuck."

"No," said Sally, "I didn't see the ten o'clock news. In fact, I pretty much never catch the ten o'clock news. Hawk's usually in bed by then, and I figure I'll survive without getting whatever the media geniuses in Denver or Casper consider the latest-breaking stories."

She sat a moment, listening, while Hawk lay facedown, cursing quietly.

"You're kidding," she said, at last. "I don't believe it."

Hawk looked up.

"Wait a second," said Sally, opening the drawer of the bedside table and fishing for paper and pencil. "I want to write this down. . . . Slow down, Dee . . . spell it out." She wrote. " 'Protease-resistant prion protein'?" She wrote more. "Wow. Where do you get this stuff . . . ? You called her this late?"

Delice said something.

"Yeah, yeah, not everybody's a no-life loser like me either. But this is impossible," Sally said. "Nina was a vegetarian. Had been for years and years. I don't get how this could happen."

More silence. "Yeah, all right. Yeah, let's have coffee tomorrow morning. You can fill me in on what your vet pal told you. Let's do it early, even though I don't teach until the afternoon," she said, and winced. "Okay. About eight, at the Wrangler. Thanks for calling."

She hung up.

"What happened?" Hawk asked.

"The Casper station had a story about the autopsy report

on Nina Cruz," Sally told him, a dazed look on her face. "Not surprisingly, it listed the cause of her death as a gunshot wound to the chest. But there was more. Evidently, the medical examiner had some concerns about her brain tissue and sent a sample to be analyzed. According to the ten o'clock news, it looks like at the time of her death, Nina had symptoms consistent with new variant Creutzfeld-Jakob disease, or bovine spongiform encephalopathy."

Hawk shook his head in puzzlement. "That can't be. She'd be the first diagnosed case in the United States."

"I know," said Sally. "It's too weird. How the hell could a vegetarian get mad cow disease?"

14

The Pork Chop Special

Blustery as it was the next morning when Sally woke up, she was grimly determined to get a run in. She was already eating way too many meals at the Wrangler, facing one more, and she had started adjusting her attitude to fit the circumstances. Pretty soon, she'd have to start adjusting the fit of her trousers. But if she told the truth, she was actually looking forward to the prospect of a large, greasy breakfast. As a one-time Californian and intermittently health-conscious human, she had a tendency to imagine each heartbeat as a strip of bacon, eaten or declined. She held out the hope that running at high altitude must counteract all the bad cholesterol and fat, even if only in penance points. And so she pulled on spandex tights and a long-sleeved T, did a couple of hamstring stretches and forward bends, zipped up the brown-and-gold Wyoming Cowboys windbreaker, and lit out for the territory.

After forty minutes fighting gusty breezes, listening to *Morning Edition* on her Walkman wasn't keeping her entertained, and getting her core body temperature up wasn't keeping her warm. She switched to a tape of kick-ass New

Orleans rhythm and blues, but the Radiators somehow weren't radiating. Her T-shirt kept riding up and leaving a gap between her tights and her top, and the windbreaker wasn't breaking a damned thing.

Time to head for the Wrangler, and the hell with mad cow disease. She might be the only person in town fierce enough to brave the place, but she didn't care. She'd stand by Delice Langham and get the breakfast she so richly deserved. Bacon and eggs, and potatoes fried in oil, if not actual lard. Tomorrow she would start in on a serious health regimen. She'd give up caffeine, maybe even cut back on the whiskey. Nothing but soy smoothies in the morning and leafy green vegetables at night. Meditation. Yoga. The works.

Tomorrow, for sure. Today, the windy old world owed Sally Alder a frigging heart attack.

If Sally was worried about the ways in which Nina Cruz's death might affect Delice's café business, she needn't have bothered with the concern. As she sauntered to a halt by the Wrangler, she noted the packed parking lot. Pickup trucks stood shoulder to shoulder. A couple of eighteen-wheelers crowded the edge of the big lot, a rare sight. Sally knew that Delice had a following among the cross-country truckers, who sometimes made a point of stopping in for a burger and a little friendly conversation. But they rarely parked in town. Somebody was making a statement. Lots of somebodies.

Outside of Jubilee Days, the annual town rodeo and drinking fest, Sally had never seen the restaurant side of the Wrangler Bar and Grill so crowded. The waitresses were running from table to table, filling up coffee cups, scribbling orders, running back to the kitchen to stack their hands and forearms with plates full of steak and eggs. Delice herself was carting dirty dishes, running tabs, circulating in the dining room to lay a hand on a shoulder here, join a conversation there. The distinction between the non- and smoking sections of the restaurant, a fairly flimsy fiction at best, had completely broken down with the onslaught of truckers and shit kickers, ranch folk come to town, townspeople stopping in for a bite before heading to work.

Yesterday, a catered vegan buffet. Today, mad cow malady and capacity crowds at Carnivore Central. Things were getting fairly weird in Laramie.

Delice motioned her to a vacant table in a corner of the one-time nonsmoking section. Sally headed over, stopping at the coffee station to snag a cup from a rack and pour herself the last tarry dregs from a near-empty pot. She grabbed a handful of little containers of creamer, sat down under a sign hand-lettered with a blue Magic Marker that said, THANK YOU, WRANGLE BAR AND GRILL, FOR BUYING MY 1124 LB. HEREFORD STEER! KITTY KLEINER, ALBANY COUNTY 4-H. Sally tore open one creamer packet after another and dumped them into her coffee. She downed a hot, bitter swallow and nearly snarled with angry satisfaction. Bad coffee, fake cream, cigarette smoke, and guys hollering at waitresses to ask if their pork chops would be ready before Jesus came back. Breakfast Wyoming style, with a vengeance.

"Pork chops for breakfast?" she asked, when Delice finally managed to join her, sitting down with a mug emblazoned with the motto, RODEO QUEENS RIDE DRAG. No steam rose from Delice's half-full cup. Delice often left her coffee sitting around all morning, returning at intervals to take a sip more out of habit than desire. You had to hand it to a woman who could stomach Wrangler coffee at desk temperature.

"Of course pork chops," said Delice. "Today's special. Three eggs any style and a pair of chops with hash browns, toast, and coffee for three ninety-nine. Right after that news report about your friend Nina, I went down to the meat locker and pulled out three hundred pounds of prime pig. We generally sell a lot of bacon, of course, but I figured this occasion called for an extra little promotion. So far, nobody's talking about mad pig disease."

"Looks like a smart move," said Sally.

"Not smart enough. We're liable to run out by noon. I may have to send somebody down to the Lifeway to buy more."

Sally looked around at women in jeans and flannel shirts clamping their jaws around cheeseburgers, men in feed caps attacking plates of fried eggs and T-bones, small children in large cowboy hats downing big glasses of milk. One little girl in a Barbie sweatshirt turned to her mother and wheedled a chicken-fried steak. "Doesn't much look like any-body's talking about mad cow disease either."

"Course they are," said Delice. "But they're all saying the same thing. See Granny Solomon over there?" Delice indicated a woman with hair so silvery and tightly rolled, she might still be wearing curlers, sporting a pastel-pink jogging suit and Coke-bottle-lens glasses with frames to match. "She probably said it best. 'Dear,' she told me, 'I hear tell that Cruz woman got the mad cow without ever having touched a bite of meat in the last fifteen years. I don't know how she got it, but I got to figure if there's one thing it didn't come from, it's good old grade-A Wyoming range beef. I'll have the Wranglerette breakfast, over easy, with hamburger patties instead of sausage, please.'"

"This is absolutely amazing," Sally observed.

"A self-selected crowd," Delice said. "These are people who set their children to teething on beef jerky tough enough to break oil-well drill bits. They can look up at that poster on the wall and tell themselves that people might not trust a steak that's been halfway across the country before it ever got to the feed lot in Omaha, or the slaughterhouse in Chicago, but they're cow-country people eating what they grow, or, at any rate, chowing down on a piece of little Kitty Kleiner's Four-H project. They figure Nina Cruz was some kind of Mexican communist chick who picked up some hideous parasite that red-blooded patriotic white folks are immune to, in some crazy place like California. If they're scared, they deal with it by pretending they couldn't give a rat's bony ass.

"But trust me. There are plenty of people in this town freaking flipping out over this. I'm guessing they won't be selling a lot of Steak Diane and Tournedos Ismail Bayeldi at the Yippie I O tonight. Even though their logic will basically suck."

"What do you mean?" Sally asked.

"I mean to tell you that there isn't much chance Nina Cruz picked up mad cow disease in the time she's lived in Wyoming. First of all, by all reports, she was a strict vege-tarian, right?"

"Not as strict as some," Sally said, thinking of Kali and Lark. "But yeah, she wouldn't touch meat of any kind, or eggs. She never made a big deal about being a vegan, so she might have eaten dairy products, but I'd guess she was more into soy," Sally said.

"Maybe she had mad tofu disease. Boy, that'd be a kick in the pants for the folks out in La La Land, wouldn't it?" Delice asked. "Because that's where she had to have picked it up—or someplace, any place, except Wyoming. I've done a fair amount of reading on the subject, being in my line of work, and last night I checked things out with my friend at the Ag Research Station. Nina Cruz had only been here two years. The experts don't know a whole lot about the disease, but all indications are that it has a hell of a long incubation period—probably not much less than five years, maybe as long as twenty. Nobody knows for sure, but they do feel pretty certain that you don't eat bad meat one day and fetch up sick yourself a day or a week or even a few months after."

"So what do you know about it?" Sally said, really getting into the spirit of the morning by polishing off her coffee and letting the waitress give her a refill as she took Sally's order. "How does it work?"

"Normal proteins mutate into something called 'prions,'" Delice explained. "The process will get started in a few cells and pretty soon triggers the same reaction in more, and after a while the animal is losing weight, and acting goofy. And then it's dead, with a brain full of lesions. The European epidemic may have gotten going when they started using ground-up cattle parts—bonemeal, spinal cord, stuff like that—in supplements they fed to other cattle. Evidently, cannibalism isn't good for cows or other living things."

"Okay then," came a voice from behind Sally. "I'll stick to eggs, and maybe those pork chops since you're pushin' 'em."

Sally twisted in her seat and beheld the placid countenance of Dickie Langham. He wasn't quite smiling, squinting as he was against the smoke from a Marlboro clamped in his teeth, but as their eyes met, he grinned and sat down, pulled a round glass ashtray out of his jacket pocket, set it on their table, yanked a nearby chair over and sat down.

"Where'd you get that?" Delice asked, indicating the ashtray in which her brother's half-smoked cigarette now rested.

"Table over there somewhere," he said, gesturing toward the smoking section.

"This is the nonsmoking section," Sally said primly.

"Guess I'll have to prosecute myself," said Dickie. "Might be a while before I come up for trial, though. One or two multiple murders, suicides, rapes, and meth-lab explosions to clear up first."

"What about mad cow disease?" Sally asked, point-blank.

"What about a tidal wave?" Dickie replied. "From what I can understand, your chances of coming up against either in Laramie are about even."

"I think the odds changed last night," Sally observed.

"I don't," said Dickie, grinding out his cigarette butt and turning to Delice. "How about some coffee here, sister darlin'?"

"How about some inside dope?" Delice asked, somehow sending a telepathic message to a waitress halfway across the dining room, who made a beeline to their table and topped off their cups, taking Dickie's order for the special, with a couple extra eggs and double hash browns.

"You want information, you'll have to apply to the medical examiner's office. They seem to be leakin' worse than a rubber on a fire hose."

"Nice metaphor," said Sally.

"Yeah. This investigation is bringing out the poet in me," said Dickie, digging in his shirt pocket for his cigarettes, tapping out a Marlboro, lighting up.

Sally decided to ignore his testy remark about leaks, and see if she couldn't get him to spew a bit himself. "So what's the status of your investigation?"

Dickie sucked hard on his cigarette, expelled a stream of smoke. "You might as well hear it from me—it'll be on the noon news, I reckon. We're looking at the death of Nina Cruz as a homicide."

No surprise there. "So what happened? What have you guys found out?" Sally was pushing. She didn't really expect an answer.

She didn't get one. Dickie sat smoking in silence. Meanwhile, something nagged at her, below the level of consciousness, a question, maybe even an answer of her own.

Sally's breakfast arrived, quickly followed by Dickie's meal extravaganza. She had a fast hallucination—the Formica table groaning and wailing under the guilty weight of so many animals fallen to human appetite. Such moments had turned many a sensitive soul onto the vegetarian path. But Sally, ever the expert self-justifier, decided to make sure that what was on her plate had not been sacrificed in vain. She picked up a piece of bacon and took a grateful bite.

By that time, Dickie had dispatched two eggs, an entire pork chop and half his toast. He swallowed coffee and took up his subject. "So you're on your way to Shady Grove tomorrow to have a look at Nina's papers," he said.

"Does *everybody* in this town know *everything* I do?" Sally asked, slamming down her fork.

Delice sipped coffee and gave her the fish eye. "Think about it, Mustang. Only yesterday you were sitting in my bar with Cat Cruz, hammering out the details. Nice score in the will, by the way."

"Okay, yeah," she said. "If I'm going to write this book, I need to know what she's got out there, and start figuring out where other stuff might be. I have to get my head around my sources." She picked up her fork and punctured an egg yolk, glad to find it runny, and scooped up egg with rye toast.

Dickie's breakfast was history. He lit another Marlboro, taking his time, framing his response. "I'd consider it a big favor if you'd make a point of letting me know when you find anything interesting in her papers."

Sally chewed another bite of bacon. "Yeah, sure, of course. I mean, anything pertinent to the case, definitely. But you know, Dick, there's liable to be lots of stuff that just isn't relevant. I don't want to waste your time with trivia."

"Or risk having somebody in the sheriff's office leaking stuff you want to save for the book, huh, Sally?" said Delice.

"I'm serious here, Mustang," Dickie said. "Whatever strikes you as interesting, even if it seems completely unrelated to her death, I want to know about it. Let me be the judge."

Sally was in a tight spot. "Come on, buddy," she said, putting a hand on Dickie's arm. "It's not just that I want to get the scoop. There are confidentiality issues here, and, of course, since I am a card-carrying college professor, some question of academic freedom. I'm not going to stonewall you, or even try to keep the good stuff for myself, and I swear I'll do everything I can to help you find the murderer—nobody wants that more than me. But this is a little delicate, don't you see? I managed to get Cat to agree not to interfere with my research, but I do feel an obligation to her to treat this project with some sensitivity and discretion."

Dickie looked down at her hand, set his cigarette in the ashtray, and patted her hand with his own. "Let me make myself really clear here, honey," he said. "I'm a great believer in free speech and privacy and motherhood and the American Dream. But in case you missed what I said a minute ago, this is a homicide investigation. Somebody murdered Nina Cruz and, I'd speculate, strictly off the record, Jimbo Perrine, too. You're about to start hanging out in a place where the murder-to-population ratio is probably higher than it is in New Orleans, and you're going to be digging around in stuff that somebody very dangerous might not want you to see. Not to sound like somebody's mother or something, but this is for your own good. If I start to get the slightest twinge of a feeling that you're holding out on me, I'll give Detective Atkins permission to do what he's pushing me to do."

"And that would be?" Sally asked.

"Get a court order and a wheelbarrow, and go out there and cart off her papers and her guitars and her shoes and any other damn thing we think of as material evidence. You'd never see so much as a grocery receipt."

"What?" Sally exclaimed.

"Nice. Very nice. You're one bad-ass cop when you wanna be, bro'," said Delice.

Sally glared at Dickie. "I could get a lawyer and challenge the court order," she said.

"You really want to go and do that? Go ahead. Sue me. Even if you could get the papers back, which is doubtful, they'd be fairly fucked up from our guys pawing through them. I'd hate for that to happen," he said, picking up the cigarette, taking a last puff, and grinding it out.

Obviously, he could do what he wanted. The fact that he wasn't seizing the papers already was, actually, a real concession to her. "I'm sorry. I really want to help. I'll keep you posted on everything."

"Thanks," said Dickie. "And I'm not foolin', Sally. I expect regular reports, and Xeroxes or originals of documents. And I want you communicating with Scotty, every day if necessary."

"Oh rapture," said Delice, rolling her eyes and pressing her hands to her heart.

"Oh shut up," said Sally, pushing her plate away and laying her forehead on the table.

15

The Hard Way

"Happy Halloween," said Hawk, having emerged from his shower smelling great and looking strong and fresh and not at all goblinlike.

"Oh crap," said Sally, "I forgot to buy candy for the trick-or-treaters."

"No problem. I'll pick some up at the Lifeway," Hawk said, pouring himself a bowl of Cheerios.

"Get some chocolate," Sally told him. "You always get stuff like Smarties and Atomic Fireballs and candy corn."

"I get what I like," Hawk answered. "I eat half of it anyhow."

"Now that you mention it," said Sally, "skip the chocolate. I don't need to be eating up my weight in Nestle's Crunch Bars."

Hawk walked over to where she was making coffee, grabbed her by the hips and turned her around. "A few Crunch Bars always look good on you," he said, pulling her against his hips and giving her a very attention-getting kiss.

"Thanks," she said, a little breathlessly. "But seriously, no chocolate. I can just make myself sick on candy corn in about five minutes."

"So you'll be back from Albany in time for the trick-or-treaters?"

"No reason I wouldn't," she said. "I can only sit and stare at paper for so many hours."

"You say that now," said Hawk, looking up from his cereal bowl, raising an eyebrow, "but the way it's been going lately, I have my doubts. You seem to be taking a perverse pleasure in putting yourself in harm's way."

He wasn't wrong. In the past month, she'd perversely set out for Nina Cruz's ranch, knowing that the weather might get ugly enough to keep her from getting home. She'd responded to the outbreak of lethal ruminant diseases by obstinately going down to the Wrangler and consuming as much animal protein as humanly possible. Now she was stubbornly arranging her schedule to spend days, perhaps months, in the vicinity of places where not one, but two people had been fatally shot, her intention being to pore over the life's records of one of the victims. Her agent had been enthusiastic about the project when she'd called, but had warned her that it sounded, well, rather dangerous.

Perverse was one way of putting it. Moronic was another.

Maybe it was hormones. They said lots of women heading out of their forties developed a penchant for taking crazy chances. She really ought to get out the blender and make one of those smoothies; maybe it would mellow her out.

Or maybe not. Sally frowned. She took the can of protein powder off the shelf, looked hard at the label, which was nothing more than a sheet of recycled paper with "Nutritional Supplement" printed in plain lettering on one side. She stuck a knife blade under the rim of the top and pried open the can.

Just powder, creamy white, looking a whole lot like the dry milk they used to buy in bulk back when she was in college, living dirt cheap in communal houses. But she remembered food co-op shelves stacked with bulk bins full of lots of stuff that looked like various shades of powders—yellowy brewer's yeast, pale mung-bean flour, agar-agar, you name it. The stuff she was looking at might be pulverized soybeans, or it might be something else.

Closing the can and leaving it on the counter, she picked up the phone and called Delice.

"What was the name of your friend at the vet lab?" Sally asked the minute Delice answered.

"Why do you want to know?" Delice said.

"Thought I might give her a call," Sally replied, evading.

"She won't tell you anything, even if you say you're my buddy. She's a pro," Delice told her.

"I'll take my chances," Sally said.

"Okay," Delice said, and gave her the name. "But if you learn anything interesting from her, promise you'll tell me instantly."

"Naturally," Sally agreed, and made the next phone call. Delice's friend allowed as how they were pretty busy. Then Sally told her the stuff had come from Nina Cruz's house, and the woman got more interested. She told Sally to bring it on by the lab and they'd give it a look. And take care handling it, by the way.

She put the can inside two plastic zipper bags, washed her hands three times, drank the last of her coffee. She probably ought to call Dickie and tell him what she was doing, but if, as was probable, the powder was nothing but ground-up soy, she'd just be bugging him for no reason and looking like a meddlesome fool in the bargain. So she put on her coat, hefted her fully packed shoulder bag, and headed out into the cold, clear morning.

Just over the river in West Laramie, Sally turned left into a driveway barred by a concertina-wire-topped security gate. A guard at the gatehouse asked her business, and she gave Delice's friend's name as her contact, saying also that she had a package to deliver. The guard requested identification, which she produced, then he searched her car and found nothing worth confiscating or even commenting on, and went back into the guardhouse and picked up a phone. Five minutes later, a white-coated technician arrived, used an ID badge to open the gate, accepted the can of powder, put it in yet another plastic bag, and walked back toward the buildings that housed the state veterinary research complex.

The whole experience was efficient, cold, utterly impersonal. She drove out the driveway, headed west, and sang along with the ever-ebullient Dixie Chicks all the way out to Shady Grove. But the Halloween creeps were upon her.

A harried-looking Cat Cruz met her at the door to the house, portable phone in hand. "I've got a call," she said, handing Sally the key to Nina's office. "And there's a bunch of business I've just got to get to this morning. You might as well go out there and get started. If you've got any questions or need to talk, just come on back in and let me know. I'll stop what I'm doing if I absolutely have to. I'll come out and check in with you later."

Sally didn't mind. If Cat was too busy to hover over her, telling her what she could or couldn't look at, think about, or publish, that was just fine with her. She let herself into the office, took a deep breath, and looked around at the tidy space, thinking about where and how to start in.

When it came to attacking an archive, a library, a document collection, some historians were methodical. They'd draw up a research plan, call for an inventory of items, and then, in calm and dispassionate fashion, work their way through, departing from design only to check back when something farther along on the list sparked the need to refer to something they'd examined earlier. Other historians were idiosyncratic, skipping around through material as fancy led them, looking for, and fastening on some detail of a place, an event, a life, that would explain the whole. Sally Alder aimed at method, but just as often followed impulse. Story of her life. Why should the archive be any different from any other place she happened to be?

Fortunately for her, Nina Cruz had been a devotee of order. There were filing cabinets full of neat, color-coded folders dealing with specific facets of her career, her causes, her personal business, year by year since 1965. In a closet in her office there were brown letter boxes labeled PERSONAL CORRESPONDENCE, again arranged by year, from 1950 to

2003. Good grief! Nina Cruz was maybe ten years older than Sally herself. And here she'd left behind more than half a century of personal mail. Sally began to feel altogether too historical.

What was surprising, to Sally, was how few boxes there were, only ten, in fact, over a period covering over fifty years. Nina must have thrown away a lot of personal letters. This was the kind of thing that made historians gnash their teeth and rend their garments. But she could see what was there, anyway, and eventually piece together a list of Nina's correspondents. Sooner or later, she'd contact the people on the list and find out if they had materials they might be willing to share.

What wasn't surprising was the fact that there were hardly any letters at all for the earliest and latest years. Nina had, after all, been only four years old in 1950, too young to send or receive much mail. And after about 1995, most of her correspondence had probably switched to e-mail.

Which meant Sally would have to try to figure out how to get into Nina's e-mail account. She'd called last night to ask, and Cat hadn't known the password. She'd look around to see if Nina had written it down in some obvious place (in a computer file titled "Passwords" maybe?). But if Nina had been at all prudent, Sally might need a hacker. Maybe the multitalented Quartz counted hacking among his interests, along with pies, French history, and accounting.

But before she thought about breaking and entering Nina's electronic correspondence, she might as well scan what was right there and easily available. Sally pulled out a few file folders at random, from different years, just trying to get a feel for the stuff in the cabinets. Once again, what she found taught a lesson in changing technology. The early business records were typed, or occasionally written out in longhand, and carbon-copied. In the middling period, greasy photocopies and dot-matrix printouts began to appear. Then computer-generated text, Courier fonts, and, ultimately, desktop-published work in increasingly elaborate form. A revolution in Sally's lifetime.

The technological transformation was, of course, just as

remarkable in the medium in which Nina Cruz had made her legend, recorded sound. When Nina had first taken to the road as a resolute young folk singer, 45s and 331/3s defined the universe of commercially available music. Tape cassettes had appeared sometime in the sixties, making music portable and personal in ways it had never been before. Anybody with a couple hundred dollars could buy a tape deck that would record as well as play, and soon you could make custom tapes, sound tracks of your own personal movie. When CDs came along, within ten years, anybody could be her or his own record producer. The advent of downloading, of course, meant that everything recorded was up for grabs.

Which made sound recordings fair game for a historian, no matter how methodical or stuffy.

Straying from the paperwork she surely should have been sitting down to attack, Sally stepped over to the shelves where Nina had stored her brilliant musical legacy. There were reel-to-reel tapes, cassettes—even eight-tracks!—along with 45s and LPs and CDs, and scrapbooks of press clippings. There was also a collection of all the recordings Nina had done with other artists, including, of course, a complete set of the recorded music of Thomas "Stonewall" Jackson.

Sally couldn't resist the albums. Over the course of the marriage, Nina had cut nine records; Stone had made five. They both sat in on each other's sessions from time to time, and had cowritten half-a-dozen songs that had made it onto vinyl. But every album had been billed as a solo outing; they'd never put out an album together. Their careers, Sally observed, were more parallel than joined.

Late in their marriage, Nina had provided a back-up vocal for Thomas's exuberant cover of the jazz standard "How High the Moon," on an album of duets he'd done with everyone from Lena Horne to Ray Price. The liner notes were illustrated with photos of Stone with his singing partners. She studied the photo of Stone and Nina. They stood at angles facing each other, hands on the earpieces of their headphones, singing into microphones that dangled from a ceil-

ing. Singing with eyes closed. When you sang with somebody that way, Sally knew, it was all about the blending of
sound. The mating of voices, not of souls. She'd fallen in
love with enough singing partners, sung with enough former
lovers, to know that, too often, it was a lot easier to make
beautiful music with somebody if you didn't have to look in
his eyes.

Soon after that session, Nina and Tom had split, leaving
behind one final testament to their years together. The title
song on a Stone Jackson record, written and sung by the
two of them, had since that time been covered, syndicated,
Muzaked, translated, karaoke'd, rearranged, and sampled a
hundred different ways. Royalties on "The Hard Way"
alone had probably made them money enough to bankroll
ranches all over the Rocky Mountains. But oh, thought
Sally, brilliant music came at a high price. *Rolling Stone*
had dubbed the song, "Our national anthem of tortured
love."

"My sister was a past master at the tortured love thing,"
came a voice, interrupting Sally's melancholy reverie amid
the records and the clippings. "But, after a while, it was
pretty clear, to me anyhow, that her lovers were taking most
of the torture. She was amazingly good at picking up the
pieces and moving on."

Sally looked up at Cat. "You're not much of one for senti-
ment, are you?"

"Sure I am. I loved—and continue to love—Angelina
more than anyone else in the world. I'll miss her every day
of my life. But I'm damned if I'll turn her into some kind of
saint. There are plenty of others willing to light the candles."

"But if she was so hard on the people who loved her, how
do you account for the fact that at least a few of the torture
victims have stuck around for more? Stone Jackson and
Nels Willen, for instance. They don't strike me as maso-
chists."

You could say the same for Cat Cruz herself.

Cat's mouth curved on one side, in something that might
have looked like a smile if it hadn't been so full of pain.
"You know, I've seen people dying of thirst in refugee

camps. They hang on for hours and days and weeks on a few drops of water, and some cynical, feeble promise that relief is coming soon."

Cat's face grew grim. "Hope can be a brutal instrument of torture."

16

Opera Gloves

Seven hours after she'd walked into Nina's office, Sally rolled her shoulders, stretched her arms high, and stood up. She walked out of the studio to the house to say good-bye to Cat, who was again on the phone. Cat waved vaguely in her direction. So Sally headed for her car, buttoning her coat and winding her scarf tighter around her neck along the way. The temperature had dropped a good fifteen degrees since morning, as it always seemed to do on Halloween. She had once observed that all Laramie children might as well decide to dress up as pumpkins. Even if Halloween day started out warm and sunny, the weather was invariably so frigid by twilight that even skinny little kids in skeleton costumes were puffed up like the Marshmallow Man with protective layers of sweaters and down vests and padded pants underneath.

Having skipped lunch, Sally spent the ride back hoping that Hawk had done something about dinner, and nurturing a smaller secret hope that he'd gone ahead and gotten those Crunch Bars. Surely she was entitled to a little chocolate binge after putting in a good day's work. She was more optimistic about the latter than the former. Apart from the fact that he'd probably had a long day himself, they were invited to the annual Halloween party hosted by the geology graduate students, a Laramie social institution featuring incredible costumes, eclectic dance music, lots of food, and lots of beer. She was usually content to wait and have something to eat there, and Hawk, who never skipped meals, would probably figure he could tide himself over with a hot dog between visits from trick-or-treaters, until the party began at nine. But tonight, the combination of puzzlement, nerves, and calorie deficiency made her ravenous.

Ravenous and curious. Who was Angelina Cruz? She'd shown so many faces to so many people. To the country at large, she'd been saint or traitor, crusader for social justice or sellout, admired by millions of people like Sally Alder for her idealism and her apparent determination to make every moment a test of right and wrong. Equally detested, by probably just as many millions (of people like, for example, Jimbo Perrine), for what they saw as her heavy-handed radicalism and self-righteous opportunism. She'd attracted a coterie of friends and admirers, and evidently courted and abandoned a long train of lovers, at least some of whom remained devoted even after, well, even after being dumped.

And what of those who'd survived and remained and more or less followed her to the wilds of Wyoming? The lovers: Stone Jackson, Nels Willen, Randy Whitebird, Kali (née Kelly Lee Brisbane). The admirers: Quartz, Pammie, Lark, and the others. And of course, Nina's sister, Caterina Cruz.

In what ways were Cat and Nina alike? Sally made a mental list of similarities: Both had made global reputations as activists and humanitarians. Both maintained ties to home and family, but at a distance (including, maybe, their relationship with each other?). Both were feminists (that covered a lot of ground, of course). Both had become rich nurturing Nina's career.

Nina had impressed Sally as both smart and capable, but without edge. They'd gotten together maybe monthly for two years, been on the verge of getting to know each other. Nina had committed her support to Sally's Dunwoodie Center early and with some heft, but she'd never tried to make Sally feel like the supplicant approaching the patron. They'd traded a little gossip along with business, chatting about the delights and frustrations of gardening above seven thousand feet.

Sally thought about it as she drove across the railroad bridge between West Laramie and the town proper. The limits of their relationship hadn't all come from Nina's side. Sally might be prone to idol worship, as her lifelong devotion to Thomas Jackson so embarrassingly attested, but she hadn't idolized Nina. Nels Willen had told her that Nina loved her. That might or might not be true. But whatever the case, Sally hadn't loved her back. Liked, yes. Admired, certainly. Respected, absolutely. But not loved. And that seemed strange, given that Nina was so evidently the kind of person with whom all kinds of people fell in love, and Sally thought of herself as a person who fell a little in love with most of her friends.

Truth to tell, Sally felt closer to Cat Cruz, after three days, than she had to Nina after two years. Cat mixed hardheaded assessments, pointed questions, and pragmatic strategies with a lot of wit and a disarming willingness to confide. She had the kind of edginess Sally adored in people like Delice and Dickie Langham, and of course, Hawk Green.

Maybe a little too much edge, though? Cultivated, over the years, by having to play hard to Nina's globally celebrated soft? Cat had loved Nina, as she said, "more than anyone"—more than anyone else had loved her sister, or more than Cat had ever loved? But Caterina Cruz's elegy for Angelina had tempered fond memory with cold truth, especially when it came to the way Nina had treated Stone Jackson.

Pulling into the garage, Sally was struck by a truth so obvious, she thought she should always have known it: Love wasn't a simple or simply good thing. She'd sung enough country songs that she should have figured that out by now; love could hurt and scar and wound and mar, as the poets said. Now, thinking about the death of Nina Cruz, she knew a certainty: Love could kill.

A chill ran through her as she walked to the house, and not only because of the frigid air. The grinning jack-o'-lantern by the door, glowing in the twilight, even seemed a little sinister. But as soon as she entered, her thoughts turned from love and death to food. The house was full of the aromas of tomatoes and garlic when she walked in: Hawk rustling up a big batch of his famous spaghetti sauce. She felt as if she could eat the whole pot. A big wooden salad bowl full of candy sat on the table in the front hall, next to the door: cellophane tubes of Smarties, plastic-wrapped Atomic Fireballs, packets of candy corn, and yes, lovely, irresistible little Crunch Bars. Sally put her shoulder bag on the floor next to the table and ate her first Crunch Bar before she'd even taken her coat off.

She'd started on a second as she walked into the kitchen. "You'll spoil your dinner," said Hawk, standing at the stove, stirring the pot.

"My mother always said that. But in my vast experience of between-meal snacking, I don't recall even one instance of spoiling my dinner. In fact, I believe I could eat mine and yours tonight."

"Go ahead," said Hawk with a grin. "Eat mine."

She grinned back, welcomed home. "Thanks for cooking," she told him.

"*De nada*," he said. "Once it started getting cold, I felt like whupping up something hot. No dead bodies today?" he inquired a little too blithely. He'd been at least a little worried.

"Nope," she said. "I got a good start. Fortunately, Nina was really well organized. It shouldn't take long to get through what's there, at least on paper. I got obsessed and didn't bother with lunch. I'll compensate with dinner," she told him, sticking a spoon in the pot and taking a bite of sweet, spicy, meaty sauce. "Obviously, you're not worried about mad cow disease either."

The first trick-or-treater rang the doorbell.

For two people closing in on the half-century mark, Sally and Hawk were fools for Halloween. They loved the kids who came to the door: tiny fairy princesses in pink tutus and tiaras and ski jackets; pint-size cartoon heroes-of-the-moment; pirates and hoboes and punk rockers and football players. Some of the costumes looked as if they'd come out of boxes from the Wal-Mart, some were elaborate home-sewing supermom productions, and some seemed to have been put together out of odds and ends and hand-me-downs and everyday clothes.

The biggest wave of them came while they were eating their dinner. They'd both get up to answer the door, exclaim over the kids, shovel out candy. The preschool kids, with hovering parents, came first. Next, the school-agers, mothers and fathers relegated to standing out by the street, as if anybody would let a couple of second-graders run around town by themselves on Freak Night.

By seven or so, the ringings of the doorbell had slowed to sporadic. Now, Sally knew, there would be large parties, families from the poorer parts of town who would come out all together, and teenagers who couldn't quite give up a childhood ritual. Since they'd bought, as predicted, far too much candy, these late visitors always made a haul. But they weren't as much fun to see. Half of them didn't even bother with costumes. By now, Hawk answered while Sally did the dishes, or they took turns while they were getting dressed for the geology party.

This party had been going on, in one form or another, for maybe twenty-five years. Sally had attended her first one in the late seventies, when revelers' creativity with costumes was generally enhanced by generous application of mood-altering substances. She had been blown away by the costumes, ranging from a person encased inside a gigantic papier-mâché mountain, to three women in matching pink evening gowns with shoes dyed to match, black bouffant wigs, and every inch of skin covered with brown makeup, a minstrel-show rendition of the Supremes that would never pass muster during these more sensitive days.

The psychedelic drug use had tapered off, and the costumes had become both more politically correct, and more risqué, although variations on planetary-science themes remained a constant. Last year she'd noted two people dressed as a stalactite and a stalagmite, a group of nine with huge papier-mâché heads depicting the planets of the solar system, a woman wearing nothing but a scattering of pebbles over the strategic spots, and a man encased in a seven-foot-tall erect penis costume. A hell of a lot of work went into these things.

Sally and Hawk weren't among those who went for either the labor-intensive production or the edge of respectability. Hawk was going as—what else?—a mad scientist. He had a white lab coat, an Einstein wig, and Groucho Marx glasses he'd adapted with lenses from an old pair of his own prescription specs. Pretty basic: The glasses were a nice touch.

Over the years, Sally had tried various approaches to Halloween costumes. She'd cross-dressed (once, memorably, as Bruce Springsteen), made political statements (an American flag-covered jumpsuit and death's-head makeup), even gone for inanimate objects. Once long ago, she and a friend had covered themselves with green makeup, worn green-dyed tights and T-shirts and garbage-bag tunics, tied their hair on top of their heads and stuck in dozens of plastic fern fronds. Pretending to be house plants, sitting quietly in corners, turned out to be a good strategy for people getting a serious buzz off some rather fresh psilocybin mushrooms.

But tonight, she was relying on her longtime passion for vintage clothing, indulged at flea markets and boutiques and junk stores and the Salvation Army over years and years. Back in Berkeley, there'd been a great vintage shop that took trade-ins. She'd swapped a fur-trimmed Cossack coat and hat she'd found at the Alameda flea market for a skin-tight, strapless black evening gown and a pair of black satin opera gloves, à la Rita Hayworth in *Gilda*. Back in the day, she'd had to lie down to be zipped into the dress, but the stitching in the seams had proven equal to an evening's wear, if she didn't take deep breaths. She'd tried it on the week before, discovered, to her delight, that she could still squeeze into it, and that it even fit a little less snug up top. She hoped that wouldn't be a problem. When a reporter had asked Rita what held her famous gown up, she'd said, "Two things."

Happily, the bodice of Sally's dress was made in the manner of what they used to call a "merry widow." It had enough boning from waist to chest to hold up a small office building, let alone a couple of things that were acceptable, but not getting any younger.

She looked in the mirror: all in all, not half bad. Her hair was long and she'd put a few waves in with a curling iron. Red lipstick. High-heeled sandals and the dress. Add the gloves and it might be, well, kind of middle-aged dynamite.

Hawk hadn't seen this getup, and Sally was really looking forward to his reaction. She'd postponed putting on the gloves until the last minute, because it was such a production, rolling them up, pushing down fingers one by one, and easing them on until they stretched from fingertip to the middle of the upper part of her arms. Once they were on, they stayed on pretty much for the duration. She was glad he'd made dinner. She didn't think she'd be able to cope with chips and salsa in her satin opera gloves, and anything more substantial might prove too much for side seams that had aged another couple of decades.

He emerged from the bathroom, showered and dressed but without the wig and the Groucho glasses, walking up behind her just as she was straightening the second glove. She heard a distinct gasp, then a faint moan. "You're trying to kill me, right?" he whispered.

She looked over her shoulder at him, feeling pretty damned sultry and wondering whether she ought to give him a few bars of "Put the Blame on Mame."

The doorbell rang. It had been half an hour since the last trick-or-treater, but as long as they were still home, even the laggards deserved a treat. "I'll get it," she said, taking a moment to stop and give him a kiss. "You finish getting dressed."

She sashayed over to the door, walking carefully in her ankle-breaker shoes. But when she opened it, there was nobody there. She looked around, puzzled, then worried that pranksters had come around to engage in some petty vandalism. Usually, that meant a broken pumpkin, but the jack-o'-lantern Hawk had carved was still glowing and grinning.

Then she spotted something. About halfway down the front walk lay a white object. She walked down the front steps and along the walk, then leaned over to pick up a small plastic bag, half full of some kind of white powder.

She was standing there, holding the bag in her gloved

hand and trying to figure out what was going on, when Hawk came out of the house. He stopped five paces from her.

"Don't even think about opening that, Sally," he said, deadly calm.

She stared at him.

"Put it back down on the ground."

She put the bag down.

"Have you touched that thing with both hands?" he asked.

She shook her head. "Just the right. Or maybe not, maybe both. I'm not sure."

Hawk took a breath. "Okay. Keep your glove on the left hand and take off the right one, and throw it on the ground."

"It'll take a while," she said, beginning to shiver in the cold night air.

"Fine. Take your time. I'm going to call nine-one-one. By the time I come back, I can help you take off the other glove."

"Hawk-k," she said, teeth chattering as she began to work at the glove. "Can you at least bring a j-jacket or something to cover my sh-shoulders?"

He ran into the house, returning with a plaid Pendleton couch throw, and draped it carefully over her shoulders, making sure not to touch the gloves. Then he went to make the call.

17

The Ornery Hagbody

It was amazing what one little packet of white powder could crank up. Within fifteen minutes, three police cars, a fire engine full of EMTs, the hazardous-materials team, and a beige Dodge sedan with WYOMING STATE VETERINARY LABORATORY stenciled on the side had rushed to the scene. Sally, by that time, was half frozen and fully terrified, her fabulous opera gloves crumpled on the sidewalk next to the scary little package.

Technicians wearing moon suits used tongs to put the packet in another bag and seal it, wipe down the sidewalk, and swab the wipe on a test strip. She couldn't see their faces, but she had the impression that they didn't like what the test strip showed. She kept telling herself that it was probably some stupid prank, a Baggie full of talcum powder or baking soda. Hell, ten years ago, anybody finding a bag of white powder would have been thinking: cocaine. And then thinking either, I must report this to the authorities! or, conversely, Yippee!

But that was before September 11, and some guy at *The Sun* opening an envelope and dying three days later.

The country had been nervous as hell for years, and it had been a damned strange fall in Laramie, what with murders and mad cow disease. And now, judging by the emergency-response team, everybody in Laramie was braced for a bout of bioterrorism.

Sally had been hustled off to Ivinson Memorial, had the Gilda dress cut off her, had her blood taken and her nose swabbed. She'd been hosed down and decontaminated, examined by a bored resident in the ER, and then again by somebody wearing jeans and cowboy boots who introduced himself as both a veterinarian and an MD. Nobody saw any symptoms of anything except slightly lowered body temperature (not surprising, since she'd been standing around scantily clad in the freezing cold), and they sent her home with two months' supply of Cipro and stern orders to call if she started feeling sick.

By now, a day and a half later, she'd endured a good twenty hours of the mightiest brain-splitting headache she'd ever had. So of course, she'd called. A side effect of the Cipro, the nurse at the hospital said. The nausea wasn't unusual either, given the headache. It should go away in a day or two. Thanks a bunch.

Thus, she wasn't in the greatest frame of mind when Scotty Atkins and Dickie Langham showed up at the house for a conversation. Sally was stretched out on the living room couch, a cold washcloth over her eyes. Scotty and Hawk sat in the chairs, while Dickie hunkered down on the coffee table, holding her hand.

"We took the sample out to the vet lab in West Laramie for analysis, and their tests confirmed the field test," Dickie told her. "The powder tested negative for anthrax. That's the good news. The bad news, of course, is that somebody played a very ugly trick on you and is obviously trying to intimidate you. By the way, even if it had been anthrax, there was no risk of cutaneous infection since you didn't open the envelope, and you were wearing those gloves."

"Oh goodie," Sally managed. "Lucky me."

"I called the doctor," Hawk said. "He says you should

continue the Cipro for ten days, but you don't need to go the whole course."

"Great. Only eight more days of feeling like my skull is getting jack-hammered."

"Beats the hell out of being dead," Scotty observed.

Sally took the washcloth off her eyes long enough to crane her neck to glare at him, then put it back and laid her head back down.

"I'd tend to agree," Hawk said, his voice tightening on "agree." The man was angry, and working hard to keep it together.

Sally was trying different breathing patterns—shallow, deep, alternating—searching for one that minimized the headache. Didn't seem to make a difference. "So who do you think brought me that little trick-or-treat package?" she asked them, breathing shallow and regular.

"We're working on it," Scotty said shortly. "We'll let you know when we find out."

There was a moment of silence. Then Hawk spoke, very calmly, a bad sign. "I would be interested in any theories either of you might have," he said.

"Hawk, I doubt we've come up with anything you wouldn't think of yourself," said Dickie. "Of course, this latest unpleasantness may or may not be connected to the Cruz murder."

"But if it isn't," said Sally, ignoring her head, "trying to figure it out is needle-and-haystack stuff. A student who didn't like the C-minus that was actually a charitable gift on my part? Somebody I pissed off when they thought I took their parking place at the Lifeway? Too many possibilities. Plus you guys have already made a point of trying to warn me off the biography project, and more generally told me to stay away from Stone Jackson and everybody who has anything to do with the Wild West. So you might as well start out by assuming my surprise package and Nina's death are related."

"Elementary, Dr. Alder," Scotty said, making her chuckle despite the pain.

"Which brings up one reason we're here," Dickie said

gently, rubbing the back of Sally's hand. "We've got a court order to seize the contents of Nina Cruz's office as evidence in the case."

"No!" Sally sat bolt upright. "You can't do that! I'm just getting started!"

"You're off the case, Professor. This is police business," Scotty told her.

"Listen to me carefully here, Mustang," Dickie crooned, taking her hand again. "This has gotten seriously dangerous. Whoever we're dealing with here likes all kinds of weapons, and doesn't seem squeamish about using them. Guns, biologicals, terror, and who knows what's next. Whether you admit it or not, you're known to be a little too smart and get a little too nosy. Two people have already died. I'm getting you the hell out of the line of fire."

"So you're treating Jimbo Perrine's death as related?" Hawk asked, a step ahead of Sally.

Scotty began, "We're not—"

"Do the math," Dickie said. "Two shootings in the vicinity of Albany, Wyoming, a town with a population less than your average Burger King. Both shot with hunting rifles. Of course we're treating them as related. It's driving us fucking crazy."

"Rifles?" said Sally, forcing down the pain and trying to follow every word. "Then your ballistics stuff shows that it wasn't the same gun?"

Scotty said, "Sheriff—"

"For Christ's sake, Scotty, it'll be in the *Boomerang* by tomorrow. Yeah, that's right. But you know how it is with guns in Wyoming. It's not a question of whether somebody has one, it's a question of how many they have."

Sally gave it a try. "Couldn't you guys just give me a week to scan some stuff, so I can get a jump on this project?" she pleaded, putting the washcloth on the coffee table and batting her eyes at Dickie, each bat producing a tiny pulse of pain.

"You've gotta be kidding," said Scotty. "She's kidding, right?" he asked Hawk.

"You know her."

"Forget about it," said Dickie. "Teach your classes. Run your center. Do your job while we do ours."

She looked at Hawk, who looked back with love and determination, and a ghost of the anger, in his eyes. "Enough's enough," he said. "For the moment. I still think you should write the biography. *After* they've caught the killer. The papers and other stuff will still be there when it's all over."

Sally snorted (a mistake—her head registered the snort at 5.6 on the Richter scale). "Yeah, they'll be there, in God only knows what shape. You might as well shred 'em right now."

Scotty smiled at her. He found the strangest things funny. "We'll do what we can to uphold your high scholarly standards. I'll be handling the examination of Cruz's papers myself. I'll even make the concession of doing an official inventory out there."

Sally was aware that the inventory was probably standard procedure, and not a concession on his part, but she didn't have the strength to fight about it. She sighed. "Okay, guess I don't have a choice."

No one bothered to reply.

It occurred to her that she should probably tell them about the can of nutritional supplement she'd taken to the vet lab. But it was clear they'd grown weary of her amateur detecting, and she didn't feel like raising the alarm about another batch of white stuff that was probably nothing more lethal than what it claimed to be.

Sally wasn't really holding out on them because she was pissed off that they were seizing Nina's papers.

"I've got a question," Hawk said. "What do you guys think about Sally going ahead and doing the benefit?"

Scotty gave an automatic response. "Bad idea."

Dickie pondered. "That's a complicated question. On the one hand, the less you, and for that matter, my brother, have to do with the Wild West Foundation, and anything associated with Nina Cruz, the more comfortable I feel. On the other hand, this is, after all, your chance to sing with Thomas Jackson. I'm not real thrilled about spending the next forty years listening to you tell me how I fucked up your one pass at canoodling with Darlin' Tommy.

"Then again, Dwayne's having some second thoughts. And so are the other Millionaires. I wouldn't be surprised if the other performers pulled out. The mention of anthrax tends to make people hesitant."

The phone rang. Hawk answered, put his hand over the receiver. "It's your boyfriend," he said, bringing her the cordless telephone.

"Very funny," Sally mouthed, though her head felt instantly a little better. She accepted the phone, still reclining on the couch.

"I heard about Halloween," said Stone. "I feel like it's my fault for getting you into all this."

"I'll be all right," she said. "It was just talcum powder. And even if it had been something bad, I was wearing opera gloves."

"You go to a lot of opera in Laramie?" Stone asked.

"More than you do in Cody," she answered.

"Maybe that's why I don't have opera gloves," he said.

"What's going on with the gig?" Sally asked.

"Well, we've had some cancellations. But nothing disastrous. Emmylou's more determined than ever to do her bit. David and Graham will be here too—David says he's living on a loaned liver, so he's got nothing to lose. We're still on."

"How about Cat?" Sally asked. "She might pull the plug for other reasons."

"Talked to her last night. She said she meant to go ahead, and hoped you wouldn't have a problem with it. Said she was planning to give you a call. She's sorry she didn't get a chance to say good-bye when you were out at Shady Grove."

"No big deal," said Sally. "She was on the phone."

"I think she's spent the last few days with her ear glued to a phone, trying to figure out what the hell's up with the Wild West. As far as she can tell, this outfit hasn't taken on a single project yet. All they've done so far is flap their jaws and cut paychecks. Cat's let them know they're history after the benefit. She'll be taking over project planning and management and putting in her own team."

"I bet they aren't real happy about that," Sally said.

"Cat's taking the position that she's giving them more than their two weeks' notice."

Sally thought a minute. "Good grief. The gig's only three weeks away."

"Yep," said Stone. "You'd better get better quick. I'd like to come down there and rehearse with the band this weekend."

"Thomas, I'm not sure that the Millionaires are going to stay on board," Sally said.

"Remind them that a portion of the proceeds will go to Perrine's widow," said Stone. "But if you can't convince them to play, you and I could just do a couple of duets."

"Duets? You and me?" she whispered breathlessly, and then noticed that all three men were watching and listening to her. Hawk's version of watching verged on a glare.

"Sure," he said. "Let me know what works out." He paused. "So how do you feel?"

She took a deep breath, pleased to find it didn't rattle her brain in her skull. "This hasn't scared me off the book project, Stone."

"I'm kind of surprised to hear that," he said.

Sally glanced at Dickie, who was watching her intently. "I'm a little surprised myself. But I really hate the idea of somebody trying to scare me off something I want to do. Something I think I *should* do." And now she looked at Hawk and smiled a little. "I'm a frigging ornery hagbody."

She could hear the hesitation before he spoke again. "Cat says the sheriff's gotten a court order to seize the contents of Nina's office. Won't that shut you down?"

That really pissed her off. And gave her an idea. "Oh, I don't know. Just because the cops have decided to yank the papers doesn't mean I can't continue doing research."

At this, Dickie and Scotty's inquiring looks turned to glares. They could glare all they wanted. "We historians aren't restricted to paper for our sources." She continued, "Since they're making it impossible for me to sit in some nice, quiet room with Nina's archive, I reckon I'll just work the oral history angle."

Now Scotty was glowering in earnest, and Dickie slumped

down, set his elbows on his knees, and put his head in his hands. Hawk burst out laughing.

"Oral history?" Stone asked.

"Oral history," Sally said. "It's an indispensable tool for anybody who's trying to work on the recent past, or on subjects who express themselves in ways other than writing. Perfect for researching the life of somebody like Nina. The methodology's pretty simple, but in practice it means being stubborn as well as subtle."

"I can imagine," said Stone.

Now she grinned, her headache almost gone. Maybe the nurse was right, and the side effect had subsided. Or maybe outflanking Scotty Atkins just made her blood run cool and easy. Or some might say she was simply pigheaded enough to beat a headache while she was forgetting good sense. "So I'd better get busy. Now that I can't just sort paper, I'm going to have to go around asking lots and lots of questions of everybody I can find who knew Nina Cruz."

18

Spawn of the Devil of the Month

As Sally had seen, the local reaction to the news of Nina Cruz's mad cow disease was a frenzy of carnivorousness. The response to her own encounter with talcum powder was decidedly more mixed. The mere mention of anthrax, even if the whole thing had been a hoax, had a lot of people acting squirrelly. Some saw her on the street and pretended they hadn't. One woman who'd kissed up to her after that story in *People* actually crossed the street when she saw Sally coming. Sally thought she knew how Typhoid Mary had felt.

Then there were those who seemed to presume she'd done something to deserve being attacked. A student group of the wacko Christian persuasion circulated a leaflet headed with a picture of her and the words SPAWN OF THE DEVIL. Since this particular group denounced somebody in Laramie pretty much once a month, Sally decided she'd consider it an honor to be Spawn of the Devil of the Month.

More disturbing was that note in her mailbox at school. A folded piece of white paper with three words typed on it: TRICK OR TREAT.

Yes, she had to admit, that note gave her some serious

heebie-jeebies. But she was damned if she'd let some asshole intimidate her. When the *Boomerang* called and asked
her how it felt to be the target of bioterrorism, she told them
that she didn't really see any point in being terrorized. Tom
Brokaw, after all, had gotten a weapons-grade anthrax letter
in the mail, and it hadn't set him back. And he, she pointed
out, was from South Dakota. As a Wyomingite, she had to
uphold state honor.

Some of the people who'd crossed the street to get away
from her began to cross back.

Much to her delight and comfort, she got a lot of support
from people who mattered. Dickie checked in daily to see
how she was doing. Delice offered to lend her a gun (Sally
declined). She was touched to the heart when a florist delivered a big vase of Stargazer lilies, with a card that read, "See
you at practice. The Millionaires."

And touched once again when she heard from more casual acquaintances. Pammie Montgomery showed up with a
box of chocolate-chip cookies, declaring she'd made them
from "the incorruptible recipe on the back of the chip package." Burt Langham called to say that he and John-Boy
wanted to buy her lunch at the Yippie I O. "We're not worried about you being a *carrier*," Burt told Sally. "Remember
that we lived in the Castro in the eighties, for God's sake. We
know something about real plagues. And John-Boy wants to
hear all about the opera gloves."

Even Arvida Perrine, who'd seemed pretty out of it a few
days ago, when Sally had phoned to talk with her about the
benefit, had made a point of calling to check on her.

Sally's students were best of all.

They gave her a standing ovation when she walked into
class.

"You go, girl!" somebody yelled.

So she did. Right after class, she went to Hoyt Hall and
started in on the first round of calls.

Nels Willen answered his land line on the second ring. He
was at home in Colorado, sitting by his woodstove, watching
snowflakes drift down. Three to five inches were predicted
for the North Park area. "But you never know . . ." he began,

invoking the ritual conversational gambit of the high country in wintertime.

Sally made the appropriate weather noises.

"I've been meaning to call you," he said. "I heard about the anthrax hoax. Must have scared the daylights out of you."

The warmth in his voice disarmed her. "Yeah. And the night-lights, too. But I'm fine. Even the headache from the Cipro is gone."

"That was a precaution. Back in my doctoring days, I'd have prescribed the same treatment. These days, I wonder if antibiotics aren't a bigger problem than the stuff they're supposed to treat. Technology's a double-edged sword, huh? We've got to the point where every problem we try to solve with a tech fix generates bigger, badder problems. Wonder drugs create wonder bugs."

"Most people don't get involved in medicine unless they believe in science and progress, but once you're in med school, they really pound that message home. What happened to make you change your mind?"

"Couldn't take it anymore. I went hunting one weekend, and the guy I was with was a pretty bad shot. Managed to wing a doe in the leg, but that deer kept running, and it took us most of the morning to find her. When we did, she was still alive, and in unbelievable pain. Must have been runnin' on three legs, 'cause the fourth was busted in half, the lower half near torn off. I put a bullet in her head.

"The next week, they bring this kid into the hospital, maybe thirteen years old. Followed her brother out onto the boarders' run, with her brand-new board. Got about halfway down the mountain, going like hell and completely out of control, before she hit a bump, went ass-over-teakettle, and ended up with a leg that looked pretty damn much like the one I'd seen on that doe. What really got me, though, was that she had the exact same look in her eyes. I had this momentary vision of myself pulling out my rifle and shooting her in the head."

"Oh my God," said Sally.

"Yeah," Willen said. "And then I had this image of handing her a gun and telling her to go ahead and shoot back. Kind of even the score."

"Wow. All this happened right in the operating room?" Sally asked.

"Yeah. I'm not sure how, but I managed to fix her up, and they told me she was walking again, six months later. But by that time, I'd quit. Couldn't make sense of the way I was behaving with animals, the ones on four legs, and the human kind. Took me a couple years of navel gazing to get my head around it."

Jesus.

But she plunged ahead. "I'd really like to talk with you about Nina sometime soon, if you're up to it."

Another pause. "Yeah. I've heard you're writing a book. Cat told me she'd agreed to cooperate with you, so I reckon I can do the same. I'm planning to come up to Albany to meet with her over the next couple of weekends, so maybe we can get together then," he said.

"That'd be great," she said. They agreed to meet at her office.

"I've got one more question for you right now, if you don't mind," said Sally. "It's about Nina having contracted mad cow disease. Do you have any thoughts on how that could have happened?"

He hesitated again before answering. "As you can probably guess, I've wracked my brain about that. After all's said and done, it isn't that easy to get bovine spongiform encephalopathy, even for your average meat eater. You have to ingest infected animal parts, and here in the U.S., we've been successful, so far, in keeping that from happening—or, at least, we think we have. The incubation period with this thing is so long that there's no telling whether people who ate bad meat products ten years ago will start getting sick in the future. Of course, there's lots of potential and real contamination going on, all the time."

"Yes," said Sally. "I saw the chicken episode on *60 Minutes*."

"Naturally, the people who ought to worry most about tainted meat are the ones still eating animals. It's tough to imagine somebody who's been a vegetarian for years being at risk. I have thought of one explanation, though," Willen said. "Remember I told you about that crazy Swiss dude who had Nina on an all-organ-meat diet when she banged up her knee? Organ meats are supposed to be the worst source of infection. And that was a time when the stuff was getting into the European herds, and nobody had any idea it was going on."

"That makes sense," Sally said. "Have you mentioned that to the police?"

Willen laughed softly. "As a matter of fact, I have. That nice Detective Atkins has been in touch quite regularly." But there was something beside humor in his voice.

"Nels," said Sally, "you're not blaming yourself for what that doctor might have done to Nina, are you?"

He didn't answer immediately. "Of course not," he said unconvincingly.

No time to think about that now.

She called the Wild West office. Randy Whitebird answered, pouring on the sympathy. "Oh Sally! We've been so worried about you. We were so glad when Pammie told us she'd taken you some cookies. What a bummer, man!"

Had she told him he could call her by her first name? But then, the guy was a Californian. "No harm, no foul," Sally replied. "I've got a clean bill of health, and nobody was hurt. It's pretty weird though, don't you think?"

"The world gets weirder every day," Whitebird replied. "But then, of course, we're trying to do something about that." He injected as much warmth as he could into the statement, but couldn't completely cover the note of self-righteousness. Or the vagueness of the message.

"Listen, Randy," Sally said, trying for cordiality. She didn't like either Whitebird or Kali, but she needed to interview them as soon as possible. He'd presented himself first. "I'm sure you've heard that I'm writing Nina's biography. The police have seized her papers," she told him, counting on his sympathy in that regard and not being disappointed.

"Yeah, I heard. What a violation of the First Amendment. Believe me, I know what you're going through. We've had cops in the office for the past week, making copies of everything on our computers and in our files. And it's taking them long enough to get this solved! With that fat-ass sheriff, sometimes it's hard to tell if this is Mayberry or Selma, Alabama," said Whitebird.

Sally was a big fan of the First Amendment, but she conceded, however grudgingly, the right of the police to investigate crime. And as a citizen of Laramie, she resented the comparison to Selma. Not to mention the fact that as a lifelong friend of Dickie Langham, she considered anyone who referred to him as a "fat ass" to be a philistine and a fool.

But once again, she squelched distaste and pursued conversation. "Since I can't work on Nina's papers," she told Whitebird, "I'm concentrating on oral history for now. I want to talk to the people who were closest to her, and I'm hoping I can take you to lunch at the Yippie I O Café, just to talk about how you might want to be interviewed."

Whitebird was willing. His schedule was pretty flexible. He was even available the next day. Sally suspected that he was the kind of guy who seldom turned down a free lunch.

On the way home, she stopped off at the Lifeway, prowling the aisles, trying to decide what to rustle up for dinner. She'd been thinking that they ought to eat more vegetarian meals, just for health's sake. But a day that had started out cool and brilliantly clear had turned to clammy, overcast twilight chill. Meat-eating weather, she determined, and picked up a couple of packages of pork chops and some potatoes and apples and broccoli, enough so she'd have a pork chop dinner she could put in the freezer for some hectic night later in the winter. This was going to be one of those square meals that would earn a *Good Housekeeping* Seal of Approval.

The pork chops were simmering away with the apples by the time Hawk appeared, pronouncing himself hungry enough to eat bean curd and barley. And then, moments later, the doorbell rang. Sally froze. The prospect of answering the door gave her a few problems.

Look, she told herself, what were the chances of another, more serious attack?

Not so remote, said her cautious self.

Cautious selves could not be permitted to run things.

But she looked through the peephole before she opened the door.

"You're just in time for dinner," Sally said. "We're having pork chops. Good thing I bought enough."

"Seems to be the season for pork chops," said Dickie Langham, and walked in.

Hawk was pouring a couple of Jim Beams. Dickie took off his hat and jacket, accepted the offer of a cup of coffee, reached into his pants pocket, and extracted a plastic-sealed piece of Nicoban gum. He put the gum into his mouth and began chewing resolutely, knowing that Sally and Hawk banned smoking in their house. Sometimes it seemed to Sally that Dickie had traded his former diet of booze and blow for a new and questionable dependence on caffeine and nicotine. But then, she supposed trading the lethal for the merely unhealthy was a big step up.

"I'm surprised Detective Atkins didn't come along with you," Sally said, grinding beans.

"We've decided to try a new tack with you, Mustang," he said as he sat down at the kitchen table. "Threats and intimidation seem ineffectual, so I figure we have two choices. One: Forget about threats. We can just cut to the chase and get a restraining order that would bar you from interfering with our investigation."

"At which point," Sally said, "it'd be easy enough to get a couple of lawyers to make you look like a free speech–hating fascist."

"Instead of a dedicated public servant trying to protect a respected member of our fine community," Hawk put in.

"Thank you for that show of support, Hawk," said Dickie, sucking on his gum and watching the teakettle she'd just put on to boil.

"I'm kind of on your side on this one," said Hawk, "being a concerned private citizen with an interest in protecting that same respected but perhaps headstrong community member."

Both glared at Sally.

"What's your second choice?" Sally asked, taking a sip of her bourbon.

"Share some information with you," Dickie said.

Sally leaned back in her chair, her hand flying to her heart. "I'm like to die of shock here, Sheriff. Does your ace detective know what you're up to?"

"Detective Atkins," said Dickie, "works for me. The minute I give him the go-ahead, he gets the restraining order. So don't fuck with me, Sally. I'm cutting you a big break here."

"And I'm grateful, but curious. To what do I owe this generosity?" she asked.

"To the fact that I'm betting that what I have to say will scare the crap out of you and get you to act like a sensible person instead of a damn fool," he answered.

Sally took another sip, put her hands in her lap, and leveled a look at him. "Give it a try," she said.

"All right. I'll ask you to remember that everything I'm telling you right now is privileged. If I hear about one leak, one tiny piece of information that somehow shakes loose, we'll put the lid down on you so tight, you'll be wearin' your underpants up around your ears. If you want to call out the lawyers, be my guest."

"Should I leave?" Hawk asked, starting to get up.

"On the contrary. Maybe if you hear this, you can keep working on her to get a frigging clue, and let her goddamn book go for a while," he told Hawk, happy to see that the water had come to a boil.

There was no defending herself from their scorn, so Sally went on the offensive as she poured water into the drip filter. "For now, let's focus on the facts. I assume you guys have checked into Stone Jackson's story about where he was the day Nina was killed?"

"A counter girl at the McDonald's in Riverton told us she remembered selling a cup of coffee to a tall, balding man who was talking on a cell phone," Dickie said. "It's not a positive ID. We showed her a picture of Jackson, and she thought it might have been the same guy, but she wasn't completely sure. When we asked her if she knew who Stone Jackson was, she guessed maybe he was the PRCA Champion All-Around Cowboy last year."

One woman's idol was another woman's bald guy on a cell phone. "How about Kali? Have you been able to pin down her whereabouts?" Sally asked as she put a mug down in front of him.

Dickie took a swallow of his coffee and smiled at her. "Going for the obvious suspects? The people who weren't in sight? I'd say that narrows the list down to, oh, say, the entire planet except the people you happened to lay eyes on that morning."

Sally hung her head. He was right. She was no detective. "I'm just trying to get a feel for who I really need to watch out for."

Dickie put the mug down on the table and leaned on his elbows. "Try this. Worry about every last one of them. Forget about trying to figure out who killed Nina Cruz. We think we know."

Sally's eyes widened. She set down her own glass. "I'd assume that ought to be good news."

"It is," Dickie said, looking anything but cheerful. "We've got the murder weapon. A Marlin Model 336, chambered for 35 Rem ammo. Lever action gun. A real traditionalist's hunting rifle—lighter than the 444. Of course, your serious gun guy will have both, and probably a couple bolt-action and pump models, maybe even a semiauto or two in his gun case. Not to mention his shotguns, and his pistols, and heavier rifles for bigger game."

"So Nina wasn't shot with Willen's gun," said Sally. "But it had been fired, and Nels claimed Nina was the one who fired it. That would get him off the hook," said Sally. "Where in the world did you find the murder weapon?"

"Nobody's off any hook right now. And we found the gun in question in the basement gun room at the residence of Jimbo Perrine. It was his rifle. He'd cleaned and oiled it, but the stupid son of a bitch couldn't bring himself to get rid of it after he shot her. It wasn't like it was his most precious possession. There were half-a- dozen rifles in his case worth twice what that one is." Dickie took a paper napkin from the holder on the table, extracted the gum from his mouth, wadded it up in the napkin, and applied himself to his coffee in earnest.

"Maybe," said Hawk, "the Marlin was just Jimbo's favorite. Accurate, powerful, fun to shoot, and the kind of gun that, if you were a decent shot, would put a hole in something and stop it in its tracks."

"Fun to shoot?" Sally asked, aghast. "Putting a hole in a human being? That's fun?"

"You know that's not what I meant," said Hawk.

"I can't believe this," said Sally. "I mean, I know Jimbo was a great hater. And I heard him talk about Nina—he especially resented her, probably because she'd bought a piece of land he'd gotten used to thinking of as a free country for Wyomingites. Maybe it's just because I know him, but I can't see him actually getting to the point of killing her. Was he that fucking crazy?"

"He might have been crazy, but we don't think that's the reason he shot her. Or put it this way. Of course he was fucking crazy. And being crazy like he was may have made him a good candidate for shooting somebody. But in and of itself, that wouldn't have been enough," Dickie said.

Sally was thoughtful. "What do you think that gun collection of his is worth?" she asked.

He smiled slightly. "Good question, Mustang. All told, maybe fifty thousand. Maybe more. And it looked like lately his tastes were getting pricier and pricier. On the day he was killed, he was carrying a spankin'-new Browning rifle worth almost a thousand dollars. Appears he'd also developed a thing for collectible guns. There was a limited edition Winchester 94 in his gun case, never been fired, never meant to. Just for looking at and fondling. We found a receipt. He'd bought both at a gun shop in Fort Collins, on October 12. Paid cash. Then again, he'd have had to. His credit cards were maxed out and had been for months. The mortgage company's about to foreclose on Arvida."

"Oh boy, that poor woman," said Sally.

"She should sell the guns," Hawk said.

"She is. And his mounts, too. He's got maybe a hundred all told, everything from weasels and assorted heads and antlers to a mountain lion and a moose. Some of them are worth a pretty penny," said Dickie.

Sally couldn't imagine why anyone would pay anything for a stuffed dead animal. Then again, plenty of women were willing to pay small fortunes for clothing made from the skins of dead animals that weren't even stuffed and mounted. "So what you're saying is that somebody paid Jimbo Perrine to kill Nina. And then, presumably, took out Jimbo himself. Who? Why?" She thought about the two sets of tracks in the snow.

"That's what we're working on right now. And at this point, we consider every single person associated with Nina Cruz a suspect."

Sally thought again. "What about the Halloween prank? It might be related. How can that help narrow things down?"

"Not much," said Dickie. "Actually, not at all."

"So you're concentrating on motive," said Sally. "Trying to figure out what kind of person would do these kinds of things, and why. Do you have any theories?"

"You might as well forget about trying to pump me, Sal. Naturally we have theories. And we have investigative techniques, and sources of information, and ways of making sense of that information, most of which is none of your goddamn business. Indeed, the less you know about the specifics of how we're handling this matter, the better for everybody concerned, including you."

She conceded the point. "Okay, no specifics. But how about generally? What inclinations or experiences or personality traits might lead somebody to pay a killer, kill the killer, and, just possibly, try to scare me?"

"I'm no psychologist," Hawk said, "but there's one kind of person I can think of. Somebody who feels so personally wronged by Nina Cruz that he or she isn't satisfied with killing her. There has to be wreck and ruin beyond the grave. That'd have to be somebody pretty twisted." He got up and poured himself another Beam.

Dickie eyed Hawk's glass involuntarily, caught himself, and slugged down a big swallow of coffee. "Twisted puts it mildly. There's something both impersonal and personal in a series of crimes like this. Police shrinks have profiles for these kinds of perps. Patterns of childhood abuse are pretty common. Religious or political zealotry can be a big factor, as you've seen before, Mustang. There might be a financial motive in there somewhere, but it's mixed in with lots of loco."

"Very creepy," Sally said, shivering as she got up to splash a little more whiskey in her own glass, check the pork chops, turn the potatoes.

Dickie nodded. "But the creepiest part is that the killer wouldn't necessarily appear to be badly bent. Some are the kinds of quiet loners who suddenly show up with a basement full of corpses, and all the neighbors saying, 'He seemed like a nice guy. Kept his lawn mowed. Kept to himself.' And others you'd have to call sociopaths—people who to all appearances are nice, outgoing, well-adjusted, productive members of society. Wonderful, charismatic people. And then you find out that there's a whole second soul inside, doing absolutely unexpected horrible things. We see that kind of thing in people who prey on children, for example. So we have to look at even the people who seem sweetest and most well meaning."

Unbidden, a fragment of Stone Jackson's beloved hit "Springtime in the Country" tripped into Sally's mind. A song with a lilting bounce, an irresistible hook. A song that made you happy just to hear it, until you listened a little closer and realized that the lyrics were about a mental crack-up.

"I can imagine," said Sally, "that the killer would be less than delighted to have his or her dark secrets exposed."

"Which is the kind of thing your little oral history interviews are liable to turn up," said Hawk. "If that doesn't scare the crap out of you, I don't know what should. Not to mention that it's worth considering whether the person who pulled the Halloween trick on you might already think you know something you shouldn't."

Dickie suddenly looked very tired. He finished off the last of the coffee, but it didn't give him any visible boost. He reached in his pocket again, popped another piece of Nicoban.

"Glad I don't have your job, amigo," Sally said, coming over to squeeze his shoulder.

"You should be," he replied. "Especially when you consider that we're about to play host to this big hoo-ha benefit, with all kinds of people coming in from all kinds of places and a local police force of maybe thirty people, between the county and the city, to keep an eye on things."

Hawk nodded, face grave. "What about help from the state and the feds?" he asked.

"They're already involved. The FBI has been working on the murders, and you ought to know that you've attracted a little of their attention since Halloween. It's always a little drifty dealing with them, because we never know when they're holding out on us, and sometimes they come in here thinking they know fuck-all about everything and screw up all our work. But we don't have any choice. They've got sources and resources we need. We're hoping we can get a hell of a lot of cops in here Thanksgiving weekend."

They all looked at one another. "Thanksgiving weekend. You know what that means," Sally said at last.

Dickie nodded. "Pray for good weather," he said.

19

Tortilla Soup

The next morning dawned cold and clear and perfectly crisp, the kind of morning that made you glad to be breathing pure, exhilarating Wyoming air. Hawk was already gone when Sally awoke, bursting with energy. She put on her tights and running bra, pulled on a long-sleeved T-shirt, got into her socks and running shoes. This was not a day to groove up slowly with Dionne Warwick singing "Alfie." She'd have to set a fast pace just to get warmed up, so she pulled out an old tape she'd made that kicked off with Van Morrison doing "Domino," and really cranked from there. From the first stride, Sally felt like she could high step it and run forever.

Why the hell was she feeling so good? Last night, Dickie had achieved his purpose of scaring her silly, all the while putting down most of the pork chops and a small mountain of pan-fried potatoes. He'd given her reason to worry that the idol of her youth was not, as he appeared, the spirit of light and art and compassion. Instead, Thomas Jackson might be a sociopath who'd had his ex-wife killed, then turned his own gun on the hired shooter, and might be continuing along some warped path of imagined revenge. She thought about the note she'd found in Nina's office. Could Stone be the one who dwelled too often in the dark?

Jackson, however, was just one of several potential candidates for Wyoming serial killer of the year, all of whom she hoped to interrogate—er, interview—in the near future. She was having lunch today with Randy Whitebird, a man who could easily turn out to be the psycho killer. Worse yet, she was picking up the check. Was she insane, or merely stupid?

You could be insane *and* stupid, she realized as she rounded the corner by the Washington Park band shell.

And yet, Sally thought as Grace Slick wailed "Somebody to Love" in her ears, if this was middle-aged crazy, she'd make the most of it. Her life had definitely gotten a lot more interesting since she'd packed up the Mustang, said goodbye to Santa Monica, and put the hammer down for the high country. She admitted she got a rush from solving real-world puzzles, although she could take or leave the close encounters with mortality. But quite apart from that, it occurred to her that here in Wyoming, she really had found somebody to love.

Wonder of wonders, it seemed as if he loved her right back. Hawk Green was a marvel, a man who could put up with the likes of her and keep her interested at the same time. Not perfect, and not perfect for her. But who wanted that? As Delice Langham had recently observed, "He's a pain in the ass, but he's probably a keeper."

Much as he might like to, Hawk wouldn't stop her from pushing ahead with the book. He might break a few dishes along the way, but he'd watch her back and help her think her way through the hard parts. As it happened, he'd saved her ass a time or two, and then proceeded to admire that same ass in ways that even now, sweaty and breathing hard, gave her some nice body flashbacks.

He was there when she got back. Sweaty, too, after his early-morning basketball bout, making a cup of coffee.

Had his back to her. The teakettle was whistling, and he didn't hear her come in. She walked up behind him, put her arms around him, rubbed against him, and ran her hands down inside the front of his shorts.

"I need a shower," he said, reaching behind him and around her to take hold of that well-appreciated part of her body with both hands.

"What a coincidence," she said, enjoying his firm grip, and the friction of body on body. "So do I."

Fortunately, neither of them had classes to teach that morning. They took their time washing each other, and then retired to the bedroom and spent a lot of time looking seriously into each other's eyes, and using their hands and their mouths on each other's body.

"This is going to sound weird," Hawk said during a slow-breathing, gazing interlude, "but being afraid of something horrible happening to you makes me want to make love to you as if I might not get the chance again. So I'm going to try to keep this slow, and do everything I can think of to please you." His hands moved, light and soft, on either side of her spine.

"God, men are so insensitive." She sighed, moving in to kiss him, exploring the inside of his mouth with her tongue, willing their bodies to melt together, slip and slide and linger over each other, melt again. She wanted to be so tangled up with him that she couldn't tell the beginning or the end. To rock together in the waves of a warm sea, to be swept, together, away.

Oh, tenderness.

To doze, and wake, and take another shower, and smile, and take a deep breath, and give each other a soft good-bye kiss, and head out the door to get on with the day.

"Please," he said, swinging his daypack up over his shoulder and turning toward the university, "be careful. Really. And if you need me, give me a call." He pointed to his belt. Much to her surprise, he'd clipped on the cell phone she'd given him. He hated the things, and it usually lived on the kitchen counter, turned off, gathering dust in its charging unit.

She smiled at him. "You're wearing the phone. You really do care."

"No," he said. "I've just decided to get addicted to betting on pro football, and I don't want to miss a call from my bookie."

He gave her hand one last squeeze and headed for his office. She had half an hour before she was due to meet Whitebird, three times as much time as she'd need to walk downtown. It was still a glorious day.

The Laramie merchants, to their credit, had held off decorating for Christmas until after Halloween. But now, as Thanksgiving neared, the streets were festooned with tinsel garlands and shiny plastic bells, and the shop windows sported elves and reindeer and candy canes and Santa Clauses of all kinds, from a religiously inspired Saint Nick in a white robe with a golden crown to the traditional fat guy in the red suit and stocking cap to the Buckhorn Bar's window painting of a jolly old fellow in a red union suit, black high-heeled boots, and a red cowboy hat with a white fur hatband.

As she walked up and down Ivinson, checking out the store windows before going on to the Yippie I O, she recognized the brown Toyota 4Runner parked in the diagonal spaces out in front of the Buckhorn: Scotty Atkins's personal vehicle. Scotty sat behind the wheel, talking to another white male in the passenger seat. Sally was dying to know who, but she couldn't get a good look without crossing the street and walking right past them. Ordinarily, she had a penchant for the obvious, but where Scotty Atkins was concerned, she'd found herself more often opting for the oblique. She registered the information and kept on walking.

As she entered the Yippie I O, she noted that Patsy Cline, chef John-Boy's particular goddess, was playing on the sound system. Burt Langham was manning the reception stand, the picture of dude elegance, as usual. Today, he was sporting pressed jeans, red cowboy boots, a vintage Western shirt (turquoise with a black yoke, pearl snaps, and black-and-white striped piping), and a diamond horseshoe in his left earlobe.

"No Christmas music?" she asked Burt as he led her to her favorite table in the corner.

"Not 'til Christmas week," he answered. "We try to be sensitive to employee morale around here. The chief employees being John-Boy and me. Christmas music makes him really bitchy. I once saw him throw a live lobster at a CD player after one too many rounds of 'O Tannenbaum.'"

Sally nodded. "Chefs can be so temperamental," she said.

"He's usually pretty mellow," Burt told her. "I'm the high-strung one. But that drove him right over the edge. You can never tell what'll set somebody off," he finished.

She found the casual remark unsettling, but shook off the shiver. "For me, it's John-Boy's tortilla soup," she said. "The very thought of it makes me want to offer myself up as his love slave."

Burt raised his eyebrows and offered a very small smile. "That job's taken, thank you very much, Sally," he said. "But after what you've been through, I'll overlook the suggestion. In fact, you can even have seconds if you want. Don't tell Delice."

Delice, Burt's cousin and more-or-less silent partner in the café, was famous for never comping a morsel of food or drink to anyone under any circumstances. When her brother and his cops stopped in at the Wrangler, you'd hear her yelling, "No coffee on the house for you freeloaders! If you want to mooch, you can haul your asses down to Dunkin' Donuts!"

But everybody also knew that both the Wrangler and the Yippie I O did a hell of a lot of charitable work. Meals on Wheels and the Salvation Army and the battered women's shelter would have been in deep trouble without the help they got from the Langhams.

Sally looked around while she waited for Whitebird. She loved the Yippie I O, with its incredible bar (vintage cowboy boots in Lucite, topped with a swoosh of crimson lacquer counter), the high tin ceiling, the sky-blue cloud-painted walls, and Moostapha, the fez-wearing moose head over the pizza oven. For the first time, it occurred to her to wonder whether Jimbo Perrine had been responsible for that particular piece of expert taxidermy. She motioned Burt over.

"I'm curious. Where'd you get Moostapha?" she asked him.

"Actually, my dad gave him to us as a restaurant-warming present. He used to hang over the mantel at my family's place out on Lone Tree Creek." Burt had grown up on a ranch near Cheyenne. He liked to observe that his upbringing hadn't been able to make him a heterosexual, but he'd by God never be a vegetarian. "I knew he would be perfect for this place, so I kind of hinted and hinted until he had the big idea. Dad shot him himself," Burt said proudly.

"Any idea who did the mount?" Sally asked.

"Couldn't say, but it must have been a long time ago, since I can't remember a time the moose wasn't glowering down at us as we opened our Christmas presents. I assume some taxidermist in Cheyenne did the work. It was actually really generous of my dad to give him to us. I mean, do you have any idea what it would cost to buy something like that?"

"Tell me," said Sally.

"I checked it out on eBay. They've got moose heads up for bid at everywhere from five hundred dollars for some moth-eaten relic to twenty-five hundred bucks for a prime specimen."

"I guess it's a niche market," said Sally.

"Yeah, but you'd be surprised. We've had customers come in here and offer us a grand right off the bat. One old guy came in with this little blonde, ordered four vodka martinis, a hundred-dollar bottle of wine and a couple of bloody steaks, and decided he wasn't leaving without the moose. Wanted to give us an absurd amount of money. I was almost tempted to take it, but, after all, Moostapha's family," Burt told her.

"Who's family?" asked Randy Whitebird, striding up to the table.

Ever the gracious host, Burt refrained from telling him it was none of his damned business, as Sally would have been inclined to do. "That there moose," he said, pointing to the wall.

Whitebird sniffed and stood up straighter, thought a moment. "You're right," he said, "All living creatures are family. And, of course, that particular family member would probably be a lot happier roaming free in the forest," he pointed out.

Something flickered in Burt's eyes, but again he showed

restraint, pulled out a chair for the self-appointed champion of fez-wearing moose heads, and set menus in front of them.

Whitebird scanned the menu. "You do have something for vegetarians besides"—he looked again— "grilled cheese?" he asked.

"Today at lunch we're doing a blue corn crepe with black beans and roasted peppers," Burt replied. "But if you're not vegan, don't rule out the grilled cheese. It's an assortment of three mini-sandwiches—cheddar and apples on dark pumpernickel, brie and tomatoes on sourdough, and jarlsberg and mushrooms on swirl rye. Comes with our confetti slaw or a side salad. We don't get many complaints," he finished, unable to repress a small sniff of his own.

Sally ordered the tortilla soup. Whitebird went for the grilled cheese. "I'm a big guy," he told Sally. "I have to work at getting enough protein."

You had to give him credit for not being a purist. And he was indeed big, and not a trial on the eyes, if you liked the type. For her part, she had a hard time getting beyond the beads (and they weren't, as Sally had originally thought, on a leather thong, but were instead strung on a piece of nylon cord. No animal products visible). Still, she could see the appeal of him, barrel-chested, long-legged, with lots of wavy salt-and-pepper hair and crinkly blue eyes. He used the eyes on her now, radiating warmth, and a voice that ran to gravelly. "I'm glad we could get together. And glad you're doing this book. Nina was fond of you."

Sally engaged her bullshit detector. "Thanks. I liked her, too, though I'd only known her a short time. How long did you work with her?"

"Just six months. But we'd met a year before that, in Hawaii. We were guests at the home of a mutual friend. Felt like fate to me," he said, his eyes misting slightly.

"Fate? Why?"

A waiter in a white shirt, jeans, boots, and bolo tie brought the beverages: coffee for Sally, a cup of hot water for Whitebird. "Because we'd both made hard journeys to the same place. Nina and I came from the same generation. We were both Western kids—I grew up in San Antonio, and she was from New Mexico. We were both idealists in our way.

"I was raised to be a patriot, man," he explained. "I did a pretty good job for a long time. Spent six years in the army Rangers, givin' it up for my country."

"Were you in Vietnam?" she asked.

"Yeah," he said, looking away. "And other places. It's not something I talk about a lot," he finished vaguely.

"A lot of guys came home not wanting to talk about it at all," Sally prompted.

"A lot of guys got pretty fucked up," he responded. "Me, too, for a while. But then I realized it wasn't me. It was the country. Got home in 1970, just in time for Cambodia, which was no surprise to me, I can tell you, and Kent State and Jackson State, which were. Couldn't believe the government would shoot at our own citizens, until I got a bayonet in the belly at a campus protest. Decided right then and there, as I was bandaging up my gut, that I'd take all the nasty, nasty things Uncle Sugar taught me and use 'em on behalf of The People."

"Which people?" Sally asked.

"*The*," Whitebird answered. "You know. The oppressed masses. Back in the early seventies, they were everywhere. In the South. On the Indian reservations. In the beat-up factory towns. Fight the underground guerrilla war that would liberate 'em all," he said, taking a sip of hot water.

"Where'd you do this?" Sally asked.

"Here and there," he said, keeping it vague. "You'd be surprised how many of us there were. People who knew how to do everything from blowing up an office complex the size of Fort Union, to poisoning the water supply of an average-size city. Guys with Ph.D.s in chemistry and physics and molecular biology, looking to smash the state. Girls who wanted to learn how to stick a knife in somebody and walk away before the target started bleeding to death. I watched the network grow. The more paranoid the government got about the underground, the more people they drove into it. And we had some decent financial backing from rich radicals," he said.

"Like Nina Cruz," Sally said.

"Mentioning no names," Whitebird said. "But I can say we listened to a lot of her music."

It occurred to Sally that neither Whitebird nor Kali had been in evidence the day she'd been out to Shady Grove to start her research. Cat had made good on her plan to evict the last of the Dub-Dubs. "I didn't see you out at Shady Grove. I take it you've found someplace to stay in town," she said.

"No choice. Cat said go, so I went. Didn't feel like crashing in the office with the others, so I just rented a studio apartment for the month. It's not so bad. It was pretty painful being out there without Nina. Not to mention all the cops stomping around," he said.

"Did you ever do anything back in the day that put the government on your trail?" she asked.

"No idea, man," he said, looking down as he fingered his beads, then looking up. "Never did anything that got me caught." He grinned.

Sally smiled back, wondering if she was starting to be charmed by him. For now, they both appeared to be playing along. "And eventually you surfaced back into the straight world," she said.

Now, Whitebird laughed. "Oh yeah. You could say that. I'd made some great contacts in the movement. First job I got was in a Wall Street brokerage firm. I turned out to be okay at the financial stuff, but better at public relations."

"Wow!" said Sally. "From the Symbionese Liberation Army to flacking for the establishment. Pretty rad transformation."

"Not really," Whitebird answered. "Think of Jerry Rubin. I'd figured out that we couldn't beat 'em, so I joined 'em. It was a matter of having a long-term plan. By the time I started working on Wall Street, I'd had enough of what we used to call creative violence. I figured I could build up a rep in the PR business, and then use my powers for good."

Sally reminded herself that the guy had been an Airborne Ranger. Those guys learned how to jump out of planes when there didn't look to be any place to land, to survive in the jungle on lichens and leeches, to kill with their bare hands.

Some of them, she imagined, had ended up as mercenaries or worse. Randy Whitebird had been a dangerous man, and might still be. "And that's what you're doing now?" she asked.

"Like I said, I'd had enough of creative violence. That's why I changed my name to 'Whitebird,'" he said. Another grin. "From Weissberg."

Probably not many Jews in the Rangers. And now, one more Anglicized brother for the melting pot. Sally had to grin herself, but then she got serious. "There sure was a lot of crap in the left, back in the late sixties and early seventies, about how great violence was. That, as much as the government repression, probably killed the movement," she observed.

"Yeah. And like everybody I met when I was under, I bought it for a while. But anybody who got woken up in the sixties, like I did, and managed to live as long as I have, has to travel the long and winding road. Mine's led to environmental advocacy, with an emphasis on animal rights. Over the years, I've worked my way up in corporate PR, but I've always done pro bono stuff for causes I support. I've just been waiting for the chance to cash in my stake, and use my skills and experience for things I really care about."

The waiter brought their lunches. Whitebird looked his sandwich platter over, then smiled at the waiter and said, "This looks great. Thank the maître d' for the suggestion."

Suddenly, he looked like a man accustomed to eating in nice places, the suit he'd once been, rather than the aging hipster he'd played so far. A chameleon, this one.

Impossibly fragrant steam rose from Sally's bowl. She took a spoonful of soup and almost moaned. She was pretty sure that in all her years of bumping around the West, she'd never encountered a tortilla soup to stand up to John-Boy's. They ought to put it in cartons and franchise it out. That'd ruin it for sure.

But back to business, she thought, noting that Whitebird seemed to be making pretty quick work of his grilled cheese deluxe. "Why animal rights?" she asked him.

"Why not?" he answered. "You're a feminist, right?"

"Yes," she answered warily, pretty sure where this argument was going to go.

"Feminism," he said, gobbling the last bite of the brie and tomato sandwich, "is one form of animal rights. We've just broadened the agenda to apply to all sentient beings. Where would you draw the line anyway, Sally?"

There were feminists who'd agree that women and animals ought to have the same rights. Nina Cruz had been such a one, but Sally wasn't with them. She figured that when it came, say, to the right to vote, or hold property, the line was pretty damned easy to draw. She shrugged and opted for Whitebird's protective vagueness. "Reasonable people might differ."

"And so they do," he said, opting for a diplomatic answer of his own. "So it's pretty amazing when you meet somebody whose ideas and passions match your own perfectly. That's where fate came walking onto the lanai at my friend's place on Maui, in the person of Nina Cruz. I'd never met anybody I clicked with so totally at first sight."

"Emotionally as well as politically," Sally said.

He nodded sadly. "Yeah. Man. Whew," he took the napkin out of his lap and dabbed at his eyes.

The man was clearly grieving, and his sorrow touched Sally's heart. She'd encountered Randy Whitebird exactly twice before, once on the horrible day of the tragedy, and again at the benefit-planning lunch. He'd been distracted, freaked out, self-protective at Shady Grove, and she began to understand the strength with which he'd felt about Nina. Give him the benefit of the doubt—he'd gone running out into the snow to try to help her.

Yet so far, she'd approached Randy Whitebird as somebody who deserved her disdain at least, her animosity at worst. And she knew why. Before she'd met Whitebird, the only report she'd had on him was from Stone Jackson, a far-from-objective source, but a person whom Sally was perhaps too inclined to please. Was it prudent to take an ex-husband's word about his ex-wife's latest lover? "So you and Nina fell in love, and you followed her to Wyoming, to work with her in setting up the Wild West."

"I'd have followed her to Antarctica," he said. "But it took a while. I was living in San Francisco at the time. Had a few things to wrap up before I could get here. That turned out to be a bummer in a lot of ways."

"How so?" Sally asked.

"Put it this way," said Whitebird. "Nina was the most compassionate creature on the planet, and that could be a problem. People just flocked to her, and some of them couldn't figure out when it was time to split. She had a really tough time breaking off things that were over."

Except, of course, in the case of Thomas Jackson. Or then again, maybe not. "So by the time you got to Shady Grove, some of her hangers-on were still hanging around," Sally said.

Whitebird gave a short laugh. "Oh yeah. I mean, yeah. Some of 'em were pretty cool, of course, like Nels Willen and Stone Jackson. But jeez, others. You met Kali."

"Nina's right-hand woman," said Sally.

Whitebird considered his response. "Yeah. They'd done a lot of work together. And don't get me wrong, I know they were involved for a long time. But that was one scene that was played out, way before Nina and I ever met. Kali just wouldn't let go, and Nina couldn't figure out how to cut her loose. I had to take matters into my own hands, man. The night I got here, Kali's stuff was still in Nina's bedroom. I just packed it up and moved it out, and that was that. Nina was grateful, but she couldn't manage to kiss her off entirely. She said she'd talked it over with Kali, and that Kali accepted that their personal thing was over, but she wanted to stay on and at least get Wild West off the ground. Nina agreed."

"That put you in an awkward position," Sally observed.

"I didn't dig it, but what could I do? It was what she wanted, and I wasn't about to get all caveman about her being my woman now, et cetera, et cetera. So I said I'd do what I could to work with Kali."

"Tough," Sally sympathized.

"No shit, Baba Ji," said Whitebird. "The woman kept pushing the boundaries. I like to get up real early, do a little meditation, a little yoga, make a few phone calls, get a head start on the day. Nina liked to sleep a little later. In fact, some days, especially after she'd had one of her 'spells,' she'd stay in bed half the morning."

"Spells?" Sally asked.

"Yes. Of course, at the time nobody would have dreamed she had mad cow disease, but she clearly had something wrong with her. Headaches, forgetfulness, fatigue, mood swings, all that kind of thing. But she also had moments of complete confusion, and sometimes that led to ugly outbursts she couldn't remember later. I was worried she might have a brain tumor. I tried to take care of her. Of course, so did a lot of other people.

"Kali just plain hated to let Nina out of her sight. And mornings were the worst. Can't tell you how many times I went upstairs to see if she was awake, and found Kali sitting on our bed—our bed!—or coming out of the room after some cozy little chat. Nina didn't have the guts to make her stop."

Sally could guess what came next. "So it was up to you to step in," she said.

He nodded. "Once Nina started talking about the benefit, I decided that gave me a timetable. Kali handled the books for Wild West, and I figured I'd take a couple of months to familiarize myself with that stuff. We'd get through the benefit, then I'd tell Kali to take a walk. I'd make Nina go to a neurologist, find out what was wrong, get it taken care of. Then we could get on with our lives."

He looked down, swallowed hard. "Losing Nina is just about the toughest thing I've ever had to deal with. Part of me went with her. I doubt I'll be staying on with Wild West after the benefit. My chemistry with Cat sucks, to be honest. But it's also that I've figured out that this isn't my spiritual home. Wyoming doesn't call to me the way it did to Nina. So for now, I'm focusing on this Thanksgiving event, as a way of connecting with her. Carrying on that little piece of the dream is about all I can do."

Sally listened for the false note but couldn't hear it. She wasn't sure this luxury Laramie lunch was buying her much in the way of stuff she'd need for the book. The way Nina's life seemed to have been, a lover like Randy Whitebird, no matter how infatuated, might not merit more than a paragraph. Still, he'd given her some decent sixties background information, a little more insight into Nina's eclectic politics. "And what was the dream?" Sally asked.

"Like I've been telling you, man," said Whitebird. "We shared the dream. Of a world where the rights of all living creatures are respected, where wild animals can be free, and domestic animals are treasured, not exploited. Wyoming's a place where everything from cows and sheep to ducks and deer and elk are born being set up for the slaughter. It's also a gigantic empty place where a few people can make a big difference in the lives of a whole lot of our fellow beings. It's time," he said, a note of zeal creeping into his voice, "to stop the madness, and end the violence."

20

The Grapevine

When the check came, Whitebird said he was sorry, but he'd have to run. Had phone calls to make, e-mails to answer. "My job hasn't gotten any easier, with all this," he explained. "As you heard, Cat wanted all the financial and legal stuff, and I had every intention of giving her everything. But Kali and she have issues with each other, and that means that every time I ask Kali for anything, she's got some objection or problem or question. As if it weren't bad enough to have those two yankin' my chain in different directions, the cops screwed up our computers, poking around. Quartz has been working on it for two days, so I'm hoping he'll have it straightened out by this afternoon, the Goddess willing."

Sally told Whitebird not to worry, that lunch was on her, and she'd see him around. "Let me know if there's anything I can do to help with the benefit," she said.

"Actually, there is. As you'll recall, a portion of the proceeds will go to the widow of that hunter who was shot."

"I know," said Sally. "I was the one who made the first call to Arvida Perrine to see how she felt about the idea of being a beneficiary. She said she could use all the help she could get. And then she kind of giggled and said that, after all, Jimbo wouldn't be around to object. I think she's in pretty deep shock, and I wouldn't be surprised if the doctors haven't given her a little something to help her through this."

"No doubt," said Whitebird, waving a hand like the executive whose time was being wasted on trivia. "But the truth is, no one in my office feels comfortable dealing with her."

How, Sally wondered, would the Dub-Dubs feel about raising money for the Perrine family once the word was out that Jimbo had shot Nina Cruz? Not to mention the fact that they'd have a hell of a PR problem on their hands, dedicating a piece of the action to the loved ones of the very fiend who'd killed the dearly lamented Nina. But Sally didn't give a damn about PR. That was Randy Whitebird's problem. The old corporate spin doctor would be earning his keep in that department. (And what was his keep anyway? Was he a paid employee? Doing some of that pro bono work he'd mentioned?)

As far as Sally was concerned, Arvida and her children were a whole lot needier than the owls or ferrets or whatever creatures stood to reap most of the bounty from the benefit. And Sally had reasons of her own for wanting to talk to Arvida Perrine again. "I'll be glad to act as liaison with Mrs. Perrine," she told Whitebird, reaching into her trusty shoulder bag to dig out her wallet and looking down to count out bills in lieu of working up a problematic poker face.

She could have used the practice. Whitebird gave her a protocol hug and strode off while she was still laying her money down. Seconds later, Delice Langham was looming over her. "What's with you buying lunch for Mr. Woo-woo?" Delice demanded.

"Don't be so snooty, Dee. Mr. Woo-woo did a few tours with the army Airborne Rangers."

Delice's eyes bugged. "The Rangers? You're kidding. Those guys are trained to eat babies."

Sally raised an eyebrow. "He had the grilled cheese. And what are you doing here? This is—what?—Thursday. You're usually over at the Wrangler for the lunch shift."

"I got a craving for tortilla soup," said Delice. "I don't

know what John-Boy puts in the broth, but he should probably be prosecuted for pushing addictive drugs." She lowered
her voice. "Did you hear? They've got the gun that killed
Nina Cruz, and it's—"

"Shhh!" Sally stage-whispered. "Don't say another word.
How did you find out?"

Delice narrowed her eyes. "How did *you*?"

"Who says I've heard anything?" Sally tried.

Delice put her hands on her hips, bracelets jangling.
"Give me a break, Mustang," she said. But then she reached
out, grabbed Sally by the arm, and said, "Maybe we should
discuss this someplace a little more private," and dragged
her through the hectic kitchen, out the back door, through a
little courtyard, and into a tiny utilitarian office. Two desks,
two chairs. They sat in the chairs and put their feet up on the
desks.

Sally glared at Delice. "I know nothing," she said, doing
her best Sergeant Schultz from *Hogan's Heroes*. "Leave me
alone."

Delice pursed her lips. "Okay," she finally said. "Let's say
you don't. In that case, are you interested in hearing what I
heard?"

"Just spill it," Sally said. They shared a penchant for high
drama, but enough was enough.

"We've been working up a new marketing approach for
the restaurants. I was down dropping off the ad copy at the
Boomerang about an hour ago when they got a press release
from my brother's office, saying that the murder weapon had
been a Marlin 336 that belonged to Jimbo Perrine.

"Of course, Jimbo hated uppity women," Delice said.
"And Californians and vegetarians, and anybody to the left
of John Ashcroft. But he'd have been hard put to get rid of
everybody who put a bug up his butt. You ask yourself, why
would Jimbo have gone and shot Nina Cruz? And then,
when he turns up dead himself, the answer's obvious: somebody paid him to shoot her, then decided to eliminate the
risk that he'd talk."

It did seem obvious. Right? Jimbo had evidently been
hard up for money. His neck was as red as they came. He

had lots of guns, which he adored as much as he loved shooting them.

Which still didn't quite add up to murder, in Sally's mind. As far as she knew, Jimbo, in forty-something years of life in Laramie, Wyoming, had shot and owned many a firearm, but had never killed a person. Could he really have been capable of doing such a thing?

But then, she'd known him. She'd been in a band with him, for Christ's sake. He was a bigot and a slob, but so, probably, were a quarter of the adult population of the Rocky Mountain region. She could easily imagine Jimbo tanking up on cheap beer and blasting a hole in his TV set during a Hillary Clinton press conference. She could not visualize him picking up a gun, killing Nina Cruz, and calmly collecting the fee for the hit.

But was Sally any judge in the matter? As Delice was wont to remind her, Sally was a real sap when it came to musicians, who were, as a species, among the lowest snail-sucking scum of the planet. Your average drummer or bass player or guitar jock had the libido of a jackrabbit and the morals of a jackal. Your below-average rock 'n' roller probably ought to be wearing a Hannibal Lecter mask. But Sally liked most of them anyway, and had loved an above-average number. Musicians were, alas, her weakness. So far, not fatal. So far. If Ted Bundy had been a guitar player, Sally Alder would probably be pushing up daisies with teeth marks on her ass.

And speaking of musicians, she wondered how the Millionaires would react to the latest development in the Nina Cruz saga? She wouldn't have long to find out. They had practice tonight. If Dickie had known yesterday, and Delice knew by today, Dwayne Langham would surely have the word within hours. In fact, the entire Langham clan, down to second cousins, would doubtless be speculating on the type of ammunition Jimbo had used before the story even hit the dinner-hour newscasts from Casper and Cheyenne, scooping the *Boomerang* by a whole news cycle.

"One more thing. Did you get anything out of my friend at the vet lab?" Delice asked.

"Nothing to speak of," Sally said.

"Look, I gotta go," she told Delice. "I'm a college professor, right? Got a class to teach this afternoon, office hours, meetings."

"Yeah," said Delice, "you professors work so hard, it makes me weep. Just remember, while you're up at the university eating bonbons, I'll be down at the Wrangler humping cases of beer and beating up drunks."

They grinned at each other as they walked back through the courtyard and into the Yippie I O's open kitchen.

"Hey, Sally!" said Pammie Montgomery from a counter where she was putting the finishing touches on an exquisite sculpture involving fresh spinach leaves and colorful fruits and vegetables.

"How's it going, Pammie?" Sally asked.

"Going great!" came the reply, as Pammie passed off the sculpture, pulled a chilled plate off a stack and moved on to her next composition. "Are you coming to Thanksgiving?" she asked.

"I haven't heard anything about it," Sally said.

"Well, Cat Cruz has been out of town," Pammie said, "and she only called me about the job on Monday. But I'm sure you're invited. It's for everybody involved in the Night for Nina who doesn't have other plans. Some of the artists and most of the crew are getting to town a day or two before the Friday-night gig. They've gotta do setups and sound and light checks and security run-throughs and all that kind of stuff," she said. "Probably they're sensible enough to worry about the weather. Anyway, they've booked pretty much every room at the Holiday Inn, and they'll park the touring buses out there. So Cat decided to throw a Thanksgiving dinner in an event room."

"Wow," said Sally. "How many people are you feeding?"

"She's got a list of about fifty at this point, but there could be more. Cat mentioned that she wanted to invite the police and security people to feel free to come by for a bite. From what I've seen, those guys can pack in enough for three people, and there could be a couple dozen or more of them. So I'm just going to make enough food for a hundred and fifty, and what doesn't get eaten there, we can take to the women's shelter and Travelers' Aid."

"That's a huge job!" Sally said. "Didn't you just start out in the catering business?"

"Sure," Pammie said cheerfully. "It'll be a challenge. But I'm hiring some helpers, and I can draft some volunteers, and I'll be really well organized." She snuck a look at Delice, who was temporarily distracted from the conversation, cadging a cup of tortilla soup from the chef. "Plus John-Boy and Burt are letting me use the kitchen here, after hours, for the advance prep work. It'll be fine. You don't turn down the gig that could lead to fame and fortune just because you haven't done anything that big before."

Sally tried to imagine a couple dozen Wyoming cops chowing down on brown rice casserole instead of turkey and dressing for their Thanksgiving dinner. "Is this a vegetarian feast?" she asked.

"Cat wanted something for everyone, so we'll have lots of options. Turkey and all the trimmings for the carnivores, a bunch of vegan goodies and veggie side dishes, great desserts. Not quite sure what I'll do for the people who don't eat cooked food—I mean, like, Thanksgiving's all about cooking! But I've got a few ideas. Any requests?"

"I feel very safe leaving the menu in your hands," said Sally. "But I'm partial to pecan pie."

"Quartz is handling the pies," said Pammie. "I'll let him know, if I see him. He's been real busy lately."

"Trouble in paradise?" Sally couldn't help asking.

"Oh no!" Pammie said. "It's just that he's working really hard. Putting in a lot of hours at the office," she said.

"I hear things are getting cozy there," Sally said.

"Yeah," Pammie answered. "A little too cozy for him. When Kali moved in, he decided to find another place to crash. He's got a room in a house with some friends of mine. But he's hardly ever there, between the time he's in the office and going back and forth to Shady Grove."

"Shady Grove?" Sally said.

"Uh-huh. His bus is still there, plus Cat has him working on getting access to Nina's computer records. I guess it's a real trick, because he's been out there three or four times, and he's gotta go back again. But at least he's got a key, so he can come and go without needing her to be there."

"That's enough chatting up the help," Delice said as she returned with her soup, hustling Sally out of the kitchen. "Miss Pamela M's got salads to plate."

By the time she got to her office, Sally had an hour before class. She had a huge stack of mail to open, maybe thirty e-mail messages in her inbox, and, of course, a final review of her lecture and discussion notes for today's class. She spent twenty minutes looking over her class notes, realized she had the material well in hand, put the pages back in their folder, and tucked the folder in her bag. She grabbed the mail and began sorting, setting the journals she really intended to read on top of the heap of previous volumes she still meant to get around to, throwing out ads for journal subscriptions and books she'd had no prayer of reading, discarding announcements of employee-training sessions (she ought to learn how to create her own websites, but she probably wouldn't), and tossing away invitations to receptions and potluck suppers she wouldn't attend. What remained were a request to review a manuscript, an invitation to give a lecture at a liberal arts college in the Midwest (they wanted to know what kind of honorarium she wanted; she always tried to highball that kind of request, and then found out they'd been willing to pay more), and two royalty checks (yahoo!). She glared at her computer screen, but the new e-mail messages didn't go away. She figured that the human race had waited thousands of years for electronic mail; her e-mail could wait a couple of hours longer.

She dialed the number at Shady Grove, hoping she might catch Quartz out there and schedule a time to talk.

An old-fashioned answering machine picked up on the fourth ring, and Nina Cruz's voice came eerily across the wires. "You've reached Nina's machine. Please leave a message. Peace."

Quartz probably wouldn't be picking up messages off Nina's machine, so she didn't leave one. She called the Wild West office, but he wasn't there either. Lark answered with a mellow, New Age, serenity voice, but when Sally identified herself, the yoga-class tone gave way to something more like an irate housewife blowing off a phone solicitor. Sally would have to try to get a home number for Quartz from Pammie, or leave a message with her.

Then she called the Perrine household. Arvida's mother answered, out of breath. But then, given the woman's bulk, it was probably an effort for her to hit the mute switch on the remote, get up out of a chair, and answer a phone. She reported that Arvida was resting. Sally decided to go out on a limb. "Ma'am," she said, realizing that she didn't know the mother's name, "my name is Sally Alder. I don't know if you remember me. I was in a band with your son-in-law. I was at the hospital," she began, knowing she couldn't bring herself to say, "the day Jimbo died."

"Oh, I remember you," said the mother. "You brought us dinner. We never did pay you for that."

"Please, don't think about it. I wish there was more I could do. I called today because I'm working with the Wild West people, and I've been in contact with Arvida about the benefit."

"The benefit? Oh, yes. Well, I don't reckon they'll be wanting to send any of that money my daughter's way once they see the six o'clock news," the woman said, sounding exhausted and near tears.

"I'm so sorry," said Sally, "I'm aware of recent developments in the Nina Cruz case. I can't speak for the foundation, but as far as I'm concerned, your daughter and her children need support more than ever. I'm going to do whatever I can to make sure that she gets the help she needs."

"Thank you," said the mother. "I'll give her that message."

Sally knew that Arvida's mother was about ready to end the conversation, but she wanted to get another word in. "I'd like to drop by sometime and see her. In the meantime, is there anything I can do?"

Arvida's mother wheezed a moment in thought. "It's good of you to offer," she said at last. "The poor girl's all tuckered out. Jimbo was a hard man, and he did love those guns of his, but we never imagined this. She's had a real time of it since the po-lice came the first time, and every time they came back it just got worse. They had her half crazy looking for the combination to the lock on that gun room of his, and she went through pretty near every piece of paper in the house and never did manage to find it. They finally had to break down the door, and they left a bigger mess than you ever did see.

"The doctor's keeping her sedated right now. She might be ready for a visit in a day or two. I'm here helping out, making sure the kids get their dinner and like that."

"Could I bring by some food or anything?" Sally asked.

"Oh honey, since Jimbo passed, we've been buried in food. Seems like everybody in Laramie has brought by a hot dish or a plate of cookies or a ham or whatever. People we don't even know. Thanks, but that ain't necessary. I will let Arvida know you called, though. And you come see her later on. I expect she'll be glad of the company."

21

Protein

The phone in her office was ringing madly as Sally tried to unlock the door while juggling her overstuffed tote bag and a big stack of freshly collected term papers. She dumped the papers on top of everything else on the desk and snatched up the phone, just as her voice message service was about to pick up.

Cat Cruz got right to the point. "Just tell me one thing," Cat said. "In your opinion, is there any possibility that Mrs. Perrine could have used her husband's gun to kill my sister?"

Sally's jaw dropped. The idea absolutely hadn't occurred to her. "I don't really know Arvida Perrine," she told Cat, "but I haven't seen or heard a thing that would make me think that was even remotely possible. Plus, I happened to talk to her mother yesterday, and she told me that when the police came to the house and wanted to get into Jimbo's gun room, Arvida didn't know the combination to the lock, and never managed to find it. So I don't believe she would have had access to the gun, let alone used it. Why would you ask?"

Cat sighed. "I had a speaker phone call from the Wild West staff. They'd held a meeting, and they all agreed that it was 'absolutely unacceptable,' under the circumstances, for any of the proceeds from the benefit to go to the family of the man who had murdered Nina. Kali and Lark were nearly hysterical on the subject. Kali was ranting about the fact that Mrs. Perrine was probably an accomplice in the whole thing anyway. Whitebird was a little calmer, but he pointed out that at the very least, the public relations side of things would be a nightmare."

"And what did they say about the fact that Jimbo himself was killed?"

"Lark said that it was undoubtedly divine justice, a hunting accident that turned the hunter into the game. A case of instant karma."

"They're full of shit," Sally said.

"Undoubtedly," said Cat. "But what's your take on the widow?"

Sally gave it a moment's thought. "I think she didn't know a thing about it. She's in utter shock, maybe teetering on the edge of a breakdown, not to mention up to her eyeballs in financial problems. The sheriff told me she was planning to sell the guns to pay Jimbo's debts, but as I think of it, if the police hang on to those guns for any length of time, she'll be screwed. She's supposedly also going to have to sell his taxidermy collection, but face it. We're talking about stuffed heads and mounted-up dead animals here. Those things are liable to take some time to move."

"So you're saying Mrs. Perrine's in dire trouble, needs help. In a sense, this woman is as much a victim of her husband as my sister was."

Sally thought about that. "Yeah, I guess." But the idea made her uncomfortable. Jimbo had been a certified sexist pig, to be sure, but she still had her doubts that he'd been a murderer.

"What do you think Nina would have done, in this situation?" Cat asked.

Without hesitation, Sally said, "She would have said that sisters have to help each other, and would have written a check."

"Yep. That's what I think, too," Cat said. "So I'm inclined

to go ahead with the plan to cut the Perrine woman in on the profits. If there are any profits, by the time this insanity plays out."

"Yeah, I guess you've got about as big a PR mess as you need," Sally said.

Cat laughed, not heartily, but it was a recognizable laugh nonetheless. "Sally, I've been in the philanthropy business a long time, and let me tell you something. Nobody's pure, even the most obvious victims of persecution. Hungry village kids in India beat up smaller hungry village kids."

"You blow my mind," Sally told her.

"I might be losing *my* mind," Cat replied. "But I swear, the minute I got off the phone with that detective, before those idiots called from Laramie, I heard Nina's voice in my head, telling me to live for peace, not anger and vengeance. Taking care of Mrs. Perrine and her kids is something Nina would have done. So we'll go ahead as planned. Whitebird can deal with the fallout. He can take the woman an apple pie with a freaking American flag stuck in it, if need be."

"The last thing they need is food," Sally told Cat, "but I catch your drift." She paused, then brought up the delicate subject on her mind. "I hate to mention this," she said, "but there's this whole question of why Jimbo was shot. That was no hunting accident."

"No," Cat agreed. "Seems obvious. Somebody paid him to kill my sister, then got rid of him. The cops are trying to figure out who, and why. Meanwhile, I've got Quartz working on the foundation's computer files and trying to hack into Nina's e-mail. I want answers, and I want them before the benefit." For the first time, Cat Cruz sounded worn down. "I don't know how much longer I can take this," she said with a hitch in her voice. "It's getting really hard. Part of me just wants to shut down this operation and go sit on a beach somewhere and cry."

"You could do that," Sally said. "I certainly wouldn't blame you, and neither would any reasonable person."

Cat gave a shaky laugh. "Right. But then, we're talking about memorializing Angelina Cruz here. Not many people would have called her 'reasonable.' I owe it to my crazy little sister to put on the big show. After that, I guess we'll just have to see."

"Does Stone know about the gun?" Sally asked, thinking it might do Cat good to talk to him.

"I don't know," Cat answered. "I'd better give him a call. I'll see you next week."

No sooner had she hung up than the phone rang again. This time it was Sam Branch, sounding as if he'd swallowed a porcupine. "Band practice is off tonight," he croaked. "I've got a fever of a hundred and two degrees."

"God, I hope I don't get whatever it is you've got," said Sally, who dreaded colds and always contracted a touch of paranoia during virus season.

"This from the anthrax poster girl," Sam said.

"It was talcum powder," Sally said.

"How about a little sympathy? But besides the fact that I feel like shit, Dwayne's having second thoughts about the gig. You gotta admit, it's a real cluster fuck, Mustang. You've really outdone yourself this time."

"Outdone myself! What the hell have I done?" she exclaimed.

"Put it this way. You're the only chick I know who could have dragged us into making an appearance on behalf of some California Bambi lovers' outfit, for starters. Then, before we even hear about your grand plan, one of the eco-freaks is killed, and next our bass player gets shot himself, and now they're saying it was Jimbo who blew away Nina Cruz. Then there's the mad cow showing up in our little community. And with all of that, we're still practicing away, acting like it's just another gig at the Elks Club. Unbelievable."

"You act like I planned the whole thing, Sam," Sally said. "That's ridiculous."

"No. What's ridiculous is your fantasy of playing with Stone Jackson, come hell or high water. Get a clue: He didn't show this week. If he can't be bothered to rehearse with us even once before the gig, we're off the bus."

True. Stone had called to say he couldn't make it to Laramie. Something about business to attend to with the Busted Heart Ranch. She'd been disappointed, to say the least.

Sam continued. "Has it somehow slipped your mind that two people have gotten killed, and you yourself recently received an extremely creepy care package? How stupid is it to still be hanging in on this one?"

Sam almost sounded as if he was worried about her. But she knew him better than that, of course. "I know you pride yourself on being pragmatic to the point of complete self-absorption, Sam Branch. But in this case, I have only two words to say to you: Arvida Perrine."

"Forget it. No way Arvida gets a piece of the take now. The tofu eaters will cut her off quicker than you can say 'Tom Eagleton,'" Sam said.

"I just talked to Nina's sister," Sally told him, feeling a wee bit smug at imparting the news. "No change in plans. They're sticking by the suffering widow."

"Yeah. Well, that's just peachy," Sam said. "I still don't know whether the boys will go for it."

"Tell them this. There's going to be a big bash the day before, for performers and crew. They'll get the fanciest Thanksgiving dinner in town, and they'll get to eat it with Emmylou."

"I refrain," said Sam, "from making the obvious comment."

Sally took the receiver from her ear and silently glared at the phone.

"You know," Sam said, "Jimbo was a racist and a sexist and a douche bag and all that, but I still can't feature him plugging Nina Cruz. It's not like she was an eight-point buck or something."

Sally had doubts of her own. She played devil's advocate. "Come on, Sam. You heard the way he talked about her, getting what she deserved and so forth."

"It's a free country. He can say whatever he wants. That doesn't mean he was a murderer. If I had a dollar for every time you've threatened to shoot me, I could buy Wyoming and Montana, too. And that doesn't even count the times you told me killin' was too good for me," he added.

"Jimbo was broke," Sally pointed out. "Somebody could have offered him a whole lot of money."

"Oh yeah?" Sam countered. "Well then, where is that money? I hear Arvida's about to be out on the street. If Jimbo scored big before he died, he must have hid the cash."

Sally thought about it. Sam was right. Things weren't adding up. "Maybe he didn't collect. Maybe that's why he was out in Albany the day he was killed."

Sam sneezed loudly. "Yeah. Whatever."

"Wait one more minute. I hate to say it, but I'm with you," Sally told Sam. "However big an asshole he was, I just don't see Jimbo having pulled the trigger on a human being."

He sneezed again. "You play detective. I gotta go back to bed."

Their conversation kicked off nearly a week of shitty weather and heavy speculation. By Friday afternoon, the cloud ceiling had lowered to about a foot above everybody's head, and it pretty much stayed there. Soon, wet snow mixed with sleet began falling, then the wind picked up, and icy crystals swirled and eddied over the ground, sticking here and there in piles and swales. It warmed up enough by Monday morning for some of the snow to melt, but another front rushed in, blowing sixty-mile-an-hour bone-shaking winds, and freezing the slush on the ground into treacherous patches of black ice. The Albany County Sheriff's Department was stretched to the limit handling one-car spin-outs and rollovers, two-car skid collisions, and cell phone calls from people who'd slipped on sidewalks and broken elbows and hips.

The Thursday before Thanksgiving, Sally opened one eye to watch Hawk waking up grouchy. He looked out the window, took note of the light snow falling, and cursed. "Look at that frigging weather. Now I'm gonna have to cancel the all-day field trip I planned for my graduate class. I'll be one major assignment short for the term and have to shuck and jive my way through the rest of the semester."

Sally listened to the first round of complaining, assessed the extent of his surly mood. She didn't have class until the afternoon, but she decided it would be worth slip-sliding through the snow to get the hell out of the house and spend the morning in her office. Still, she suggested he pick her up at noon and take her to lunch at the Wrangler.

"I'd rather go to El Conquistador," he said crankily. "I don't feel like a grease burger."

Opting for lard-laden beans and deep-fried tortillas over burgers and onion rings wasn't exactly choosing the path of virtue.

She had a productive morning, grading her way to the bottom of the stack of term papers, plowing through mail and messages, returning phone calls. She tried again and failed to find Quartz, but this time, when she called the Wild West office, Kali answered.

"I'm so glad I got you," Sally told her, trying for cordial, but wondering if she'd overdone it and ended up more in the range of effusive. "As you've probably heard, I've begun working on a biography of Nina. I'm hoping to interview as many of the people who were close to her as I can, and I've talked with most of your colleagues already. They've been very forthcoming, although of course there are so many different angles," Sally said, hoping that might inspire Kali to want to tell her version of the story. "I know how busy you must be, right now, but I'd really like to get your thoughts." She put a little extra emphasis on the word *your*.

"There are a lot of demands on my time," Kali answered in her usual whisper. "I don't really know when I'd be able to fit you in."

"Just half an hour would be great," Sally said, hoping that once she got Kali talking, she'd be able to keep her going. "You were so important to her. I've learned a lot from my conversations with others, but it's so hard to separate feelings and biases from fact. It's really crucial to me to have your perspective." Sally was determined to let Kali know that she was getting other sides of the story of Nina Cruz, and given the sniping and jealousies she'd seen and heard about, she figured Kali would take the bait. But was that laying it on too thick?

Maybe it was. Or maybe not. Kali hesitated before responding, and when she did, there was a note of wariness in her voice. "All right. Half an hour"—shuffling of papers—"at eleven, on Monday. I'm going out of town for a few days, and will be very busy when I get back, so don't be late." She hung up without bothering to wait for Sally's answer.

Leave town? The week before the benefit? Where would Kali be going at such a time, and why?

"She may not be going anywhere in this god-awful weather," Hawk observed when Sally briefed him over chips and fire-breathing salsa at El Conquistador. "In case you haven't checked your e-mail, they're closing the university early this afternoon. They're predicting gale-force winds and snow mixed with rain. Anyway, looks like both of our classes will be canceled."

"Bummer," she said, and motioned the waitress over to order a Dos Equis with her chicken taco and chile relleno. Hawk opted for a Negra Modelo with his enchilada platter.

El Conquistador wasn't the rumor mill that either the Wrangler or the Yippie I O were (perhaps that had something to do with the presence, or absence, of Delice Langham), but at tables all around Sally and Hawk, people seemed to be offering up their theories on who had shot Jimbo Perrine. A grizzled man in gray twill work pants and shirt, eating tacos with a younger version of himself, claimed to have overheard a state game warden say that the only way to stop poachers was to shoot 'em. And everybody knew how Jimbo felt about legal limits on game. The younger man replied that maybe the answer was to shoot the game wardens.

Sally's cell phone rang.

"Can you turn that stupid thing off?" Hawk said.

She looked at the display. A number she thought she'd dialed sometime, but one she didn't recognize. "I'll be back in a second," she told Hawk, getting up and walking across the restaurant to an empty dining room as she answered the call.

It was Delice's friend from the vet lab. "You didn't ingest any of that nutritional supplement by any chance, did you?" she asked, nerves plain in her voice.

"No," Sally told her. "I only opened the can once, looked at the stuff, and then put the lid back on. I washed my hands a whole bunch after."

"Good," said the woman, sounding relieved. "I wanted to get that squared away first thing. You see, we ran some tests on the powder. It's protein all right," she continued, "but not soy. It's bovine material."

"Bovine? Dried hamburger?" Sally said.

"Hardly. More like bonemeal, spinal cord, organ tissue," said the woman. "We have to run some more tests, but we're concerned that there might be abnormalities in the chemistry."

"What do you mean?" Sally asked.

"Some problems with the proteins. I don't want to say any more, but I did want to get back to you, in case you had more of the stuff. You don't want to keep it around, and we'll want to see if this sample is an anomaly, or if there's a larger problem. We'll be glad to come to your house and pick it up."

"That's all I've got," said Sally. "But there's more of it out at Shady Grove. And I want to make sure I'm understanding you. Problems with the proteins—does that mean you think there are prions in this stuff?"

"I'd rather not speculate," said the woman. "You can understand that the last thing we want to do is cause a panic."

"I won't say anything to anyone. And since I was the one who brought it in, at least tell me this. Are you concerned that this material came from diseased animals?"

"You didn't hear it from me," said the woman. "I'm calling the police now." She hung up.

Sally ended the call and stood a moment, staring at her phone. Experience told her that the counterculture had embraced a lot of wacky ideas about health. She'd known a woman who swore by something she called Magic Mud to cure her children's diaper rashes, and it had turned out to be bentonite clay. Nina Cruz might have thought that cow powder would keep her skin smooth and her joints lubricated. Might have, that is, if she hadn't been a devout vegetarian. She couldn't have known what was in that can. How in the world had she gotten hold of the stuff?

Dickie's cell number was programmed into Sally's phone. He answered on the first ring.

But now people were coming into the empty dining room, seating themselves at tables.

"I've got something I need to talk to you about," Sally told him. "I can't talk now, but I can meet you at the station right after lunch. This is really important, Dick."

He said he'd meet her in half an hour.

"We have to go to the sheriff's office after lunch," she told Hawk, looking around at the crowded restaurant. "I can't explain now."

"Okay," he said. "Should we leave now?"

"Dickie won't be there for a little bit. We might as well eat up."

Somehow, the taco and relleno didn't seem quite so appetizing. But she finished her beer.

Outside, the wind had died down, but the snow had thickened. Hawk and Sally stopped to clear the windows and windshield of Hawk's pickup before taking off for home, snow falling so fast now that his wipers could barely keep up. Visibility was so bad that he had to pump the brakes hard and slide into the other lane at Third and Ivinson to keep from plowing into a skidding minivan.

Sally's purse flopped over, spilling its contents out all over the floor. "Shit," she said, bending down to stuff things back in, a fair undertaking. Later, she would reflect that her overloaded tote bag and the terrible weather had probably saved her life, since she was still bending down when the bullet shattered the back window of the pickup and slammed out the front.

22

Cold Facts

Sally would never know how Hawk did it, but he managed, somehow, to get the truck to the side of the road without further damage. Talk about grace under pressure. Then he was brushing chunks of safety glass out of her hair, and then he was hugging her so hard she thought her ribs would break.

It was some time before she realized she was crying. It would be much longer before she stopped.

Ordinarily, there would have been plenty of witnesses to a shooting in broad daylight, two blocks from the beating heart of downtown Laramie. But the weather had kept most sane people at home, and the fast-falling snow obscured visibility and slowed reaction time. A ski parka–clad woman pushing a very bundled-up child in a baby jogger had seen the glass explode, and she'd stood on the sidewalk and watched a light-colored car veer around Hawk's truck and turn north on Fifth Street. But she'd been so stunned, she hadn't really noted the make or model, let alone the license-plate number. She was the only eyewitness.

The police arrived quickly, closed off four blocks of Ivin-son Street, and got busy working the crime scene. They took about a million pictures of the truck, inside and out, the tire tracks in the snow, the bullet hole in the windshield. While Sally and Hawk demonstrated the positions they'd been in when the shot was fired, a deputy set out to follow the tracks of the light-colored car around the corner at Fifth. He disappeared into the veil of white, only to reappear minutes later with the bad news that the tracks had led back to Third Street, where the driver had evidently turned south. Third Street being one of two or three streets in Laramie that had any kind of traffic that day, more cars had since driven by and obscured the tracks.

And so they'd lost the trail.

Sally thought Scotty Atkins might have left them shivering in the blown-out truck cab, using their discomfort to advantage as he questioned them about the shooting. But Dickie Langham had taken the job of working with them, and he was nothing if not compassionate. He noticed their blue lips and, as soon as he could, took them to his Blazer, where the heater was cranking nicely. For a few minutes, he sat quietly, watching them carefully for signs of shock and hypothermia. Once he was confident that they were thawing out, he observed, "It's a fucking miracle you weren't killed, Sally."

She nodded.

"I've pretty much had it with this whole thing."

"Me too," said Hawk.

"Mind if I smoke?" Dickie asked.

"It's your truck," Sally said.

With hands that trembled a little, he went for his cigarettes, managed to shake one out of the pack, got it lit, shook out the match, blew out a stream of smoke. "Okay. I want you to tell me everything you can remember, from the time you left the restaurant to the moment that bullet hit. Everything."

They told him.

"You didn't notice a car following you? Weren't looking in the rearview, worried somebody might get out of control and rear-end you?" Dickie asked Hawk.

Hawk thought it over. "Yeah, of course I was checking the rearview. And I guess I remember a car there. But I don't recall being too worried about it. I must have decided they were following at a safe distance."

Dickie regarded the glowing tip of his cigarette with narrowed eyes. "You were wrong."

"Evidently," Hawk said.

"Do you remember anything about the car or the driver? Were there any passengers?"

Hawk thought hard. "Nondescript sedan, I think. Not dark, but I can't remember the color. No passengers. But I'm not completely sure. I was pretty busy coping with the guy who skidded out in front of me at the light at Third. You know how it is. You avoid an accident and your adrenaline starts pumping, and it takes a minute to take it all in. Plus Sally was all over the floor dealing with all the crap that had spilled out of that suitcase she carries around."

"Why do you always carry so much shit?" Dickie asked her.

"I don't. Every woman's got a big bag that's the mother ship, full of littler bags you might call the dinghies and dories. Sometimes you can get away with just a lifeboat or a tender."

"Yeah. Well, you're gonna be picking safety glass out of the fleet for the foreseeable. Now you—what do you remember?" Dickie said.

"Clearing off the windows and worrying about the visibility and the traction," Sally replied. "Hawk's the best driver I know, but it's the other fools who scare me. Then Hawk started pumping the brakes to avoid the guy who skidded, my purse capsized, I bent down to try to put everything back, and the next thing I knew I was covered with broken glass."

"Don't worry, honey," said Hawk. "I'm sure my insurance will cover the repairs."

"Very funny," said Sally.

His mouth went hard. "Sorry. Guess I'm just one of those people who cope with attempted murder by making stupid jokes."

She could almost see his internal temperature rise. She'd seen him in this state before. When he got this mad, he had a tendency to break things. She reached for his hands. "We'll get through this."

"Damn straight," he said. "But I might have to shoot somebody before it's all over."

"I wouldn't advise it," said Dickie.

"Oh, go ahead, Hawk. I mean, it's clear guns are a great thing. Why, everybody in Wyoming seems to be shooting somebody this fall. Why should you be any different?" Now it was her voice rising, the pressure building in her chest, lights exploding behind her eyes. "This is just a fabulous flaming festival of shooting and killing and killing and shooting!"

The tears gushed again. Hawk wrapped her up tight, again. It took a while to get her calmed down.

Then, as if he'd waited out her hysteria, Scotty Atkins got in the Blazer, and made them go through the whole sequence of events all over again.

And now Sally said to Dickie, "I need to tell you why I wanted to meet you at your office."

"Does it have something to do with the call I got a little while ago from a woman at the state vet lab?" he asked.

"Yes. So you're aware I took a can of what I thought was some kind of soy powder out there to be tested, and it turned out to be animal product, from cows, they seem to think. And they're worrying about abnormal proteins."

Hawk looked at her in amazement. "That stuff you brought home from Nina's place? The powder you said she used in her breakfast drinks?"

She nodded.

"You didn't actually swallow any of it, did you?" Hawk said.

"No. I kept meaning to whip myself up a power smoothie, but I never got around to it."

"How did you happen to come by it?" Dickie asked.

"Pammie gave it to me," she said. "There's a lot more of it out there."

Scotty stared out the window at the worsening weather. "We'd better get somebody out there before the highway guys close the road."

Dickie picked up his radio transmitter and dispatched a deputy to Albany.

"Would you mind telling me," Scotty asked Sally, "why you took that stuff home with you?"

"I didn't even think about it," Sally said. "It was like borrowing a cup of sugar from the neighbors."

Scotty closed his eyes and ran his hand over his head.

"A cup of sugar," said Dickie. "Fine. But why, then, did you get suspicious enough to take the stuff out to the lab? And why, oh why, oh why, did you choose to withhold from us the fact that you had done so?"

"Because I didn't want to look like a fucking idiot when it turned out to be nothing!" Sally exploded. "Because you've been very clear that you don't want my help, don't want me anywhere near the investigation!"

"Do you recall my telling you that I expected you to tell me anything and everything you learned, with regard to the life and death of Nina Cruz, no matter how insignificant?" Dickie asked her.

"Yes, of course I do. Just before you seized her papers and told me to bug off," Sally answered.

Dickie reached out and took her hand, making her meet his eye. "I'm only going to say this once. Never, ever, withhold information in a police investigation."

"Especially," Scotty added, "when it would appear that somebody has gone from playing tricks on you to trying to kill you."

"Okay," she said. "I'm sorry. Really. You're always accusing me of taking stupid risks, and I guess you've had reason to do that. But isn't it equally foolish for you guys to be holding out on me when I'm obviously in danger? I need to know everything—I mean it, Scotty, no holding back—if I'm going to be able to protect myself. What I don't know *can* hurt me."

Dickie and Scotty exchanged glances. "She's got a point," Dickie said at length, and lit yet one more cigarette soon to be reduced to a crushed-out butt in the Blazer's reeking, overflowing ashtray, a lingering pall of smoke.

Scotty said, "Do I have to recite the warning about leaks and confidentiality and compromising our investigation?"

"No," she said. "You don't."

"I guess not. All right." He glanced from Sally to Hawk and back again, reluctant but resigned. "To begin with, the moment Nina Cruz moved into the county, we had her under surveillance."

"Surveillance?" said Sally. "What do you mean? Tapping her phone? Video cameras in her woods? Bugging her e-mail? Airplane flyovers?"

Scotty scowled at her. "We're not at liberty to divulge that information."

"It's all pretty boring stuff anyway, Mustang," Dickie said, trying to placate her.

"Yeah, fascists are real boring," Sally shot back. "That's one of the secrets to their success."

"Don't get carried away, Sally," Scotty said, refusing to take the bait. "It wasn't that elaborate."

"At least before September 11," Dickie muttered, but Scotty left that remark alone, too.

"Why?" Hawk asked. "Apart from the fact that she was involved in left-wing politics, of course. I mean, she might have kissed a Viet Cong or two, many long years ago, but why snoop on her now? So she never gave up on trying to change things. So she threw herself into feminism and environmentalism and animal rights. It's not like she was downloading specs for nuclear weapons off the Internet. That seems a little extreme to me."

"Did to us, too," said Dickie, joining in. "But the feds were absolutely insistent. They showed us something they called a 'very partial dossier' on her, going back all the way to the sixties. Twelve file boxes full of folders with labels like 'Visit to Algeria,' 'Black Panthers,' and 'Ditches.' "

Hmmph, said the historian in Sally. The feds had kept more paper on Nina's life than Nina herself had. She'd have to file a Freedom of Information Act request for this book project, and given recent political developments, the government would very likely stonewall her request. "Ditches?" she asked.

"Yeah," said Dickie. "Ditches. Evidently, at one time Nina agreed to sponsor a ditch-lining operation in New Mexico—some cousin of hers or something, marketing a product that would line and cover irrigation ditches, which would decrease evaporation and absorption, theoretically saving water, and saving ranchers and farmers a lot of money. Nina wrote them a letter telling them she approved of green-resource management and saying she was enclosing a check. They went broke nine months later."

"A lot of people tried to get their hooks into her," Sally said wonderingly.

"A lot succeeded. Most were harmless. A few seem to have been doing good things, and doing them well. But a few of Nina's pet projects weren't so benign," Dickie said.

"I heard about some of that from Cat and, less directly, from Randy Whitebird," she said. "Some of the people she subsidized used her money to do things like smuggle dope, buy weapons, and build bombs. But I didn't hear anything that made me think that she knew ahead of time, or approved of that sort of stuff. And for quite some time, her sister's been keeping a pretty close eye on where the money goes. That's a woman who doesn't suffer fools gladly," Sally pointed out.

"True," said Scotty, "but recently the pattern has shifted again, toward more questionable enterprises, including this Wild West Foundation. The FBI has been interested in a number of the people involved in this project for some time."

"They're interested in everybody left of Rumsfeld," Sally grumbled.

"Don't blame me. I voted for Gore," said Dickie.

"You and seven or eight other people in Wyoming," Scotty remarked.

"About the FBI being interested in these people," Hawk said, trying to keep them on track. "Who and why?"

Sally jumped right in. "Randy Whitebird, for one, has a political history that makes Nina Cruz look like Condoleezza Rice. Joining the student left and then moving into the most radical cadres. Clearly he engaged in some violent actions, and then went underground. When he came back up, he was a Changed Man in a Gray Flannel Suit. But I wonder if all the years while he was polishing his corporate image, changing his name, he kept up the old school ties, so to speak."

"Did you learn all that from your 'oral history'?" asked Scotty.

"He was vague on the details," she said, "but, yeah, I did. Do you have more?"

Dickie spoke up. "Charter member of Earth First! and the Animal Liberation Front, in a very quiet way. He's not the one out there pouring sugar in bulldozer gas tanks or releasing rats from research labs, but they're cashing his checks, and maybe even crashing at his pad when they need a place to cool down. Four years ago, two dudes who'd blown up a construction trailer at a new development in the Arizona desert were arrested at the Mexican border. They were wearing Hugo Boss suits and driving a late-model BMW, but the border guys got suspicious when they found grocery bags full of broccoli and bulghur in the trunk. The car was registered to Whitebird. He claimed they'd stolen both the suits and the vehicle."

Hawk cocked an eyebrow and said, "What about the groceries?"

"How about Kali?" Sally asked.

"Utah native with a biology Ph.D. No arrest record, and in many ways, an inspiring success story for you modern career gals. She's worked her way up the research side of the biotech industry, to become a senior vice president at a fast-growing Wasatch Valley firm called BIOS. The company does a lot of business with the government," Dickie told her.

"What kind of business?" Sally asked.

"The FBI wouldn't tell us, and if we did know, we wouldn't tell you," Scotty put in.

"So, nyah-nyah," Dickie added.

Sally rolled her eyes. "Kali didn't strike me as a paragon of patriotism."

"Come on, Sally. As you know, the West is full of people grabbing up fistfuls of government dollars just as fast as they can denounce federal tyranny. As far as the folks in Salt Lake City are concerned, she's a model citizen, with one small quirk. She's an outspoken animal rights activist," Dickie said.

"I can't imagine that goes down smooth in Utah," Hawk observed.

"She's found a way to make her politics palatable to the more conservative element in Salt Lake by making common cause with the antiabortion movement," Scotty answered.

"That seems pretty far-fetched," Hawk said.

"You'd be surprised," Sally said. "There's a faction of the ecofeminist movement that would be right at home at a Right to Life prayer vigil."

"According to her FBI file, Dr. Brisbane has attended any number of those prayer vigils," Dickie said. "But what's more interesting is that she's made several trips to Europe, ostensibly either to do business or to go skiing, where she's had contact with members of radical fringe Green groups. The feebs wouldn't have known about her involvement, but, for once, the CIA tipped them off. The spooks were keeping a close eye on a couple of German players, and she showed up in some of the surveillance pictures."

Sally found herself imagining grainy photographs of slack-haired people in trench coats, meeting at dingy cafés. Or maybe snowsuit-clad Valkyries and Vikings lounging on ski-lodge decks? "Photos? How would they ever manage to track her down?"

"Secret-agent stuff," said Dickie. "We could tell you, but then we'd have to shoot you."

This was an ill-advised remark, given where they were and why they were there. "Sorry," said Dickie, leaning over to squeeze Sally's hand as she let loose once more.

Sally finally squeezed back, took the handkerchief Hawk offered, blew her nose. "Forget it." She took a deep breath, shook her shoulders. "What about Lark?"

Scotty spoke up, resuming business. "Another animal lover—met Kali at a PETA conference. But she got her start with that Deep Nature bunch in Oregon. Did some time up there for tree spiking."

Hawk grimaced. "Very nice. The monkey-wrenching technique they use to slow down timbering in old-growth forests. You pound big nails or spikes into trees that are slated to be cut, and when the loggers come through with their chain saws, they hit a spike and it busts the chain. Problem is, sometimes a piece of flying chain or spike will hit the logger. It's a pretty ugly way of saying you love the planet," he said.

This was what they called tree hugging? "But not all the Wild West people are like this," Sally said. "Nels Willen wouldn't approve of spiking. From what I've seen, he's an incredibly thoughtful, not to mention nonviolent, man."

"I talked to a couple of people I know in environmental groups," Hawk said. "Willen's given millions to environmental organizations. He seems particularly interested in funding outfits that bring people who think they hate one another together to work out solutions to tough problems, starting at the local level."

"There are a couple of red flags where Willen's concerned. The animal rights connections, of course—lots of donations to various groups, some of them sketchy in the extreme. But that's not the main concern with him. Do you know why he quit being a surgeon?" Dickie asked.

"Yes," said Sally. "He told me about his epiphany."

"Did he tell you about his malpractice suit?" Scotty asked. Sally just stared.

"Sorry to burst your bubble," said Scotty. "Obviously, you're taken with the guy. But epiphany or no epiphany, Willen quit fixing blown-out knees shortly after a five-million-dollar suit against him was settled out of court. Some kid broke her hip snowboarding, and her parents claimed that Willen deliberately botched the surgery so the kid wouldn't get out on the mountain again and break her neck. The lawyers had witnesses who claimed to have heard Willen say that somebody needed to do something to save the rich from themselves. But Willen was his own worst witness. He'd said in a deposition that when it was all over, he'd have to find a way to live with the fact that he'd made a fortune off ski developers' urge to wreck mountains, and helping people hurt themselves."

"That's a serious load of guilt," said Hawk.

"Beyond serious, I'd say," Dickie said. "If they made a statue of Guilt, it'd look like him."

"Willen, Kali, Lark, Whitebird." Sally ticked them off on her fingers. "What about Quartz? You can't possibly tell me the kid's some kind of ecoterrorist, and he hasn't lived long enough to be driven crazy by guilt."

Dickie answered quickly. "Nope. Quentin Schwartz, it seems, is just a nice, bright young man who wants to do good in the world. Guess there are a few of them left."

Sally looked at Scotty. He nodded. "We're not concerned about Schwartz."

She'd learned her lesson. She really was going to stay away from the Dub-Dubs. But if, somehow, that wasn't possible, she might keep an eye out for Quartz. In that crowd, a nice, bright young man might need some looking after.

Hawk spoke quietly. "You haven't said anything about Stone Jackson," he said.

"Nothing there," Dickie said. "Politically, anyway. He's what he appears—a liberal Democrat, a moderate but devoted greenie, a solid citizen."

Scotty looked at Dickie, something flickering in his eyes. "Personally, it's a different matter."

Dickie lit another cigarette.

"So what's the personal angle?" Hawk finally asked.

Dickie sighed. "As you're no doubt aware, being in recovery is a day-to-day thing."

Sally could see the pain passing through her dear friend. "And you're saying Stone was out of recovery some day or days, in the not-distant past?"

Dickie closed his eyes, tipped his head back, exhaled a stream of smoke. "A little something the surveillance on Nina turned up. Last June, she called him in Cody. Her phone records indicated that she hadn't called him there before, and there were no previous calls from any of his numbers to her at Shady Grove. So we're surmising that they'd been out of touch awhile, and she'd initiated contact. Two days later, the Cody cops arrested him for DWI. He went straight from the Cody jail to a very private treatment center in Colorado." Dickie lifted his head and opened his eyes, darting a cold glance at Scotty. "Generally speaking, of course, that ain't nobody's business but his own."

"But specifically speaking," Scotty said, "Jackson's fall off the wagon had come across the FBI's screen. And what was interesting is that the only person to visit Jackson at the Colorado facility was a Ms. Cruz."

"Cat went to see him?" Sally asked.

For a second, Scotty looked startled. "How did you know?"

"The way she looked at him at the Wild West meeting. The way she talks about him. I wouldn't be at all surprised if the feeling wasn't mutual, and they're both feeling guilty as hell. So she went to be with him when he was falling apart? Doesn't surprise me a bit."

"Surprised us some, if for no other reason than that she had to fly from Lagos, Nigeria, to New York, then to Denver, then charter a plane. Evidently, she stayed in town a week, went to see him every day, and then flew back to Africa."

"And I'm assuming Nina never called or went down to see either of them," Sally said.

"Not that anyone could discover," Scotty answered.

And yet, when the time had come to plan the benefit, Nina and Stone had been in touch. She'd called on him for help, and he'd come. And, by all accounts, by that time, he was back on the wagon and feeling strong, and Cat, Nina's sister and closest confidante, was, well, who knew where. Passing strange.

"What I can't figure is, how the hell does Jimbo Perrine fit into all this?" Sally wondered.

"Old Jimbo had a few side businesses to go along with his taxidermy thing. Ran a little dope, did a little quiet business in 'lost' weapons and ammunition. Had some survivalist buddies out in the back country who used him as a middleman for everything from guns to beans and bacon. The FBI has been watching him, too. We're tracing possible links with animal rights types, as unlikely as that seems," Dickie said. "But when the going gets weird, sometimes the weird get together."

"What I would really like to know, right now, is why Sally's become a target," said Hawk.

Everyone sat silent for a moment.

Then Scotty Atkins broke the silence. "It would appear that, acting entirely on her own, your friend, Dr. Alder, has piled up a fair bit of information on Nina Cruz and the people around her. And she has even taken it upon herself to handle evidence pertinent to this case."

"I really am sorry for not telling you about that can of powder. But don't forget, when I found that note in Nina's office, I turned it right over to you," Sally said.

"As was only fitting," Dickie said. "The problem now is that among the many things you've learned, and, by now, I dearly hope, have told us, is something that has led some person to try to kill you."

What did she know? Who knew she knew it? Sally had to answer those questions, before it was too late.

23

Twenty-nine Messages

The weekend before Thanksgiving started out surprisingly normal, considering that she'd nearly been killed the day before, that Hawk too might have been hurt or worse. She got up early, had her coffee, saw that the snow had piled up and the skies were gray and low, so she went to the gym. Nobody bothered her there; nobody ever did. Today was no different. She sweated out an hour of cardio, lifted weights for a while, lingered a little longer in the steam room than usual, but nothing wildly out of the ordinary. Spent the rest of the day working in her office, taking time out for lunch with a couple of colleagues. Typical college professor day. Except that much of the time, she was wracking her brain to figure out why somebody was shooting at her, and who that somebody might be. It was a little distracting.

Hawk suggested going out that night, but she didn't really feel like it, so they made dinner, rented a movie, watched it, and went to bed. Their lovemaking that night went on and on, rocking from gentle and sweet to hard and fast and back again, as if they were checking out each other's existence, reminding each other they were still there, still whole, still feeling, feeling every which way.

She fell into a heavy sleep, and slept far into the morning. When she finally opened her eyes and contemplated getting out of bed, she discovered that her body wouldn't move. It wasn't just that she didn't want to move. She couldn't. For some time she lay there, absolutely still, wondering how she'd become an inanimate object.

Hawk came in with a cup of coffee. "I thought I'd let you sleep late. It's almost noon."

"What's noon?" she asked, utterly serious. It turned out that she could speak, but time measurement concepts weren't computing.

Hawk looked at her more closely, setting the coffee on the night table. "Middle of the day," he said. "Sun's highest in the sky. Look," he told her, pulling the window curtain aside.

She stared out at a sky so brilliant blue, the sight hurt her eyes. She closed them.

Hawk got into bed, rolled her onto her side, pulled her back to his front, and held her a long time, saying nothing. She remained motionless where he'd put her.

Eventually, he got up, picked up the now-cold coffee, and left the room. She still didn't move. As the afternoon wore on, the sun moved across the dazzling sky, but Sally remained where she'd been all day.

She might have dozed; she wasn't sure. But sometime in the late afternoon, she realized that she could feel at least one part of her body. Nature's call brought her back into herself, and she got up on leaden legs to go to the bathroom. She managed to drink a glass of water, but it was all she could do to drag herself back to bed. She collapsed onto the bed and was almost instantly asleep for the next ten hours.

When she woke in the middle of the night, she thought she must be in the middle of a tornado. There was a roaring in her ears like a train speeding by, ten inches from her head, and the bed was shaking hard. It took a minute to realize that Hawk was sitting on her, holding her down, until the shaking let up.

"What was that?" she asked him.

His eyes were worried. "I think you had some kind of fit. I'm wondering if I should take you to the hospital."

"No," she said, sounding remarkably like herself. "I'd just get sick." And, after a minute, she added, "I had a bad dream."

He hugged her hard, and the trembling started again, much more gently. But then she realized that this time, it wasn't her. He was crying, his chest shuddering. Hawk Green, Man of Steel. She was flooded with love that brought her back to life again, and eventually she slept in peace.

Sunday morning found her ravenous, sitting at the breakfast table inhaling her first cup of coffee while he worked up eggs and potatoes. "Take a look at the *Boomerang*," Hawk told her, glancing over his shoulder from his station at the stove. "Front page."

She looked at the banner headline: GOVERNOR PROPOSES TAX INCREASE. This was big news, of course, especially in Wyoming. The voters had inexplicably elected a Democrat to the statehouse, and the guy was doing far-out radical things like suggesting that Wyoming raise property taxes just a touch, in order to buy chalk for the schools and pay teachers enough so they wouldn't have to moonlight at Wal-Mart. "Guess the gov doesn't plan to run again," she said.

"Not that story. Below the fold," Hawk said.

There were three stories. A Centennial woman had won $10,000 in the New York State lottery. A tanker truck carrying hazardous chemicals coast to coast had flipped over somewhere west of Laramie, and they'd had to close the interstate for six hours while they got the mess cleaned up, sort of (officials were advising motorists to keep their windows closed in the vicinity, at least for a few days).

The third story, a couple of paragraphs in the lower left-hand corner of the page, dealt with a corporate bankruptcy. The BIOS corporation of Salt Lake City, a biotech firm that had ridden a combination of top-secret government R&D contracts and medical research projects to rocketing success, had filed for Chapter 11 status.

"BIOS?" said Sally. "That's the company Kali works for, right?"

"That's my recollection," said Hawk.

"Hold the eggs," Sally told him. "I want to see what more there is to this story."

She went to the desk in the corner of their living room, opened up Hawk's laptop, connected to the Internet, and clicked her way to the *New York Times*.

The story had actually made the bottom of the front page, continued in the business section. BIOS stock, which had been trading at $36 a share as recently as September, had taken a plunge sometime in late October, when word got out that the FDA was going to deny approval for the marketing of Madicin, a BIOS-developed wonder drug designed to treat spongiform encephalopathy in both animals and humans.

The wire-service report quoted an unnamed BIOS official: "Once again, government red tape stands in the way of progress," the official said. "With the spread of chronic wasting disease across the West, and concern about the possibility of a mad cow outbreak, you'd think they'd understand the gravity of the situation. People and animals are getting sick and dying out there. Madicin's time has come."

When she told Hawk what she'd learned, he said, "I bet our friends at the sheriff's department knew this was coming. It'd be interesting to know why they didn't tell us, and what they're thinking."

Sally frowned. The fuckers had held out on her again. "I'm going to call Dickie," she said, getting up and going to the phone. But when she picked up the receiver, it was dead.

"Phone's not working," she said, a little tremor starting in her stomach.

"Oh. Oh yeah. I forgot. I unplugged it yesterday. Given the shape you were in, I didn't want you disturbed." Hawk was busy with his potatoes, didn't see the fear in her eyes.

Much relieved (and a bit ashamed about leaping to panic), she plugged it back in and heard the stuttered ring that signified voicemail. "You have twenty-nine new messages," said the pleasant mechanical female voice.

Four were from Delice, charting an emotional course from warm sympathy ("Heard what happened this afternoon. Can I do anything? Call me.") to concern ("Anybody in there? Are you guys okay? Give me a call as soon as you get this.") to annoyance ("Come on, Mustang. Quit screening calls and pick up the goddamn phone. I just want to know that you're all right, for Christ's sake. Pick up or I'm coming over there!") to resignation, and more friendship ("Hi. I left some flowers on your porch. Hope you're okay and you get this before they freeze. Call me if there's anything I can do.").

Sally looked up and noticed the vase of gorgeous lilies and irises and mums.

"They didn't freeze," she said.

"She dropped them off last night. I heard her come and go—she didn't even ring the bell. I brought them right in."

A little more life flowed back into Sally.

As it turned out, half the people she knew had called to see how she was doing. There was even a message from Arvida Perrine's mother, which struck Sally as remarkably sweet. Her friend and boss, Dean Edna McCaffrey, left a message that just said, "I'm canceling your classes next week. Don't know what you've gotten yourself into, but sounds like you need some time to get out of it. Let's have lunch when you're up to it." It was a thoughtful offer, although Sally's only class was on Tuesday, given the Thanksgiving break. And given the fact that half the students had already gone home, having no intention of attending Thanksgiving-week classes, lots of Sally's colleagues just scheduled "independent research" days on the assumption hardly anybody would be around.

Sam Branch had called, too. "This is it, Mustang," the message said. "The boys took a vote, and it was unanimous. For your own good, whether you like it or not, we're pulling out. I've already called the Wild West offices and let them know. Sorry to say, but the woman who answered the phone didn't seem all that disappointed. By the way, if I were you, I'd take a nice long vacation somewhere far away until these fuckin' Californians go back to the swarm they came from."

That was a disappointment, she guessed. But she had to

admit, it was also a relief. Now that the bullets had started flying her direction, she certainly didn't want to put anybody else in harm's way. And now she had the perfect excuse to extricate herself from the Night for Nina and from anyone and everything having to do with the Wild West. Her life would go on whether she played music with Thomas Jackson or not, whether she wrote a book about Nina Cruz or didn't. Enough was enough. Good-bye, Stone. Adios, Cat. Farewell, Angelina.

Except that several of them had called.

Pammie Montgomery: "Hey, Sally, how are you? The chef wants me to bring over some tortilla soup. Call the restaurant when you want a delivery, and I'll be there in a flash."

Quartz: "Sorry I haven't been able to return your calls, but I've been kind of tied up. Really bummed to hear about the latest attack. Hope you're all right. Peace—out."

Nels Willen: "Boy, this just keeps getting worse and worse. My opinion, it's time to fold up the tent and ride off into the sunset, but then, I'm afraid it ain't up to me. Anyway, I hope you're doin' okay. There are a couple of things I need to share with you. I'll be around on Monday. How 'bout I come to your office in the morning?" He left a number to call.

A nearly inaudible woman's voice: Kali. "I am so sorry about this latest violence. The whole thing is just terribly upsetting. I'm sorry, too, that I won't be able to meet with you this week—I have an emergency trip out of town. Be well, sister."

Sister? If Sally were Olivia de Havilland, maybe, contemplating Joan Crawford.

Thomas Jackson: "Now that the weather's cleared up some, I'm packin' up to head down to Laramie for the week. I heard about you being shot at. Also hear the Millionaires have bailed out of the benefit. Hey, Sally. I feel just horrible about involving you in something that's turned out to be so dangerous. I'm not sure how to make it up to you. . . . Anyway, I'll be in Sunday night. I'm staying out at Shady Grove. If you're willin', I'd like to come into town and visit with you. Maybe even work on a couple of songs, if you still want to play."

If she still wanted to play. With him. Hoo-boy.

Cat Cruz had called twice, the first time on Saturday to say she had heard about the shooting. She doubted there was anything she could do to help Sally out, but if there was, she wanted to do it. The second call from Cat had come in earlier Sunday morning. "I assume by now you've seen the newspaper," she said. "If you're still planning to write my sister's life story, which I hope you are, we've found out a thing or two about this BIOS company that might interest you. Call me."

She wouldn't call, damn it. She was determined not to call. Especially given the last message in the queue, sent just minutes ago. "Sally, this is Scotty Atkins. Bet you've been feeling low. Don't obsess about it. We're pursuing our investigation and expect to have things wrapped up very soon." A slight pause. "Take it easy," he said, and hung up.

Well, sure. Uh-huh. She would take it easy if it killed her. Don't talk to Willen. Don't think about singing with Stone. Don't call Cat. Have a little breakfast, lie around the house, maybe read a good book. Spend a week of enforced leisure catching up on that big pile of paperwork that never seemed to get any smaller. Plan a quiet Thanksgiving dinner with Hawk, or find out where the Langham clan was gathering to feed and get herself invited. Focus on turkey and stuffing.

Yeah, right.

"Think I'll skip the eggs this morning," she told Hawk. Tortilla soup sounded good.

"Good timing," said Pammie Montgomery when Sally reached her at the Yippie I O. "I'm just finishing up my shift. I should be there in half an hour or so. I'm supposed to pick up Quartz, so maybe I'll bring him by."

If Cat Cruz had somehow found out things about this BIOS business, chances were it was Quartz who'd found them. Sally felt a little guilty about using Pammie to get to him, but only a little.

Hawk had taken off for his office by the time Pammie arrived with two one-quart cartons of soup and a dozen smaller containers of condiments and accoutrements—tortilla strips, little chunks of cheese, chopped cilantro, diced tomatoes, extra chiles, sliced avocado, lime wedges. "Mix and match," she said.

"I just dump in everything," said Quartz.

"This soup's full of chicken!" Sally said, taken aback. "I thought you were a vegetarian."

"I've fallen from grace," Quartz admitted. "I'd even drink a cup of satanic coffee right about now."

"Beats the hell out of powdered soy smoothies," said Pammie. "Did you ever give that stuff a try, Sally?"

"Um, nope," Sally said. "Guess I'm just a creature of habit. Speaking of habits, you wouldn't have any idea how Nina got started with her power drinks, would you?"

"I haven't been around long enough," Pammie told her. "Any idea, cutie pie?" she asked Quartz. He shook his head. "You could ask Kali or Lark," she suggested.

Yes, Sally certainly could. At the first opportunity.

"Speaking of Kali," said Pammie, "did you see the paper this morning? That company of hers turns out to have been working on a cure for mad cow and chronic wasting disease. Isn't that bizarre?"

"Yeah," said Quartz. "What an outrageous coincidence."

Both Sally and Pammie just looked at him. "You gotta be kidding," Pammie said finally.

"Okay, I admit there's something going on here. Heck, maybe Kali suspected what was wrong with the woman she loved, and had gotten her company involved in a desperate search for a cure," Quartz allowed.

"That's a romantic's-eye view of the situation," Pammie told him, patting him on the hand. "But I doubt things work that way. After all, how long has Nina been acting strange? And how long does it take a major medical research program to get up and running? I don't know."

Quartz looked sad. "Well," he said, "you never know about timing. But at any rate, looks like they don't have the cure, and the company's going broke. No wonder Kali's seemed so off balance and distracted lately. As if losing

Nina weren't enough, the poor woman's got a bunch of other shit to deal with."

No surprise, then, that Kali was back and forth to Utah so much. A thought suddenly occurred to Sally. "According to the newspaper story, BIOS stock went in the toilet. Executives these days take a lot of their perks in stock. I wouldn't be surprised if Kali hasn't lost a fortune in the last couple of months."

"Her and all the other people who owned shares, which probably includes everybody from secretaries at the company to little old ladies in Iowa. But think about it, Quartz," Pammie said. "Kali's a senior vice president and a scientist. She knows how this stuff goes. Do you think she knew the FDA approval for—what's it called?—Madicin . . . do you think she knew it was in trouble?"

"Gee," said Quartz. "I suppose it's possible."

"Boy, I tell you what," said Sally, "if it were me, and I had a bunch of money invested in something I thought was likely to go south, I'd be pretty tempted to dump my stock while it was still worth something."

Quartz took a swallow of coffee and said, "You might. But then you'd be sitting in the cell next to Martha Stewart, trying to figure out what color bar warmers to crochet."

"You guys know Kali," said Sally. "Do you think she's a candidate for Martha's cell mate?"

"Hell, I don't know," said Pammie. "I've only been hanging around the Wild West bunch because of my darlin' here." She grinned at Quartz. "But from what I've seen, just judging by the way she eats, Kali's pretty much of an absolutist. I can't imagine her bending the rules, even to save her own skin."

Sally thought another minute. "But consider the fact that her company does biomedical research. Obviously they must have to use animals as experimental subjects. That seems completely out of line with her politics. How do you suppose she works out that contradiction?"

"I think her focus is computer simulations," Quartz said. "She doesn't do any work with animal subjects. But, of course, other researchers at the company must be using animals." He looked at Sally and Pammy, eyes somber. "Who in the world doesn't have some contradiction to work out? Nobody, but nobody, is made of pure love and light, no matter how noble they try to be." And almost as an afterthought, he added, "I guess, in the end, everybody's got something to hide."

24

Monday, Monday

She didn't call Cat, made no attempt to get in touch with Thomas Jackson, never contacted Nels Willen. She told herself that she was taking a step back, trying to collect her wits. The day had dawned gorgeously clear and unexpectedly warm. She crunched along on melting snow glittering in the sun, bound for her office, humming the Mamas and Papas' anthem to the day of the week. Piled-up paperwork and cascading e-mail awaited her.

Her intentions were good, though admittedly not pure. Sally sat at the computer table, perpendicular to her desk, methodically working her way through e-mail messages. She'd left her office door half-open, and she wasn't a bit surprised when Nels Willen walked through it.

He looked ten years older than he had the last time Sally had seen him. Still, he managed a smile that made her understand why Nina had sought refuge with him, and he sat down in her funky easy chair. "You doin' okay?" he asked.

"No physical damage," she replied, swiveling from the computer to the main desk to face him. "I'll admit to being a little skittish at times. A car backfired in front of our house last night, and I was half under the bed before I realized how I'd reacted. Now I know how dogs feel on the Fourth of July."

Willen nodded. "With what you've been through, you've probably got a little post-traumatic stress."

"Oh!" said Sally. "Is the trauma over?"

Willen shook his head. "Some traumas take their time about it. Some don't end, it seems. Guess that brings me to what I wanted to say to you. There are some things you need to know, if you're gonna write about Angelina."

She cleared a space on the desk and leaned forward on her elbows, lacing her fingers and resting her head on her hands. "Nels, I don't really know if I am going to write that book."

"But there's still a chance you'll do it. Cat wants you to do it. So does Stone."

Sally searched her heart, and admitted she still wanted to write about Nina's life. "Yeah, there's a chance."

"Okay," said Willen. "I suspect you know why I took that rifle up to Shady Grove the morning Nina died."

Sally waited a beat. "I think I do. You were pretty sure you knew what was wrong with her, and where it would lead. She was exhibiting the symptoms of variant Creutzfeld-Jakob Disease, which you assumed she'd contracted in Europe, the years she ripped up her knee. You felt responsible. You were her doctor then. And more," she ventured.

Willen closed his eyes, slumped in the chair. "I've loved Nina Cruz for a quarter of a century. Not in a possessive way, you understand. There was more love in that woman than any one person could hold. All I've wanted was a little of her light shining on me. She gave me that. And more."

"She took a lot, too," Sally said. "That's become increasingly clear to me."

"And why not?" said Willen. "She gave away so much, she was entitled to a little back. She couldn't find it in her heart to hurt anyone."

"What about Stone?" Sally asked. "What about the famous 'Get a life, Tommy' note?"

"The man was killing himself," said Willen. "Trust me. That was the only thing that could've shocked him out of the tailspin he was in. I knew them both. I saw what he was doing to himself. Leaving him was the most loving thing she could have done. The pain of it quite nearly killed her, too."

Sally nodded. "I believe you. That must have been incredibly hard for her. You can hear the whole history of their life together in the music."

"Yeah," Willen laughed thinly. "They did it the hard way."

Sally thought about it. "Uh-huh. And you know what? Since then, have either of them taken the plunge, let somebody in, been so vulnerable? You'd know better than me."

Willen shook his head. "Not Nina, anyhow. And believe me, I tried. I thought I could be the one to help her heal. But she said she'd never again risk giving somebody everything. She couldn't hurt that much, or hurt anybody else so deeply."

"So instead, she portioned out love in addictive little doses," said Sally. "A self-protective, pretty effective strategy. She'd make only partial and temporary promises to people like you and Whitebird, like Kali. That way, she could move on, or come back, or move around, and not feel like she was betraying a trust. Anybody who wanted more, or felt hurt, well, that was their problem. And if they chose to hang on and hang around, that was fine, too. She didn't mind surrounding herself with people who adored her."

"I accepted her rules. She made 'em pretty clear." He leaned over and put his elbow on the chair arm, his head in his palm. "Angelina was an unusually clear person in so many ways. That's why it was so horrible to watch her blur and fade. I couldn't stand it."

Sally's fingers clenched. She pressed her lips together. "So you were going to do the humane thing. She'd asked you to bring the rifle, said somebody was trying to kill her. Obviously, her mental state was deteriorating. Paranoia strikes deep."

"In the end, Sally," said Willen, "humans are nothing more than animals. She was a suffering animal. When I was a hunter, if I saw a deer with a broken leg, or one of my dogs got sick, I put it out of its misery." He took a breath. "I figured it was my job to end Angelina's torment, since I'd been the one who caused it in the first place."

How could anyone stand living under the burden of guilt this man hauled around? "You didn't cause it, Nels. If, indeed, she got mad cow disease after she wrecked her knee, some Swiss quack caused it. And he certainly had no idea what he was doing. All you did was try to help her, the best way you knew how. It blows my mind that you were willing to go to prison, for the rest of your life, to end her pain," Sally said.

Willen sighed heavily. "No. In the end, no. I couldn't do it. I put the guns down years ago. I'm not the man I was. And, as it turned out, she wasn't quite as crazy as I thought, at least not all the time. She thought somebody was trying to kill her. Guess she was right."

Then the man who'd been so brave, so competent, on that terrible morning at Shady Grove, put his face in his hands and cried his heart out. Sally sat for a bit and watched him, then got up, walked around her desk, knelt on the floor, and put her arms around him.

For the second time in little more than twenty-four hours, Sally found herself comforting a crying man. If that didn't break your heart, she thought, what could?

"Sally," said Willen. "Don't blame Angelina for trying to spread her love around. There were so many people who wanted a piece of her. She was so committed, so devoted, so luminously gifted. She'd walk into a room, and everybody in the place would just crave a little touch. Most people were content with just that. There were only two people I know of who always wanted more. And they undoubtedly deserved it."

"Stone and Cat," said Sally. "The love of her life, and the sister of her heart."

"Both of them gave Angelina everything they had," Willen said. "Somehow, she couldn't handle it. They were made different from her."

It was the old Eric Clapton conundrum, and she asked the question out loud. "Why does love have to be so sad?"

Willen shook his head. "Maybe it doesn't always. Looks like Stone and Cat were made for each other."

So Willen knew, too. And it hadn't taken Sally any time at all to figure it out. Had Nina known?

* * *

"Of course she knew," Cat Cruz said, when Sally called her an hour later, and asked the question.

"How?" Sally asked.

"I told her. She'd been keeping him on a yo-yo for years, and it wasn't doing Thomas any good. They hadn't seen much of each other recently, but last spring they were both at some charity event in Boulder, and I guess the sight of her shoved him off the wagon. He needed plenty of help, but she wasn't into giving any. So he called me, and I came back to the States, and that's when we got involved. She deserved to know. And do you know what she told me?"

Sally said, "No."

"She just kind of smiled and said, 'You're in for a tough road. But that old boy deserves the best, so don't screw up.' Then a month after he got out of the clinic, she was calling him up about the benefit. Reeling in the line. She couldn't let him go."

"That must have been infuriating," Sally said.

A pause. "Yeah. That's one word for it. Plus there was the fact that I was beginning to worry about the financial stuff. I had only the vaguest inkling then, but in the past couple of weeks, Quartz has dug up a ton of really disturbing information. She was buying and selling stock, cashing in securities, and not penny-ante transactions either. While I was in Colorado, spending my days in some hick-town hotel room waiting for my hour of handholding with Thomas, she was moving money around. And then, when I was back in Africa, facing all that misery and worrying that, while I was away, the ever ingenious Stone Jackson would finally find a way to kill himself, my beloved sister contacted some lawyer in Seattle about drafting a new will."

"Seattle?" Sally said.

"Yeah. Some guy she probably hid in her basement, back when he was a bomb-throwing anarchist. Now he's a trusts-and-estates expert. I had no idea that shit was going on until she sent me a draft. We weren't talking, and when I left the country on another UN gig, it seemed distinctly possible we'd never speak to each other again.

"But she called me two days before she was killed. Said she loved me. Said we had a lot to talk about. Said she really needed my advice on plans for the Wild West Foundation. Needed someone she knew she could trust. Begged me to come out for the big Thanksgiving-weekend festivities. A lot of things had come clear to her. She loved me. She loved Stone. She . . ." Cat's voice faltered, and she took a big breath. "She said she hoped we could make each other really happy, because we both deserved the love we knew how to give. She was writing us a song, and she planned to perform it at the benefit. She hadn't written a new song in five years. She sang me a couple of lines. It was beautiful. We found some lyrics in a computer file. The cops confiscated all her tapes and CDs, but I called up your pal Atkins. Her last dated tape had a recording of what she'd done so far. He made a copy for me. I thought that was really nice of him," Cat said.

"Actually, it was," Sally said, touched by the uncharacteristic gesture.

"She didn't get to finish it, Sally," said Cat. "But I played it for Stone. I think he's planning to finish it for her, and play it on Friday."

Sally was swamped with sadness. But she got hold of herself. "So what did you learn about Nina's financial wheeling and dealing?"

Cat's voice turned hard. "Appears she'd been slipping around, at least in a small way, for a while, apparently at the urging of the wonderful Kelly Lee. Five years ago, she bought a substantial interest in BIOS. The stock rose slowly and steadily for a couple of years, and then really took off. All the while, she'd buy a little more here, a lot more there."

"So she was bankrolling Kali's company," said Sally.

"Evidently. But in typical Nina fashion, always generously enough to require a hell of a lot of gratitude, but keeping her options open. The week before she died, she set up an account with an online broker. I think she was getting ready to dump the stock."

"Why?" Sally asked.

"I think somebody'd tipped her that the company was about to take a dive. She didn't want to go through the broker we usually use, because we'd been working with him for years and she didn't want to get him in trouble. If it came out that she had inside information."

"So you're assuming Kali told her, so she could get her money out in time."

"Yeah. Ever the devoted acolyte. I assume she took care of her own business, too, although it's possible she felt like she had to go down with the ship, if for no other reason than to keep from going to jail later on."

"It'd be very interesting to know whether Kali stayed in or got out," said Sally.

"You'd have to think the FBI either already has, or will have, the answer to that question," Cat pointed out.

"And did Nina actually sell the stock?" Sally asked.

"No," said Cat. "Before she got around to it, somebody murdered her."

25

The Reeling Monster

Hanging up the phone after talking to Cat, Sally tried to clear her head. Had it really been only a few weeks since Stone Jackson had walked into her office? Since she'd driven through the snow to watch Nina Cruz die? Since Jimbo Perrine had been shot? Since she herself had narrowly escaped death? It seemed an age since she'd slept out a blizzard on Nina's office floor, found the mysterious note that she'd been sure had held the key to a killer's identity.

She still could not manage to convince herself that Jimbo Perrine had murdered Nina Cruz for money. And even if he had, that didn't answer the question of who might have paid Jimbo to commit homicide.

Maybe Nels Willen couldn't fire the shot himself, but that didn't mean he might not have found somebody to carry out his deadly plan.

Maybe Randy Whitebird had sensed that his days as Wild West director and Nina's main squeeze were numbered, and he'd sought a Ranger-turned-radical solution to looming rejection.

Maybe Kelly Lee Brisbane had found out that Nina was

planning to dump her BIOS stock, not to mention dump Kali herself. But what about the mad cow connection? Sally hadn't exactly warmed up to the woman, but maybe if she'd had the chance to talk to her, one on one, she would have caught a glimpse of what Nina had seen in her. What if Kali had known what she was seeing as Nina succumbed to the ravages of spongiform encephalopathy? What if, as a biologist, she had thrown herself into looking for a cure out of love (and the knowledge that even one case of mad cow disease would send the company that found the magic bullet into the financial stratosphere)? In that case, Madicin was much, much more than a drug to Kali: it was both a potential fortune, and a desperate attempt to save her beloved's life.

And what would have happened when she realized that the wonder drug wasn't going to work? A woman who wouldn't eat cooked food seemed an unlikely candidate for hiring a hit man. But then, there were the snake earrings, the choice of a pseudonym. You never knew, did you?

Even Nina's own remarkable sister, or the famously tormented man who'd spent a life loving Nina, might have finally had enough, finding in Jimbo Perrine a willing tool of their rage. How would someone go about locating an assassin-for-hire in Laramie, Wyoming? How would they discover that the redneck, bass-playing taxidermist was willing to kill for dollars?

Any one of those people might have been the dweller-in-the-dark who'd written the note Sally had found that cold morning, a few very long weeks ago.

Sally sat brooding about what she'd learned, about a murder weapon in Jimbo Perrine's gun case, and about at least one can of tainted protein powder in Nina Cruz's pantry. Nina might, as Nels Willen believed, have acquired bovine spongiform encephalopathy from diseased organ meats during her long-ago convalescence in Switzerland. Or she might just as easily have gotten sick from long-term exposure to a lethal dietary product someone had passed off to her as soy supplement. Sally had to find the connection between mad cow disease and Jimbo Perrine.

Scotty Atkins was, no doubt, running down every possible

link. And he could, and surely would, find the answers. Sally didn't have his skills or his resources, or his authority. She ought to leave the job to the pros.

But she could think of one person she could talk to. A person who might, or might not, be willing or able to talk freely with the cold-blooded Detective Atkins. Someone who might know something she didn't know she knew.

Time to see how poor old Arvida Perrine was doing.

For an impetuous person, Sally Alder had experienced very few compulsions. But this was one. She didn't hesitate. She didn't stop to call. She didn't even give it the infinitesimal pause between a first and second thought. She hurried home, got in the Mustang, and drove straight to the Perrine house, a battered little stucco affair with a detached garage, on a muddy gravel side street in West Laramie.

As Sally approached the front door, she could hear a large dog barking inside. She rang the bell, hoping the Perrines weren't the kind of family that went in for vicious Rottweilers. Arvida answered, filling up an ample white sweatshirt silkscreened with an image of a black Labrador retriever and holding an identical barking dog by its collar. "Chill out, Zeppo," said Arvida. "It's just a lady who used to play music with your daddy."

Zeppo quit barking, but he strained against Arvida's hold, wagging his tail like crazy and looking as if he was just dying to jump up on Sally and give her face a lick.

"Jimbo liked to think he was a great hand with hunting dogs," Arvida explained. "But that man couldn't train a dog to save his life. This one never quite understood the command 'Drop it.' Ate every duck he was ever sent to retrieve. He took early retirement. Kids love him. Come on in, Sally."

They walked into a living room that was cluttered but clean, littered with cardboard boxes and stuffed animal heads. "I'm just packin' up the mounts. Up 'til now, I haven't had the energy, but the kids are at school and I feel like I can finally get around to it. I'm hopin' I can find somebody to buy the whole collection, and not have to sell 'em off one by one. I'd even be willin' to throw in all the things in his taxidermy workshop out there in the garage, although whippin' that stuff into shape's gonna take some work. Jimbo wasn't much on neatness to begin with, and he was in the middle of a couple big projects. The cops were in there right after he died, but it's been closed up ever since. I just opened the workshop door for the first time, and it about flattened me. Probably have to air the place out for a week before I'll be able to stand gettin' in there to clean up."

Sally shuddered involuntarily.

"Yeah," said Arvida. "I know what you mean. Want some coffee?"

"That'd be great," Sally said.

Arvida let the dog loose, and, as expected, he leapt up, put his front paws on Sally's chest, and lopped out his big tongue. Sally'd always had a soft spot for black Labs. She let him give her a sloppy dog kiss, then removed him from her body and shoved his rear end down on the floor, issuing the firm command, "Sit."

Zeppo sat.

"Would ya look at that!" Arvida said. "Maybe you should train hunting dogs."

That was all she needed. "Think I'll stick to history. How are you, Arvida? How are the kids?"

They went into a kitchen that hadn't been updated, oh, maybe ever. Yellow paint, harvest-gold appliances, gold-and-brown linoleum floor, a wood-grained Formica table with V-shaped metal legs. But cozy enough on a cool fall day. As Arvida put on the kettle and got out the jar of Taster's Choice and two shiny brown ceramic mugs, Zeppo paced the kitchen. Arvida opened a back door and let him out. "The kids are still in shock. So'm I, truth to tell. My mom thinks we oughta get a therapist."

"Probably a good idea," Sally said, reminded once again that Wyomingites were not cartoon stereotypes of themselves. Therapy: it wasn't just for neurotic Coastals anymore.

"I'm gonna call our doctor and get some names today," Arvida said. "Think I'm finally ready to talk to somebody."

"I can't imagine what you've been through," Sally said, sitting down at the table.

Arvida sighed, settling into a chair and leaning her chin

on her hand. "It's bad enough him getting killed. But now they're sayin' he murdered that woman. Jimbo was a lot of things, but, I tell you, Sally, the man wouldn't of done it. We always been hard-pressed for cash, and he might of done one or two skanky things to make a little extra money. But even for a million dollars, he wouldn't kill a person, no matter who they were. He might of hated her and everything she stood for. But I still can't see it. And I reckon I knew him better'n anybody."

"What do the police say?" Sally asked.

Arvida's mouth hardened. "They think I'm just some damn dumb redneck's damn dumb wife. Somebody shot Nina Cruz with Jimbo's rifle, and when they came to search this place, they found the weapon in Jimbo's gun room. Their way of thinking, must've been him."

Sally faced a dilemma. Scotty had lectured her about leaking any information he gave her. And he'd told her about Jimbo's illicit gun trading. Surely the man's wife must at least have had her suspicions. She'd as good as admitted she knew he was slipping around outside the law. Telling a person something they probably already knew wasn't a violation of confidentiality, right? "Jimbo used to buy and sell guns, didn't he?" she asked as Arvida spooned instant coffee granules into the mugs and poured in boiling water.

Arvida nodded. "People came and went. He had it mixed up with his taxidermy. I expect some of the big UPS shipments he sent and received weren't elk racks or whatever. But I never asked him for details.

"He once told me that there were two kinds of people in the world; men and women. Women should stay home and raise their kids and keep a clean house, and leave everything else to the men. He tried to be a good provider, but there was always something. One time he got hurt at work, and the insurance company refused to pay the workman's comp—they said he was liftin' too heavy a load, and he should of known. We didn't have no money to pay the doctors, let alone a lawyer to sue their sorry asses at the cement plant. So he'd moonlight. And we wouldn't talk about it."

Sally thought a minute. "Maybe he bought that gun from

somebody who used it to shoot Nina Cruz," she said. "Can you think of anybody it could've been?"

Arvida shook her head. "No, and it'd be hard to find out. He didn't keep no records. And any rate, the police talked to some of his hunting buddies. One guy said he'd admired that Marlin 336 last year when they went out after deer. Jimbo'd had that rifle awhile."

Sally sipped at the coffee, which did nothing to improve the bitter taste in her mouth. "So what are you going to do?"

Arvida rocked a little in her chair. "Don't know. But I gotta pull myself together. My mom's been great, but the kids need me. It's funny. In a way, I have to get back to where I once belonged. I been pretty much a mom and nothin' else for the last ten years. Every penny we had came from Jimbo. But I supported myself from the time I got outa high school, and I worked right up to the time Jim junior was born. I've done everything from wait tables to work in an office, and I can do it again. Might even take a couple business courses over at L Triple C," she said, referring to the community college in Cheyenne. "Mom says she'd watch the kids."

"Do you need anything?" Sally asked.

"Nah. I was a big mess at first, but I'm gettin' it together." And then, much to Sally's surprise, Arvida giggled. "It's kinda weird. I used to be a big-time stoner. Before the kids, me and Jimbo used to smoke so much weed, we were in a permanent fog. Then, once we were parents, we pretty much quit—or at least I did. He probably got loaded on hunting trips and like that, sitting around the campfire, for all I know. Me, I haven't even seen marijuana in years. So it blew my mind that when people started dropping off all that food after Jimbo went, somebody left us a nice little shoebox full of dope brownies."

Sally started. "You're kidding," she said.

"Nope. Really good ones with chocolate chips. Just left 'em right on the front doorstep. I knew it the minute I smelled 'em. It ain't a smell you forget," she observed.

Sally recalled the time in college she'd decided to give Alice B. Toklas's famous recipe a try. The rank herbaceous odor of baking marijuana had filled the kitchen as soon as the brownies began to cook and had gotten increasingly strong. By the time they were done, the thought of actually eating one had made her want to puke. Fortunately, she was living with roommates who prized a good buzz far above a palate-pleasing experience. The brownies had disappeared in ten minutes.

"I know what you mean about the smell," Sally said. "It's a lot easier to think about choking one down if you haven't been around them when they're actually cooking."

"No kidding. And even so, I thought about throwin' 'em right in the trash. But I guess I kind of fell back on my old bad habits. Took 'em into my room so the kids wouldn't get 'em. And whoever made 'em must of done something right—cooked the dope into the butter or something—because these were delicious.

"At least I paced myself. In the old days, I'd've just been gobblin' 'em up. Probably put myself into a coma. But I guess you get a little wiser, or at least older. Kept myself to two a day. Perfect dosage, I thought. Heck, I was so zoned, half the time it was all I could do to get up and go to the bathroom. Finished 'em off two days ago. Finally feel a lot better today. I'm ready to start coping now."

Arvida drank a little coffee, shaking her head. "But it was good, I think. I needed to space out. I think my mom knew, but she didn't say anything." She giggled again. "I got a real kick out of being stoned on my ass while the cops were trying to grill me. I think Jimbo would of appreciated it."

"Wow," said Sally, aware that she was sounding a little loaded herself. "Who do you think left them?"

"I don't have a clue. I can think of a few who might have done it ten years ago, but pretty much everybody I know has straightened out, or at least keeps up a good front. Like I said, Jimbo might of had some buddies who're still smoking weed."

Suddenly, there was a huge racket in the backyard. Clanging, banging, the sound of something heavy and hard running into something big and unstable. A big crash, rolling and sliding sounds, the tinkle of breaking glass.

"What in the name of the Lord is going on out there!" Arvida exclaimed, rushing out the back door with Sally hot on her heels.

Something, or someone, had gotten into the garage.

"Zeppo!" Arvida yelled, waddling as fast as she could toward the workshop entrance, "You dumb dog! What the hell are you doing?"

And then she burst out laughing. By the time Sally joined her at the door, she was nearly hysterical. It wasn't hard to figure out why.

Looking in the door to the taxidermy workshop in the garage, Sally was greeted by the sight of a reeling monster. Jimbo's last mounting projects had evidently included a fine elk head capped with a magnificent set of antlers. Zeppo had somehow dislodged the head from wherever it had been perched, inserted his own head completely inside it, and gotten stuck. Now he careened around the workshop, the antlers clearly too heavy for his Labrador neck, wreaking havoc. He'd already tipped over a large wooden shelf, and the shattered remains of glass containers and their contents lay in chaos on the rapidly flooding cement floor: animal parts, plastic syringes, sewing miscellany, objects Sally couldn't identify. The place reeked of decomposing animals, spilled chemicals, and stale cigarette smoke.

Zeppo whirled, trying to remove the elk head, and an antler swept across a workbench, catching a huge jar full of glass eyes and hurling it through the air. They watched as the jar flew up, hurtled down, and smashed on the floor, eyeballs bouncing and scattering as the floor began to flood with a crazy mix of powders, crystals, and liquids, mingling promiscuously, hissing and sizzling in spots. In the midst of the spinning eyeballs, a small piece of white paper drifted down at the edge of a spreading puddle of bubbling yuck.

Arvida grabbed Zeppo by his antlers and yanked. The elk head came off with a slurping pop, and he rushed out the door, yelping.

"Hey, Sally!" yelled Arvida. "Hurry up and help me get the little bastard!"

Sally snatched the piece of paper before it got soaked with

whatever hideous concoction was brewing on the floor. Something was written on it, but she didn't stop to read. Hastily stuffing the paper in a back pocket of her jeans, she ran out of the garage to find Arvida collaring Zeppo and turning on a garden hose. "I'll hold him," she told Sally. "You hose the hell out of him."

By the time they were done washing him off, they were all drenched and shivering. Clouds had scuttled in to cover the sun, and the temperature was dropping fast. The stench of mingling chemicals was getting stronger.

"Christ!" yelled Arvida, dragging the dog toward the house. "I hope whatever shit he was using on the animals doesn't catch on fire or something!"

"I'll call nine-one-one!" Sally shouted back.

26

The Bill of Sale

Two full-scale fire engines, an ambulance, and a hazardous-materials team arrived within minutes. The hazmat guys insisted that everybody clear out while they secured the toxic scene, and the EMTs weren't listening to any talk about everyone being unharmed. Once again, Sally found herself standing in the freezing cold while they examined her on the scene, and then rushed her off to undergo decontamination at Ivinson Memorial. One of the EMTs told her she ought to program 911 into the speed dial on her cell phone. It was getting old.

Better safe than sorry, she guessed. She and Arvida seemed to have survived the encounter with the Chimera, and Zeppo himself had been shipped off to a vet to be treated for exposure to noxious substances. At the very least, he'd no doubt stepped in nasty stuff and gotten himself a snootful of formaldehyde. That couldn't be real good for anybody.

The police had come, of course, and questioned both of them. They told Arvida she wouldn't be able to go back to the house until the chemicals had been completely cleaned up. She'd better make other arrangements. "We can stay with my mom a few days, I guess," she said, drooping with renewed exhaustion. She said almost nothing after that, and when her mother came with the children to pick her up, they let her go.

Hawk had brought Sally some dry clothes, and once again, she found herself in the bleak hospital cafeteria, facing down a scowling Scotty Atkins. This time, Dickie Langham had joined the party. Except for them, and a lone worker in a hairnet closing out the cash register, the place was deserted.

"This one's a regular angel of mercy, isn't she, Sheriff?" Scotty asked Dickie as they sat sipping the nearly undrinkable hospital coffee.

"A good neighbor, at the very least," Dickie agreed. "Really nice of you to go out there and see how Arvida was doing."

Sally looked down into her plastic foam cup. "I'd have said she was doing better until her home turned into a Superfund site," she said.

"What, exactly, *were* you doing out there?" Scotty asked.

"Paying a condolence call. Looking in on a bereaved acquaintance." She gave up the pretense. "I figured she might talk to me. Tell me things she wouldn't tell you guys. Her husband obviously thought of himself as some kind of rebel outlaw. You think she'd spill her guts to a tight-ass cop like you, Scotty? Or how about you, Dick? I mean, you're a really nice guy and all that, but you think she was completely unaware that you all were keeping an eye on Jimbo? The woman's not a complete moron."

Dickie sighed and cracked open a piece of his nicotine gum. "Mustang, when I tell you the FBI's put somebody under surveillance, don't automatically assume I'm sneaking around in a trench coat, planting bugs under the coffee table. I hate to have to admit it, but, you know, sometimes those guys don't share their little projects with us. It gets in the way, if you really want to know."

"The feds are famous for keeping secrets from local law enforcement," Hawk put in.

"Everybody's an expert," said Scotty. "Okay, Sally. I'll

admit, I don't have a lot of patience when it comes to interviewing witnesses. Sometimes, maybe, I even resort to a little bullying."

"A little!" Sally exclaimed.

"Don't bully back, Sal," Hawk said mildly.

"We're dying to know, Sally," said Dickie. "Did she tell you anything you think we might not have known?"

Sally looked at the three men. Almost as one, they folded their arms on the table, waiting for her answer. "You promise she won't get in any trouble?" she asked.

"No," said Scotty.

Dickie tossed him an exasperated glance. "Maybe," he amended. "Depends. Probably not, okay? Assuming she hasn't done anything really terrible."

"Is eating dope brownies really terrible?" Sally asked.

All three men burst out laughing, Scotty included, catching Sally completely by surprise. "She's been cooking up marijuana brownies?" Dickie finally asked.

"Not cooking them. Somebody brought them to her, right after Jimbo died. Why do you suppose anybody would do that?"

They thought about it. "A well-meaning pothead friend?" Hawk said.

"Maybe. But she didn't seem to have any idea who that might have been," Sally said.

"Or malicious mischief at the very least," said Dickie.

"Or maybe there was more in there than just weed," said Scotty. "Maybe somebody wanted to poison her."

"I doubt that," said Sally. "She seems more or less healthy. She's just been zonked for weeks."

"I noticed that she seemed dazed and vacant when I interviewed her. Figured she was in shock and mourning," said Scotty. "And maybe really stupid."

"Yeah. She could tell. It wasn't exactly flattering to her. But you should have seen how quick she got on that dog when those eyeballs started bouncing around." Sally started to laugh, and then remembered the piece of paper in her jeans pocket. "Hey. I forgot something. It was in the jar full of glass eyes. When the jar broke and all the stuff started spreading out on the floor, I picked it up to keep it from getting soaked, and stuck it in my pocket. Can I have that bag please?"

Hawk reached down and picked up the white plastic bag the hospital had given Sally for her wet clothes.

"There was something written on it. Hope it didn't get too wet to read," she said, pulling her jeans out of the bag, sliding her fingers into the pocket, carefully pulling out the limp paper and handing it to Dickie.

He smoothed the paper out on the Formica-topped table and leaned over it, peering down. "Lucky for us, this was written in ballpoint pen, not felt-tip. Didn't run much."

"What is it?" Hawk asked.

Dickie pored over the paper. "It's a bill of sale, handwritten. For one Marlin 336 rifle, to be shipped to a post office box in Aspen, Colorado. Paid for in cash. Dated September 25 and initialed JP."

They all looked at one another.

"But there's more. He's written down below, 'Rifle returned October 7. Customer didn't give reason, but wants cash refund, in person.' And that part's dated October 11. The night before Jimbo Perrine was shot."

"Goddamn," said Hawk. "He didn't do it."

"And he departed from his usual practice and wrote up a receipt. After the fact, no doubt. Must have gotten suspicious when the customer sent the gun back and asked for the cash. In person, no less. And the goddamn fool, he went to the meeting. But then he was still nervous enough that he hid the bill of sale in his eyeball jar. Jesus!" said Sally. "So which of the suspects have connections in Aspen, Colorado?"

Scotty rolled his eyes.

"Would you believe, all of them?" Dickie asked.

A moment of silence. Then Hawk said, "Aspen's the Kevin Bacon of western towns. Nobody's more than six degrees of separation from it."

"This is going nowhere," Sally said.

"Au contraire, as we say in Wyoming," said Dickie. "We now know that Jimbo Perrine was set up, by somebody using an Aspen drop, at a particular time. Even though it could've been any number of people, that gives us our best lead yet. The feebs will be ecstatic."

"In fact," Scotty said, "it's likely just about enough to blow this thing open. So thank you very much, Dr. Alder, for once again provoking a ridiculously dangerous situation that puts a useful piece of evidence in our hands."

"You're welcome," Sally said solemnly.

"I think that'll be enough assistance from you on this one," said Dickie. "Your hero medal and McGruff Crime Dog Fun Pack will be in the mail."

"Send it to Baja or the Bahamas," said Hawk. "I think a tropical vacation is in order. Like immediately. Maybe we could get a last-minute Internet deal for Thanksgiving weekend."

"No way!" said Sally. "You think I'd give up the chance to meet Emmylou and sing with Stone Jackson?"

All three men stared at her in horror. "Consider the circumstances. Briefly: nasty pranks, bullets, devious murder plots, even, for Christ's sake, a toxic spill. Somebody who already killed at least twice wants you out of the picture, Mustang, and you're acting like a lovesick groupie, throwing her undies over the fence where the Rolling Stones are holed up. Get a fucking grip, would you? Getting out of Dodge would be the prudent thing to do," Dickie finally managed.

"Or we could just lock you up until we make the collar," Scotty said placidly. "It'll probably only be a few days. Given the current political climate, I could probably get a warrant to arrest you for hanging around with radical environmentalists. That's practically terrorism. We wouldn't even have to let you talk to a lawyer. In fact, we could probably arrange for you to spend the Thanksgiving break in a chain-link cage in scenic Guantánamo Bay. Thank God for the Patriot Act."

"Come on, guys," said Sally. "I've got things to wrap up at school this week. So do you, darlin'," she told Hawk.

"Can the sweet talk," said Hawk. "Save it for the beach at Bimini."

She sighed. "Sorry, guys. I'm not going anywhere. I'll keep out of sight for the next couple of days, so you professionals can do your work. And I can do mine. Then, I swear on John Lennon's grave that I'll be careful. I'll go to the Thanksgiving dinner and the benefit, but other than that I'll hole up at home or my office. Hawk will look out for me, won't you?"

"Look what a great job I've been doing so far," he grumbled.

"I'd say you've been a saint, Hawk," said Scotty. "Most guys prefer women who don't have to undergo emergency decontamination procedures."

Scotty and Sally exchanged mock smiles.

"We're getting real close here, Sally," Dickie said as patiently as he could. "Can you manage to get the hell out of our way for at least a few days while we wrap this up? Then you can do whatever you want. Write your book, spend Nina Cruz's money on a mink coat, quit your job and move to Cody to be Stone Jackson's towel girl. That is if the Cruz money's still there, and Jackson isn't in jail," he finished.

"He didn't do it. Or Cat either. I'll bet you a hundred dollars," Sally said. "Look. It seems pretty obvious that whoever killed Nina and, presumably, Jimbo, knew what was in the can of stuff Nina used to make her breakfast power drink. By the way, has the lab finished the analysis?"

"Yes, as a matter of fact, they have. It was protein all right," said Dickie. "But not soy. Ground-up spinal cord and brain tissue from diseased cows. I doubt Ms. Cruz knew what she was putting in her morning milk shake."

"No," said Sally. "But she did know she was sick. She may even have suspected what was wrong with her. If she thought she had mad cow, she might have been willing to try anything to get better. Having passed several years of my wayward youth in hippie houses, I can testify from personal experience that counterculture types like Nina are pretty susceptible to dietary cures.

"People with terrible illnesses look for miracles where they can find them. She might have been hoping that those smoothies would save her life. In that case, whoever knew what was really in the cans must have been playing on Nina's hopeless hope. How cruel is that?" Sally asked.

Maybe not cruel in the eyes of a killer who saw Nina Cruz as a woman who wielded hope as a weapon of torture.

Sally groped at an answer, just out of reach.

"Thanks for that expert testimony," Scotty replied. "And I hope it will be your last attempt to involve yourself in this *police matter.* Go flunk some freshmen or something."

She stood up, put on her coat, walked out into the hall. The three men took a moment longer to get ready to go out into the cold night, pulling on gloves, exchanging soft words. Sally's hearing had suffered from too many years of standing in front of too many speakers, being blasted by too much rock 'n' roll. But she caught snatches of the conversation. "Incorrigible idiot." "Curious to a fault." "Taken out back, tied up, and whipped." And "extra protection."

Maybe it was the surreal moment in the taxidermy workshop, complete with monster and witches' brew. Maybe it was the knowledge that Jimbo hadn't been a murderer, that the dowdy Arvida was a complicated and interesting person, that even the Dub-Dubs had their virtues, and their reasons.

Or perhaps it was the fact that the halls and offices of the University of Wyoming were vacation quiet, her Tuesday class all but empty, most of the students having started the break the weekend before.

Or, possibly, it was the confidence of Dickie Langham and Scotty Atkins that they would soon know who had killed Nina Cruz and Jimbo Perrine, and why. For the first time in weeks, Sally enjoyed some peace of mind.

She even got a little of the holiday spirit. She wasn't cooking Thanksgiving dinner, of course. That task was in the capable hands of Pammie Montgomery, who was, despite Delice's grumbling, managing both her day job and the madness of the massive catering assignment with grace, efficiency, and a seemingly superhuman power to forgo sleep. According to Delice, Pammie was getting her prep work done at the Yippie I O between four and eight in the morning, when no one was there except the café's bakers, Quartz the soul mate and catering sous chef, and the indefatigable John-Boy. Delice didn't mention it when they talked on

Wednesday morning, the day before Thanksgiving, but Sally felt certain that John-Boy must be helping Pammie out. For that matter, if by doing nothing more than grumbling and looking the other way, Delice was giving Pammie a little boost, too. When Delice said something about "people who spend all their spare time caramelizing squash and toasting almonds and conning other people into chasing down fresh turkeys and organic brussels sprouts in Colorado," Sally suspected that Delice might have even made a helpful phone call or two.

"She'll have to clear out today, though. We're booked solid for Thanksgiving. So she'll move the whole operation over to the Holiday Inn tonight. It's fucking incredible, Mustang. This girl thinks she can pull off Thanksgiving dinner for a hundred and fifty, with full-scale meat-eater, vegetarian, and vegan menus. She's dealing with so many special dietary requests, you'd think she was running a hospital commissary. Those guys at the Holiday won't know what hit them! They probably think arugula is some kind of horrid skin condition."

"What do you think, Dee? Can she manage it?" Sally asked.

"Yeah. Probably. Although the kitchen will be chaos. She's got only four assistants, plus any volunteers she can snag. I guess she talked a couple of the Wild West weirdos into helping out."

"Which ones?" Sally asked.

"Her boyfriend, of course. Got him on the pies. Kid's got a good hand with pastry, but he gets distracted. Slave to his cell phone. Yesterday, he got a call and took off in the middle of rolling out dough for a dozen pecan pies. Stuck the dough in the fridge, but didn't even wash the flour off his hands. Came back an hour later, and didn't say a thing about where he'd been, just got back to work with the rolling pin. Pammie was pretty pissed, but then, he's working for free, so he can do as he damn well pleases."

"Who else is helping?"

"A few of her friends from college, and the two crackpots who don't eat cooked food."

"Lark and Kali? They're cooking?" Sally was taken aback.

"The blonde one won't touch anything that isn't raw. But the other one seems willing to deal with heating up vegan ingredients, as long as she doesn't have to eat what she cooks. It's not that weird. Remember that anorexic roommate you used to have, who cooked huge fattening meals for everybody else and then wouldn't eat a bite? Some people are just strange about food," Delice said.

"Sounds to me like Pammie could use some more helpers," Sally decided. "I can't make it tonight, but I could go over there tomorrow and give her a hand."

"What've you got going tonight?" Delice asked, assuming, as always, that everything was her business.

"Stone Jackson's coming over. We're going to run through a couple of songs."

Delice guffawed. "At last! Your lifelong dream come true. By the time you're done rehearsing, they'll have to put your knickers in the Laramie landfill."

"Many thanks for that delicate insight," Sally said.

"I presume Hawk will be there to chaperone?" Delice asked.

"Sure. He says it's a private performance he wouldn't miss. We'll work in the living room while he gets some grading done at the kitchen table."

"Good," said Delice. "Aside from any lascivious designs you may have on darlin' Tommy J, there's the little matter of whether the man killed his ex-wife. And then set up and murdered Jimbo Perrine, for that matter."

"How'd you hear about that?" Sally asked. The cops had decided, for the moment, not to release the information about Jimbo to the public.

"My brother told me, idiot. He figured I'd find out anyhow, and he wanted me to know so I could help keep an eye on you. You're not supposed to be alone with these people, girlfriend."

"What are you?" Sally said. "Deputy for a day?"

"Nope," said Delice. "I'm just a woman with an ounce of common sense, unlike you."

27

Running Without the Ball

Thomas Jackson arrived at the Eighth Street house carrying a guitar case and a large plastic to-go mug of coffee and looking haggard. He'd lost weight since Sally had seen him last, hadn't shaved in a couple of days, and he appeared to have slept in his .clothes. His skin was like parchment, his bones showing through. "I look like shit," he said as she let him in the house.

Actually, she was ashamed to admit, she found his worn-out wasted look appealing. It seemed to say, "I need help," and of course, she'd lived the better part of her life fantasizing about rescuing Stone Jackson from whatever devils pursued him. "You had anything to eat in the past week?" she asked him.

"I don't know. Probably. Could you try an easier question?" he asked.

"How about a toasted cheese sandwich and some tomato soup?" she said. "And I can make some more coffee."

He smiled wanly. "That'd be swell," he said.

And so he sat at the kitchen table, eating and chatting quietly with Hawk. It occurred to Sally that the two hadn't met before, and Hawk seemed anything but intimidated by the living legend sitting across from him, slurping canned tomato soup. Stone, for his part, expressed curiosity about the lab exercises Hawk was grading. They were hitting it off just fine.

She smiled. Dream Man meets Real Life. Considering the events of the past few weeks, Real Life was looking quite good.

But once Stone had fortified himself with a few calories, and the color had come back into his face, the dream took over again. They went into the living room, tuned up their guitars, and, without doing anything at all overt, without even buttoning the top two buttons of his rumpled flannel shirt, Thomas Jackson transformed himself from a fallible, flawed, exhausted human into a perfect vessel for the music of the cosmos. For a blissful time out of time, she gave herself to the magic.

Stone had decided they'd open the show by performing two of Nina's sweetest songs. "Morning for Women" was a feminist ballad so pretty, it almost made you forget the message. The second, "Wake Up Again," was about the inevitability of pain and change, and the eternal possibility of joy and renewal. "Wake Up Again" told one version of the story of Stone and Nina, one lesson about the relationships of humans who, despite everything, tried their damnedest to care for each other.

Other performers would take on Nina's darker material, her more outspoken political tunes. Toward the end, Thomas and Emmylou would do the soul-wrenching but soaring "Hard Way," and then Thomas would close the show with the song he'd finished for Nina, "Home at Last." The song was ostensibly about finding her way to Wyoming, to a home place she'd never known was there. Then again, it could be read another way: as the testament of a woman accepting imminent death as a kind of peace. It was hard to tell what Nina had left behind, and what Stone had added to "Home at Last."

Sally knew the old songs, of course. She'd been singing them for years, often as solo numbers when she'd played restaurant gigs and happy hours, almost always wishing somebody had been there to trade verses, put in the harmonies. She'd performed "Morning for Women" at potlucks and fund-raisers for women's groups, and you could pretty much count on getting everybody in the place to sing along.

But now, for the first time, the voice she'd always sung with in her head was right there in the room. Taking a solo break on a guitar whose sound she knew by heart. Singing with her as if they'd done it half the days of their lives.

Damn, the man was good. He was so good, he made her sound good. Which made her feel very good. Which made her sing and play better, maybe, than she ever had in her life.

"I think that'll do," he said after an hour and a half. "If we do half that well Friday night, we'll get things rolling nicely." He took a big swig from his coffee mug. "I hope to hell I can get through this. It just gets worse and worse. If they don't get the person who killed Nina and Perrine soon, I don't know what I'm gonna do."

"So you heard about the gun," Sally said.

"Yeah," said Stone. "The sheriff called me. Wanted to know what I thought about it."

"And what do you think?" she asked.

"I'm beyond thinking," he answered. "I'm on autopilot. I'll think after the gig."

"In the meantime," Sally said, "you'd better take real good care of yourself, Stone." She took a deep breath, knowing she was probably stepping over the line. "You might think about going to a meeting."

He closed his eyes, nodded his head, smiled. "Already did. And going to another one tomorrow morning. And every day, if I need to, until I don't."

"It's good to have backup," Sally said, thinking of Hawk in the other room, working over the lab exercises.

"It's life and death sometimes, Dr. Alder," said Stone, opening his case and putting his guitar away. "We'll run through those once or twice tomorrow sometime, then again at the sound check Friday morning. I think we'll be good."

"Thank you, Thomas," she said.

"Don't thank me. It ain't over until we do it the hard way, one last time," he answered, taking his leave.

She went into the kitchen. Hawk looked up from his papers, eyes luminous, shaking his head.

"That," he said, "was the most amazing live musical performance I have ever heard. You sounded beautiful. That man sings like heaven on earth. Thank you for letting me listen in."

"Thank you for loving me," she said, wrapping her arms around him, kissing him very gently, and smiling. "There are several ways I would like to express my appreciation. Would you come to bed with me now?"

Maybe Thomas Jackson had left some of his magic in the house. Or maybe they were making their own, out of the ache and wonder of living on the planet, of bad and good fortune, of still having the capacity for amazement. Eventually they dozed off, nested like spoons, and slept peacefully and deep, waking in the brilliant sunlight of Thanksgiving morning.

It'll happen today, Sally thought as she laced up her running shoes. She knew it. They'd get the killer today.

"Hey, there," said Hawk. "What are you doing?"

"Putting on my shoes," she answered genially.

"Maybe I'll come along," he said.

She cocked her head and gave him a look. "You know how you feel about running. You say you can't understand why anybody would do it without a ball being somehow involved."

"I play basketball. Sometimes you have to run without the ball," he said.

"True. But then you have to anticipate what the other guys are going to do. Even when you're a team player, it's more fun to have the ball," she said.

"Okay. So today I'm all about the team. You can entertain me."

Laramie was holiday quiet, traffic nearly nonexistent. She knew Hawk could run a lot faster than she could, if he chose. But he loped along companionably, discussing everything from the latest political comedy in California to Wyoming basketball (the Lady Pokes' chances looked pretty good).

Everything, that is, except the main thing on their minds. She noticed he'd stuck the cell phone in the back pocket of his shorts, prepared for an emergency. At least he'd left the Smith and Wesson at home.

"I've got a feeling," she said at last. "They're going to catch the murderer today, Hawk."

"I think so, too," he said. "So why don't you relax and let Dickie and Scotty do their jobs, and you can help out Pammie, eat some great grub, and rub shoulders with the rich and famous?"

"My plan, exactly." She nodded for emphasis, and fell silent for half a block. "But I've been thinking," she began again, "about the question of what I know about Nina's life and death, and why somebody is so scared that I know it, that they'd try to kill me."

"I admit," said Hawk, "that I've wondered about those things myself."

"I keep going back to two things: the note I found in Nina's office, and the can of protein powder."

"What about that day of research out at Shady Grove? And what about all the interviews and conversations you've had?"

They were heading north now, slightly uphill. She huffed and puffed and thought awhile. "It's possible somebody might think I found something in Nina's papers, but they'd have no way of knowing what I'd looked at. Sure, there might be something there that would expose the murderer. But I didn't find it. The tough part about being a historian is that you usually have to noodle around in stuff for quite a while before you either happen across what you're looking for, or realize that something you've already seen matters."

"But the Halloween prank—" Hawk began, as they turned to loop around LaBonte Park.

"Suggests that whoever pulled it wanted to scare me away from digging further."

"Wouldn't they be better off with you poking around in Nina's stuff than, say, Scotty Atkins and his crew?"

Their feet slapped on the dirt track worn in the park grass. "Maybe. Scotty has more resources and a good enough brain. I just don't think the papers are the issue. And as for the interviews," she said, "any one of these people could be afraid of what somebody else might have said to me. But what I've learned doing oral histories over the years is that they generally consist of stories the interviewees feel like telling. People very rarely blab out things they don't want known. I need to assume that the people I've talked to told me exactly what they wanted me to hear. Consider old Randy Whitebird, for instance. The guy's made a career out of manipulating information to his advantage."

"There's no reason to think that the others wouldn't at least try to do the same," Hawk agreed.

"So, let's focus on the note and the powder," Sally said. "The only person who saw me with the note was Lark. Unless she wrote it, she probably wouldn't have known what it was. But she might have told somebody that I'd picked up a piece of paper in Nina's office. And the most likely somebody, from what I've seen, is Kali."

"Although at that point, from what you've told me, everybody out at Shady Grove was in shock. You were an outsider. She was one of a bunch of insiders. Lark might have told anybody. And it sounds like Nels Willen was pretty much holding things together out there," Hawk observed.

"Even though Whitebird made a point of saying he was in charge," Sally said. "Now about that powder. If that was the source of the prions in Nina's brain, she'd have had to have been taking it for a long time. Whoever was giving it to her must have known her awhile." Sally made a list: "Cat. Stone. Willen. Kali. I don't know for sure how long she's known Whitebird or Lark."

"Who knew you had a can of the stuff?" Hawk asked.

"Pammie gave it to me. Quartz was there. But they might have told anybody I'd taken it. I admit, poisoned powder doesn't seem like Cat's style. And I have a very hard time imagining Stone saying to Nina, 'Try this fabulous new health food product,' while he's snorting up lines and chasing them with Chivas."

"What about after he cleaned up his act?" Hawk asked.

"Still seems like a remote possibility. By that time, she was involved with Willen, and then with Kali, and with God knows who else. And we have to consider the possibility that the powder wasn't the source of Nina's disease. There was that Swiss doctor, force-feeding her organ meats after that skiing accident way back when."

"Have you asked Stone about that?" Hawk inquired, as they took the final turn around the park and headed back home.

Sally searched her memory. "Actually, no. The only source I have for that information is Nels Willen."

"The same Nels Willen who brought the rifle to Shady Grove. The same guy who may well have ended his medical career with an intentional act of malpractice."

"Which brings me back to that powder. Seems pretty clear. Somebody knew what was wrong with it, and also knew I had a can. Somebody who wanted to kill Nina Cruz slowly, but then decided to use bullets instead, on both Nina and Jimbo Perrine. Somebody who claims to hold life sacred, but doesn't, in the end, have much regard for human beings. Very scary disconnect."

"Now you see what it's like, running without the ball," said Hawk.

28

Turkey, Tofu, and Bull Balls

Pammie Montgomery's kitchen was pure madness.

The first person Sally spotted was Randy Whitebird, wearing a white chef's jacket and yelling into a cell phone. "T.K.? What was that? Seven of the crew are what?" He listened a moment, said "Hold on," and yelled, "Seven of the roadies are on the Atkins diet, and two of the people from the lighting company are hi carb. So some of 'em want a steak, and the others are requesting pasta or rice. We've also got three on the crew who are lactose-intolerant, and a sound guy who keeps kosher."

"Oh, for Christ's sake!" Cat Cruz hollered from the sink, where she appeared to be hosing down a large object in the sink. "Kosher? Like there's any kosher food in the entire state of Wyoming."

"Pickles?" Sally ventured. "You can always find pickles."

"I can't fucking believe it!" exclaimed Pammie Montgomery, picking up a large pale, roundish object from a long steel table and dropping it back on the table with a clang. "These fucking turkeys are frozen solid! How the hell am I supposed to be able to cook them by tonight? The fucking supplier *promised* fresh organic turkeys!"

Sally walked over to the table. Five turkeys, wrapped in plastic and plainly labeled *fresh* and *organic,* sat stonily side by side. She pushed a finger into the surface of one, and found it frigid and unyielding. "Maybe these are extra-virgin turkeys," she said.

"Why don't you just send somebody down to the Lifeway and pick up a few turkeys? They always keep some around for Thanksgiving cooks who don't plan ahead. Hell, you could probably get the whole dinner with all the trimmings, precooked and packed to go," said Hawk.

"But they won't be organic!" Pammie screamed. "How do I explain that?"

"You don't," said Hawk. "You fake it. Don't tell anybody. Maybe extend cocktail hour for good measure. A few extra tequilas and they won't know an organic turkey from a turkey buzzard."

"I like this guy," said Cat, grinning at Hawk, who beamed back. "Quartz, go on down to the supermarket and pick up five turkeys. We don't care if they're hooked on crack, as long as they're thawed. If they don't have 'em, see if they'll sell you a bunch of turkey dinners. If you don't want to serve up the mashed potatoes and dinner rolls, Pammie, you can skip the extras."

"I really don't think that's a good idea, Cat. You'd be surprised how many people can tell the difference between the real thing and the birds that have been shot up with a million hormones and then pumped so full of grease so they practically slide off the shelf," said Quartz, wrinkling up his nose.

"We don't have a choice. I'm not going to spend the next two hours giving these stupid birds warm baths and hoping they come around," Pammie decided. "And if the ones they have at the Lifeway happen to be self-basting, that's okay with me. That is, if I can remember to check when the little timer thing pops up. I always forget, and then they cook themselves to charcoal. Be a love, Quartz, and go get them."

"I really don't think I should leave, sweetheart. I've got focaccias and ciabattas—"

"I can deal with your dough, son," said Nels Willen, a chef's hat atop his braids and a white jacket hanging off his skinny frame. "Go get the lady's turkeys."

"How are those potatoes coming over there?" Pammie yelled to a girl at another sink, peeling potatoes out of a huge sack.

"I think these actually are organic," came the reply. "Half of them are rotten."

"That's a good sign," Lark offered from a counter where she was slicing up cabbages. "They haven't been sprayed or inoculated with preservatives."

"Jesus, preserve my sanity," said Pammie. "Are you going or what, Quartz?"

Grudgingly, the young man shucked off his white jacket, pulled on a coat, and said he'd be back as soon as possible.

Things only got crazier from there. Pammie gave Sally and Hawk white jackets to wear ("I want my kitchen staff to look professional") and put Hawk in charge of hauling boxes of things out of and back into the walk-in refrigerator. Sally was put to work chopping onions and garlic, chiles and ginger, for a sweet and hot deep-fried tofu noodle dish sure to please the palate of the most discriminating vegan. Kali stood tending the fryer, transforming cubes of bean curd from bland little chunks of health into crispy morsels of deep-fat goodness. "How do you feel about that?" Sally asked as she brushed off her garlicky hands and delivered a bowlful of chopped stuff to Pammie, who was creating the sauce.

"About frying up what would otherwise be perfectly good food?" Kali shrugged, sending her earrings into a little snaky dance. "I wouldn't touch the stuff if you paid me. But at least it started out life as a bean," she said, and sighed heavily. She looked tiny and vulnerable, despite the dangling reptiles framing her pixie face. "I guess you do what you have to do."

"I'm really sorry I haven't gotten a chance to hear your story yet," said Sally. "I hope you'll have time for me soon."

"I doubt it," said Kali. "Cat has made it clear I'm not welcome here, and as you're probably aware, I have other things to deal with." She dipped a strainer into bubbling oil and lifted out golden morsels of tofu.

Sally selected an onion, began chopping, and took a chance. "So it wasn't just coincidence that your company was working on a cure for spongiform encephalopathy?" she asked.

Kali glanced up from the fryer, her expression pained. "No. Of course not. Nina had begun exhibiting symptoms several years ago."

"But the kinds of symptoms she evidently had could have been lots of things. Why would you suspect mad cow disease?" Sally asked.

"If you knew anything about the death trade in animals," Kali told her, "you wouldn't have to ask that question. Nina had been a carnivore for much of her life. I myself grew up eating flesh, and not just supermarket stuff—my dad used to take me hunting every fall. Everyone who uses animals for food is at far greater risk than they know," she finished.

Hunting every fall? Kali, Willen, who else? How many of these animal rights people had come by their politics after they'd taken their finger off the trigger?

As for the dangers of meat eating, sure, there were reasons to tread lightly at the top of the food chain, but Sally was pretty sure Kali was overstating the case. Even if the fried tofu was looking better than it had a moment ago. "So once you started to have suspicions about what was wrong with Nina, you went to work on a cure?" she asked.

Kali searched Sally's eyes. "If the person you loved most was facing death, wouldn't you do all you could to save her? I'm a biomedical researcher. Nina was desperate. She knew I'd give it everything I had, and I did. She supported the work. We were close, very close, to a breakthrough. Then somebody killed her."

"Why?" Sally asked her. "Who do you think could have done such a thing?"

"I couldn't say," Kali replied, returning her attention to the fryer. "But I comfort myself with the knowledge that at least she never knew I'd failed."

Sally was struggling to come up with a subtle way to ask Kali about the protein powder, but she never got a chance. "Hey there, honey child," hollered Delice Langham, coming in the door, and toting a turkey in a plastic mesh bag in each hand. "I ran into the lad here at the market," she said, tossing her head back at Quartz, who had followed her in with three more big birds. "John-Boy had run out of Jimmy Dean sausage for his stuffed mushrooms."

"What are you doing here, Dee?" asked Sally, looking around for Kali and cursing her missed opportunity.

"I figured if you were reduced to running to the supermarket for industrial-grade turkeys, you could probably use a hand," said Delice. "When we dropped off the sausage, it was clear that John-Boy's got things under control at the café, and Thanksgiving at the Wrangler's just business as usual. Besides, I'm not about to miss out on Emmylou."

Hawk emerged from the cooler with a large, heavy cardboard box. "Hey, Pammie!" he said. "What were you planning to do with these oysters?"

"I figured I'd serve 'em raw, on the half shell. Lemon and fresh horseradish and cocktail sauce on the side. That ought to at least satisfy the Atkins diet roadies, huh?"

Hawk put the box down and gave it a dubious glance. "I don't know about raw. And they don't have shells. Don't know who your supplier is on this one, but they sent Rocky Mountain oysters."

Sally gave a hoot. "Bull balls! Perfect! Those roadies will be throwing amps through the windows by the time it's all over."

Cat collapsed in hysterics. Even Nels Willen was giggling. Pammie, meanwhile, had fallen onto a stool and pulled her chef's jacket over her head.

"Don't sweat it, honey," said Delice. "Somebody give me a cell phone. Sam Arnold down at the Fort in Denver sells like a million of these babies a year to people who pay a week's wages for a buffalo steak. Don't know exactly what he does with bull balls, but evidently it's incredible. I'll find out. Then you'll all have to try a taste."

Nearly everyone laughed. Kali and Lark paled and left the room. "Just kidding!" Delice hollered after them, moving to the fryer to take up Kali's abandoned position. "What's in here?" she asked, shaking the fryer basket.

"Tofu," Sally said.

"Eww. Gross," said Delice, never one to pass up a cheap shot.

"That was really mean," Quartz told Delice. "I'm going to see if they're all right." He scurried out after the two women.

"He's a doll," Sally told Pammie.

"Yeah, he is. I think he's going to move back to Oregon after this, though," Pammie said, tasting her sweet and hot sauce, nodding, then taking it off the heat and moving to another pan.

"That's a drag," said Sally.

"Yeah. Maybe. I've been thinking about ditching UW and going out there to go to culinary school. And John-Boy knows chefs in both Portland and Eugene. He said he's sure I could get on at a great restaurant."

Love. It could change your life.

As the afternoon wore on, the atmosphere grew more and more hectic. But dish by dish, the Thanksgiving feast began to take shape. Pammie's menu, posted on the wall, was staggering: polenta tortas and pumpkin flans and curried vegetable stews; brussels sprouts with brown butter and almonds; wild mushroom ragouts and winter-squash risotto; Chinese tofu and fresh cabbage confetti slaw. Garlic mashed potatoes, sweet potato gratin, bread stuffing with apricots and golden raisins, cranberries five or ten ways, pies and pies and pies. No steak, unfortunately, for the Atkins enthusiasts, but the aroma of roasting turkey perfumed the air.

And the kitchen grew ever hotter, noisier, more crowded. As the production crews at the stadium finished with their setups and sound checks and light checks, hungry roadies and techies and security people wandered in looking for snacks. The local police had accepted the invitation in droves, a notoriously ravenous bunch. Pammie had to get someone to find Dickie Langham to get them out of her way. For his part, Quartz seemed to have appointed himself kitchen cop, and he chased out visitors with an aggressiveness that surprised Sally.

All the while, Sally smashed and skinned and chopped what seemed to her a nearly endless pile of garlic cloves. As her hands began to sweat garlic fumes, she asked Quartz, "Is there any reason this couldn't be done mostly in a food processor?"

"Pammie likes it done by hand," he said simply. "Would you rather do more chiles?" And then he moved over to chase off an electrician who'd sidled up to a counter and was helping himself to a piece of pecan pie.

Stone Jackson, in his role as chief talent and co-producer, had been supervising the technical run-through, and he showed up with Terry Kean, the concert promoter. They seemed preoccupied, but confident. Pammie offered to fix them a snack, but they allowed as how they'd stopped off at the Wrangler for eggs and bacon. "That's some good grease they got there," said T.K.

Delice stepped forward, beaming, to introduce herself to them and explain precisely how much pride she took in her grease.

Sally interrupted Delice. "Stone, could I ask you something?" she said, putting down her knife and wiping her hands on a dish towel.

"Sure," he answered. "It's pretty noisy in here. Let's go outside."

Sounded like a good idea. Sally finished up, washed her hands, rubbed them with lemon. Then mint. Then parsley. Then lemon again. No good. Garlic. No wonder it worked on vampires. It was immortal, too. She'd have to make sure Hawk ate a lot of those mashed potatoes.

As she walked out the door, the cold air hit her like a blessing, and she realized just how hot it was in the kitchen. "This is going to seem like a strange question," she told Jackson, "but I want to ask you about the time Nina tore up her knee, skiing in Switzerland."

"That was pretty terrible," said Stone. "I wasn't a whole lot of help, I'm sorry to say. I was barely aware of what was going on with her. I mean, I was such a mess, I even tried to hustle her doctors for drugs."

"Did they give them to you?" she asked.

"To their credit, no," he said. "One guy tried to get me into detox, but I wasn't having any of that. Another one suggested a diet of organ meats to replenish lost brain cells." Stone smiled. "Might've helped. At least it would have been solid food, something I wasn't seeing much of at the time."

So Willen's story about the Swiss doctor checked out. "You know, Thomas, Nels Willen thinks that Nina got mad cow from the diet that doctor put her on," she told him.

Stone nodded. "He told me as much. And he's still beating himself up about it. But what could Nels do? By the time he got there, the guy had been treating her for two weeks. And who knew anything about mad cow disease at that time? This is all twenty-twenty hindsight. Nels needs to let himself off the hook."

The door opened, and Willen himself came out. "Hotter than heck in there," he said, taking off his chef's cap, pulling a bandana from the back pocket of his jeans, and wiping his face.

"Hey, bro'," said Stone, clapping Willen on the shoulder. "You doin' okay?"

"Yeah, yeah. I'll be fine," Willen said. "The chaos helps. By the way, Thomas, Terry Kean's looking for you."

"I gotta get back in there," said Stone. "Be excellent unto yourselves." He opened the door to the kitchen and disappeared inside.

"Nina would have loved this," Willen observed quietly. "She liked a big crazy scene like this as much as she liked being all by herself in a beautiful silent place. She loved being alive."

"You miss her a lot, don't you?" Sally said.

"Yeah," he answered. "But I'll get by. And whatever happens to the Wild West, I've got the means to carry on the work we both cared about. It's not like it's the first time I've had to deal with tragedy. I'm worried about some of the others."

She looked up at him. "Stone's really been through it," she said.

He nodded. "So has Cat, although she tries not to show it. Likes people to think she eats nails for breakfast, but she wouldn't spend all that time in refugee camps if she didn't give a damn."

"I think Mr. Whitebird will survive," Sally said.

Willen gave a half smile. "That guy seems like the kind who could survive an atom bomb, and crawl out from under the rubble selling radiation as a cure for carbuncles."

Sally laughed. "But he loved her, too. At least he was sincere in that." She thought a moment. "And what about Kali?"

Willen shook his head. "She's devastated. I mean, we all loved Angelina, but most of us understood that she was a woman no one person could hold. Kali, well, she never gave up hoping. Poor thing's like to die of a broken heart. But then, I've known her a few years now, and she's never been what you'd call a ray of sunshine, exactly. Think she wears all that white 'cause the darkness comes in pretty close to where she lives."

Sally's vision hazed over in red.

Hawk burst out the door. "What the hell are you doing out here alone with him?" he said.

"Oh, come on now, Green. I like your woman a lot, but she's too young for the likes of me," said Nels.

"For God's sake, Hawk!" she said. "He's no danger to me. Listen—"

Hawk glared and grabbed her by the arm. "Come on in. Emmylou has entered the building."

Back in the kitchen, the quiet was deafening. Pammie was giving a taste to a huge pan of rich brown gravy, adding a swirl of salt and giving the sauce a whisk, turning the burner down to low. The five turkeys, golden and gorgeous, were lined up on the counter, set to rest and gather their juices before they could be carved for the feast. Everyone else had apparently gone into the ballroom to gawk at the Queen of Country. "Let's go meet Her Highness," Pammie said, wiping her hands on the dish towel at her waist. "And then it'll be showtime."

"Where's Kali?" Sally asked her. "I really have to find her."

Pammie furrowed her brow. "Haven't seen her in a few minutes. Probably out making her curtsy like the rest of us. Come on. Let's have a minute of fun. Then we'll do what we have to do."

You do what you have to do. And if you live on the dark side, that could include anything. If you fashioned yourself into the goddess of death and destruction, the other half of the cycle of birth and creativity, you might have to do just about anything.

And if you knew that the person you loved almost more than life was dying of a horrible disease, you might devote your life to trying to find a cure. And when you failed, maybe you took life into your own hands.

"Hey, Pammie," Sally said. "Did you happen to mention to anybody that I'd taken a can of Nina's soy powder?"

Pammie thought a minute. "Yeah, actually I did. I was out at Shady Grove right before Halloween, picking up some kitchen stuff Cat was giving me. Kali showed up, said she'd left some things behind, and opened the cupboard where Nina kept her stash of the supplement. Kali sat there a minute, and then said she thought there must be one can missing. I told her you'd taken it. Did I get you in trouble?"

"No," Sally lied. "Thanks."

Pammie nodded. "It's time to go curtsy to the Queen," she said, heading for the ballroom.

So now Sally knew. Kelly Lee Brisbane, zealot, acolyte, scientist, searcher after magic bullets, was capable of loving someone to death.

The party was in full swing, and dotted with celebrities. Sally passed a group clustered around Graham and David, telling stories about previous charity gigs. But it was easy to locate Emmylou by the crowd gathered in one corner. Sally caught a glimpse of abundant silver hair and a flashing smile as the white-jacketed Pammie made through the throng for her introduction. She saw Emmylou hug the chef.

"Maybe I can get a hug," Hawk said. "I'm not usually pushy in crowds, but I could make an exception."

"Later," said Sally. "Right now, we've got to find Kali. She's the one, Hawk. She killed Nina and Jimbo. I'll explain later, but I've got it figured. Have you seen Dickie or Scotty?"

"Not in the last few minutes." He scanned the crowd. "Don't see Kali either. She's kind of small to spot," he said.

"But she ought to be easy to find. She always wears all white," Sally said.

Hawk looked down at himself, and then at her, in their chef's jackets. "That's not going to be a lot of help in here today."

"Maybe she's back in the kitchen," Sally said. "I'll go take a look."

"No, you don't," said Hawk. "Let's go find Dickie or Atkins first. The woman's already shot two people, you say, and you're going after her?"

Sally took a breath. He was right. How stupid could she be?

Dickie Langham turned out to be right where she should have expected. She could see his Stetson hat sticking above the crowd, right next to Emmylou, Stone Jackson, and, of course, Delice. Sally shoved through the people, Hawk in her wake, and found Dickie telling a law enforcement joke Emmylou was apparently enjoying.

She didn't even stop to introduce herself. "I'm really sorry," she told Emmylou, "but could I borrow the sheriff here for a minute?"

"I'll look forward to resuming our conversation, Sheriff," Emmylou said graciously, as Dickie tipped his hat and Delice moved between Emmylou and Stone, hooking her arms through theirs and launching into a joke about cowboys and chewing tobacco.

Sally dragged Dickie into the kitchen. Most of the help had drifted back in to do the final preparation for dinner. Kali was nowhere to be seen.

"You've gotta find Kali, Dick," Sally told him.

He frowned and said, "Okay."

Pammie, meanwhile, was in a state.

"Sally Alder!" she yelled. "You were the one chopping garlic. Did you put a bunch of fucking garlic in my gravy?"

Sally looked at her in puzzlement. "No. I didn't touch your gravy," she said.

"It's ruined!" Pammie wailed. "Somebody came in here and dumped garlic in my perfect gravy! Smell this!" She waved a hand over the gravy pan, wafting fumes Sally's way.

Sally walked toward the stove, but she didn't really need to get close. The whole kitchen reeked of garlic. "Wow," she said. "That's pretty strong."

"I can only imagine how it tastes," said Pammie, her chef's curiosity leading her to pick up a spoon, dip it into the gravy, put her other hand under the spoon to catch drips, and raise it toward her lips.

"Don't! Don't touch that stuff! Do not taste that gravy!"

Quartz's voice. Coming from the doorway between the kitchen and the ballroom. "I mean it, Pammie. You're right, somebody's been at your gravy, but that's not garlic you're smelling. It's poison!"

"Arsenic," said Dr. Nels Willen. "Smells like garlic when it's heated."

Pammie paused, spoon halfway to her mouth, staring at Quartz. Everyone followed her gaze.

And there stood Quartz, pressing a large pistol to the neck of the woman who called herself Kali.

Cat Cruz, standing next to Pammie, grabbed the spoon and hurled it against the wall, just as Scotty Atkins burst in, gun drawn. Dickie grabbed Kali by the arms and held her while Scotty cuffed her hands behind her back and began to recite the Miranda warning.

"Quartz?" Pammie said, her face the picture of puzzlement. "What's going on? What's with the gun? Where are they taking Kali?"

"She's under arrest for murder," he said shortly, in a far less mellow tone voice than Sally had ever heard him use.

"Ladies and gentlemen," said Dickie, "we'd like to ask you to remain where you are, while we secure the premises. Much as it pains me to say this, we ask that nobody touch any of the food. We'll be conducting brief interviews and gathering evidence. When we're done with you, you'll all be free to go about your business."

"What about the feast?" Pammie said.

"I'm sorry. Nobody's to touch a thing. We have reason to suspect that this food has been subjected to malicious tampering. It would be very stupid to think about eating it," Dickie answered.

"What about the stuff people have already eaten?" Cat asked, alarm blooming on her face.

"We're suggesting that everyone stay here. A medical team will arrive shortly to check people out and offer advice."

"About what?" Sally asked.

"Symptoms of poisoning," Scotty said.

Everyone froze.

"I can start checking people right now," said Dr. Nels Willen, breaking the collective paralysis. And then he addressed Kali. "Why? Why would you do this?"

Her eyes were bright, but strangely unfocused. Her voice, usually nearly inaudible, rang out. "Great causes demand great sacrifices, Nels," she said. "Nina was willing. She knew we'd never be able to convince the public that animal rights mattered until there was a human martyr to the cause, somebody to put a famous face on it. A Rock Hudson or an Arthur Ashe. Why not Nina Cruz?"

"And you made sure she'd be a martyr, didn't you?" Sally put in. "With that little protein supplement you kept supplying her. She didn't even know you were poisoning her, did she, Kali? She thought you were trying to find a cure."

"I was!" Kali protested. "I tried! Madicin had incredible potential. Nina knew that. The supplement should have worked!"

"The supplement?" Sally said. "It was full of prions. You were giving her medicine that had as much potential to kill her as to cure her?"

"You'd be surprised," said Nels Willen, "how common a pharmacological strategy that is."

"You used my sister as a guinea pig!" Cat had pushed through the crowd. "What did she do, Kelly Lee? When she realized that you'd failed, did she tell you she was selling out of BIOS? Cutting you out of her will? That'd be like Nina. Noble intentions and a quick exit. But you couldn't let that happen, could you?"

"She was doomed anyway, Cat. She was willing to offer her life to a higher purpose. My work had to go on."

"Your *work*! You shot at me!" Sally said. "And you killed

Jimbo Perrine. Who doesn't count as a sacrificial lamb, when it comes to your work?"

"I didn't know what you might find in Nina's stuff. And then, of course, you had the protein powder. I had to act." Kali looked around, eyes on fire. "I'm just sorry," she said, "that all of you who came to honor Nina Cruz by eating slaughtered animals won't have the honor of following her to the other side."

"That's enough." Dickie turned to Scotty. "Take her away," he said, gesturing at Kali. "I'll be out there in a minute." Then he turned back to the people gaping at him from around the kitchen. "We're sorry. We appreciate your help, folks. I'll be back in a little while. In the meantime, would you all please cooperate with the investigating officer?"

They all looked at one another.

Quartz hitched up the hem of his chef's jacket, stuck the gun in his belt, and pulled a wallet out of his back pocket. He flipped it open, revealing an identification card and a shiny badge. "Agent Quentin Schwartz," he said, "Federal Bureau of Investigation."

29

Snowing. Again.

After the Thanksgiving dinner that never was, the benefit concert was almost an anticlimax. For one thing, once the dinner guests learned that every morsel of the feast Pammie Montgomery had conjured up was to be disposed of as hazardous waste, they had to do something about dinner. Delice invited everyone down to the Wrangler. ("It won't be fancy, but to our knowledge we haven't killed anybody yet. At least not directly. At least not in the restaurant.") And just about everyone went. By the end of the evening, the cast and crew of the Night for Nina were so excited and satisfied, they hauled out their instruments for an impromptu jam. Those few lucky Laramie folk who happened into the Bar and Grill got a treat Sally would never in her craziest fantasies have imagined. Delice said she'd never, ever forget the sight of Emmylou sitting on one of her very own bar stools, crooning "I'll Be Your San Antone Rose."

Cat paid the bar tab and kept a close eye on Stone. He ate three cheeseburgers, but stuck to coffee.

And the next night went off without a hitch. No technical problems, no performers too loaded to perform, not even the usual flaming egos on display. Some people were a little freaked out by all the extra security people Cat had insisted on bringing in, but for Sally's part, that was just fine. From Sally and Stone's opening duet to the encore, with everyone on stage singing and crying their way through Bob Dylan's "Farewell, Angelina," everything went so well, Sally, perversely, was almost disappointed. The benefit made enough money to cover costs, without a penny to spare for the cause, of course. The annual blizzard even held off.

Until Saturday, when a fast-moving wall of snow slammed in from the West, shutting down the countryside from Salt Lake City to Omaha, from Flagstaff to Amarillo. Some of the out-of-towners, heading off in rental cars bound for Denver International Airport, in buses and semis and VW vans, had left right after the gig Friday night, trying to beat the coming storm. Those who had dallied were likely to be stranded somewhere on the road, or joining other Thanksgiving weekend travelers enjoying an extended stay in DIA.

Snowing. Again.

The world outside the house on Eighth Street was blanketed in white, the early afternoon light diffuse and dusky.

"So there's one thing I still don't understand," said Hawk, cracking open a Budweiser and sitting down at the kitchen table. "How did Kali work the setup with Jimbo Perrine? How did she find him in the first place?"

"Seems like Jimbo had a little business going, buying and selling guns off the books. You could do it on the Internet," said Sally. "Nobody knows who anybody is in cyberspace."

"Right. They'd never even have to meet in real space," Hawk said. "You could do pretty much everything anonymously, using encrypted electronic transmissions and a global freight delivery service."

"Up to a point. Kali must have decided that even the anonymous transaction didn't give her cover. She had to clean up the last loose end. Probably told herself that anybody who dealt in black-market guns had it coming," said Sally. "Weird. That's pretty much what Jimbo said about Nina Cruz. He and Kali had more in common than he'd have ever believed."

"Yeah," said Hawk. "But Jimbo never killed any people." He paused. "For what it's worth, I don't think she was planning to kill you at first. I think she just wanted to scare you off with the Halloween thing. Then she got desperate when it didn't work."

"Oh, I don't know. She struck me as pretty strange from the moment I met her," Sally said.

"Precisely my point. She's a head case, clearly, but recall the business she was in, and her connections to international bad guys."

Sally's eyes got big. "Oh. I see your point."

"Yeah," said Hawk. "If she'd wanted to kill you on Halloween, she might not have had that much trouble getting real anthrax."

She reached across the table and grabbed his hand. For a little while, they sat without speaking.

"She couldn't let her go," she said at last. "If Kali couldn't have Nina, nobody could."

"More likely, if Nina was going to sell BIOS short, she'd lose her life savings. What a way to stop insider trading," said Hawk. "It would be really interesting to know who told the police that Kali was in Salt Lake City the morning Nina was killed."

"Probably somebody who's on the way to Stuttgart with a suitcase full of Euros. Recall that Kali showed up in government surveillance photos of radical animal rights groups," Sally observed. "There are more of them out there, Hawk." On that note, she got up and opened a Budweiser of her own. "For that matter, remember that the FBI has been interested in the Wild West bunch for quite a while."

"Right," said Hawk. "The FBI. Including undercover agent Schwartz."

"Now that I think back on it," said Sally, "it must've been Quartz I saw sitting in Scotty Atkins's 4Runner, out on Ivinson. Talk about hiding in plain sight!"

"You know, I wondered how Pammie would take the news that her soul mate was a willing tool of the fascist state," Hawk said.

"From what I've seen, she doesn't appear to be interested

in politics, one way or another. Anyway, it sure didn't look like it bothered her any last night."

Quartz and Pammie had been hugging and kissing at the wrap party after the benefit, an affair featuring food flown in from Stone's favorite Nashville barbecue joint. Pammie just didn't have it in her to kick out one more bash, though she vowed she'd cook again, and she was still thinking about moving to Portland. Quartz said he was going to ask the Bureau for a desk assignment.

"So what do you think about the dope brownies?" Hawk asked.

"I guess Kali could have sent them, just to keep Arvida from noticing anything that might help the cops pick up the thread. But somehow, I don't see Kali whipping up a batch of pot brownies. Maybe it really was somebody else, and they just don't want to own up to it," Sally said. "I'll have to keep an eye on the boys in the band. Any of 'em show up for practice looking extra goofy, I might mention the matter and see how they react."

The doorbell rang.

Two bundled-up figures stood on the front step, frosted with fast-falling snow. Thomas Jackson and Caterina Cruz.

"We stayed in town last night so we could go grocery shopping," Cat explained as they shook off the snow, pulled off knitted caps and gloves, and walked in. "We're on our way out to Shady Grove before we can't get there. But we wanted to stop in and thank you for sticking with this thing."

"Ah shucks," said Sally.

"And we made a point of telling that lovely Detective Atkins we thought you'd been a big help," Cat said.

"Great," said Sally. "I bet he was really delighted to hear that."

"Sally only did it because she's been in love with you her whole life," Hawk told Stone.

"That happens with a lot of women," said Stone. "But they usually get over it once they meet me."

"Not me," said Cat.

"Me either," said Sally. "But I'm afraid you're in line behind the big guy here." She pulled Hawk close and gave him a squeeze.

"So it's sloppy seconds for me," said Stone.

"Hey! What do you think I'm settling for?" Cat said, looking up at him.

Stone gazed at Cat, with more peace in his eyes than Sally could have believed possible for Thomas Jackson, world-famous victim of bad love. "How about the undying devotion you deserve from somebody better than some old broken-down Tin Pan Alley hack?" he asked.

"Land's sake," said Cat. "You'll turn my head."

"You guys are really cute together," said Sally. "Now get out of here, while you still can."

"Hey," said Stone. "We just heard some news on the radio. Seems the Game and Fish Department found the poacher who shot the deer. A seventeen-year-old kid. He said that after he fired the shot, he noticed that the animal was sick and decided to take off. Appears he was driving his father's Dodge Ram, and the game warden managed to track down somebody who'd seen him skedaddling and recognized the truck. He's evidently cooperating with both the Game and Fish and the Albany County Sheriff's Department, at the suggestion of his father, a municipal court judge."

So much blood, that fateful morning at Shady Grove.

Sally had to ask. "So what's going to happen with Nina's place?"

"I'm going to hang on to it for the moment," said Cat. "I kind of like it out there. Though there are a lot of ghosts. Who knows? Maybe I'll make it a wildlife refuge. Or become a developer and subdivide it."

Sally and Hawk grimaced.

"Just kidding," said Stone. "Right, darlin'?"

Cat smiled enigmatically.

"Boy," said Sally, deciding a change of subject was in order, "it's too bad the benefit didn't make any money. Poor old Arvida Perrine's going to need all the help she can get."

"We're setting up a fund for her," Cat said. "Nels said he'd get the ball rolling. Says it'd be a good way to start coming to terms with walking out for his morning constitutional and finding the man's body in Nina's woods. Between the three of us," she said, looking up at Stone, "Mrs. Perrine will be pretty well taken care of."

"I'm glad to hear that," Sally told them. "She's a cool person. Now seriously, the weather's getting worse and worse. You'd better go."

"We'll be in touch," said Cat. "As soon as the police release Nina's papers, we want you going to work on that biography."

"Jeez," said Sally. "You know, I almost forgot I was supposed to be doing that."

"You're doing it," Stone said. "We need your help."

Sally stared at him. "I was really suspicious of you the first time you told me that," she said. "I'm still suspicious."

"Too late," said Stone. "I've been in touch with a movie guy I know. Had him call your agent. The screen rights are pretty much locked up."

For once, Sally was speechless.

"Gotta go," said Cat, putting on her hat. "Bye, honey," she said, hugging Hawk and turning to Sally for a little bit longer hug. "Bye, bye, love."

Here's a sneak preview
of Virginia Swift's new novel
HELLO, STRANGER

Available soon in hardcover from
HarperCollins*Publishers*

Chapter 1

The Rule of Thumb

The Rule of Thumb was one of those grotesqueries of English common law. For centuries, it had stood rock-solid, entitling—no. Make that, *obliging* a man to "correct" the misdeeds of his wife and children with physical force, but holding that the instrument of household justice be no bigger around than a man's thumb. Some kind of limit, that. A switch cut from a tree, hickory or willow; a leather whip, braided rough; a well-knotted piece of rope; objects close to hand, within the reach of a modest man. A prince might have more means at his disposal: the blade of a fencing foil, say, or a length of iron chain. Such things would certainly remind a woman of her duty to submit to her husband's authority. As God and nature and the Bible and everybody had decreed.

The hell you say, thought Professor Sally Alder.

Whenever Sally taught the course titled "Women's Rights in America," she opened the class on domestic violence with a few minutes on the Rule of Thumb. Talking about the Rule made her a little sick to her stomach every time she gave the lecture, but it was something that had to be done. The students needed to know, or at the very least, to be reminded, that history could be a horror show. That a woman's right to be secure from bodily abuse should never be taken for granted. Even in the twenty-first century, there was plenty of reason to assume that not everybody had gotten the message.

Some students stared vacantly back at her, or surreptitiously checked their cell phones. More scribbled busily in their notebooks, knowing that this Rule of Thumb was likely to show up on a test. She might just as well have been telling them the names of the states, or the atomic weight of zinc. But at least the scribblers would have some memory of this lecture, unlike the girl who'd taken out an emery board and spent most of the class happily filing her nails.

Sally brooded all the way back to her office, huddled into her coat against the wind. Did she really imagine that bearing history's lousy news was actually doing any good? They had given a new meaning to blasé today, she thought as she entered Hoyt Hall and climbed the stairs to the fourth floor, headed for her office hours.

She already had a customer. Sally had put a chair in the hall outside her office, a molded plastic thing with a fold-down desk, so that students waiting their turn to see her wouldn't have to hunker down on the floor. Just now, a girl slumped uncomfortably in the chair, a knit cap pulled down over her head. She'd put a backpack on the desk and lay on top of it, her head on her arms, motionless, the picture of dejection.

What in the world had happened to Charlie Preston?

This was the first time Sally had seen the girl in nearly a month. Charlie was registered in Sally's class, but she hadn't been around before spring break, hadn't returned in the week after.

Plenty of students bagged lots of classes. They dropped out, or failed, or contented themselves with Cs and Ds. But Charlie hadn't struck Sally as your typical half-assed student. A third of the time she didn't show, true, and she'd missed a number of assignments. She never said a word in class. But she listened. And it seemed like she got it. And

Sally's real measure for intelligence in a student: she laughed at the professor's jokes.

When Charlie did turn in the work, she showed real spark and insight. She'd come to Sally's office hours more than once, simply to talk about women's history. Sally'd been delighted, encouraged her interest. Charlie was only a freshman, but Sally was already imagining writing recommendations to get her into graduate school.

"Charlie?" she said, touching the girl on the shoulder. "Are you okay?"

A moment passed.

The girl raised her head, and it was excruciatingly obvious that she was not close to okay. The cap covered her ears, but revealed a face that was a mass of bruises, darkening, it seemed, before Sally's eyes. Her lower lip was cut and swelling fast, and one eye was nearly closed. It occurred to Sally that the spike Charlie wore through the eyebrow, the ring through the lip, would be trouble soon, if she didn't get them off.

It wasn't the first time Sally had seen a woman who'd been beaten up. Back in her own student days, she'd run the University of Wyoming Women's Center, which had taken calls for the local shelter. More than one woman had called up crying, asking what to do, where to go. And more than one woman had shown up at the Center, grim or shaking or shame-faced, mumbling something about having walked into a door.

This was the worst she'd ever seen.

"Come in with me," she told the girl, bending over to rub her back, briefly, before unlocking the office door. "I'll call an ambulance, and go with you to the hospital. And we'll call the police."

Charlie hefted her backpack, an effort that cost her, and followed Sally in. But then what Sally had just said seemed to sink in. A look of terror swept Charlie's face. "No!" she exclaimed, grabbing Sally's arm, grimacing at the pain that opening her mouth had caused. "I can't. Can't go to the hospital. No cops." Tears sprang into her eyes, leaked down the sides of her cheeks.

"Charlie," said Sally, as gently as possible. "Sit down a second."

The girl collapsed into the broken-down easy chair in front of Sally's desk, the backpack slipping to the floor with a clunk. These kids. Sally bet there wasn't a backpack at the University of Wyoming that weighed less than forty pounds. They'd all be in back braces by the time they were thirty.

Sally took off her coat, hung it in the closet, moving deliberately to calm herself down. "You're badly hurt," she said, turning back to Charlie. "You need medical attention. I know you're scared, but let me help you. Let the police help. Sheriff Langham's a really, really good friend of mine, a truly incredible person. Trust me, he'll take care of you."

"Yeah, right," said Charlie Preston. "Just like they always take care of me. Nobody ever believes me. Every time I manage to get away, they always send me back to him and the bitch. He's such a great liar, I even believed him this time. He's all, 'All I want to do is help you,' and I fucking believed him. I must be the stupidest person in the world."

Sally set her briefcase and purse on the floor next to the desk, sat down in her chair. "You've got to see a doctor, honey. I'd drive you myself, but my car's at home. I could call a friend, if you don't want an ambulance." She thought a minute. "You wait tables at the Wrangler, don't you? I'm sure Delice wouldn't mind giving us a ride."

Delice Langham, owner of the Wrangler Bar and Grill, was one of Sally's best friends, known for being a demanding, but compassionate boss. Sally knew that on more than one occasion, Delice had slipped a waitress money to get away from a loser boyfriend, had called the cops when angry men showed up looking for "their" women, had been known to take them on herself, with a bag of quarters, or even the Colt .45 she kept below the counter. Sally was also aware that Delice had fronted the down payment for one of the bungalows used by the Laramie SafeHouse. Delice was probably at work now, but she would leap into her Explorer and speed over in five minutes flat if Sally called.

But Delice was also the sister of the Albany County Sheriff, Dickie Langham. Charlie shook her head. "I got a car," she said. "I can drive myself. I'll go to a doctor, I swear. But not the hospital. They ask too many questions. And I'm serious, there's no need to get the police involved."

Sally looked at the girl, very steadily. "Listen to me, Charlie. Somebody hurt you, a whole lot. Nobody's entitled to do that. They need to answer for it."

Charlie bristled, tried to sit up very straight, wincing. "I got it. I can take care of myself. I know a doctor I can go see. She's helped me out before."

Sally asked the obvious question. "Then why didn't you go straight to her?"

"She's not in town. She's somewhere else—I don't want to say where."

"You're in no shape to drive a long distance."

"It's no big deal, Dr. Alder," said the girl. She looked down, shook her shoulders, looked up again, screwing up her courage. "I'm sorry I missed class again. I didn't want any of the kids to see me. I knew you had office hours after, so I waited here. I almost waited outside the classroom, but I thought I might miss you. I couldn't go to the Wrangler. I didn't know who else to ask."

"For what?" Sally said.

"Money. I need money, Dr. Alder. I need to see a doctor, all right. And I need to get out of here for a while, figure out what to do next."

"Your parents . . ." Sally said, pointlessly.

Charlie just glared.

"Okay. What about the SafeHouse?"

"They know where it is," said Charlie. "It's not safe for me."

"There's more than one," Sally pointed out.

"It doesn't matter. They'd find me." Charlie slumped in the chair.

"Your friends . . ." she tried.

"My dad scares the shit out of them, and my stepmother makes them think they're all going to hell." She sat up straighter, and Sally had to admire the effort. "Please, Dr. Alder. Help me out this time. I swear I'll pay back every cent."

"It's not the money, Charlie. Do you promise to call and let me know where you are, as soon as you've seen the doctor? To keep in touch with me? You can't just run away. And you don't have to."

"I can handle myself!" the girl insisted. "I just need some cash."

Sally took a deep breath. "How much?"

Charlie took a breath of her own, but the air caught in her lungs, hitched out in a small grunt. Broken ribs too?

"How much do you have?" Charlie asked.

"Just a second," said Sally. She reached down for her purse, took out her wallet, extracted bills. She'd just been to the ATM. She had more than two hundred dollars. It wouldn't be the first time she'd given money to a woman in trouble, no questions asked. She handed over the cash.

Charlie stuffed the money in her pants pocket and closed her eyes when the tears came again, blinked them away. "Thanks," she said, not looking at Sally. "I really mean it, Dr. Alder. This is the best thing you could do to help me."

Sally sincerely doubted that. She reached for the phone. "One more time. Please let me call the police and the ambulance. It's really the smart thing to do."

"If it were the smart thing to do," said Charlie Preston, "I wouldn't be in the shape I'm in. I gotta go now. I'll be in touch, I swear to God. You don't know what this means to me. Just promise you won't call the cops. Please."

"I can't make that promise. This is the best I can do," said Sally.

"Just a couple of days? Please?"

"This is a terrible idea," Sally said.

"Look. I gotta get going." The girl got up. She was wearing a snug T-shirt, low-slung jeans, Doc Marten shoes. The knit cap. No coat. Sally heard the wind, howling through the budding branches of April trees, banging loose doors and rattling the window casings, the kind of wind you had to lean hard into, just to stay upright. "Where's your coat?" she asked.

"I'm fine," said Charlie. "It's warm out."

Right. And Sally was Maurice Chevalier. "You can't go driving off to who the hell knows where without a coat. Take mine."

"Really. I'm good. I got it," said Charlie.

"Goddamn it, Charlie. I must be crazy to let you out of here at all. At least take my coat, and stop acting like a moron," Sally told her, getting up to go to the closet.

"Won't you be cold walking outside?" the girl asked, taking the soft black wool coat with the warm liner.

"I'm good," said Sally. "I got it."

A few more tears. Sally opened a drawer, pulled out a box of tissues, put it on the desk.

Charlie got up, put on the coat, took a wad of tissues and jammed them in a pocket. She leaned over, pain in every movement, and picked up her backpack. "Thank you," she said. "You don't—really, I can't—anyway, thanks. See you."

And she was gone.

Sally picked up the phone. She'd agreed not to call Sheriff Dickie Langham. She hadn't made any promises about the sheriff's sister.

Delice answered on the third ring. "Oh, it's you," she said when she heard Sally's voice. "I'm waiting for a call from my meat guy. It's blowing like hell up in the passes, and the truck with my order had a problem somewhere between here and Denver. Hamburger all over the highway."

"Can you come to my office?" Sally asked. "There's something I need to talk to you about, and it requires some privacy."

"I can't really get away," Delice told her, "but it sounds like an emergency. Can you come down here?"

"No car," said Sally. "I'd walk down, but I don't have a coat."

Delice was silent a moment. "I'll pick you up," she said. "This is something bad, right?"

"Yeah," Sally answered. "I'm going downstairs now. I'll be watching for you out in front of the building."

Ten minutes later Sally was sitting in Delice's tiny office, hands around a cup of the Wrangler's terrible coffee, listening as Delice ripped a new orifice in a meat supplier who'd had the bad luck to lose a truck to the balmy breezes of a Rocky Mountain spring.

"I don't care how many orders this sets you back!" Delice hollered into the phone. "You're going to get my goddamn stuff up here by dinnertime, or you're going to start looking into the butcher protection program." She slammed down the phone, jangling a dozen silver bracelets, took a swig from her own coffee mug, and looked at Sally. "Okay. What's up?" she asked.

"Charlie Preston," said Sally.

"She's supposed to be working four to midnight," Delice said. "She's missed some shifts, but she usually calls ahead. What about her?"

"She won't be coming in," said Sally.

Delice pursed her lips, thought a bit before she spoke. "She's got some problems."

Sally leaned her elbows on Delice's desk. "The latest problem is that somebody beat the hell out of her. She came to my office, looking like a train wreck. She wouldn't let me take her to the hospital or call the police. She claimed she knew a doctor who could fix her up, but she needed money."

"So what'd you do?" asked Delice, eyes somber.

"She seemed like she was at the end of her rope. I gave her all the cash I had."

"Gave her your coat too, huh?" Delice said. "The really cool one you got last fall on sale at Bloomingdale's. The coat I want to kill you for."

"It's just a coat," said Sally.

Delice nodded. "I'd probably have done the same. And I'm not just saying that to be reassuring. Sometimes there isn't much choice."

"I couldn't keep her in my office," Sally said.

"Uh huh. If they're gonna run, they'll run. I can tell you two things. One is that you'll never see that money again." Delice drank a little more coffee.

"It wasn't a loan," said Sally.

"The other thing is that there's a better than even chance you'll never see Charlie again," Delice told her.

"I know. That's what worries me. She was really messed up, Dee."

"Yeah. I can imagine," Delice replied. "But at least she admitted she needed a doctor, and had some idea of who she could go see. How much do you know about her?"

Sally shook her head. "Very little. She's bright, but frustrating. She misses lots of classes. She works for you."

"She's also been a tough case since she was a little kid. She ran away from home, probably not for the first time. Her father and stepmother reported her missing, and a trooper picked her up hitchhiking on I-80, just west of Green River, in the middle of a snowstorm. She was half frozen to death, but from what I heard, she wasn't exactly oozing gratitude for the ride. She clammed up and wouldn't talk, and they took her straight home. After that, she just fell into trouble, a couple of shoplifting incidents, and a real problem with running away."

"How do you know so much about her?" Sally asked.

"Last year, the parents gave up and agreed to temporary foster care. She was living with Mike and Julie Stark when she came in here asking for a job. She had that look in her eye—wounded but brave. I like that. I hired her on the spot. Mike and Julie filled me in on the background later."

"Mike and Julie Stark? Maude's nephew and his wife?" Sally asked.

"Yeah. Nice people. They've got a fourteen-year-old daughter, always wanted more kids but couldn't have them, so they take in foster children now and then," Delice explained.

"So did Charlie keep running away because she was being abused at home?" Sally asked.

"She didn't talk about it with me," said Delice, "and the Starks didn't go into detail. But it's what I suspect. For their part, the parents claim they've tried everything, but she's an incorrigible juvenile delinquent who runs with a rough crowd, a pathological liar and thief."

Sally thought a minute. "From what she said, it sounded like she was living with her parents again."

"For about the last month, yeah. I don't know what happened, but I guess, somehow, they managed to talk her into coming home. I know they bought her a car—maybe that had something to do with it. Bradley Preston has bucks."

"Bradley Preston?" Sally frowned. "The name rings a bell, but I can't place him."

Delice made a face. "He's a heap-big bwana corporate lawyer and a pompous jerk. You'd never know I had to kick his ass out of my bar twenty-some years ago."

"Wait a minute. There was a guy who used to hustle pool and hassle waitresses. Bad Brad. Used to work as a roughneck on drill rigs, right? You're not saying he's Charlie's father?" Sally said,

"Same guy, but different M.O. Quit the oil patch, went to law school, married and divorced his secretary when she ran off and left him with a three-year-old kid. Faster than you can say 'rebound,' he married an upright Christian woman and got born again. He represents insurance companies who want to deny claims to little old ladies and Cub Scouts."

"He was a rude bastard, back in the day. I recall him getting a huge snootful of Yukon Jack, reaching across the bar, and ripping the T-shirt off Lizzie Mason when she was in the middle of making a tequila sunrise," said Sally.

"And that," said Delice, "was the last time he set foot in my place. Stupid son of a bitch."

Nobody messed with Delice Langham.

"What about the stepmother? If the father is a batterer, where does this good professing woman fit in?" Sally asked.

"Who knows? Beatrice is probably too busy minding other people's business to notice," Delice said with a sneer.

"So she's that kind of Christian," said Sally. "Maybe she just doesn't want anything to do with the leftovers of Brad's first marriage."

"Or maybe it's easier for her just to see nothing. You know how it goes. Family members look the other way so it doesn't come down on them." Delice picked up a pen and drew circles on her desk blotter.

"Or maybe she's convinced herself that the kid deserves what she gets," Sally said.

Delice put down the pen, sighed heavily, looked up. "It happens," she said.

"I'm feeling better about giving Charlie the money," said Sally.

"And the coat," said Delice. The wind was really kicking up by now, pounding the dingy little window of Delice's office with dust and gravel from the Wrangler parking lot. "She'll be glad she's got that coat. It's getting really evil out."